Medusa's Shame

The Sacred Throne Series - Book One

By
Robert Southworth

*With thanks to Paula, Jtf and Rob. Through these
difficult times you have kept me going.*

Chapter 1

'A Journey of Discovery'

S cripos was not much larger than many fishing villages. In the minds of its populace, however, it was so much more. They believed that it was destined for far greater things than merely surviving on the day's catch. Riches had come to Scripos in the form of religion. A new temple in honour of Hera had been built on a nearby hill. Pilgrims from the surrounding lands now came to pay their respects and present offerings. With each visitor, Scripos gained wealth and the priests gained influence. The elders, who were not averse to taking bribes, soon convinced most dissenters to fall silent. A small standing force of twenty men were enough to ensure those more stubborn voices were not heard for very long. In truth, few complained at the sudden wealth. The priests may have amassed too much influence, but the fishermen and other traders never wanted for customers. The occasional undesirables being silenced or moved on, was a small price to pay.

The boy, an individual that many would describe as an unwelcome addition to Scripos, was being observed.

His actions had been scrutinised for several days, by more than one resident. One set of eyes watched with amused interest; another set, viewed with a building prickly annoyance. He'd gone about his task oblivious to the watchers and with no deviation from his routine. He would arrive at the fountain that stood at the centre of Scripos. Within a short time, he began to attract a crowd. Initially, the onlookers had mainly comprised of children, but as the days passed, men and women began to swell the ranks. The diminutive figure was a few years short of adulthood and displayed the signs of too many missed meals. Cheek bones and ribs were only thinly covered in flesh. The eyes seemed to sit too deeply within the skull and the limbs looked as though they could break should a strong wind press against his fragile frame. Clearly, it was not his looks that drew the masses. The boy had a skill; a talent for spinning a tale.

The day, like those before, passed with him receiving the odd coin from an appreciative passer-by. As the crowd filtered away, he gathered his earnings. A few coins and two flat breads. It meant that hunger would be avoided. It was at this point, he looked toward a partly concealed figure that had clearly been observing him from the confines of their home. He gave a wry smile, clearly sensing an opportunity to add to his haul. He placed the coin in a small purse at his waist and took a bite from one of the flat breads. Casually he strode toward the stranger.

"Would you like to hear a tale?" he asked, bending his neck in a failed attempt to get a better look at the figure hidden within the shadows of their small household.

"I have been listening," came the reply in no more

than a whisper.

"Oh…" His disappointment was obvious, "I won't trouble you further." He turned to walk away.

"The bread looks dry. Come take a drink." The figure turned and disappeared into the interior without waiting for an answer. The young storyteller knew better than to trust a stranger when he had coin in his purse, especially if that person seemed reluctant to be be seen. However, the bread was dry. He licked his lips as he decided whether to follow the mysterious stranger or retire. Then he slowly took a step to his front. The temptation of a cooling drink had been too much for him, nonetheless, he still moved with caution.

With a little trepidation, he entered the dwelling. His eyes searched the interior, almost expecting an attack. However, it was his nostrils that were assaulted, as a delightful aroma overwhelmed his senses. He glanced around for the source of the sumptuous aroma, but the lack of light barred any chance of revelation. Suddenly, a lamp flickered into existence, the figure with its back turned, was gradually illuminated. But frustratingly, he could not make out any features.

"Take a seat. I think I can offer you more than dry bread."

"Thank you," he replied. He pulled back a small bench and took his place at the table. The movement caused the unstable surface to rock and he shot out a hand to prevent a jug from tipping.

"Forgive me. The table, like much of this place, is not best suited to entertain guests."

"It is better than I am used to." As he spoke, he leaned forward trying to see his host's face. Nonetheless, being in closer proximity, his keen hearing allowed him to make some observations. The tone of voice, though no more than a whisper and containing a certain huskiness, led him to believe his host was female. The form before him seemed haunched over, as though many years weighed heavily upon its spine.

"Your tales are very entertaining, if a little inaccurate."

"My former master was regarded as a man of knowledge. Some say that his tales were a gift from the gods who took pity on him for his blindness."

"Pity from the gods? Now that would make a great story." The figure turned to face the boy. "Who was this man?" she asked.

For the first time he could see his host. "Homer. He was not a man of influence or substantial wealth, but a man of learning. More than that, he was a good man." He paused for a moment, then compelled to speak further, said, "It is not wise to anger the gods, old woman."

"Do you think that those seated in Olympus await my words with abated breath?" She gave a mischievous smile.

"Perhaps not, but those that serve the gods may hear you. They're not known for their mercy. They rarely forgive and lack compassion for anyone without plenty of coin. In Iona they tormented my master, turned the people against him. He was already old and crippled, then one night a crowd, encouraged by the priests, threw both insult and rocks at him. A blow from one, took the little sight that he possessed." His face flushed with anger betraying the love he felt for his former master.

"And how did you come to know him?"

"My mother received a few coins, and a room in payment for cooking meals and keeping his home clean. When she took ill and died, he allowed me to stay and taught me the stories of Troy and its heroes. He was not a king or warrior, but Homer was a great man."

"Praise indeed. So, tell me, teller of tales. Do you intend to become a *great man* too? What name should my ears be pricked to heed?" she asked.

The boy's eyes narrowed, he wondered if the old woman was teasing him.

"That kind of life is for others. I wish only for a full stomach and a comfortable place to sleep. My name is Aetes, an unimportant name for a boy that seeks neither fame nor fortune."

"Aetes?"

"Yes."

"Aetes is a fine name." She reached out a hand and placed it over the boy's heart. "There was a hero called Aetes, his endeavours matched those performed by the likes of Hector, Achilles and even, Odysseus."

"Then why have I not heard of him?" he asked.

"Perhaps like you, he did not seek fame and fortune. Truth be told, he deserved plenty of both."

Aetes chewed on his lip. The room fell to an awkward silence. He wanted to ask a question but felt unable. His face reddened slightly.

"W-w-w ... would you tell me about him?" he stuttered.

She smiled; the grey wisps that once served as eyebrows raised high on her forehead.

"And what would I receive in return?" she asked.

Aetes looked around the room in which he sat.

"I will clean for you," he blurted out. "And journey to the market," he added quickly.

The host raised a jug and poured water into a goblet. However, when the vessel was full, she did not stop. The liquid overflowed the small goblet. Aetes watched. His eyes widened, as he realised that the jug seemed to have a never-ending supply of water. The old woman continued to pour, but her eyes never left her young guest. When finally she stopped and placed the vessel on the table surface, she took her seat without acknowledging the miracle. She gave a loud cough, breaking Aetes's focus just for a moment. When he returned his gaze back to the jug, all seemed normal.

"If I tell you, then you must know all. The story will be told from the beginning, because it there that the seeds are sown for all that follows."

"I want to know all," he replied eagerly.

"Even if the truth breaks apart the words of your beloved, Homer?"

He sat up upright at her words. As though it would be a disloyalty to hear his former master's tales disproven. However, moments later, his eyes narrowed, and his jaw became set.

"I want to know more."

"Very well, Aetes. We will begin tomorrow. I grow weary and require sleep. You may lay your head wherever you find comfort."

A sharp rapping at the door drew the attention of both Aetes and the old woman.

"Despite the lateness of the day, it seems the gods have no wish for me to enjoy an undisturbed sleep," she announced.

The knock sounded again, with more ferocity.

"Whoever it is, they do not seem happy."

"Then we had best not keep them waiting. Open the door, Aetes."

"Me? I am not sure…"

"Come now, Aetes. Bravery begins with a single step."

"So, does running away," he replied.

She gave a bark of laughter that ended as suddenly as it had begun.

"Open the door." She eyed the boy.

He moved reluctantly towards the door. The timbers shook in response as the rapping on timber sounded for a third time. Aetes raised a hand and grasped the handle. He took a deep breath and as he did so, pulled the door open and hastily retired to a safe distance.

"Where are you, old woman?" a voice bellowed. It belonged to a short, rotund man. His jowls wobbled in unison with his annoyance. His white robes fitted poorly as they stretched almost to breaking point to cover such an impressively rotund gut.

"Bretos, I thought you had forgotten me." She stepped forward. "It seems so long since you were last hammering at my door."

"You were told that your presence is not welcome here," Bretos replied. He glanced at Aetes. "And now I see you are taking in strays."

"He needed a place to lay his head. Besides, you should be thankful. He has a talent for telling a tale. The people need respite from those tedious ceremonies at the temple."

"Be careful, it is not wise to offend the gods. Hera is not known for her mercy."

"I am old, Bretos. The gods have no interest in one as ancient as me. Besides, I doubt I have reason to fear a bloated fish, like you."

Aetes coughed to prevent his laughter being heard. Bretos moved forward, his anger clear to see. He pushed Aetes out of the way in the process of closing on his insulter, which sent the boy sprawling to the ground.

"How dare you," Bretos began.

The old woman cut him short, "I suggest that you

help Aetes to his feet." The dry humour was gone now, her voice held a deep menace.

"Know your place. I am a priest, servant of Hera." Bretos was clearly too enraged to heed the tone within her voice.

A moment later and the old woman had covered the ground between herself and Bretos. One of her hands held his jaw tight as her other held a blade against the soft flesh of his throat.

"What say you, Bretos, should I open that throat of yours? It's a messy death, but relatively quick. Or perhaps I should take my time and remove each limb slowly? I doubt anyone would shed a tear at your passing. Well *priest,*" the word was laced with as much venom as possible, "how would you like to die?"

"No... please," he pleaded.

"Then go away and do not return." She released him.

"Yes... forgive me." He stumbled away from her reach.

"And Bretos."

"Yes."

"Help the boy to his feet."

Bretos lifted Aetes to his feet and even brushed the dust from the boy's garment. Then as quickly as his ample size would permit, he left.

"What... who?" Aetes struggled to find the words. He could not believe how she could move so fast. She was clearly no ordinary woman.

"Rest, we have a tasking day ahead of us." Without another word she extinguished one of the lamps., signalling that the conversation was at an end.

*****

Aetes stirred the next morning to find that in the night someone had covered him with a number of furs. Despite the hardness of the floor, it had been a long time since he had enjoyed so much comfort as he slept. It was not until the door was flung open that he sat upright, allowing them to drop away.

"How do you expect to hear what I have to say, if you don't greet a new day?"

"I am ready to learn," Aetes replied as he jumped to his feet. "Would you like me to prepare something to eat first?"

"I have already eaten. It is not wise to travel on an empty stomach," she replied.

"But I thought you were going to tell me."

"Not tell. I will show you, but not here," she interrupted as she turned to leave.

"But..." he faltered.

"Come or stay, the choice is yours," she called out as she exited.

Aetes raced towards the door. Outside, as the light of the new day hit his eyes, causing him to pause. Slowly, his sight returned, and he observed his host climbing aboard a small cart. At its front, a donkey missing one ear and most of its coat, stood patiently waiting for the order to move on. The woman cackled at the look on the boy's face.

"He's stronger than he looks."

"W-we haven't got far to travel, have we?" he stuttered. He clearly doubted the beast would survive a substantial journey.

"We go the distance that is required, not one step further."

As the day marched on, so did the small cart. It was not until the night began to creep in that he asked his first question.

"Do we near our journey's end?"

"For this day, our roaming is over." She called out instruction to the donkey and the cart turned off the track. "We will need a fire, find some wood."

Aetes glanced around at the trees that stood oppressively near their chosen camp site. The boy may have been young, but he was no fool. He knew that the location would be an inviting place for robbers to fall upon weary travellers. She bent and collected a small branch that had fallen to the ground.

"We will gather wood, together," she announced in a far gentler tone than he had become accustomed. The old woman must have guessed the reason he was reluctant to stray from the cart. Aetes nodded but his eyes roamed from tree to tree. "The heroes of Troy were not the beginning or for that matter the end." Aetes turned to look at his travelling companion. "The destruction of the house of Priam, and the great city was no more than a chapter in a woeful tale. A terrible game in which god, human and creature played their part, but it began with the gods... It always starts with the gods."

"Should you talk of the gods in this manner, are you not afraid?" As he spoke, he picked up scatterings of twigs and branches from the ground for the fire.

"Fear?" She gave a rueful chuckle. "When all that you love has been taken, even the gods cannot bend you to their will. No Aetes, I do not dread reprisals from the gods." Her face showed no sign of defiance or anger, only sadness dominated her expression.

"So how did it begin?" His arms were becoming over-loaded.

"All will be revealed to those willing to see. We have collected enough, time to rest. I am too old to allow the cold of the night on my bones. It will be good to sit near the flames."

"What is your name?" Aetes asked.

"I have had many," she replied.

"But surely you must have a name?"

"Really?" She raised an eyebrow. "If I must have one, what would you suggest?"

"Err..." The boy's brow wrinkled as he pondered.

"How about... 'old woman'?" She suggested.

"That's not a name," Aetes replied, his tone suggesting annoyance.

"It's as good as any, and fitting don't you think? I am alas old and," she grasped one of her breasts with her free hand, "without a doubt female. Yes, *old woman* I like it."

The two of them returned to the camp site. Aetes watched his companion. The remainder of the night was spent consuming a stew that was warmed on the open fire. Flat bread was employed to mop up any remaining juices. Furs were laid upon the ground just a few paces from the flames and both the travellers settled down, eager to soothe their tired sinews. Aetes took one lingering look toward the trees, but the day's exertions had made him weary. His focus began to blur and slumber soon followed.

*****

One day turned into many. Like the drips of rainwater from a leaf, the old woman released parts of her story. On the seventh day the cart was called to a halt and the two companions sat in silence as they stared into the distance.

"Is that..."

"It was *Troy.*" In the distance stood the ruins of a city. Many people have tried to call it home since Priam sat upon its throne. The gods, however, seem determined that it should crumble to nothingness. Each time it begins to thrive the ground begins to shake. Both new and old walls crash to the ground, and the people are driven out." She urged the beast to move forward, ensuring the creature took a path that led away from the ancient walls of what was onceTroy.

"Are we not going to the city?" Aetes asked.

"No, there is nought but the spirits of the dead in that place. We journey to a location that housed no king, prince or warrior. Nonetheless, I will wager it has withstood the ravages of time far better." The cart trundled along the overgrown track for no more than one hundred paces before once again being called to a stop. "From here we walk. Release the beast, he will not wander far."

Aetes did as he was instructed. Several items were then thrust into his arms, without a word being spoken, he followed the woman into the undergrowth. As they moved through the overhanging branches that obstructed their progress, glimpses of a small wooden entrance cut into the side of a hillside that seemed to appear from nowhere.

"Who lives here?" he asked as they neared. There was a slight tremble in his voice.

"No person has stepped through this door for centuries." She paused before the entrance. Stretching out a hand, ancient knuckles rapped against ancient timbers.

"I thought you said nobody lives here?"

"I said no person *resides* within." She knocked again, but this time in a different place. Aetes remain perfectly still, his eyes growing wide with amazement as writing appeared on the age-weathered timbers. The woman stroked the letters one by one as she muttered a language that Aetes did not understand. As her hand passed over each symbol it glowed golden with such intensity that Aetes was forced to squint. When all the letters were alight, the woman ceased speaking and rested the palm of her hand against the door. The noise of a large bolt scraping free from years of lying dormant sounded from the other side of the timbers. The lettering's glow faded as the door began to move inward. The old woman moved through the entrance, but after five or six paces turned to see that Aetes had not taken a single step.

"W-w ... what are you, a sorceress?" he stammered.

"I am an old woman. All those years gives knowledge that many do not possess. You have nothing to fear from me. Besides, if I wanted to kill you, then you would already be dead."

"But..."

"Aetes, come inside, or be on your way. I require food, not conversation." She turned and proceeded into the tunnel that led into the heart of the hillside. Every few steps that she made, a torch erupted into flame, lighting the way as she progressed. As her shape disappeared into the distance, the echo of her voice reached the ears of Aetes. "You must put all that you think to be natural in this world to one side, if you truly want to learn the truth."

Finally, Aetes took his first timid steps. As he moved inside, the door to the outside world closed and the brightness of the day was lost to him. His journey took him along a winding passageway. Other than the torches that provided the comfort of light, it was devoid of any other adornment. The air that met his nostrils, however, was adorned with all manner of differing odours. The woman had only just entered the underground corridor moments before him, but somehow, she had created a heavy mix of different aromas. He pressed on, eager to investigate what his companion was doing. A soft blueish illumination, subtly different to the one produced by the wall torches appeared in the distance. This new form of light seemed to distort the walls of the passage. He held out a hand, yearning to touch the magical glow. As he neared, the delicate illumination fell upon his skin. Each of the hairs on his arm stood proud, as though they were basking at the illumination's touch. Trance-like, Aetes moved forward, all concern that he was entering the lair of a sorceress driven from his mind. He was met with the sight of the woman moving energetically between various pans, each giving off plumes of smoke and wondrous fragrances.

Aetes moved toward his host. The corridor opened out into a room that was only slightly better lit than the passage to his rear. He wanted to ask questions, but he could not find the words, so bewildered with the sights and smells that collided with his senses. An eagle-like screech ripped Aetes from his trance-like amazement. His now fearful eyes peered into the gloom in search of the beast that made such a terrifying sound. They came to rest on a dark cloth that hung from ceiling to floor, hiding what lay beyond.

"What is it?" he asked.

"You have eyes. Look for yourself," the woman replied busying herself with her potions.

The boy raised a trembling hand and grasped the cloth within his fingers. Reluctantly, he moved the ancient fabric to one side.

"Hector would not have been so timid," the woman called out.

The boy's jaw clenched. His annoyance triumphant over his fear, he pulled the cloth away. Startled, he jumped backwards as the creature beyond became apparent. Aetus stared at the monstrous shape that remained perfectly still. It was approximately half his height, and its skin resembled old weather-worn leather, dark as night. Upon its back were two wings, one of which was much smaller than the other. The face almost human, contained wide, staring, yellow eyes. The mouth was unnaturally large, with teeth that appeared capable of easily tearing flesh from bone.

"What...?" The boy struggled to find the words.

"She's a harpy." The woman moved forward and placed a hand on the creature's cheek. "She is also my dearest friend."

"But I thought that they were part human, part bird," the boy replied.

"She is an anomaly. When I found her, she had been cast aside by her kind. She survived on insects and small rodents. Bigger prey was out of the question. Her wings have never fully formed."

"Do her kind not devour men?" he asked.

"Only those with deceit in their heart. Are you deceitful, Aetes?"

"I... try not to be," he replied nervously.

"Then she may simply take a finger or two."

Aetes quickly moved away, placing his hands behind his back. The woman laughed as she stepped closer and continued to caress the creature's cheek.

"I have missed you." No reply was forth coming, but the old woman continued as if there had been. "Yes, I have been away far too long, and no, the boy is not food."

"Does she understand you?" Aetes asked.

"Yes, and I her," she replied.

"But..."

"Harpies are not like you or I. When they speak, they do so, within the confines of your head. The only sound they make is born from emotion. Rage and fear will make them shriek, it is those sounds that many men have heard. It is possibly why these creatures have an unbefitting reputation."

"But you said her own kind cast her out?"

"The harpies have been hunted to near extinction. They cannot afford the luxury of caring for the weak. She bears them no ill will for their actions. For my part, I am less forgiving."

Aetes plucked an apple from the table. "Will she allow a gift?"

"Well, that's the question. Are you pure of heart, young Aetes? I sometimes think that if all the great halls throughout each land had a harpy, then deceit would be driven from this world."

He took a large gulp and a less than confident step forward. Slowly, he raised his hand, clearly mindful to keep his fingers flat and away from the edges of the fruit.

"What's her name?"

"I call her Rock, which is what I mistook her for the first time we met. Besides, her real name is far too difficult for my tongue to navigate."

Aetes took another small step.

"I mean you no harm," his tone highlighted his trepidation. Suddenly, his head jerked upright as if slapped in the face.

"She spoke to you," the woman announced excitedly, bouncing from foot to foot. A wide beaming smile erupting on her weather-worn features.

"Yes," he replied.

"It is most unusual for it to happen so quickly."

The boy, however, was not listening. At least, not to the words spoken out loud. His face was contorted, as if the concentration required, caused him physical pain.

"I am sorry, I do not mean to stare. Your wing... does it hurt?"

Rock turned her head to the side, never breaking eye

contact with Aetes. Then she moved her head from side to side in answer to his question. Aetes moved his hand to Rock's cheek and any trepidation between the two seemed to disappear.

The remainder of that night was spent consuming food and the three of them engaging in an uncommon conversation. Rock was an intelligent creature; however, she could only converse by speaking into the mind of a singular human. This meant that either she had to repeat her words again or the recipient passed on the message. Despite the awkward nature of the conversation, it was not long before all three were sharing their experiences and feelings. They were unaware that the day had turned to night as they enjoyed each other's company.

Chapter 2

'Tell the Tale'

Aetes slowly opened his eyes. He had fallen asleep where he had been seated the previous night. He looked across to Rock. Her head was tucked beneath her one good wing and was obviously still asleep. He carefully got to his feet in an attempt not to wake her. His efforts, however, were in vain as a crash sounded from the corridor and was promptly followed by several colourful curses.

The old woman emerged, her expression more than equal to the darkness of the corridor beyond.

"Are you hurt?" Aetes asked.

"Only my pride. I have walked that passage more times than a boar has hairs. It seems that my memory is not what it used to be." She ran a hand down the front of her garment. Pulling the cloth away, the flesh was stained red.

"You are bleeding!"

"It is the blood of Adonis. I am unharmed."

"Adonis?" Aetes asked, his interest pricked.

"The legend says that while hunting alone, Adonis was mortally wounded by a wild boar sent by the goddess Artemis. Apparently, she was angered because Adonis had entered her realm. As he lay dying, blood from the wound dripped to the ground. Aphrodite, who loved him, sprinkled that same earth with nectar and her tears. From that spot a red anemone sprouted."

"And you believe the flowers contain his blood?" Aetes asked.

"I have no thoughts on the truth of the legend. I travel to a place that lies in the woods near an ancient city that thrived long before Troy. There, the flower only grows with red petals and to a size far larger than normal. With just a few petals squeezed, I can fill two vessels. Fortunately, one vessel will suffice."

"What is its purpose?"

"You are."

Aetes suddenly looked concerned.

"I do not intend to poison you. Surely you know that I wish you no misfortune by now. I merely meant that its properties will aid me in revealing the past."

"But how?" he pressed.

The woman held up a hand to prevent him from speaking.

"Patience, Aetes. First, we will eat and then you shall receive the answers. Perhaps even see the truth regarding gods and men."

Aetes wanted to ask further questions. but then reluctantly nodded his head in agreement.

*****

Despite her declaration that Aetes would know all, she seemed in no rush to begin his education. Aetes spent the time conversing with Rock, but with frequent sideward glances to his host as she consumed her meal. As time passed, she rose and then busied herself with various vessels and the contents within.

Suddenly, Aetes and Rock leapt in the air as the woman gave a part shriek, part laugh. She held aloft an amphora, which could easily fit into the palm of her hand, declaring that she was ready to begin. Without uttering another word, she walked to the far side of the room. Her free hand reached up high and grasped an unseen object. It wasn't until she pulled her hand down that it became apparent that a fabric, as dark as the darkest of nights, hid what lay beyond from all prying eyes. Aetes stood as an audible gasp escaped his lips. He stepped cautiously until he stood at the woman's shoulder, gaping as he observed what lay to his front.

An archway stretched from ground to ceiling. It was not carved from stone, like many such structures throughout the known world, but sculptured from bronze. The borders were adorned with all manner of symbols, writhing around each symbol were the bodies of snakes. Only one head was visible, jutting out from the arch. Its mouth open with fangs bared, as if ready to sink into the flesh of a careless passer-by. At the apex, a carved head of an individual known throughout every land. High cheek bones framed eyes, which though sculpted from metal, could send shivers down the bravest man's spine and instead of hair, a multitude of vipers. The unmistakeable image of the feared Medusa was instantly recognisable.

The structure was not a gateway to another room or passage. Its centre, like its frame, was made of bronze, but this was not cold and unyielding. It was in a liquid state as if waiting to be poured into an expectant mould. The surface shone and reflected the room in which Aetes, Rock and the woman stood. The latter took a step forward and placed a finger into the pool, watching the ripples as they washed toward the structure's edge.

"What is it?" Aetes asked.

"A doorway - one that is specia, I grant you. But in essence just a door," she replied.

"But how do we pass through?"

"With knowledge and a little faith." She raised the small amphora to the snake's gaping maw. In one movement she tipped in the entire contents. The mouth closed and suddenly the reptilian bodies that occupied much of the column began to move. The undulating mass moved towards the mask of Medusa. The snakes crowning her head began to writhe and her eyes glowed red. From the corner of each eye a single crimson teardrop flowed downward, and then dropped into the pool of bronze.

"Are you certain that you wish to know the truth, Aetes?" she asked.

"I am," he replied, his gaze never leaving the archway.

"Then take my hand."

The teardrops acted like boiling water on ice. A small

hole grew as the bronze simply melted away.

"Make clear what is hidden. Remove the shroud of lies and reveal the secrets, no matter their keepers." She stepped forward and Aetes allowed himself to be pulled through the archway, although he closed his eyes, fearing what lay ahead.

*****

"You can look now, Aetes."

He did as instructed. Gone was the gloom of a home cut into a hillside, gone too was the bronze work of the arch. In its place, a pathway, flanked by more traditional columns stretched into the distance.

"But how?" He made no attempt to keep the amazement from his voice.

"It is quite real – at least, it is not a dream. Gods can do many things, but they cannot turn back the passage of time. However, they can create places that survive outside the rules that the world of men must obey. Medusa was cursed and forced to live in exile. Her two sisters were lesser gods but not without power. They created this gift so that she could look back on more joyful times. But Medusa had grown angry, her heart filled with rage at her mistreatment. She used her own powers to mutate the archway and then cast it into the sea. For good measure, she ordered her sisters never to return."

"How did you come to possess something created by gods?"

"That is a question for another time. This day we will

learn of the deities. You can decide for yourself if they deserve the admiration of men." She raised a hand and instructed that he should follow her down the path.

The track led along an unknown coast. Despite seeing the waves crash just beyond the columns, the two travellers could not feel the water's spray or smell the odours that usually accompany a large body of water. The pillars of stone continued to frame the pathway as it meandered on to a promontory. At the cliffs edge the columns curved around to form a courtyard. At its centre there was a single stone bench. The old woman, showing more care than usual, took Aetes by the hand and led him to that bench, indicating that he should sit. As he did as he was instructed, the space between each set of pillars burst into life. Each space showed a different scene, but the images were hard to discern. It was like looking through a heavy mist, the shapes of individuals could be seen, but their identity and precise actions were obscured. The old woman took her place next to Aetes.

"I cannot see," Aetes announced.

"You will." She raised an open hand at one of the scenes. She then closed her fingers tight, as though grasping fruit from a tree, and then drew the empty hand to her breast. The scene she had selected suddenly moved to its right, pushing the image that had held that spot further right. Again, it moved, and again until at last it came to rest directly before them. "This will show you the true measure of the gods. Do not speak or ask questions, allow yourself to become part of the visions you observe. With practice you will learn far more than just what you see and hear." She stretched out her hand once more and pointed a skeletal finger. "Reveal," she said, in no more than a whisper.

*****

A muscular man emerged from the pool. He was clearly an individual at ease with his own body. He did not race from the waters and seemed content for the female who sat patiently on the bank, to admire his form.

"You have no need of me, Zeus. I doubt I could ever match your self-devotion," she announced. But her tone was without malice.

"This is not my true form. I only wish to please you," he replied as he shook the water from his dark, tightly curled hair and impressively trimmed beard.

"Then come and sit next to me." The female gave the ground a gentle pat.

"You trust my intentions?" He gave a wry smile.

"My sisters say that you're definitely not to be trusted, but I will take the risk. After all, you claim to love me."

Zeus moved quickly from the water's edge to be at her side. He dropped down and gently took her hand.

"It is no falsehood. I may be a god, but I have never felt so vulnerable." He looked into her eyes, his stare never faltering.

"Is it me that you love, or do you crave the experience that I have denied you?" She fixed him with a stare.

"I am Zeus. If all that I wanted was lay between your

legs, then I could simply take it."

"You could take the flesh, but not me," she replied defiantly.

Zeus appeared to falter, his earlier confidence wilting away.

"Medusa, how can I prove that my love is real? Shall I forsake my powers? Live at your side as a mortal?" His tone was almost pleading.

She raised a hand to his cheek.

"Do that and you would surely grow to hate me. I do love you, but I would not demand such a sacrifice. I would not allow it."

"Then let me create a home for us. A place where our feelings can never be ignored or spoiled," he replied.

"No... I cannot live a life of solitude. Locked away wondering when you would return to my arms. Never knowing if you had finally tired of a once beautiful mortal. Besides, you know that the other gods are jealous and seek power, they would use my mortality to weaken you."

"Weaken me... how?" Zeus asked indignantly.

"I would make you vulnerable. It is not hard for a god to harm a mortal, even one protected by the mighty Zeus. If you love me, as you say you do, then harm bestowed on me would also be bestowed upon you."

"Then how can we be together, there must be a..." Zeus attempted to speak. But she placed a hand against his lips.

"We simply cannot be."

"But..."

"I am sorry." Medusa replied, tears welling in her eyes. She rose to her feet and without another word, strode way.

Zeus did not chase after her; he fixed the pool with a rage-filled stare. The skies above turned black, matching his mood. Then a deafening thunderclap sounded before lightning erupted from the ominous clouds. It streaked downward, colliding with the surface of the water and exploded. The glow was so bright that Aetes was forced to close his eyes. By the time they were opened again, Zeus was gone, and the image was fading into shadows as the mists rolled down.

Aetes opened his mouth to speak, but the image to his front suddenly cleared to reveal a different scene. It was night, but a full moon lit a small track, on which, a solitary figure journeyed. The features of the individual were hidden, but it was clear to see that they were in a hurry.

The path led to a large temple. At its entrance stood an impressive statue of the goddess, Athena. The figure climbed the steps that led to the interior. Once there, it raised two hands and removed the hood that had covered its face. Medusa glanced nervously around as she stood alone in the centre of the place of worship.

"Zeus, I have answered your call. Where are you, my love?" she whispered.

"My brother cannot be here this night. Perhaps I can

stand in his stead?" An impressive form spoke as it emerged from the shadows.

"Who are you?" she asked, her excitement turning to fear.

"I am Poseidon," he gave a playful bow, "I am sure that I can be a more than adequate replacement for my brother."

Medusa did not reply. She pulled her hood back into place and made to leave. Poseidon grasped her by the arm, his strength preventing her from pulling free.

Medusa struck out at Poseidon's face.

"If you hurt me, Zeus will tear Olympus apart to get his hands on you."

"You think that I fear my brother's wrath or that he would risk war for a mortal?" He ripped her tunic down exposing her breast. Once more she hit out at him. "I love a woman with spirit." He brought his free hand around and caught Medusa across the cheek. She was knocked from her feet, landing on the cold surface of the temple floor.

Aetes rose to his feet, determined to rush to Medusa's aid. The old woman, however, held him firm and made him re-take his seat.

"These images are nought but shadows of the past, Aetes." The boy reluctantly settled back onto the bench, his eyes watching the mists arise on the scene and hiding the fate of Medusa. Thankfully he observed another image begin to emerge.

The pool was covered in thick ice and the surrounding countryside held a shroud of white. Medusa cut a sorrowful form as she sat upon a tree stump, staring out across the frozen water. Two women stood close by, but she paid them no mind, lost in her own thoughts. The thick cloak protected her against the cold, but it could not hide that she was heavily pregnant. Suddenly, lightning struck the ground and when the smoke cleared, Zeus and two others emerged. Medusa for the first time took an interest in proceedings. Her face suddenly etched with hope as she looked towards Zeus. He gave her a brief encouraging smile but turned quickly to the figure on his left.

"I commanded that he should attend, Athena." Zeus announced.

"I sent word," she replied.

"I do not see why any of us are here," the individual to his right announced. His tone suggested that he was bored.

"Because I deemed it necessary!" Zeus raged.

"Oh... An order from the father of the gods. How could we refuse?"

Athena quickly intervened. "Hades, we are here because Medusa is mortal," she explained.

"My point exactly. When did the lives of mere mortals weigh so heavily on our shoulders?" Hades asked.

"It matters..." Zeus spoke through gritted teeth, "it matters because Medusa's family are immortals and Medusa was under my protection."

"Oh! I see. Someone has plucked the ripe fruit from the tree before you," Hades replied.

Zeus's eyes glowed with rage. Sparks of lightning raced ominously across the heavens.

"Be warned, Hades. This is not the day to test my patience." Zeus eyed his brother with obvious menace.

The lord of the underworld gave a small bow of submission, but a look of defiance never left his face. Further interaction was cut short by a thunderous, cracking sound. The pool's ice was splintering and breaking apart. The broken surface was arranging itself into a walkway that stretched to the water's edge. Poseidon arose from the very centre of the pool, trident in hand and wearing full battle armour. His face displayed a mask of displeasure.

"What a surprise. Our brother has gone for the dramatic entrance," Hades remarked sarcastically.

Zeus ignored Hades and stepped forward.

"Why have you come prepared for war, Poseidon?" Zeus asked. His hands balled into fists. Small strand of electricity raced between his fingers, as though preparing to do battle.

"Why do you take the word of a mortal over that of your brother's?" Poseidon replied. He met his brother's stare, unflinching in his defiance.

"I want the truth," Zeus demanded.

"I have already told you that I have not lain with this girl, forced or otherwise."

"And yet her stomach swells," Zeus pressed.

"Not from my seed. I tire of these accusations," Poseidon replied, his anger clearly rising. Reacting to the god's rage, the waters of the pool burst through the ice. The usually tranquil pool resembled that of a raging ocean.

"One way or another I will have the truth in this matter."

Poseidon gripped his trident. The knuckles of his powerful hand turning white, declaring his anger to the world.

Athena stepped to her front. "Before we slip into war, may I make a suggestion?" she asked.

"What is it?" Zeus replied, never allowing his glare to leave Poseidon.

"Atropos of the Moirai can read the very depths of the mind, even that of a god. If Poseidon agrees, then Atropos can prove Poseidon's guilt or innocence."

The lord of all the oceans held his ground; his hand still gripped his mighty three-pronged weapon. All present watched him, waiting anxiously for his decision. Finally, he permitted the trident to fall unceremoniously to the earth.

"Fetch Atropos, let there be an end to this foolishness," Poseidon announced.

Athena nodded and vanished from view. No words were spoken by those that were left behind. Even Hades kept his tongue.

Fortunately, Athena completed her task promptly. She arrived with the diminutive figure of Atropos at her side. The woman seemed less than happy at being summoned.

"I am too old to take part in your games," she announced to all rather than an individual.

"We will not keep you long," Athena replied, taking Atropos by the arm. "Poseidon, will you come closer please."

Atropos was blind, scarred tissue stood where eyes should be. Nonetheless, she seemed aware of all that stood around her.

"Ah! the God of fish. Unfortunately, my nose works far better than my eyes."

Poseidon bit his lip. "Can we get this over with," he uttered.

"Take a knee. You can't expect an old woman to reach to your height," Atropos demanded.

Poseidon shook his head in exasperation as he knelt before Atropos.

"Do you know what is required?" Athena asked.

"I am Moirai, I know all from birth to death. I witness all, but if we are to condemn someone then proper respect must be paid. She reached out and plucked a hair from Poseidon's head. She tied a knot in one end of the hair and with a circular movement between thumb and finger, rolled the remainder of the hair around the knot. She placed the knot on her own brow and spoke beneath her breath. Then suddenly, she popped the knotted hair into her mouth, before placing a hand on either side of Poseidon's head.

"Tell me King of the fish, did you force yourself on this poor innocent girl?"

"No," Poseidon replied defiantly.

"Was she willing?"

"No... I mean I am innocent. I have not lain with this girl."

Atropos let her hands to drop to her sides.

"I believe I am ready to return to my home," she announced.

"But what did you discover?" Athena asked.

"What I knew all along."

"Which was?" Athena asked, clearly becoming frustrated.

"Innocent. Poseidon did not touch the girl."

Medusa began to sob.

"I think that I am no longer required." Poseidon retrieved his trident and without another word, walked into the pool and disappeared beneath the surface.

Zeus leaned close to Athena and whispered.

"Not death." Without looking at Medusa he took Atropos by the hand and simply disappeared.

Athena approached the sobbing Medusa. Her face

was set like stone oblivious to the young woman's woe. "To falsely accuse a deity is bad enough, but for that accusation to be levelled at a god of Olympus then the crime is both grave and reckless. To compound your lies, you defiled one of my temples. Zeus has asked for mercy, an act that you do not deserve." She paused as though considering a suitable punishment. "You have used your beauty to enchant Zeus. I shall remove that beauty. You have deceived in order to place yourself at the centre of your betters. I shall ensure that you will never command an audience. You wished to deny your mortality. I will grant you that wish, so that you will learn the error of your ways with every passing day. A never-ending life of solitude without so much as a kind reflection to gaze upon."

Medusa's sisters cried out their misery, they rushed forward to plead for mercy.

"Get back!" Hades ordered. "Know your place."

"Wait," Athena held up a hand to quell his rage. "Your sister's crime is not yours. I feel sorry for them. This creature has created such pain. I will grant you one day in each year. You may visit her and for that day she will be as you see her now." She turned back and glared at Medusa. "As for you, I tire of your presence. Be gone."

Medusa did not raise her eyes from the ground as her image faded from sight.

*****

For quite some time Aetes and the woman sat in the cavern without speaking. The boy's eyes were red raw from his attempt at not crying.

"I don't understand," he finally spoke. "We saw Poseidon force himself on Medusa. Could Atropos be mistaken?"

"No, the act was not carried by Poseidon. Even the gods cannot hide the truth from the Moirai. We saw someone claiming to be Poseidon. If you wish to know the truth then you must learn to see what isn't there. Someone wanted war between Zeus and Poseidon. Medusa was merely a useful tool."

"But Medusa was innocent," Aetes replied.

"Mortals make useful sacrifices."

"But surely someone could prove that she was innocent?"

"Someone did know," she replied.

"Who?"

"Atropos, did you not hear her call Medusa innocent? Gods become deaf when their pride is wounded. Zeus had laid the blame at Poseidon's feet. When he was proved wrong, he lost face. The fate of a mortal is insignificant compared to the childish pride of a god. I am not sure those that inhabit Olympus are capable of love."

"It's..." Words failed him.

"I did not show you the fate of Medusa to add weight to your heart, Aetes. I wanted you to see beyond the obvious. I also wanted you to see that gods have all the failings that mortals possess. Pride, jealousy, and greed flow like wine in Olympus." She paused for a moment.

"Tomorrow, you will enter the archway alone."

"But why?"

"I want you to witness the past without my presence swaying your opinion. Besides, if the Adonis Blood is to work then you must be alone."

"It worked today," he replied, confusion spreading across his face.

"It was only given to the arch. Tomorrow you will consume the blood and will become one with the arch. It will enable you to experience what those within the arch feel. You will experience their joy and their sorrow."

"Will it hurt?"

"You are not part of their world. No harm can befall you. If you are to truly understand the likes of Hector and Achilles, you must know their heart. But that is for tomorrow and this night we must eat and rest for the day ahead."

*****

The following morning arrived and Aetes rubbed his eyes. Sleep had not come easily the previous night. Medusa's fate and that of her unborn child had weighed heavily upon his mind.

"Here drink this," the woman pushed a goblet into his hands. He spied it with obvious caution. "It is just warmed milk with a few herbs."

"Thank you," he replied.

"Today will differ from your experience yesterday. As I said, the blood of Adonis will make you part of the arch. You will not have to journey along a path or select of image from the columns. It will know what to show you because you will be the arch. You will have a sense of who the individuals are long before you observe their actions."

"I don't understand."

"Have you ever seen a man and without speaking to him know that his life has been hard? That look in his eyes, the way he holds himself. Well, the arch will focus your senses. You will behold sights and witness many actions. Some, you will not immediately comphrehend."

"When will I know to stop?"

"You will know and so will the arch. Remember that within there is no time. You will not feel hunger, grow old or require sleep." She held up a small amphora. "I collected more blood this morning. Are you prepared?"

"What now?"

She smiled at him. "Yes, but be warned, it tastes foul."

Part One

'ORIGINS'

Chapter 3

'The House of Tantalus'

Mycenae

Since Tantalus, former ruler of Mycenae, had been consigned to the depths of Tartarus, Mycenae had rarely known stability. Despite having a formidable army, it was never able to grow beyond its borders because of the threat from internal enemies. Rulers came and went, usually at the point of a blade. This night would be no different...

King Atreus stood motionless as he looked beyond the city defences. His gaze was fixed firmly on the dark and foreboding countryside. His sibling, Thyestes, had sought the throne for himself, and now Mycenae was embroiled in a violent and bloody civil war. Just two days earlier he had met his brother in battle, driving his forces from the field. Since the victory, he had been beset with unease. It gnawed at his very soul. He had no love for his brother but recognised that Thyestes possessed skill and experience on the battlefield. So why did the battle seem such an easy victory? It was little more than a few small skirmishes. Thyestes seemed content to probe for weaknesses, reluctant to commit to a full-scale attack. It almost seemed as though his brother was ensuring that he preserved his troops. Atreus stared into the darkness, he knew that within the shadows an army lay, ready to strike.

"Where are you, brother of mine?" he whispered to himself.

"I'm sorry?" came the reply from a man that never left his side.

"Nothing, Pallas. Just thinking out loud," Atreus replied, his eyes never leaving the shadows beyond the city walls.

"We have strengthened the defence and doubled the guard," Pallas replied. The seasoned warrior seemed to know the doubts that had settled in Atreus' soul.

"Good, let's hope the night passes without incident." As he spoke, Atreus watched a flame rise from the city. It rose high into the air, arched over the defences and disappeared into the countryside beyond. For a moment, confusion flooded his mind, but then his eyes widened as he understood the flames meaning. "A signal!"

"What?"

Atreus ignored the question.

"Call out the army, everyone to their positions!"

"What is it, my king?" Pallas asked.

"They are already within the walls. They didn't meet us in battle because my brother's troops were slipping into the city." Pallas drew his sword, but the king grasped him by the hand. "No old friend, I have another task for you. Take your place at the side of my children, help them flee the city if necessary."

"But my place is at your side." Pallas tried to resist his King's wishes.

"We have been deceived, Pallas. The enemy is upon us, and the city may fall. If this is to be my last night, then I will go to the next world in the knowledge that you watch over my kin."

"But..."

"Thyestes has infiltrated the Mycenae. He could not have done this without help from within. I need my children to be with a sword that they can trust. Please my friend."

"It will be done," Pallas replied.

Screams began to shatter the stillness of the night. Atreus drew his sword.

*****

Menelaus and Agamemnon were attempting to put on the last of their armour. Their mother, Aerope, burst into the room. Although she held herself with a calm dignity, the eyes betrayed her and let those near see the fear she felt for her loved ones. Three bodyguards to her rear in close attendance.

"With haste boys, we must leave the city," she announced.

Agamemnon thrust a hand through his long hair. "But I am ready to fight."

Menelaus fumbled with his sword, managing to catch it by the hilt before it clattered across the floor. He recovered his composure and then declared, "We will not run away and leave our father."

"Your bravery is to be applauded and not one citizen of Mycenae would question it, but your father has ordered that you remain safe from harm." Before they could reply she added, "Even if you can defy your father, you cannot defy your king." She smiled clearly trying to reassure her sons. The smile, however, turned to shock as a blade burst the base of her throat.

Agamemnon screamed with rage and raced forwards, his weapon already rising above his head. As his mother dropped to the floor, his attack became apparent to her killer. Agamemnon's blade took him just below the jaw line. The guard died before the shock could register on his face. The two remaining guards advanced on Agamemnon, but one was brought to an abrupt halt as a spear struck the would-be assassin in the chest. Casting the leather tunic aside with ease, the spear tip crashed through flesh and bone. The guard dropped to his knees, slipped forward only to be suspended from the ground by the shaft of the spear. Menelaus who had thrown the spear, now moved alongside Agamemnon, blade in hand.

Agamemnon glared at the assailant. "You should have brought more men. We are not children for the slaughter. We have been trained since we took our first steps, by our father's own hand," declared Agamemnon.

There was a momentary flicker of concern in the guard's eyes, then he rallied and gave a roar of defiance. He recklessly swept his blade at both young princes. It was a reckless lunge, and he was punished for not taking care. Menelaus blocked the strike, as Agamemnon dived low and then used the tip of his sword to pierce the guard's thigh. Before the would-be killer could react, Menelaus struck him across the jaw with the hilt of his sword and the fight was over. The guard slipped semiconscious to the floor.

"Menelaus, watch the corridor," Agamemnon ordered.

The younger brother nodded his reply as he leapt over the unseeing body of the guard.

Agamemnon looked at the unconscious assassin, and then glanced towards the body of his mother. The sinews of his arm tensed as he gripped his blade. Despite his rage, he did not deliver a killing blow to the treasonous guard. He waited until his foe's senses had returned.

"Before your end, know that I will return to this city. Each man and woman that sold their king to my bastard of an uncle, will perish. They shall regret their treason." He raised the blade, and in one powerful blow removed the guard's leg just below the knee. "But it will not be an easy death." He announced over the screams. Hacking downwards, he detached the other leg without the slightest sign of hesitation. "I will take back this kingdom, bit by bit if I must." His victim offered no more screams. Pitiful whimpers emanated from the man as his eyes watched the weapon rise for a third time.

Menelaus returned to the room, as the guard's head skidded across the bloodied floor. He looked at his brother's armour showing the signs of the slaughter. Menelaus then glanced to the remains of the would-be assassin; his face paled at the sight.

"Errr... I believe we will soon have uninvited guests."

Agamemnon went to his mother, placing a hand on her cheek. He closed his eyes and made a solemn vow to avenge her death. Allowing his hand to drop, he grasped the necklace that hung about his mother's throat, pulling it free from the surface of the flesh that was already beginning to turn cold. Then without a word, he returned to Menelaus.

Agamemnon and Menelaus stepped into the corridor. No conversation took place, but it was clear that they needed to find their father. Their progress, however, was brought to an abrupt end as six warriors entered the royal quarters.

"Come on you bastards!" Agamemnon screamed.

A figure pushed his way to the front of the men. He sheathed his sword and removed his helmet. He dropped to one knee, showing that he was no threat.

"My prince, we are here to ensure you escape the city. By orders of the king."

"Pallas! Menelaus lowered his sword and raced toward him. For the first time that day, the young prince showed emotion, tears welling in his eyes. "Our father is he..." words failed him.

"He was alive the last time I saw him. Where is the queen?" Pallas asked.

"She's dead," Agamemnon announced, as he raised the necklace to prove the point. "Lead us from this place, Pallas."

*****

Atreus ordered his warriors to fall back. He had attempted to reinforce his men at the main gate to the city, but the enemy had emerged from every corner. Slowed by each surprise attack and archers hidden on the roof tops that had rained down death on his men, his attempt had utterly failed. Receiving word that the gate had fallen, and the enemy had reinforced their numbers, he was forced to retreat. His troops were scattered around the city, many of his loyal commanders had been killed leaving pockets of his men without leadership.

"Orders? My King." Cineas, was one of the few commanders that had managed to survive the assassins, he was also one of those most loyal to Atreus.

"We need to concentrate our forces. We will retire to the palace and collect as many as we can along the way. Send out runners, try to get the word out to all those that are loyal."

"We could get you out. If we wait much longer then…"

Atreus grasped Cineas and pulled him close.

"I have given orders that the princes be taken to safety. If we stop the fight now, then our enemy's attention may be drawn elsewhere. We must keep their focus upon us. Besides," he raised his voice so that his men could hear, "I am not ready to yield the city. We may still be a thorn in my brother's side." It was a false confidence purely for the benefit of his warriors. He knew that the battle for his beloved city was over the moment the main gate was laid open.

There was a scream as another man fell to a hidden archer.

"Bastards!" Cineas cursed the unseen attackers.

"We need to move now," Atreus replied.

Both king and commander urged the men back along the narrow streets. Now and then they would be forced to stop their progress as the enemy emerged. Often no more than a handful would strike from the shadows. The skirmishes only lasted a short time, but each assault would leave injured or dying men. Warriors that Atreus could ill afford to lose. It was a gruelling and costly journey to the palace.

Finally, they reached the courtyard, a large expanse of open ground that lay before the palace walls. Atreus called out to his men to halt. He eyed the surrounding buildings, searching for signs of the foe. Then he stared at the palace. He knew that it offered protection, but ultimately it would be the end of his reign. There would be nowhere left to run, his brother's troops would eventually force their way over the feeble defences. He wondered if Thyestes had already taken the palace and patiently lay in wait. That sickly, arrogant smile etched upon his face that so frequently occupied his sibling's features. Atreus forced thoughts of his brother from his mind to concentrate on what had to be done.

He held up his hand, constantly watching for signs of his brother's troops. A tremendous thirst overcame him, he licked his lips, tasting the dry skin beneath his tongue. He was aware that he was feeling an inner dread The heart pounded within his chest, he could feel the sweat between his grasp and sword hilt. It was an uncommon experience. He had fought in battles many times, but he was so consumed with giving orders that his mind was usually divorced from the potential dangers. This day was different, there was no possibility of victory. Glancing to the warriors at his side, he realised that the fear was not for himself. Serving him had condemned each of them to a terrible fate.

"I think we need to move," Cineas advised.

Atreus looked back towards the palace.

"Run! Don't stop until you get inside," Atreus ordered. He burst into a run. If there was a trap within the palace then he would spring it. Perhaps if he was to fall, then his brother would be merciful to his men?

Atreus could hear his warriors in close proximity, their sandals heavy on the cobbled courtyard. He estimated that he had at least fifty men under his command, far too many to cross open ground without being seen. Speed was the only option; he hoped the gods would look kindly on the desperate move. He had reached the halfway point before hearing the first scream. Chancing a sidewards glance, one of his men was clutching the shaft of an arrow that had buried itself into the flesh of his thigh. Cineas caught the man before he fell and was helping him reach safety. Atreus cursed before coming to stop.

"Keep going," he urged his men forward. As he spoke, he observed an enemy break from buildings to his right. Atreus placed himself between the advancing attacker and Cineas.

"Leave us, my King!" Cineas called out.

"Just move. I will cover your retreat." Atreus replied, before plucking the sword from the injured man. He turned to face the enemy; a blade grasped in each hand. He waited for the adversary and in the distance observed more of the enemy advancing. He walked backwards, no more than a few paces from Cineas and the injured warrior. He required room enough to do battle but needed to be close enough to guard those he protected. A quick glance over his shoulder showed that the first of his troops had entered the palace, he silently prayed that the foe did not lay in wait. A scream of rage brought his attention back to the more pressing danger. The enemy was bearing down on him, Atreus stopped his retreat and prepared to meet the attack. His foe slowed as he neared, sweeping his weapon from right to left trying to remove Atreus' head. It was a clumsy assault; Atreus didn't even need to offer a block. He danced aside, the warrior's weapon flailing in the air as Atreus' own thrust ripped into the flesh of his enemy's belly. Atreus twisted the blade, tearing the man's insides to pieces, and then withdrew. He allowed the warrior to drop to the ground, which was becoming slick with blood and torn intestine. There was no need to deliver a killing blow. The attacker posed no further threat and would not see another day.

Atreus looked at the distance Cineas still had to cover. The three attackers who had emerged from the shadows, still posed a threat. Atreus had confidence in his ability with a blade, but he knew that three against one rarely ended well. As they neared, it became obvious that one of the attackers was avoiding battle and was going for Cineas. Atreus was forced to block a lunge. He took a step back, raised a blade and threw it at the flanking assailant. He wasn't permitted the time to see if it was successful, a blade swept down catching him a glancing blow to his upper arm. It spun him around, but years of training enabled him to keep his balance. He continued his turn, brought the second sword around. It took the throat from his foe, a dark crimson spout of blood, erupting from the wound. It splattered into the eyes of the third attacker. Atreus reversed his swing and delivered a deep wound to the man's gut. Atreus stepped forward. He lifted the man's head, ripped off the helmet, and drew back his own blade, ready to strike. However, he didn't finish his enemy. The face, partially covered in blood was one that he recognised.

"Keteus, you serve in my ranks," Atreus whispered. He could not hide his hurt at the betrayal. He felt as though he had been kicked in the groin. His hand slipped from the man's head; the anger required for battle leaving him. In its place a nothingness settled within his chest.

"Forgive me, my King," Keteus replied.

"Why..." Atreus began to ask but changed his mind. "Go, you may survive if you reach a healer in time." He pushed the man away and without haste, walked to the palace, too unsettled at the betrayal to fear further attack.

*****

Agamemnon, Menelaus and their escort had escaped the city and were making their way through the surrounding countryside. It had been no easy task avoiding the patrols that were loyal to Thyestes. However, this was no time to be overconfident. If the city had fallen, then it would only be a matter of time before the land was swarming with the enemy. Thyestes would not permit heirs and potential challengers to his throne, to survive. Pallas was leading the small troop. Suddenly, he held up his hand and brought them to a halt.

"What is it, Pallas?" Agamemnon asked.

Pallas wiped the sweat from his forehead. "There is a clearing just ahead, and it seems to be occupied."

"How many men?"

"As far as I can tell, just one."

"Then kill him and let's be on our way," Agamemnon ordered.

"I am not in the habit of killing without good reason," Pallas replied.

"The good reason is because your prince ordered it," Agamemnon snapped.

"At this point you are neither prince nor a man. I promised your father that I would keep you alive. So, I suggest that you remain quiet before you alert the enemy to our position."

Agamemnon's hand drifted towards his sword, but Menelaus placed his hand on his brother's arm.

"We could just go around the clearing," Menelaus suggested.

"That we could, but why is this man sitting alone in a land torn apart by war? A fire rages alerting one and all to his position, and yet he hasn't even raised his head to look for potential dangers. Remain here I will approach him alone." Without waiting for reply or argument Pallas stepped into the clearing. He strode without trying to conceal his approach. When he was no more than ten paces away from the stranger, he gave a cough. The figure remained perfectly still; his features concealed by a hood. Pallas was forced to move closer.

"Stranger, I am Pallas, a commander in the King's army. I have you surrounded and demand to know your name."

"You are truly a talented commander. To surround a clearing with five men and two others that have the blood of Atreus."

A shocked Pallas felt that he was losing control of the discussion. Hand drifting toward the blade at his hip. "Who are you?" Pallas asked, his tone stern.

"There is no need to reach for your sword. I meant no disrespect. My name is not important, but what I can offer, however, that is a different matter."

"And what can you offer?" Pallas replied, his hand remaining close to his hilt.

"The troops of Thyestes press on all sides. Despite your skill and devotion, you cannot save Agamemnon and Menelaus, but I can. I have knowledge of a route that will see you all safely beyond the enemy patrols and these lands. I can also place them beyond the reach of their wretched uncle."

"If you can do all these things, what is it that you will want in return?" Pallas asked.

"Payment," came the brief reply.

"We have nothing to exchange."

The figure laughed.

"I have no need for physical goods. I offer a service, one that can be repaid when the sons of Atreus are in a position to offer a service in return."

"What kind of service?"

"In truth, I do not know. The time may well never arise that I need their help, but if this night proves anything, it is that the future is uncertain. Perhaps I should put my proposal directly to them?"

"They're just boys," Pallas protested.

"Not any longer, Pallas. They must become men and in all haste. Bring them closer. The fire has done its work well on this plump rabbit. Whether or not my offer is accepted, you will all need a good meal to face the trials ahead."

Pallas looked over his shoulder toward the trees, unsure if he should call the small band of men toward the fire.

"If I wanted you dead Pallas, I could have informed your enemy the moment you left the city. A task that would have seen Thyestes pay me handsomely. I offer you nought but friendship, trust me, you are in dire need of friends. Especially, ones with skill and influence."

Pallas stared at the figure, he wished that he could look into the man's eyes. Finally, he gave a whistle to signal the others to come forward.

Chapter 4

'All Things Change'

Atreus watched the movement of shapes on the far side of the courtyard. He could not understand why the enemy had not launched an attack. He wondered if Thyestes was merely playing a cruel game. Atreus knew that the battle was over, and it would not be long before his brother was in complete control of Mycenae. Thyestes was no fool, he must be aware that he had gained victory. As a child, his older brother had treated him with disdain and cruelty. For years, Thyestes' enjoyment seemed to revolve completely on the amount of pain he could inflict on any poor soul. Atreus remembered all too well being the main target. Raising his hand, he touched the scar that ran close to his left eye. One of many injuries caused by his brother's violent attacks. If Pallas had not caught Thyestes in the act, then the beatings would have continued for many more years. Thyestes was sent away, but the reports the king received about his behaviour resulted in him losing his right to the crown.

Atreus was selected as heir and groomed to be king. In truth, he never wanted the crown, nonetheless, he became king following the death of his father. Almost immediately, the question on how to deal with Thyestes' behaviour and public rants of having the crown stolen from him had been a constant thorn in his side in the early years of his reign. However, Thyestes had seemed to have a change of heart, his attitude changed and all talk of the claiming the crown stopped. He had risen through the ranks of the military and had defended the lands of Mycenae. As his brother's reputation grew, so did those that saw him as the true king. Atreus, despite his closest advisor's recommendations, had refused to agree that his brother should be put to death for treason.

"I wish I had listened to Pallas," he whispered to himself.

"I wish that I had a bow," Cineas announced. He pointed to a figure across the courtyard.

He looked in the direction that his commander had pointed. The unmistakable image of Thyestes came into view.

"It wouldn't help, you are a bloody awful archer."

Cineas laughed. "Perhaps the gods would guide my aim," Cineas replied.

"I think they have forsaken us this night. I shall go and speak to my brother."

"You cannot trust the man. Stay. We will fight the bastards," Cineas pleaded.

"There have been too many deaths, Mycenae has lost too much blood already." The carnage had to stop, no matter the cost to himself.

"But we still have men in the city. They will continue

the fight," Cineas replied.

"Look." Atreus pointed beyond the courtyard, towards the city. "Mycenae is burning. Its people are dying. Thyestes will not stop. He would rather the city is nought but dust than give up his claim to the throne. My time as king is at an end."

To Atreus, it looked as if Cineas wanted to shake him until he changed his mind. Finally, however, it seemed that his friend was resigned to agree to his actions. Atreus watched as Cineas straightened his back, pushed out his jaw and took in a deep breath, then called out.

"Open the gate!"

Atreus walked out into the open space. At ten paces he stopped and waited to see what Thyestes would do. To his surprise, Thyestes dismissed his bodyguards and set off across the courtyard alone. For a moment. Atreus considered the possibility of killing his sibling. Would he have enough time before the bodyguards could react. Thyestes was a fine swordsman, his skills honed on the battlefield. Atreus knew that his brother would not be an easy man to kill. Thyestes rarely left things to chance. Atreus could not see the archers he knew would be hidden, but they would be present, ready to at a moment's notice.

"Brother!" Thyestes called out as the distance between them closed. "It is brave of you to venture out to meet me. Our father is no longer here to protect you."

Atreus ignored the insult. "It is a beautiful night. A walk is good for clearing the mind."

"And what thoughts play on your mind?" Thyestes replied, as he came to a halt.

"How to stop the city from burning and our people from dying," Atreus replied.

"All things come to an end, Brother."

"That is so but tell me Thyestes. How will the crown you seek rule nought but ash?"

"Then surrender. Give up the crown and save both city and those within."

"And watch as you slaughter all that were loyal to me?" Atreus shook his head.

"I have no wish for more deaths. I would have all serve me, as they have served you."

"Then declare it to all. Give them the freedom to remain or leave without fearing for their lives."

"And what of their king?" Thyestes asked.

"We both know my fate."

Thyestes smiled.

"And your sons?" The usurper's eyes narrowed.

"I cannot bargain away what I do not possess. I can only place my life in your hands. However, you should know this Thyestes. If you refuse, then I shall order my men to fight to the last. This city will burn. Every burnt ember, every dead body will be testament to your inadequacies as both man and future king. However, if you agree I will order my warriors to accept you as their new ruler. You will have victory, the crown and a city to rule."

"You will instruct your men through-out the city to lay down their arms?" Thyestes seemed genuinely surprised at the offer.

"We both know that I am not leaving this place. Cineas is trusted by my troops, he will ensure that all hear my orders."

"Cineas is alive? It seems I need better assassins." Thyestes laughed. "But I need good men, and he is a fine commander. How about that old rogue, Pallas?"

"Dead… He fell as we tried to reach the main gate." Atreus lied.

For the first time, Thyestes' eyes left Atreus. He seemed deep in thought, pacing back and forth.

"Very well Atreus, I will honour this agreement. Those loyal to you will be free to remain in the city or seek their fortune elsewhere. But they should know that I will not tolerate disloyalty. The mercy I have shown this night, will not be repeated. They must yield to my will."

"I shall inform my people within the palace and return shortly. You should inform your men that the war is at an end. It would be unfortunate that hostilities arise from a misunderstanding." Atreus did not wait for a reply. He turned and strode toward the palace. He knew that his fate as a man was sealed, but with this last act, those that survived the night might look kindly on him as a king,

*****

It was not long before Atreus emerged from the palace gate. At his side walked Cineas, minus his sword. Atreus had listened to the speech his brother had made to his troops and realised that he could do no more to protect his people. This agreement relied on Thyestes keeping his word.

Thyestes was waiting in the centre of the courtyard. Far more torches now burned, ensuring all could see the passing of the throne from one brother to the other. As the three men came together, the warriors loyal to Atreus left the palace, dropping their weapons to the ground. Those loyal to Thyestes that ringed the courtyard, gave a cheer.

"It is a noble act you do this day, Atreus," Thyestes announced.

"A king must place his people before himself," Atreus replied.

"We both share a love for Mycenae and those within its walls. Even if we could never share the love of brothers."

"I have always loved you, Thyestes. Even when you showed me only hatred. I doubt that you are even capable of love. That is the reason the crown will sit poorly upon your head."

"We shall see soon enough. I have spoken to my men, and I see that Cineas is ready to visit your warriors about the city and declare the war is at an end. Is there anything else?" Thyestes asked.

"No, I think..." Atreus began to speak.

Drawing his sword, Thyestes plunged it into the chest of Atreus. He twisted the blade, but Atreus refused to scream.-Thyestes stepped in close and whispered, "I will honour our agreement, but I will hunt down your sons. Trust me Atreus, they will scream so loud it will wake the dead."

Atreus managed a grim smile.

"Fear Agamemnon, brother."

"And why would I do that?"

"Because he is just like you."

Atreus slumped to the ground and died where he fell.

Thyestes signalled for his men to approach. For a moment, he pondered his brother's final words. An involuntary chill raced down his spine as he thought of vengeful princes seeking his death.

"Take Cineas around the city and have him give word that the war is over. There is to be no more killing," he paused for moment, "but first, take this," he kicked the lifeless body of Atreus, "and hang it from the city walls. People should know not to oppose the will of Thyestes."

*****

Pallas had agonised over whether to trust the stranger. The princes, however, had been less reluctant to hear their new host out. Pallas could not deny that the chance of reaching safety was only improved by having a plan and he hadn't the time to devise one. The stranger had spoken of a mine that lay in the east of the lands of Mycenae. A once productive, but now abandoned silver mine, known as the River of Artemis. So called, because the silver flowed from the mine like a raging river. Pallas had scoffed at the idea that the mine could be navigated, but the stranger insisted that he knew every twist and turn it had to offer.

"How do you come to know so much of this mine?" Menelaus asked.

"I have had reason to visit it many times. Most of its tunnels have collapsed, some have even filled with water. I do not wish to belittle the danger. It is not without jeopardy. But the risk provides us with an opportunity." The stranger poked the fire that made the flames reach up and caress the rabbit carcass cooking on the spit.

"How does danger provide an opportunity?" Pallas asked.

"The mine was a source of great income to many past kings of Mycenae. Each day the mine burrowed deeper into Gaea's flesh. Those that dug so feverishly in search of their fortune, were not aware that a plethora of caverns were sat directly beneath their mine. Tunnels lost their stability, bringing down the earth onto unsuspecting workers. Before long rumours started that a beast roamed the tunnels seeking victims or that Artemis was angry that her silver was being pillaged. It was nonsense, but soon miners were unwilling to raise their tools or even place a foot in the place. Their concerns were of course foolishness, but it meant that the mine was abandoned. However, if you have the right guide, you can use the caverns that sit beneath to travel almost to the coast. If fortune is especially kind, that guide will also have a vessel waiting to carry you from harm's way."

"You seem to have this all planned out," Pallas pointed out.

"It is what I do. I also like to eat rabbit. Let's consume this fine animal, then I shall leave you alone to discuss the matter. I will be leaving before nightfall. The full moon will provide enough light to travel. If we avoid the main routes, we should stay clear of the patrols. We could reach our destination within three days."

Menelaus' eyes were wide. "Three days!"

"Better slow than dead," Pallas announced. He still didn't trust the stranger. Especially, as the man insisted on keeping his face hidden beneath his hood. Yet the only plan in the offing was the one offered by a man that they had only just met. It made Pallas feel uneasy, but he remembered that the city had been lost because of the disloyalty of men that he had called friend. He was also aware that he needed to assert his authority. The stranger and the princes needed to be reminded who was responsible for ensuring that they made it to safety. To do that, he needed each of them to act swiftly, and without questioning his orders.

"No need for discussion. We have no idea what has happened within the city and an attempt to find out may well place us all in danger. So, we must assume the worst and leave Mycenae behind. We will have to place our lives in your hands at least for the time being. We will travel with you through the mine. Once we have safely navigated to the other side, we shall discuss our next move."

"Excellent! Now let us eat for the night presses on," the stranger replied.

*****

Their guide had been correct when he said the journey would be slow. During many hours spent travelling they spent much of their time hiding from riders in the distance, especially as night became day. Pallas noticed that the troops belonging to Thyestes were too numerous to be merely regular patrols. Although he did not share his fears with the princes, he knew that it meant that the fight for the city had not gone well for Atreus. Pallas also knew that his king would never abandon his people to the cruelty of his older brother. Secretly, Pallas concluded that Atreus must be either prisoner or dead.

Travelling through the night was proving to be difficult. The terrain tricked both sight and footing. The cold bit at exposed flesh, and the succulent taste of rabbit seemed too far away. Pallas heard his own stomach growl its discontent. He turned to look at the princes, both were approaching manhood. Indeed, they would be considered men if they were not part of the royal household. They were used to the life that being a member of nobility offered. Both had tremendous skill with a whole range of weapons, but neither had spent a single night in discomfort.

"It's getting light, we should look for somewhere that will hide us from the patrols," Pallas announced, not wanting to highlight his concerns to the rest of the group.

The stranger stopped his progress. He raised a hand

and pointed to a small gully.

"At the end of this track, there is a sharp incline that houses a number of small caves. The largest of them will give us ample room and enable us to light a small fire, without it signalling our enemy. The climb will be tough, I admit this night is wearing upon my old limbs."

Pallas doubted the stranger felt any exhaustion, his pace had remained constant, never any sign of flagging.

The gully's earth was wet and stuck to feet and lower legs adding unwanted weight to the travellers. As the steep climb began Pallas decided to drop back, allowing the stranger complete control on their direction. Entrusting someone to to take the lead went against his natural instincts. Pallas loathed having to take the action, but he needed to be close to the princes. He fell in alongside Menelaus who seemed to be struggling more than his older brother. Pallas wanted to offer an arm, but knew that like their father, both were filled with pride.

"Pallas," Menelaus said, as his brother continued ahead. He spoke through the heavy intake of breaths.

"Yes, my Prince."

"My father," he paused, as if he wasn't sure that he wanted to utter the words, "is my father dead?"

Pallas felt a weight upon his heart far greater than he had experienced before.

"You ask a question that I cannot answer," he replied. He had tried to speak in a gentler tone. It was not easy for a military man.

"But you know my uncle. If the city falls, will he allow my father to live?"

Pallas remembered the words of the stranger. 'They must become men and in all haste.' Pallas did not want to speak the words. If he admitted the king was dead, he would also be admitting that terrible fact to himself. He suddenly felt so very weary. He had been a warrior since he was not much older than Menelaus. He had served their father and Aetreus' father before him. Duty had always come before his own family, and so, those he served became his family. He loved Atreus like a brother, he had even loved Thyestes once, it was that love that had blinded him to the acts of cruelty Thyestes inflicted on Atreus for so long. Then Atreus had two sons, and Pallas had loved them as sons.

He turned and looked at Menelaus. "Your uncle is a brutal and unforgiving man. We must strengthen our heart to accept the possibility that your father may be dead. In answer to your question. No, I do not think that Thyestes would allow anyone that was a threat to his rule, to survive. That is why we must honour your father's wishes and get you and your brother to safety." To his surprise his words did not bring Menelaus to tears.

"If he has killed my father, then the walls of Mycenae will not protect him," Menelaus replied.

"Then you must grow strong. Pay attention to your body and mind. The time will come that you have the opportunity to have a reckoning with Thyestes."

The boy nodded and began to climb once again. Pallas watched him go. He raised a hand and wiped the tears from his eyes.

Chapter 5

'The River of Artemis'

The terrain on the third day permitted them to travel during the day. Heavy woodland protected them from prying eyes. The sun had begun its descent towards the horizon when the small group came to a halt.

Pallas and the others looked down from the hillside. To the east, the silver mine known as the River of Artemis, could clearly be seen. However, here was an obvious problem. In the valley between their position and their desired destination, at least twenty soldiers had set up camp. Pallas stared at the back of the stranger and wondered if a trap had been laid in advance.

"I am not responsible for this, Pallas. But our plan remains unchanged," the stranger announced. It was as though he could see into Pallas's thoughts.

"And how do you suppose we pass unseen? The terrain does not lend itself to concealment," Pallas replied.

"Then we will use the day to our advantage."

"What do you mean?" Menelaus asked.

"We cannot risk being seen. The mine is too far from our enemy's position, we will be chased down before we can reach safety. We will have more of a chance If we cross the valley before sunrise whilst they are still asleep.

"No, there is another way," Pallas interrupted. "They have only two guards, one at either end of the camp. If we get close enough, we can kill them all before they can place a hand to blade. It is the only way to ensure that our path is clear, and we are not pursued. We haven't the strength for a chase."

"You only have five men, Pallas," the stranger replied.

"No, I have seven. Eight if you can handle a blade," Pallas gave a determined reply.

"Alas, my mind is sharp, but my fighting prowess far too blunt."

"Then you can act as lookout. Come closer," he motioned to the group, "the camp isn't far from that cover, do you see it?" He pointed at a certain part of the terrain. "I suggest we work our way to that point and wait until dark. First, we will rest for the remainder of this day, as we intended to do. As night falls, we will advance on the camp. Our group will split in two. We will take out the guards and then fall on the other men. They must all die and not be given the opportunity to escape and tell of our position."

"Are you sure?" Menelaus paused briefly, then added. "And do you think they know we are close?"

"Thyestes would have offered a substantial reward for your death or capture. If they believed we were nearby, then they would not be sitting on their arses," Pallas replied.

"These bastards are traitors! I only wish there were more of them to kill," Agamemnon announced.

"Now is not the time for fury, Agamemnon. We must be measured and kill without emotion, and above all, in silence," Pallas advised.

"You will not find me wanting," Agamemnon replied.

"Then rest. I will take the first watch."

The day passed without incident. Pallas had hoped that the enemy would break camp and leave the way to the mine clear, but they remained in the valley. The stranger sat down next to him.

"Are you sure that this is the right course of action?" he asked

Pallas sighed. "I am not sure of anything. The past few days have been a little demanding."

"Your king, Atreus. What kind of man was he?"

"I am not a young man, though not as old as many think. I was only a sapling when Atreus' father brought me into his household. Despite my age, I had shown a talent on the battlefield, and he wanted that knowledge passed to his sons. In the early years I found Atreus to betoo quick to tears. It soon became apparent that the reason behind his sensitivity was the cruelty he faced at the hands of his brother. Thyestes was sent away. It was not done out of hate, but partly to save Atreus, but mostly in the attempt to force Thyestes to change his ways. It failed miserably, but Atreus prospered from the separation. He gained a great deal of skill, both in diplomacy and military tactics. Fine attributes in any man."

"Indeed, but what kind of man was he?" the stranger asked again.

"What kind of man? He was a good man, a man that prized his honour above reward. He did not look to the gods for guidance or blame but took responsibility for his actions. He was more than a king to me - he was loved as much as any son or brother."

"And Thyestes?"

"Talented in the field of battle, possessed of an intelligence that few could match. But his ambition knows no boundaries. Honour and friendship have no place in his cold heart. The man is nothing but a loathsome bastard." Pallas spat upon the floor as if to show his disgust. "He believes he is a direct descendant of Zeus and as such, all men should bend a knee in his presence."

"And what of Agamemnon and Menelaus?"

"What about them?"

"Would the good King Atreus agree with sending them to kill?"

"Atreus is not here. He is more than likely dead. If the princes do not want to go the same way, they must embrace death. They must be prepared to send men to the other world. They cannot be like Atreus. Do you not agree?"

"I think that Thyestes will one day regret making an enemy of Agamemnon and Menelaus. The time approaches that we should begin our journey into the valley. I wish you good fortune in your task." The guide rose and brushed his robe clean, indicating that the time for talk was at an end.

*****

The group had made their way down into the valley and waited for the camp to fall to slumber as the night pressed on. Pallas watched the guards as they rested on their spears. Finally, he turned to Menelaus, who stood at his side.

"Stay close to me. Do not hesitate, and when you strike, do so at the throat. It's hard to call out when you're sucking on a blade."

Menelaus nodded.

"Let's move," Pallas ordered.

The group split into two as it moved forward. The guards fell with little more than a whimper. Seven figures drifted through the enemy's camp. Now and then the dying flames of the camp's fire glinted on a length of a rising blade, and then disappeared as the weapon fell. The flames also highlighted the pale face of Menelaus, as he made his first kill. Pallas watched as the boy showed no hesitation in the terrible act but thankfully, neither did he display enjoyment. The slaughter did not take long, the foe never rousing from their sleep to take up arms. They died where they lay, ignorant of their upcoming journey to the next world.

Twenty men lay bloodied on the ground, as seven shadows slipped from the camp and made their way towards the mine. Not a word was spoken between man or boy. Not even as the stranger emerged to show them the way forward.

*****

The sun was rising as the entrance to the mine came into view and they were forced to come to a halt. Pallas looked at each of men. The blood of the victims covered much of their garments. He noticed that even the seasoned warriors carried a look of revulsion. Only one figure seemed at ease at the night's gruesome work. Agamemnon cleaned the blade of his sword with the bottom of his own tunic.

Pallas crossed to Menelaus and wiped a splash of blood from the boy's cheek. "You did well."

Menelaus' face was as white as fleece. "Did I?"

"You did not turn away, despite the task. Now, try to put it from your mind." Pallas turned to their guide. "Do we have supplies?"

"Hidden a short way into the mine," the stranger replied.

Pallas glanced down at his own eyes red-stained hands. "We have to wash this night away. We need water."

"I think I can provide you with more than a little water. Follow me." The stranger took off through the entrance and down the first tunnel.

There was an audible groan as the group moved their aching bodies into the tunnel. As they progressed, the light of day began to lose its reach and oppressive darkness began to close around them.

"Do not fear the darkness, I have some lamps hidden

with the supplies," the stranger announced.

"Is it far?" Pallas asked after colliding with one of his own men.

"You have my word, there is comfort close by, and I promise it will be worth the wait. But first we must choose the correct path. Just up ahead the main tunnels bear to the right, but we seek a smaller, less travelled path. Move over to the left side of the tunnel, place your hand upon the wall so as not to miss the entrance. Thankfully it is the only tunnel that branches left, but it pays to be careful in a place such as this. It would be unfortunate to become lost in this place."

Pallas moved to the front of his men. He knew the guide was leading, but if there was danger or treachery to be faced, then he would place himself between it and his men. Besides, he thought that the princes would need to hear a familiar voice in the darkness. As Pallas moved into the gloom, he understood just how easy it would be to become lost. The darkness assaulted the senses. He placed a hand upon the tunnel wall, the solidity providing comfort. He moved slowly, fearing the unknown to his front.

Finally, he gave a silent thanks to the gods when at last he located the entrance to side tunnel.

"I have found it," he alerted those to his rear. "Call out when you reach the entrance," he ordered. Pallas continued forward and was relieved as each of the party announced that they had successfully found the entrance. Time moved on, and with each step, Pallas became less sure of the direction of travel. He was certain that they descended deeper into the earth. He could feel his thigh muscles ache as they resisted the downward slope and the urge to break into a run.

"Wait here!" the guide called out.

Pallas heard the stranger's footsteps fade. The sound of the footsteps was replaced by his own breathing as the heavy darkness weighed upon his nerves. He could not see the faces of those behind him, but he sensed their discomfort. He wondered if the recent slaughter played on their thoughts. Such an oppressive atmosphere easily conjured up snarling ravenous creatures, determined to seek vengeance for the slain. Pallas had killed many men in his life, mostly as an an act of self-preservation. But did those men of the camp deserve to die at the hands of an unseen enemy? Was it simply expedient to commit slaughter? For a moment, he wondered if those men had died to soothe the personal anger he'd felt at the loss of both his king and friend.

Abruptly, his thoughts were interrupted. In the distance a light appeared, driving the memories of the dead from his mind. He was obviously not alone; he could sense the relief of those his rear. Deciding not to wait for the stranger to give a signal, he moved forward, keen to escape the darkness. The illumination seemed to grow in its brilliance, forcing Pallas to protect his eyes. When finally, he dropped his hand he was amazed by the image before him. A pool of clear water glistened in the lamp light.

"I thought that the opportunity to bathe and fill your bellies would aid you for the journey ahead." The guide poked at a meal that cooked above an open fire.

"This is..." Pallas struggled to find the words.

"Wondrous?" The stranger suggested. "I have visited this place many times. I bring another lamp whenever I journey through the mine and stay a while. This place seems to cleanse more than just my flesh. I doubt the meal will match the setting, but it will be warm and filling."

"Thank you," Pallas replied. He was still struggling to take in the astonishing scene. The rest of the group, however, were less transfixed. Armour and garments were discarded, naked figures rushed to pass Pallas, obviously eager to feel the cool liquid on their skin. Pallas could not deny the urge to dive into the waters any longer. He stripped and strode into the pool. He ducked his head beneath the surface and closed his eyes, enjoying the solitude that the caressing water brought. As he emerged, he observed those nearby. Most held their tongue, concentrating on removing the blood and dirt from their flesh. Agamemnon, however, resembled a boy that was merely enjoying a daily bathe. He was not exactly smiling, but his face was devoid of the haunted look that afflicted the others. Pallas wondered what raced through the boy's mind. The prince had always been difficult to second guess. He had always been a secretive child who seemed to set himself apart. Not cruel like Thyestes but withdrawn from all but his younger brother.

The bathing continued for some time. It was only the smell of food that tempted Pallas and the others from the pool. Gradually, the group began to interact, even if the conversation was a little stunted. The meal was finished and one by one the group members began to slip into slumber. Pallas was one of the last to fall asleep and

wasn't too impressed at being woken so soon after closing his eyes. He looked up to find the stranger standing
over him, a finger pressed to his lips.

"Be warned, Pallas. We are not alone." He motioned
towards the tunnel. "Wake the others."

"Dog's balls!" Pallas replied. "We should have hidden
the bodies." He hurried to each of the sleeping figures
and roused them from their slumber, but mindful not
to let them cry out. The group dressed in haste, collect-
ing the supplies needed for the journey.

"We must leave now. It seems that most of our uninvited guests have ventured down the wrong tunnel.
They will find that this place can be treacherous," the
stranger announced as he strode back to the group.
"Fortunately, they do not block our path." Without another word he hurried to the far side of the pool. Cut
into the floor was a hole that was only wide enough to
allow the passing of one person. A ladder made of rope
disappeared into the gloom below. He waved them forward. "Pallas would you lead the way. I have an idea that
may dissuade our pursuers from following."

Pallas stepped forward without hesitation. He
lowered himself into the opening, grasping the ladder
in each hand.

"Send the princes after me," he ordered.

"Wait!" The stranger called out. "Take this." He held
out a lamp, the like of which, Pallas had never seen before. The oil burned brightly, but the clay pot in which it
was housed, was in turn held firm by an outside cage. A
hook attached to the top of the cage made it easy to be

fixed to the body, leaving the arms free to do whatever they wished. "My own design, ideal for times like this."

"Much appreciated," Pallas replied. He took the lamp and began his descent. At first the ladder seemed stable enough, but as the other men joined the descent, it bucked and jerked wildly. Pallas, looked up anxiously toward the princes. He tried to move in the rhythm of the moving ladder, but quickly realised that it was chaotic and impossible to judge. "Slow and sure. Make sure of your foothold before you move," he called out to those above. Pallas knew that the ladder was unsuitable for carrying so many at once, but the proximity of the enemy removed the luxury of a gradual descent. He pressed on. Now and then he would glance to the gloom below and then upwards to those men that struggled above. However, for the most part he concentrated on the ladder directly to his front. His hands were beginning to feel raw, but he gritted his teeth and pressed on. After what seemed an age, his foot landed on the firmness of the cavern floor. He held up his oil lamp to provide better light for those still climbing down.

A shadow loomed from up above; a scream rent the air. A body came hurtling toward Pallas, only his quick reactions enabled him to dive out of harm's way. He spilled the lamp sending it rolling about the cavern floor. Pallas regained his footing as the light of the lamp span all around him. For a moment, he refused to look at the body, fearing that one of the princes lay crumpled, bones broken by the deadly fall. But look he must and forced himself to observe the body. As the light settled, he could make out the form of Dryas. A good man that Pallas had known and liked for many years, despite the loss, Pallas felt relief. For the time being at least, he was fulfilling his pledge to Atreus and keeping the king's sons safe. He crossed to the fallen, but there was no sign of life.

"Is he dead?" Agamemnon asked as he stepped from the ladder.

"That he is. Hold up the lamp to aid the others," Pallas replied. As Agamemnon retrieved the lamp, Pallas straightened Dryas' limbs. He silently thanked the man for fulfilling his duty and remaining loyal. He placed a hand on his cheek. "Swift journey my friend."

The remaining members of the group waited for the stranger to reach the bottom of the ladder. As he did so, he took the lamp from Agamemnon. He removed it from its cage and then held its flame on the rope. Initially the strands stubbornly refused to light, but then the fibres began to smoke. Finally, the flame took hold and raced up into the darkness.

"I have coated the top half of the rope with oil. It will come as quite a shock should they try to follow us."

"Then Dryas will have company on his journey. We should move," Pallas announced.

*****

The soul of Dryas emerged from the broken shell that was once its home. He watched as his comrades turned away to continue their journey. He tried to follow, but for some reason he seemed rooted to the spot.

"That is a path that you cannot walk," a voice echoed in the cavern.

"Who is there?" Dryas asked.

A black clad figure manifested itself in the empty space. Dryas recognised the shape before him. He looked once more to his friends.

"But how can that be? You are there," he pointed to the group, "but now you are here?"

"I am *Death*. When the flame of life is extinguished, I am present."

Dryas' face twisted with confusion.

"Then why are you with my friends?"

"Because some are doomed to walk with *Death* as a constant companion. Look no more on this world and prepare for your voyage to the next." The dark form waved a hand. A golden doorway appeared in the solid rock of the cavern wall. Any further questions that Dryas wished to ask were forgotten as he was compelled to leave the world of men.

*****

All but one of the small band had survived the descent into the lower caverns. They were not permitted the luxury of grieving for their comrade. The stranger took the lead and navigated the many twists and turns that the mine had to offer. Every now and then a cry of woe would echo through the darkness.

"This mine has claimed many," the stranger announced, as they paused to take a rest.

"I will say this for them, they are persistent," Pallas replied.

"I doubt they still give chase. No... I think the screams are of those that have lost their way and have met with an unfortunate accident."

"Well, they won't get pity from me," Agamemnon added.

"Brother, they are still men," Menelaus replied.

"No, Menelaus your brother is right. These men would have been paid handsomely for gutting you like a fish. They've also sold out their king. Save your mercy for those more deserving." He spat on the ground as he thought of their treachery. "Those bastards deserve nothing but death." Pallas' words poured cold water on the conversation and soon the group were once again travelling through the depths of the mine.

*****

Time meant very little to Pallas, for the darkness gave no clue to what part of the day it was. When the ground began to incline, he realised that they must be heading toward the surface, but it was a full three more sleeps before fresh air was to brush against his skin again. Still, they had not reached their journey's end. The stranger told them it was a further day's walk to the coast, and the waiting vessel.

A small cove played host to the stranger's craft. Its crew were camped on the sand, the smell of roast boar filled the air. It was with tangible relief that the small group of travellers were welcomed and offered nourishment.

The stranger approached Pallas. "I have news," he announced, as he passed one of two bowls of steaming hot stew to Pallas.

"Gratitude. I will not lie, it smells good. What is the news?" Pallas asked. He half expected some impending doom, the last few days had been relatively easy.

"By morning we will have another vessel in the cove. It presents us with an opportunity."

"In what way?" Pallas asked.

"We have been fortunate to escape the attention of Thyestes, but it would be foolish to believe that just because the princes are free of his lands, they're also free of his wrath. When we first met, I told you that I had the means to not only get them to safety, but to keep them alive."

"I remember." Pallas nodded.

"It seems to me that not many states will be willing to risk the fury of Mycenae's military. However, a state that is powerful may be persuaded."

"But which state would be willing to protect the princes? What is there to gain?" Pallas asked.

"A state or states that wish to have royal sons and not just daughters, one where marriage will ensure their loyalty. Or perhaps owe a debt to the late King Atreus."

"I know of no debt, but Priam of Troy and Atreus were more than rival royals. I believe they shared a true friendship. Besides, the princes will not like being whored out to the highest bidder." Pallas replied, but inwardly his wards had little option.

"Highest bidders? They will be fortunate to find more than one willing to risk Thyestes' wrath. I understand they will be reluctant, but they need strong arms about them until they can take the fight to Thyestes."

"If I can get them to agree, what did you have in mind?"

"Sparta. King Tyndareus is in my debt." The stranger reached inside his robe and pulled out a wooden disc, carved symbols adorned its surface. "Place this in his hand and he will know that I wish him to help you."

Pallas felt confused. "So why do we need a second vessel?" he asked.

"Because this is where we must part. My men are good sailors and loyal. They will see you and Menelaus, safely to Sparta. I will take Agamemnon to Troy. If the princes are housed within two states, then Thyestes may be reluctant to wage war on two fronts."

"And if Priam refuses?"

"Then I will see him carried safely to Sparta and your warm embrace."

"And if Tyndareus refuses?"

"He will not. The debt he owes me will compel him to offer young Menelaus protection. Besides, he has no love for Thyestes.

Pallas did not reply immediately but stared for some time at the hooded figure.

"I do not know your name. I could not even fully describe your features." Pallas held out a hand. "But you have saved Agamemnon and Menelaus. For that you have my gratitude and friendship."

"Your friendship honours me, Pallas. I do not conceal my name and face for deceitful reasons. You were unsure about trusting me. Likewise, I did not know that those within your group were loyal. Holding my identity close was a necessary act." He raised his hands and removed the hood. "I consider myself a fine judge of men. I now know that you're loyal to Agamemnon and Menelaus. I will do all that I can to aid them reach safety. But remember that I may call on the princes to honour this debt in the future. I must admit to finding enjoyment in causing Thyestes torment."

"You have met Thyestes?"

"I have encountered many of those that have suffered from his deceit and savagery. The man has a gift for causing misery," replied.

"That he does, but it will be his undoing. They will return one day, and that bastard's wall or army will not be enough to save him."

"The princes have a determination that is rare in ones so young. I believe that this land will be returned to them. But first, we must keep them alive, and so, they must travel to different lands."

"To new lands then," Pallas agreed.

Chapter 6

'An Uneasy Friend'

Agamemnon had not enjoyed the sea voyage. His host had clearly tried to ease his concerns, but the prince missed his brother. His father and mother had been ripped from this world, and now he must remain separated from his only remaining family. He silently admitted to himself that he was apprehensive about living within the house of another royal family. He had only met King Priam once, and that had been a brief affair, an embarrassing moment when Priam's son, Hector bested him in a contest with a spear. A humiliation made all the worse because Hector was younger by several years. In Hector's defence, he didn't gloat, quite the opposite. He'd helped Agamemnon with his stance, and it was not long before Agamemnon's performance improved. Nonetheless, for a boy who had grown accustomed to winning, it had left a sour taste within his mouth.

Agamemnon forced the memory of the shame from his mind. He looked toward the land that had come within view. Leaning forward, he tried to make out the detail upon the shore. As he did so, the wind began to strengthen. It raced across the water's surface and hit him with force. His feet began to slip. Agamemnon grasped the rail to avoid toppling overboard. His heart pounded at the near calamity, breathing heavily, he licked his lips, tasting the salt deposited by the strong coastal breeze. His mouth suddenly felt dry. He wondered if it was the salt or the thought of begging Priam for protection.

"Take some water." The stranger had approached unseen.

"My gratitude," Agamemnon replied as he took the water skin. He looked at the stranger and wondered why he had never managed to catch sight of the man's face. Why was he so keen to hide his features? Or perhaps he was merely as ugly as a cow's arse. Agamemnon smiled at the thought. The stranger turned and glanced about the deck. Then in an instant the hood had been thrown back to finally reveal the handsome features beneath. The white hair stood in stark contrast to the darkness of his attire.

"As I told Pallas before we left Mycenae shores, I do not hide my face to conceal my deceit," the stranger announced.

"Then why?" Agamemnon asked as he studied the features of the man that stood to his front. The hair and beard were mostly grey with flecks of black that hinted at a lost youth. The jaw was square and strong and the skin tanned, suggesting that the stranger did not always hide his features.

"The reasons are many. I too have people that I wish to protect, keeping my identity can aid it that task. I admit that it be advantageous in making deals. When you negotiate, it is best to unsettle those that wish to take advantage. It takes their mind from the task at hand."

"Is that not a type of deceit?" Agamemnon replied.

"I suppose, but my word is my bond. A deal struck is pinned to the earth with the strongest of blades. No amount of pressure, be it through the threat of violence, temptation of wealth or flesh will compel me to withdraw that blade."

"I commend your dedication to honour. I fear few men in this world can honestly claim the same, especially, in the royal households I have encountered. For many, the truth is like a blade within the fires, ready to be bent to the will of its master." Agamemnon spat over the side of the vessel, as though his words caused a sour taste upon his tongue.

"It is true that many men are untrustworthy. But that is the world," the stranger paused and pointed into the sea "Look there!" Agamemnon did as he was directed, observing a huge shark circle and devour an unfortunate fish. "Think on that scene. Imagine that fish was a man, would it matter if he was honourable?"

"Are you saying that honour does not matter?"

"No, I'm saying that holding it aloft like a banner will make little difference. Be the big fish with the sharpest teeth. Honour may help you sleep soundly at night, but it will not keep you safe."

"My father was a honourable man. He would not like me to stray from the correct path."

"Forgive me, Agamemnon," he placed a hand on the

prince's shoulder, "but your father is dead. Much of his city is nought but ash, and those who once called him king, now bow before another. I am not saying discard your honour or your father's teachings. I merely believe it is best for you to be your own man, let your victories and your defeats be your own." The mysterious man raised up his hands and replaced his hood, once more concealing his features from the world. "Forgive me, I have preparations to make before we reach land."

Agamemnon nodded. After watching his host replace his hood and make his way down the deck, Agamemnon switched his attention to the coastline growing on the horizon.

"What kind of man are you, Priam?" He whispered the question. "Will you honour your friendship with my father or will you be fearful of my uncle's wrath?"

*****

Agamemnon stepped from the vessel, grateful to feel the stability of the wooden walkway beneath his feet. They had landed some distance from the city of Troy. The settlement was one of many that had sprung up to take advantage of the plentiful trading opportunities. With that in mind, it came as a shock to Agamemnon, to see Priam striding in his direction.

The stranger appeared "We are most fortunate that Priam was not within his palace. If that fortune holds, we may be able to conclude our business before nightfall."

"For a king, he travels with too few guards," Agamemnon replied.

"Under Priam's control, the people of Troy enjoy hands filled with coin and stomachs filled with food. A happy people rarely take a sword's edge to what brings them contentment."

"They love him?" Agamemnon asked.

"As much as any person can love a man that can take your life on a whim," the stranger replied.

"Does he have such whims?"

The stranger seemed to consider the question at great length. Finally, he broke the silence. "Priam rarely acts without careful thought. He is rare amongst not only kings, but men. That does not mean he is without fault. His answer to you this day will not be given in malice or to honour a friendship. He will do what is best for his people. He places their lives and his city above all. Now go and discover if Troy will be your new home. I shall return to the ship and ensure that it has adequate supplies should your request be denied."

Agamemnon nodded and slowly began his walk toward the oncoming King of Troy.

Priam's face was one of delight as he welcomed Agamemnon to his shores. "I recognise the boy that I met in more joyful times. You are most fortunate to find me. I have been travelling my lands for three days, I have only just decided to return to Troy's warm embrace." Priam paused and looked at Agamemnon. "Your journey cannot have been easy. Come take refreshments with me. I will ensure that those upon your vessel are well fed," Priam placed a hand on Agamemnon shoulder and guided him away from the others on the dock.

"You heard of my father's fate?" Agamemnon asked. The smile on Priam's face fell away, his sadness seemed genuine.

"Your father was a dear friend. One that will be missed."

"He is definitely dead?" Agamemnon asked. It was a pointless question. His uncle was not the sort of man who knew mercy or would allow a threat to his power to linger too long in this world.

"He gave his life so the slaughter would end. It was an honourable death." Agamemnon could have sworn that he saw a tear in the king's eye. Priam turned away and plucked some fruit from a nearby cart. "I regret advising your father not to end his brother's life. I see now that so much misery could have avoided with just one death."

"You told my father to keep Thyestes alive?" It was more accusation than question.

"Thyestes had loyal followers. I felt it would be prudent to keep him alive." Priam's face was a mask of sadness as he spoke. Just for a moment, he seemed lost in his own thoughts but then rallied to look at Agamemnon. "Tell me, why have you come to my shores?"

Agamemnon fought back the anger, within he wondered if his father's death had been because of Priam's advice. "Thyestes wishes to send my brother and I to the next world. For our safety, it has been decided that we place ourselves under the protection of powerful men. I come to you Priam. I know that you held my father in high regard. He always trusted you. I had hoped that the friendship that bound you together could be extended to his son."

"On my friendship you can rely on..."

"But?" Agamemnon sensed Priam's hesitation.

Priam placed an arm on the young prince's shoulder and turned him around to look toward a far range of hills.

"Just beyond that horizon lays Troy. It has become prosperous, not because its people have a gift for trade or a mighty army to bend others to its will. It prospers because of its location and the fact that I do all that is in my power not to create enemies. If I take you within those walls, and trust me Agamemnon, nothing would give me greater pleasure, then there is no doubt that your uncle will set sail with murderous intent. The lure of your young head and the wealth within the walls, would be too much to resist. No Agamemnon, I cannot offer you protection. For it is not within my power."

"You side with Thyestes?"

"If that was the truth, then your head would already be sailing back to Mycenae without it's body."

"You could try and take it!" Agamemnon hand shot towards the blade at his hip. Priam's arm was far swifter. His powerful fingers clasped around the thin wrist of Agamemnon.

"If you are to survive and reclaim your father's throne, then you must save your rage for your enemies. It would also be prudent not to offer violence to those far more experienced in battle. Do not mistake a man who wishes to avoid war, with one that cannot make war." Priam released Agamemnon and the smile returned to his face. "I am not your enemy, Agamemnon. You must realise that my first duty is to my people. If their weight was not upon my heart, then I would take up the sword and cut the crown from your uncle's head and place it gently upon yours."

"Words... nothing more than empty words, Priam. You dishonour my father." Agamemnon was interrupted as a man raced to Priam's side and whispered in his ear.

"Forgive me, Agamemnon. I must leave for Troy at once."

"There is no more to be gained from further words anyway." Agamemnon did not wait for a reply. He turned and walked back towards his vessel without another glance to Priam. The king called for a horse and Agamemnon thought that he sensed panic within the man's voice. Nonetheless, he refused to turn, Priam had turned his back on his father's friendship and one day he would regret that dishonour.

Chapter 7

'A King's Loss'

Nobody saw the powerfully built, dark-cloaked figure walking silently within the royal palace. Its inhabitants oblivious as he entered the gardens and approached the luscious produce that sat waiting to be consumed. He drew out a small flask, removed the stopper and the emptied its poisonous contents over the fruit. Without a word the unknown person slipped away.

A woman and children played within the garden, oblivious to the uninvited visitor. The female was a beauty to behold, and although not so young anymore, still cut an elegant figure, delighting in the attention of the children. She begged for a rest, and they allowed her a few moments to take a drink and a slice of sumptuous apple. After swallowing one bite a great pain wracked her stomach. She looked at the fruit within her hand and then to the children. Through the terrible agony seizing her body, she tipped the vessel containing the remainder of the produce on the ground, crushing it beneath her feet. The pain became unbearable, she fell, her vision failing as she hit the ground. Servants raced to the fallen form and gently lifted the unconscious woman. They carried her with great care to a place of comfort.

By the time Priam had reached the royal quarters, the woman he loved since childhood, had slipped from the world. Turning his eyes from her and without uttering a word, he made it clear to all they should leave.

The door closed, alone with his love, he moved to her side. His breathing quickened and his throat dry. He was a proud king, used to concealing emotions, but the hairs on his arms began to rise and a tremble afflicted his bottom lip.

"Come my love, rise from your bed," he pleaded. When no answer came, he fell to his knees. "Please my beautiful, sweet Hecuba." He reached out a hand and placed it upon the cold flesh of the queen. "All these years, I have protected you. Do not make my labours for nought." Hecuba's eyes were open, but they could not see the grief of her husband. Priam had other wives, but Hecuba was his queen and his love. Their marriage was not made for the good of Troy or to fend off potential enemies. Hecuba had held his heart since they had been children. Now Priam's world seemed no more than a shattered amphora.

As time passed, Priam refused to leave Hecuba's side, denying others entry. The king was lost in his misery; his gaze never leaving his beloved wife. His tears rolled freely. Some of that sadness fell onto Hecuba's unflinching cheek to give the impression that she shared his woe.

A full day had passed before a disturbance took place in the corridor beyond the royal quarters.

"The king must not be disturbed!" A voice sounded in

the corridor.

"I helped bring you into the world, Kadmos. You're beginning to make me regret that action," sounded the reply.

"I have orders!"

"Yes – your orders are to move out of the way before I take that sword and stick it..."

The door to the royal chamber was wrenched open. Priam stood staring at the owners of the voices, his jaw set like granite, his displeasure impossible to ignore.

"Forgive me, my king. I was unsure how much force to use," the soldier flushed with embarrassment as he spoke.

The visitor to the palace replied "Force! Be gone with you before I slap your arse. You're nought but a child,"

"What do you want, Maeja?" Priam looked at the elderly woman and then to the worried master of guards. He realised that the man's fear was not because of a displeased king, but because of the woman that many called sorceress. "The queen is dead. Can a man not grieve for his wife?" Priam asked, determined that he would show no fear.

"A man may, but a king must look to his subjects," Maeja replied.

Priam turned to the guard. The man was loyal and the son of one of his most reliable generals. However, he lacked his father's intellect and was out of his depth when it came to dealing with the likes of Maeja. "Kadmos, stand down I will hear what the woman has to say."

"Oh, hear me you will. Time is short and the people need their king," Maeja interrupted.

"What do you mean?" Priam asked, his temper beginning to rise.

A voice sounded from further down the corridor, "What's happening, Father?"

Priam looked and observed his eldest son, Hector. He quickly turned and closed the door to the royal quarters to prevent his son spying the lifeless body of his mother. Hector had been present in the gardens when Hecuba was taken ill, Priam would spare him further pain. He returned his gaze to Maeja. "Well?"

"The frightful ones are on the move," she replied.

At her words Priam's hand instinctively moved to where his sword usually hung at his side. "Are you sure?"

"Who are the Frightful Ones?" Hector asked.

"They are the Mormo. Creatures that do not belong in this world or the next," Maeja responded. "Some say spirit, others say demon. I just call them nasty little bastards with a taste for blood." She moved closer to Hector and cupped his jaw with her deceptively powerful fingers. "They hunger for children," she turned his head from side to side, "but you own too many years, they would likely just slaughter you," she snorted.

"They could try," Hector replied defiantly. He shook his jaw free from Maeja's hand.

The old woman's creased face broadened with a huge smile that revealed a mouth empty of all but a couple of teeth.

"Ah! The bravery of the innocent. How I miss the days when consequences and the dead did not weigh heavily on my mind. I suppose age makes cowards of us all. To be young of limb and pure of heart again." She ruffled Hector's hair. "I like this boy. He has his grandfather's spirit."

"Enough! Maeja, where will I find these creatures?" Priam demanded.

"They dwell beneath the old city, but be warned my king, they have taken children captive. We must move with all haste before they disappear into the tunnels that lay beneath the old ruin and take their captives with them."

Priam knew that it would take too long to raise the army. "Kadmos, how many men do we have guarding the city?"

"No more than twenty, surely not enough..."

"Each will be mounted and ready to leave by the time I reach the courtyard. Give the order and then send word to the army. You will follow with the main force."

Kadmos did not reply. He turned and raced down the corridor.

"You have my sword, Father," declared Hector.

"No, my son. One member of our household chasing these foul beasts is enough."

Maeja placed a hand on Priam's forearm.

"A man that has recently suffered a great loss can sometimes throw his life away far too cheaply. The presence of his son would focus his mind and ensure he returns home to his people and his family. Besides, the boy may be young, but his skill cannot be matched by any in your ranks."

Priam went to argue but stopped himself. Instead, he looked at Hector. He knew the boy would feel shame at being left behind. The king fought against his natural urge to protect his son. "Very well, Hector. Get your armour and meet me in the courtyard." Priam watched his son race away and wondered why the young were always so determined to risk their lives. Without taking his eyes from the back of Hector he spoke to Maeja.

"You will look to my son's safety." It was not a request but an order.

"What can an old feeble woman do, when the horns of battle blow?" she replied.

"You may well be old - you were when my father was a child. We both know that you are no ordinary woman, Maeja. As a prince of Troy, I grew up listening to stories about the old woman that dwells beneath the ground. It is rumoured that you cannot die, but I promise you that if my son is harmed this night, then I will put those rumours to the test."

Maeja gave a chuckle. "That may well be the price of failure, oh great and powerful king of Troy. But tell me Priam, what will be the reward for success?" She gave a wry smile.

"Reward? I thought you were beyond earthly riches?"

"There is more than gold or power in this world," she replied.

"Bring Hector home safe and I will grant you all that is in my power."

Maeja nodded. "Then I shall do all I can to ensure that Hector returns. But you know that the Moirai already know our fate and we cannot change the path on which we journey, Priam."

The king looked to the royal quarters and thought of the lifeless body of his love that lay within. "None of us can escape our fate or lessen the hurt of those left behind," he whispered solemnly.

"Hecuba was a fine woman. Loved by both subject and her children, but I think by the man at her side most of all." She raised a hand and performed a strange gesture within the air. "She will not wither while you're away. You will have time to say your farewells when you return."

Chapter 8

'A Kiss from the Dead'

It was not long before Priam, Maeja and the palace guards were on route to Troy's ancient palace. It had been abandoned long before Priam had taken the crown. The lands were susceptible to earth tremors and the ancient home for Troy's royalty was placed too precariously on coastal cliffs. After part of the palace was cast down into the depths of the sea, priests claimed that Poseidon was displeased with man entering his domain. The palace was abandoned, and it wasn't long before fearful rumours started. Mysterious deaths and children disappearing gave rise to the belief that the Mormo now prowled the shadows of the old ruin. In the reign of Priam's great grandfather, the rumours turned to fear as several children were taken from the warm embrace of their beds. The old king was forced to send his best warriors to track down those who had become known as the *Frightful Ones*. The warriors did not return, but the attacks ceased, and so, the Mormo were consigned to cautionary tales to frighten children into good behaviour. Only the royal household were made aware of the real threat, each generation warned those that followed, to remain vigilant.

Priam and his men moved at a lively pace, but despite

Priam's authority, it was Maeja that gave the orders for the men to either stop or increase their pace. Now and then she would raise a hand, stop her horse and dismount. Wolf-like, she would sniff the air, crouch low and study the terrain. Then without saying a word, she would remount and wave the troops forward. Priam doubted that any of his men could match her skills at tracking and was content for her to take the lead. However, as the forest that barred the way to the ancient ruins came into view, he felt compelled to speak.

"Are we gaining, Maeja?" He had to shout to be heard over the movement of the horses.

She raised a hand calling the group to a stop. Priam could not help being amazed at the speed she could dismount; it was jarring to see an elderly woman with such fluidity in her movements.

"Maeja?" Priam pressed.

She crouched low and plucked some of the grass from the ground. First, she sniffed and then dropped all but one strand of grass. She raised it to her mouth, her tongue seemed unnaturally long as it traced each side of the grass, then it curled around the plant and took it into her mouth. Priam grimaced as he watched the display.

"They're near, but we will have to enter the forest. I had hoped we would catch them before entering that foul place," she replied.

"You can tell that from eating grass?" Priam asked, his face displaying his astonishment.

"What? No, I just like grass. It's very refreshing."

"You are a strange creature," he replied, shaking his head with dismay.

She gave a high-pitched cackle, but then stopped abruptly. Maeja walked about twenty paces, her head weaving from side to side. Now and then she would caress the ground obviously aware of signs that Priam could not see.

"They have separated into two groups. The larger group have taken the main path," she pointed towards the main track that ran towards the forest. "The smaller one that contains the children has for some reason moved in that direction."

"Why would they carry out such an act? It rarely makes sense to split your force."

Maeja did not reply immediately. She stroked her chin as if in deep thought. She looked toward Hector and gave him a wink.

"The young ones are important to them. If they believed that their prize could be lost, they might wish to keep it from falling into the wrong hands. I would suggest that the Mormo know that we give chase. I imagine that they plan to fall upon us as we make our way through the forest." There was an audible concerned rumbling from Priam's men.

"How many of the creatures guard the children?" Priam replied, ignoring the fears of his men.

"Difficult to be certain, they do not move like men or leave the same impressions. However, I would say no more than three," Maeja replied.

"What do you mean they do not move like men, are they in possession of more than two legs?" Priam pressed.

"Many tales of the Mormo suggest that they are spirits. That they float above the ground, as though dancing upon the breeze. I can only tell of the time that I saw them with my own eyes. I was nought but a girl and had wandered too close to the forest. Fortunately, I spied them before they saw me. They do indeed have two legs, but they do not walk as we do. Each movement is like a dance to music that only they can hear. A journey from one point to another does not take the shortest route. They meander like a stream through the mountainside."

Priam was lost for words. He was used to facing his foe on the battlefield. An enemy could move with speed and move from side to side, but often they came straight on. You stood your ground and faced your foe. With the blessings of the gods, skill, and good fortune you would live to see another day.

"Maeja, take three of my men. Rescue the captives, the rest of us will put an end to these demons."

She nodded and walked back to where the men had dismounted. Her diminuitive, bent frame holding their attention. Walking by most of the warriors she remained silent or shook her head as she glanced in their direction. Finally, she nodded at an individual.

"Name?" she asked.

"Galen."

"You will do." She motioned that he should fall in behind her and then continued to inspect the men. She tapped another man on the shoulder. "Name?"

"Erastus."

She motioned that he should fall in, and then continued once again. She stopped and studied a warrior for some time. "What is your name?"

"Aetes," he replied.

"Hmm I sense the gods favour you. Do not leave my side because I'm certain that they have no love for me. You might keep me alive."

"Or you might get me killed," he replied.

Maeja laughed. "It's a strong possibility but growing old can be tiresome." She strode away from the main path with the three warriors hurrying to catch up.

Priam watched them go and then gave the order that the horses should be tethered. He watched as his soldiers struggled to bring their mounts under control. He was suddenly aware that these men were not the finest warriors that Troy had to offer. They were used to comfort, only a few could boast of experiencing real battle. He also knew that it was too late to turn back. As the men filtered back to him, he motioned for them to come closer. He kept his voice steady, devoid of emotion.

"I know that many of you have not faced an enemy, never mind the terrible foe we may battle this night. You are warriors of Troy and the creatures that lay within this forest threaten your loved ones. I do not ask you to be mere soldiers. I ask that you to show me that you are men. We will fight as one, let them crash against our shields. Stand your ground and do not break. No matter what happens – stand your ground. Follow me." He turned and strode purposely up the track.

"We are better than you think, Father. I have worked them on the training ground," Hector announced as he fell into step with his father.

Priam placed a hand on his son's shoulder.

"I meant no disrespect, Hector. Training is important, but it is no replacement for the taste of battle. Until they face that terror, we will not know whether we fight alongside lions or sheep."

"I hope I will not let you down, Father."

"Impossible – you are my son. My blood runs through your veins, which means you will do your duty. Of that I have no doubts. Besides, you are a match for any man with the blade. I pity any enemy that attracts your fury."

*****

Aetes watched as Maeja held up her hand as she bent low to the ground. He moved to her side, desperately trying not to make a sound.

"What is it?" He whispered.

"Look in the clearing," she replied pointing to her front.

A mist was rolling along the floor of the forest, but in the distance four children were sitting by a large tree. His gaze searched the surrounding area for the creatures responsible for the abduction. Then two figures appeared from around the tree. At the sight of them, Aetes caught his breath. They floated above the ground, the mist hiding their feet, but their movements suggested they were at the whim of a non-existent breeze, moving as a sail dances in the wind. Their faces were indiscernible, but they seemed to be female and not what he had imagined.

"I see only two creatures," he whispered.

"Yes, that is a concern," Maeja replied. "Perhaps the other one is hidden in the trees or beneath the mist."

"How do we get close without placing the children in harm's way?"

"It is time to test how blessed by the gods you are Aetes. Erastus and Galen scout your way around the edge of the clearing. Stay out of sight until, well until it's time to be seen."

"And me?" Aetes asked.

"You need to discard your armour and tunic," she replied.

"What?"

"You are not much older than a child. I am hoping that these creatures do not possess great eyesight. They will be interested to see a young boy walking alone. Hopefully they will want to investigate."

"And if they don't?" he asked with panic rising in the pit of his stomach.

"Then they will kill you and I will need another plan."

Reluctantly Aetes removed his clothing and was

about to step into the clearing when he felt the skeletal hand of Maeja grip his arm.

"We are about to encounter vicious creatures. It would be foolhardy not to take your sword. Just keep the blade slung on your back."

"And what will you be doing?" Aetes' annoyance was beginning to triumph over his fear and embarrassment.

"I will be at your side." She pointed at the floating vapour. "Well at your feet would be more accurate."

Aetes slung his sword over his shoulder, the leather strap creating discomfort as it lay against his bare flesh. Maeja slipped beneath the mist, and he felt even more exposed and alone. He bent and retrieved a dagger from his garments. Small enough to hold within his hand, he positioned it so that the blade was hid along the inside of his forearm. Taking a gulp of air, he stepped forward, his eyes never leaving the creatures. He wondered if Maeja had been right about the third Mormo, was the creature hidden beneath the mist too? His concentration switched back to the two figures to his front. They seemed to have become aware of his presence. They moved towards him, their bodies performing a snake-like dance as they closed upon his position. As they neared, the differences between them and the women that Aetes knew, became apparent. Taller than any human he had known, but slender and wearing the thinnest of robes that left nought to the imagination. Their skin was as pale as the mist on which they seemed to float. They could almost be described as beautiful, until he noticed the long, dagger like nails that protruded from their fingers. At first, he thought they were smiling, but as they neared, Aetes realised their mouths were far wider than any human's, and filled with long, flesh-tearing teeth. No more than five paces away they came to a stop. Aetes fought his fear and wondered if they sensed Maeja beneath the mist. He did not, however, lower his gaze for fear of giving away her position. Slowly they began to move again, much more cautious than before. Now, as they came closer, he felt the breath of the nearest Mormo on his skin as it leaned its head forward. The nostrils twitched as a dog sniffs a tasty bone. Suddenly it straightened as though startled and confused at the same time. Then it plunged downward with such speed it was not afforded the chance to scream. Aetes looked down, but the Mormo had disappeared beneath the mist. There was no sound of battle or cries of agony, but the mist where the Mormo had disappeared, now seemed to have taken on a shade of crimson. A terrifying scream made Aetes jerk his head up to look at the second Mormo. To his terror, it was rushing towards him. He panicked trying to grasp the sword that hung on his back. The creature rapidly bore down upon him. The arms of the beast held up high, the clawlike talons ready to tear at his flesh. The mouth widened to bare its teeth as Aetes struggled to reach his sword. No more than a pace away, it leapt towards him, and he was forced to abandon his search for his sword and defend himself with the small dagger within his hand. He took one step back, never thinking for a moment that he could avoid his inevitable death. Suddenly, the beast stopped in mid leap. Without hesitation, Aetes drove his blade upwards. It took the creature under the jaw, smashing bone and ripping flesh. Before Aetes could tell if he had killed the creature, it slipped beneath the mist.

He scrambled for his sword dropping the dagger in the process. Drawing the larger blade, he was unsure to his next action. A shape began to emerge from the low cloud of mist. His heart raced, but quickly began to calm as he realised it was Maeja. The sorceress held out a bloodied hand, it held the dagger.

"Are you injured?" asked Aetes.

"The blood is not mine. Be on your guard I sense another creature is close." As Maeja finished speaking a dreadful scream emanated from the trees on the far side of the clearing.

"I think that was Erastus, he needs our help!"

"He is beyond help, get to the children," she replied.

Maeja once again slipped beneath the shroud of vapour and Aetes was engulfed with the feeling of vulnerability again. Maeja may be an old woman, but he would rather she was close. He picked his way towards the children, a task that proved more difficult than it first seemed. The mist hid the forest floor. Roots and stones became a barrier to an easy passage. Finally, he reached his objective. To his surprise they showed no signs of ill treatment or even upset. In truth, they did not seem to notice his arrival. They sat without making a sound. No tears of woe or gratitude for their rescue.

Another scream broke the silence. Aetes realised as the cry died away that he was now the only member of the palace guard left alive. He watched the tree line, as he placed himself between the captives and where the scream had emanated. Then he saw it. The Mormo dripped with the blood of his fellow guard. But Aetes guessed that the beast's thirst for slaughter had not yet been quenched.

The Mormo could not be mistaken for a beautiful woman as it raced, teeth bared, towards him. He wanted to run, but with a look to the children he knew that he must stand and fight. Despite the cold of the night, he could feel the hilt of his blade slipping in the sweat of his hand. He doubted that he could defeat the but hoped to die bravely. Better to go to the next world with his honour unblemished.

As the Mormo passed the only other tree in the clearing, the beast suddenly stopped. Aetes watched as it was pulled downward. The creature, however, obviously had no intention of slipping beneath the mist. It clamped its talon-like nails into the trunk of the tree. Aetes observed as the creature was time and time again yanked downward, but resiliently refused to be dragged to its destruction. Then the tussle stopped, the Mormo seemed to be looking around in search of its invisible attacker. Aetes noticed that the beast did not loosen its grasp on the tree, and the rage disappeared from its features. Now there was only fear upon its face.

A loud crack broke the silence, followed by a scream of obvious pain. Aetes watched as another crack sounded and the creature dropped slightly into the mist. As the third crack sounded, Aetes realised with terror that the cracks were bones being smashed apart. The battle was at an end, the fight had been driven from the creature and within moments it sunk down beneath the swirling mist. Aetes was thankful that silence descended, and the Mormo's screams brought to an abrupt end. Aetes could tear his eyes from the scars that adorned the gnarled trunk of the tree.

"There is nothing to see out there," a voice sounded from his rear.

Aetes sighed with relief. "I thought I was going to die."

"We are all going to die, but not this night," Maeja replied.

For the first time, he tore his gaze from the tree and turned to face the old woman.

"You did not need me. I think you could have destroyed these creatures without my presence." Aetes' hands shook. Facing the creatures had been terrifying. The fear had almost overwhelmed him. If it hadn't been for the children, he would have run and not looked back. But the young did not deserve to be left to their fate, and so, he had held his ground. Now that the threat had passed, he realised how close he came to death; so near to being torn limb from limb. "I was... I was terrified."

"Those that do not feel fear cannot be brave." She stepped closer and placed a finger against his chest. "Do not underestimate what you have done this day. Those young ones would not have seen another day if it was not for your actions."

"But..." he tried to reply.

"We need to go to your king's aid. Dress with haste," she ordered.

"We cannot take them into battle," Aetes pointed to the captives as he replied.

"They will remain here."

"Surely they will be in danger?"

"The Mormo place their victims in a trance, they will not move until the sun rises."

"But there are beasts other than the Mormo," Aetes replied, horrified at the thought of leaving the children unprotected.

"Is there? Tell me have you heard the rustle of creatures in the undergrowth? Have you seen the birds in the trees or heard their song?"

For a moment Aetes remained silent as he pondered her questions. "No... no I haven't."

"The Mormo have survived in these parts for centuries without satisfying their hunger with children. I imagine they would have substantial appetites. Animals will have learnt over time to stay away from the Mormo, they will have learned to steer clear of their scent. Alive or dead they will still have the stench of danger about them. That stench will protect the children until our return."

It somehow made sense to Aetes, despite going against every instinct to leave the children. He went to get dressed, but then turned once more to face Maeja. His cheeks flushed crimson.

"I am not sure the Mormo considered me to be a child. Removing my clothes served no purpose."

"I did not think they would," she replied, and then smiled.

"Then why?"

"I'm an old woman. It is not often I get to see a young warrior in all his glory." She burst into laughter.

Chapter 9

'Hold the Line'

Priam was ignorant of the fate of the children or Maeja. He was more concerned with his men. Despite Hector's declaration that he had trained the palace guard, he could not ignore that these troops were not natural warriors. They were more used to calming drunken guests than fighting an enemy wishing them nought but destruction. Thoughts of his men evaporated as the trees thinned and the beginnings of the old palace came into view. The full moon helped him survey his surroundings. The mist that had been a constant companion as they had marched through the forest was far lighter near the ruin. For a moment, he wondered if Maeja had been mistaken. *Had the Mormo forsaken their plans for ambush, and merely raced to the catacombs below the ancient building?* However, the sound of horrific cries to the rear of his men proved the old sorceress had been right.

"Form up!" Hector called out his order.

Priam could not deny the speed that the guard had reacted to Hector's command. As he and his son stood in the centre of the makeshift circular formation, he assessed the threat that they faced. Trees on both sides of him swayed and parted as Mormo poured from the forest toward his flanks. Priam glanced back toward the ruins and to the doorway of the catacombs. Was that the plan? Force his men beneath the palace where the tunnels would cause them to become separated and lost? The Mormo could then pick them off, attacking from the shadows.

"Father," Hector's tone and worried expression suggested he understood how grave the situation had become, "what are your orders?"

Priam licked his lips as he searched his mind for answers.

"Men listen to me. Their numbers are too great to fight in the open. We will head for the catacombs but be warned we must stay together. When we reach the entrance, half of us will face the enemy, the other half will prepare for attack from within.

Looking across at the trees the Mormo seemed to be holding their position. He turned to his men. He would look at their faces. "When I give the order, break formation and run. Do not stop or look back."

But his men were looking over his shoulder. The horde of Mormo was parting and from within their ranks a figure was emerging. It was taller than the other Mormo, its flaming red hair stretched down below its waist. Even at that distance royalty was identifiable. The creature was without doubt the queen.

It moved with supreme confidence and her subjects could not take their eyes from her form. The queen continued her path and left her subjects behind. She did not stop until she was within twenty paces of Priam and his men. She was beautiful and lacked the beast-like appearance of her followers. The thin white tunic that adorned her body, only served to enhance the magnificent figure beneath.

Her voice was as sweet as honey. "King Priam. I am delighted that you have chosen to visit our..." she used her hands to highlight her followers, "home."

"You gave me little choice. Your... people," he could not think of a better word, "should have remained in the ruins and forest."

"Perhaps? But it seems to me that it is you that has strayed from your path and with so few men."

"An entire army approaches. If you want to survive this night, then return from where you came and never enter my lands again." Priam knew it was piss and wind, but sometimes all you had was bluster.

"By the time your army arrives, you and your men will be dead," she replied.

"Then the army of Troy will tear down every stone and uproot each tree to take a bloody revenge."

Her face suddenly took on a mask of sadness.

"Even royalty have their masters, Priam. We must all face our fate." She turned and began to make her way back to her followers.

"Hector, now!" Priam ordered.

The prince stepped forward and with all his might threw his spear at the queen. It soared through the air and Priam thought that it must strike its target. At the last moment, the queen leapt into the air, twisting her body to avoid the deadly missile. The spearhead drew blood on the queen's shoulder, but not knowing that it had failed to kill its intended target, it continued its brutal trajectory. It took the next Mormo in the throat and the one to its rear in the stomach. As the slain toppled to the ground a strange stillness settled on the combatants. Then a scream of rage sounded from the Mormo ranks.

"Run you bloody fools!" Priam screamed.

His men took off towards the entrance to the catacombs. All around him men ran for their lives. Armour and weapons clanged in the charge for safety. Priam ran too, ensuring Hector was always to his front. A man fell to his left, calling out his woe, but Priam dared not slow his retreat to assist Approaching the entrance, his men were already forming a shield wall. Hector slipped through the man-made barrier. Priam gave silent gratitude to Zeus for his son's safety. He darted through the gap made by Hector and turned to observe the enemy. The Mormo were dragging away two of his wounded men.

"Hector, set up a defensive line to our rear." Priam looked to the walls of the catacombs and noticed several torches hanging on the walls. "See if you can get those lit. If the clouds cover the moon, then we will need light to see the enemy."

A voice sounded from the front of the catacombs. "Here they come!"

Priam moved to observe the enemy. The entrance was wide enough for eight men to stand abreast, shields locked against the horde. That left seven, including himself, ready to fill the gap left by anyone falling in battle.

"Front line, hold your ground! Do not yield a single step. Those inside, use your spears to help protect those ahead of you. If one falls then take his place. The enemy must not break through." Priam looked towards the charging Mormo. They could not be mistaken for women now, teeth and claws bared, spittle forming at their mouths as they sensed blood. "Make ready, ready..."

The Mormo smashed into the heavily armoured palace guard. Many of those at the fore of the charge were driven on by those to their back onto the waiting spear tips. They died quickly but were soon replaced. Priam and his men in the second row struck at the savage beasts from relative safety. The creatures tried with savage intent to break the line to allow their superior number to pour torrent-like through the gap and wash the warriors away.

Priam could see little. This was no dignified duel with a trained opponent. It was the chaos of battle. Claw, tooth, blood and spittle and above all, the haunting cries of those about to die. He hacked the arm from a Mormo threatening to break through and as the creature let out a terrible scream, the pressure of the attack suddenly lessened, and then was gone. The Mormo were to their front one moment, then they streamed back towards their queen, the next. Priam wiped the thick, sticky blood of the Mormo from his breastplate. Its consistency reminded him of the golden liquid of the holy tree. But that was where the resemblance ended, for it was as black as the night, and the stench of it made him turn his head from the foul substance.

Priam understood why the queen had pulled her followers back. The Mormo were powerful of limb. Natural weapons at their disposal that could deliver untold damage to the flesh. But the creatures had no weight. Slight and built for speed they could not use the mass of their bodies to force an opening. The Mormo would attack using speed to create enough force to smash his line. If it faltered then the Mormo would retire, reform, and then charge again. Each attack would weaken the line. Eventually, the creatures would find a way in. He looked at the condition of his men. One had died, his throat opened wide to the night air. Three others nursed wounds. He ordered them to the back line and reinforcements to take their place. Those fresh troops had only just taken their place when a roar erupted from the Mormo lines. The horde surged towards Priam.

*****

The battle continued to rage. Five attacks had thinned the Mormo ranks, but Priam now found that he and Hector were the only ones left in the back line. Each of the men under his command was nursing several injuries. Deep cuts were evident on most of the exposed flesh. His men breathed heavily, wincing as they felt the effects of so many wounds. He stared into the distance to see an enemy that had suffered from the slaughter too, some lay dying, others screamed their discontent at severed limbs or deep punctures to the flesh. But they would charge again. Priam doubted that his men could withstand another onslaught. Panic started to grip-his insides.

"King Priam," the queen called out. As she did, the two captured men were brought to their knees in front of the Mormo ranks.

"I thought the talking was at an end?" Priam replied. He sensed what was coming but could do nothing.

"Your men have fought well, why see them slaughtered. I will grant them safe passage."

"And what of the prince?"

"You and those of your blood must fall. The valiant Hector must remain."

Priam thought it was a strange reply. Why would a creature that dwelled in the shadows wish the destruction of his family? What could she have to gain by such an act? He turned towards his men.

"You are being offered safe passage. The choice is yours."

Dromoclese, the eldest man in the guard cleared his throat. "Turn tail like a whipped dog. What man could live with that shame? I say let them come, the bastards will bleed before they lay a hand upon the prince." His words were met with nods of agreement from the other men.

"You have your answer," Priam called out as he turned to the queen.

She did not reply. Waving a hand to the Mormo that guarded the prisoners, she showed no emotion as the two men had their throats ripped out. Their bodies cast into the dirt.

Priam felt rage building within every sinew of his body. He placed a hand against the entrance wall, trying to calm his vengeful spirit. The thick gloop covered its surface. He recoiled from the Mormo blood but then raised the hand to his nose, smelling the vile substance. He recalled a story told to him by his grandmother when he was no more than a child. He began to form a plan.

Chapter 10

'Darkness Falls'

Snarling, ravenous beasts charged forward. Priam watched as they neared, knowing that the moment he gave the order, would either save or condemn his men to death. He glanced into the catacombs at Hector, a burning torch in his son's hand.

"Are you ready?"

Hector nodded.

The Mormo were dangerously close now. Priam sensed his men's fear, knowing that they wanted nothing more than to turn and run, but knew they would remain until ordered otherwise. He needed the Mormo to be completely committed to their charge.

"Steady men." He spoke in a calm, authoritative tone. "Steady."

He waited until they were close enough and then screamed, "Fall back!"

His men did not need to be told twice. They raced passed Priam as he turned to give the order to Hector. His son, however, had anticipated the order and threw the blazing torch towards the Mormo bodies. It landed just moments before the charging Mormo reached the entrance to the catacombs. Priam was horrified as nothing happened and the flame seemed to die. He turned and raced back to his men as they hurriedly reformed their shield wall. A great force hit him in the back, knocking him sideways. He not only struggled to his feet, but also, to replace the air that had been forced from his body. As he turned to face the Mormo, he narrowed his eyes as a roaring flame engulfed the Mormo, both living and dead. Their terrible screams dampened any elation felt at the success of his plan. The blood of his enemy attracted flames like priests to gold. Trying to see through the smoke, he hoped to count how many of the enemy remained. But as the fire began to die away, thick black smog filled the catacomb entrance.

"Back! We must find another way out!" Pallas screamed.

Hector seized the only lit torch from one of his men and took the lead. The thick acrid fumes seemed to follow them with each step as they moved further into the catacombs. Most of the tunnels were wide enough for two men to walk side by side, but others squeezed the men into single file. Priam kept glancing back into the gloom, wondering how many of the enemy had survived, and if they stalked the tunnels. He wanted to be at his son's side, but it was essential to keep the men together. To that end he was better placed bringing up the rear.

*****

Maeja had maintained an unrelenting pace. Aetes wasn't surprised. There was obviously a lot more to the old woman than her frail exterior portrayed. As the dark shape of the ruins came into view, Maeja stopped and seemed to be watching something that he could not see.

"What is it?" he asked.

"There was a battle here," she replied.

Aetes stared into the darkness. Cloud had mostly obscured the moon and he could not see any evidence of her claim.

"How..." he began.

"I feel their pain. The dead do not hasten to the next world. Those that fall victim to a violent death are often reluctant to leave a familiar place."

"Who - what dead?"

"Sometimes you must look with more than your eyes, young warrior. Mormo and the king's men died here. Can you not sense their anguish? Sadness is on the breeze. It lies upon the rocks and in the grass."

"I can't see anything," he replied.

"Then we shall move closer." Maeja strode forward. Aetes thought her unconcerned that danger may be lurking within the shadows.

He ensured that he never dropped too far behind, despite fearing what lay ahead. The safest place was at the side of the sorceress.

"Watch your step," she announced without breaking her stride.

The warning, however, came too late. Aetes' foot snagged on an object, and he tripped, powerless to prevent his fall. What he landed on was far softer than the ground. His hands groped the form and recognised the attire of a palace guard. As they travelled across the torso and towards the head, he met a cold, sticky substance he knew was blood. Despite, the urge to vomit he continued until he came upon the cold, unflinching flesh of the fallen man's face. He must have known him. He would have no doubt that he'd drunk far too much in the man's company. Perhaps even met his family. The darkness robbed him from knowing the guard's identity, but that did not deter the feeling of wretchedness as it washed over him. He was lost in that gloom until a hand grasped his shoulder.

"We cannot linger. There are two here that cannot be saved, but we may prevent the deaths of others." Maeja's tone was devoid of its usual scorn or sarcasm. It suggested that she knew the heavy weight upon his heart.

"Of course, forgive me." Aetes forced himself to rise. He made a silent promise that he would return to this place, collect the bodies of his comrades and return them to their loved ones.

The rest of the journey to the old ruins was in silence. Aetes's mind was filled with the fate of his friends and of the king. He took little notice of where Maeja was leading him. It wasn't until the vile stench of burnt flesh met his nostrils that he became aware of yet more slaughter. Like many other citizens of Troy, he had heard the stories of the catacombs beneath the old palace. Eyes adjusting to the dark, Aetes picked his way through the scatterings of distorted limbs and torsos. Shivers ran through him as the dread crept through his veins. He knew that his friends lay among this abominable horror.

Maeja crossed to the wall and plucked what he thought to be an ancient torch from its ensconcement. He couldn't be sure, the lack of light made recognising the simplest of objects difficult. He did, however, recognise the sound of the sorceress rummaging in the leather pouch that hung at her waist. Moments later, the torch suddenly erupted with light. Aetes knew it was no ordinary flame that gave so much light from one small torch. It also burned bluish white. It was as though she had captured a part of the moon and set it alight on the very tip of the torch.

Aetes was now able to observe the true extent of the slaughter. Bodies of both Mormo and the palace guard lay distorted at the entrance to the catacombs. Judging by the smell of burnt flesh there must have been an intense fire. Some of the bodies remained unburnt. However, at the furthest point into the catacombs, all the bodies were blackened, twisted beyond recognition. His heart leapt at the thought that King Priam lay among the disfigured forms.

"Your king is not here," Maeja replied, as if knowing his thoughts.

"How..." He was about to ask how she knew what he was thinking, but remembered who he was speaking too, and so, changed his question. "What happened here?"

Maeja did not reply immediately. She drifted between the dead. Aetes pondered if she was tracing the actions of the battle. Her body swayed here and there, one moment standing, the next bent low.

"King Priam took up position at the entrance." She pointed to where many of the fallen were free from the effects of fire, lay. "The Mormo attacked, time and time again. The king lost men, but despite being driven back the line did not break. As the Mormo delivered its final charge, someone in the ranks appears to have known that Mormo blood attracts fire like flies to the dead."

"So, Priam lives?"

"The smoke would have driven him and his men into the catacombs. Not all the Mormo are dead. Tracks lead away from the entrance. I believe they have another way in."

"How many?"

"Five or six, but the number is not important."

"What do you mean?" Aetes asked.

"The king will be watchful to his rear. He will expect any attack to come from there, but the Mormo will be free to choose the moment and place of their assault."

*****

Hector called a halt. Stretching before the men was a slender, wooden slatted, rickety bridge. Priam forced his way to the front wanting to know why the men had stopped. Hector placed a hand on his chest, preventing him from taking another step.

"Careful, Father."

Priam squinted in the light of the torch as he looked at the obstacle, and then into the chasm. The depth of the natural obstacle was hidden as it disappeared into the darkness. He used his foot to topple a rock over the edge. He heard it clatter over the side. The silence that followed was deafening.

"I think that we had better cross with great care." Priam took the torch from Hector and passed it to Dromoclese. "Take this and show the way. Hector and I will guard the rear."

Priam drew his sword and watched as Dromoclese moved across the precarious chasm. The ropes and wood creaked as the guard took each step. As Dromoclese finally placed a foot on the solid ground. Priam ordered the next man across. It was taking too long; any advantage the fire had given them was being eaten away by the painfully slow progress. "We must hurry, men. Fill your hearts with courage and trust in the gods for sure footing."

Priam was not sure if his words would hurry his men along. After all, if the gods had their welfare at heart, then surely, they would not find themselves pursued by creatures. Priam's attention was split between the bridge and the oppressive darkness that closed in from behind.

It was with no small amount of relief that he saw the last of the guard begin the perilous crossing. A noise sounded to Priam's rear, and he span around. He stared into the darkness, his hand tightening on the hilt of his sword. He gave a silent curse, knowing that the Mormo could be within striking distance and remain completely unseen. A thunderous crack followed by a terrible scream split the air. Priam turned to see the last warrior clinging by one hand from the bridge ropes. The wooden planking had given way and the guard plunged downwards and now held on to a single rope.

"Hang on!" Priam called out to the warrior. "And made to move toward the ancient crossing.

"No, my king." Dromoclese handed the torch to one of the other men. "I will go."

Dromoclese began to edge his way across the bridge. He moved towards the broken planks, trying to distribute his weight across the ancient timbers. As he neared the stranded man, he slowly lowered himself into a crouched position and stretched out a hand.

"Go back, Dromoclese!" Hector called out.

"I nearly have him," Dromoclese replied. As he spoke, the sound of the individual strands of rope snapping echoed through the tunnels.

Priam moved to the edge of the chasm, but it was an impotent act. He looked across the bridge at Dromoclese. There was nothing he could do. Their eyes locked. The guard's face showed that he knew his fate was sealed. One moment, Priam was looking at a loyal servant of Troy, the next, both men and bridge had disappeared into the darkness.

"No!" Hector screamed. Priam grasped his son by the shoulder, fearing that he would slip over the edge.

"We cannot help them," he whispered.

"We have to try!" Hector replied, shrugging free of his father's grip. His face was full of anguish as he looked over the edge into the blackness.

"You cannot help the dead. We must look to the living." Priam turned his attention to the men on the far side of the chasm. "Find your way out. If the tales are correct, then the catacombs lead to a coastal path."

The remainder of the palace guard looked at the king and then each other. One reluctantly spoke up.

"But my king, we cannot..."

"Prince Hector and I will find another way out." Seeing that his words had still not motivated his men into leaving, his tone hardened. "Am I not still the King of Troy? Go now!"

Slowly, the men moved away, taking the only source of light with them. Priam felt the darkness close around him. He rushed to cut some of the rope from the remnants of the bridge.

"Hector, take this." He passed one end of the rope to his son, "We will soon be feeling our way along these tunnels. There was a side tunnel fifty paces back the way we came, we will seek it out. It would be unfortunate if we became separated."

"Father..." Hector began and then fell to silence.

Priam reached and found his son's cheek. "What is it?" he asked.

"I... I am scared."

"That is how it should be."

"Are you?" Hector asked.

"Hector, I have already told you. Bravery is not the absence of fear, but the ability to act despite its presence.

Besides, you are a prince of Troy."

"And that matters how?"

"There is a reason our bloodline has ruled Troy for many years. We do our duty when others turn their back and run. Now we must do our duty once again. Let us find our way out of this wretched place."

"You did not answer my question, Father."

"Am I scared? Be thankful that the darkness hides the colour of my attire. In all honesty Hector, I could easily soil myself." Priam laughed. However, the brief humorous moment was broken by a scream that raced along the various tunnels and invaded their ears. "We must not delay, come on."

In the shadows they retraced their steps to find the side tunnel. Talking was kept to a minimum with just the occasional word from Priam to keep Hector's moral up. This was made more difficult as more screams were heard in the distance. Then Priam held his arm up and waited for Hector to walk into it.

"Look, a light, Priam whispered.

"Do we head towards it?" Hector asked.

"What choice do we have? No talking from this point and stay close to the wall."

Priam started off towards the light. Priam wondered if the Mormo could see in the dark. If that was the case, he knew they had no chance of survival. His mind drifted to the screams. Had the Mormo come across his men? Surely, they would have encountered him and Hector first. They must have found another way into the catacombs. That would mean that the beasts could be anywhere.

*****

Dromoclese stared down at the broken and bloodied form of himself. Confusion strode through his mind. How could he behold his own body? Raising a hand to his face he noticed that he could see through his extremity to the cavern wall. A strange light, which reminded him of the light of a new day, emanated from every part of him. His eyes returned to his broken form. Finally, realisation dawned upon him that he was dead.

"Dog's balls! Of all the ways to die."

"I've seen worse." A voice sounded from the darkness.

Dromoclese instinctively reached for his sword. "Stay back!" he called out.

"Do you fear that you may die for a second time?"

"Who are you?" Dromoclese demanded.

"I am the end for all." A black robed figure stepped from the shadows. "All that set out on their final journey must first cross my path."

"Hades!" exclaimed Dromoclese.

"No not Hades. You think the master of the underworld has journeyed to give you a personal escort to the next realm. Is that likely? I see that death has not diminished your feeling of self-importance."

Dromoclese held up a hand in protest. "This is my first time being dead. It is not as though I was expecting to die. If I was, I would have sought out a priest and enquired as to the order of things."

The clad figure rolled his eyes to show he was bored with the proceedings. He waved a hand to reveal a gateway in the cavern wall.

"Wait! What about the man that died with me?" Dromoclese asked.

"Fear took him long before the fall's end. He has already started his journey."

"That is a pity. I would have liked to have company."

"Time is pressing, and I have other duties, so..." The figure pointed towards the gateway.

Dromoclese walked forward, but then stopped and looked over his shoulder.

"You never told me your name."

"Does it matter?" the figure asked.

"No... I don't suppose it does."

Dromoclese left the world of men.

Chapter 11

'The Ruin of Royalty'

Priam and Hector crept toward the light, certain the tunnel was coming to an end. His worries intensified as the light they approached grew. He thought it was strange, the darkness had seemed so oppressive, but now he feared the upcoming light far more. Despite that fear gnawing at his insides, he pressed on. He knew that he must bring an end to this nightmare. Life or death were both preferable than wandering around endlessly in the darkness never knowing when tooth and claw would seek out his flesh. Then it dawned on Priam that the fear he felt was for his son. If Hector had not been present, then he would have made his stand at the entrance to the catacombs. He and his men would most probably be dead, but at least it would have been a glorious death. His thoughts suddenly made him chuckle. 'A glorious death', what a fool. Death in battle was nought but blood and pain. The clanging of blades is rarely accompanied by cheering, but by the screams of the dying and the blank expressions of the dead. Even the joy of victory is born from the relief of being alive, rather than the victory itself.

Priam stopped just short of the light that invaded the tunnel. He could see that a large open space lay just ahead. He could hear voices but had no clue as to whom they belonged. Hector came to his shoulder.

"What is it, Father?"

"There is someone or something up ahead, but I can't..." He felt the rope that had bound the two together go limp and drop to the floor. He glanced sideways, to see his son dash across to the opposite side of the tunnel. "Take heed, Hector."

"These parts of the catacombs are enormous, Father. Wait! I can see movement on the far side!"

Priam watched as Hector's mask of determination turned to one of obvious shock, paling at the view before him. Priam needed to see what lay ahead. He crept forward, ensuring he kept close to the tunnel wall. He stared into the light. Initially, he felt amazement at the size of the underground cavern, guessing that it could easily house Troy's throne room. His gaze stopped at one point in the distance. The bodies of six palace guards littered the cavern floor, four Mormo including the queen, seemed to take great delight in their demise.

As Priam continued to watch a fifth Mormo entered the cavern from a tunnel beyond the queen. It dragged a guard by the leg.

"Is it him?" Priam heard the queen screech.

The king watched as the Mormo dropped the guard at her feet. The man was still alive and tried to rise. The queen had obviously realised that her captive was not who she sought. Brutally, she threw the man back to the ground and brought a powerful foot down, crushing the man's throat.

"Father."

"Yes, my son," Priam replied trying to quell the anger rising in every sinew.

"I believe I have had enough of running," Hector announced.

Priam placed his shield on the ground, retrieved the spear that was slung across his back, and raised the weapon to his shoulder.

"Make your aim true boy. It would be to our advantage to face three rather than five."

"Yes, Father." Hector replied as he raised his own spear, and then nodded that he was ready.

*****

"In you go." Maeja pointed to the ruined well.

"Why did we not enter the catacombs at the same place as the king?" Aetes replied.

"Why are the young so unwilling to embark on adventure? When I was young the opportunity to climb down a well shaft and enter the beast's lair would have been impossible to refuse. Pfft... I despair, I really do."

"I am willing," Aetes replied hurriedly, as he swung a leg over the well's stonework. "I simply thought it would get us to the king sooner."

"We are not looking for Priam."

"But you said that his life was in danger."

"It is, but we search for those that wish to do the killing. Their tracks disappeared close to the well. This may or may not be where they entered the catacombs, but I'll wager two rabbits for my cooking pot that it is damn close." As she spoke, she pulled an ordinary pebble from her leather pouch. She closed both hands about the stone and whispered through her fingers. "Selene, goddess of the true light." She breathed through her fingers. "Allow your blessed illumination to show the way." Immediately, pale blue beams of light escaped Maeja's clutches. Without ceremony the sorceress tossed the pebble into the well. "That should aid your descent."

Aetes began his journey into the catacombs. The descent was difficult but did not take too long. Aetes let out a sigh of obvious relief when his foot made contact with the ground. He turned from the wall of the well only to be startled by Maeja standing directly in front of him.

"You forgot your spear." She handed over the weapon.

"But... how did you...?" Aetes stuttered.

"Aetes, you must accept that from the moment you set out on the mission to rescue those children, the world that you thought you knew had changed. You must not only think with your head, but your heart, and most importantly your gut." She pressed a hand against his stomach. "Even your eyes and ears can be deceived. Sometimes we must feel our way through life. If we survive this night, then more dangers will follow, and our enemies may well pose far greater threat than a few Mormo with teeth and claws."

"Is that not bad enough?" Aetes asked.

Maeja chuckled. "Well perhaps we will die this night, then the nightmares of the future cannot harm us."

"I'd rather not," Aetes replied.

"Now let us find these bastards and put an end to it." Maeja bent low and plucked the blue stone from the ground. Holding it high, she strode down the nearest tunnel.

*****

The spears cut through the cavern's ancient and musty air. They reached the pinnacle of their arc and then turned downward as they raced toward their intended targets. The Mormo had not reacted to the act of violence, clearly oblivious to the presence of Priam and Hector. However, that presence was announced as the tip of a spear burst through the spine of the nearest Mormo. Its screams did not prevent flesh and bone being torn apart, they did nonetheless, give warning to the other beasts. The alarm was not in time to save another creature as the second spear took her in throat. The power of Priam's rage became evident as the Mormo was carried along with the missile at least six paces, pinning it the ancient rock of the cavern. The slaughter was met by screams of fury from the remaining Mormo. The queen pointed toward their uninvited guests, and her last remaining subjects charged toward Troy's royalty.

"Any words of advice, Father?"

"Just kill the bastards." Priam drew his sword and advanced on the closest Mormo. He heard Hector screaming his battle cry and could not help feeling pride that the boy had vanquished his fear. The Mormo to his front, soon brought his attention back to the battle. The claws swept down in a savage attack and only Priam's experience at using a shield kept him from being opened from chin to groin. The opportunity to strike back at the beast was limited, as time and time again it slashed at any exposed flesh. Priam contented himself with blocking the blows and moving, hoping that the creature's rage would sap its energy. He chanced a look sideways. As he did so, he saw Hector slice off the hand of an enemy with a perfectly executed attack. The screech it emitted made Priam's own opponent look to the side, giving Priam an opening. Darting to the left, he brought his blade up, and then swept it downwards. The Mormo screamed as Priam's blade cut through flesh and smashed bone. It tried to remain standing, but with the knee nought but bloodied pulp, it fell without ceremony. Seeing his chance, Priam blocked the desperate flailing arms of the beast with his shield and plunged his sword deep into its breast. He knew that the fight was won, but his rage had not yet subsided. He raised his blade one last time and decapitated the foul creature.

Priam took in deep breaths, the exertion and excitement of battle was an experience he had thought was consigned to history. He glanced over at Hector. His son stood unmoving, looking toward the queen, his jaw set in obvious defiance. To Priam's surprise, Hector was suddenly moving at pace.

"Wait!" Priam shouted. Feeling the gnawing sensation of panic grip deep within his guts.

Either Hector did not hear, or he ignored the warning.

Priam raced forward, eyes flitting between the waiting queen and the onrushing Hector. As his son neared, Priam witnessed the once beautiful Mormo queen, change in size and shape. Her limbs swelled and lengthened. At the end of each finger, the already vicious looking nails, elongated becoming what could only be described as talons. The jaw jutted forward,–which forced the mouth wide to display teeth capable of tearing a man in two. Hector's battle cry screamed through the air as his son threw himself at the queen. The terrifying she-monster swatted the prince as though he was no more than a troublesome fly, and screeched her triumph as Hector crashed to the ground with a nauseating thud.

Priam

closed upon his enemy, ensuring the queen did not have the time to deliver a fatal blow to his son.

"Finally, the great Priam has grown tired of men dying in his stead," she snarled.

"What wrong have I done you?" Priam asked as he maintained a defensive position.

"You...," the creature seemed to struggle to find words.

"You have doomed your people and do not know why?"

"The words were spoken." She looked in genuine pain as she tried to reply.

"What words and by whom?" Priam demanded to know.

"They come to me and each of my children. Each night our sleep was filled with the same voice. The words will not stop until you and your bloodline are dead."

The rage came back to the features of the queen. She raised her hand and with a terrible force, swept down toward Priam. He used his shield just in time, but the power of the blow knocked him from his feet. He scrambled to his feet. A second blow came, and he dived out of the way. But just a fraction too slow. He felt the queen's claws tear at the flesh of his thigh. He wildly swung his sword hoping to slow his attacker's assault. To his horror his arm was caught by the queen's powerful grasp and he was unable to pull it free. The agony he felt next was like no other, as a powerful jaw clamped onto his forearm. Screaming he brought the shield round. It smashed the powerful jaw and broke the queen's hold.

Priam tried to move away, but his legs faltered, and he fell once more. Afraid though he was, he would not await death with his back to the enemy. Fighting the pain, he turned over, and felt the cold, unyielding ground beneath his spine. His sword arm was useless. He cast away the shield and pulled a dagger from his belt. He knew that it was a forlorn hope, but he begged the gods for one chance to draw blood on the creature. Then the queen was screaming. Priam raised his head to see Hector with sword and shield standing in defiance of her rage. He wanted to stand at his son's side, but his sight became blurred, and darkness overcame him.

*****

The sound of battle had made Maeja increase her pace.

Aetes was struggling to keep up, not that he would admit to being outpaced by an old woman. Suddenly, the sorceress came to an abrupt halt. Aetes swerved to avoid crashing into her.

"Why have we stopped?" Aetes asked.

"Two tunnels... I admit I am unsure which to take," she replied.

"Well, we can take one each."

She turned to face him.

"I will not be able to protect you," she replied.

Aetes thought he saw a glimmer of concern in her eyes. "I gave my word that I would protect the king and his family. Even if it meant my death. It is the life of Priam and Hector that matters, not mine." Without waiting for a reply, Aetes turned and took the tunnel to the left.

Aetes was far less confident as the darkness closed in. If only he had remembered to ask Maeja for the blue light. He pressed on; with each step the sound of battle grew louder. He could not rush, the lack of light saw to that, but he maintained a constant pace without concerning himself with what lay in the shadows. The time for caution was at an end. The life of the king and prince may depend on him, and he would not be found wanting.

Eventually a brightness appeared in the distance. Aetes did not slow his pace. His hand gripped the shaft of his spear with increased pressure, which did not stop until the end of the tunnel was in sight. His eyes needed time to grow accustomed to the light. It was sometime before a large cavern appeared before him. The sounds of battle had diminished but his gaze was drawn to a figure that lay, lifeless upon the ground. With dismay, Aetus recognised his king. As he continued to stare, two figures came from behind one of the large columns that reached into the heavens of the cavern. Hector was doing battle with a terrifying beast. The prince was not attempting to attack, his shield and blade being used to keep the foul creature away from Priam. Suddenly, it dawned on Aetes that he was not moving to aid his prince, frozen like a statue as he watched those he served in mortal danger.

Move! he told himself. There was no time to lose! He forced himself to take a step, and then another. Soon he was running; his gaze never leaving the battle ahead. As he closed within twenty paces, he saw the queen rip Hector's shield away and deliver a blow that sent the prince sprawling. Aetes gasped, he dropped the spear and shield, discarding their safety for greater pace. A figure moved to his right. *Gods! Let that be Maeja!*

He pressed on and watched as the creature raised her hand to deliver death to Hector. There was no alternative, but to throw himself forward, placing himself between beast and prince. One moment he was flying through the air, the next his body came to a jarring halt. What in the name of Zeus was happening to him? It was as though he were standing on air! He looked at the prince who was seemed to be staring back, but not at his face. Aetes dropped his gaze, shocked to see the creature's talons protruding from his own chest. There was no pain until he was flung against the large column. Smashing into the unyielding masonry, the bone in his arm broke and pierced the flesh. Aetes slithered down the column and remarkably ended up in the sitting position.

He watched as the queen turned her attention to Hector, ignorant as the flailing figure of Maeja arose to her rear. The old woman grasped the creature by the hair with one hand and plunged her free hand into the creature's chest. Aetes was joined in his stare as Hector, and the beast all looked at the clasping hand of Maeja. The fingers slowly opened to reveal the bloodied mass that was the ruler of the Mormo's heart. The hand withdrew and the queen stumbled and fell. Her head landed in Aetes lap. He stared down at the disgusting sight, his consciousness beginning to fail.

"Don't die on me boy."

Maeja's words forced himself to stay awake.

"I am not sure I have a say on the matter," Aetes replied. The waves of pain now began to wash over him. He felt Maeja's hands on him. "No! Look to the king."

"Priam is in no danger," Maeja replied.

"But the king..."

"Is just a man," she interrupted. "Now be quiet."

*****

Maeja had waited a respectful amount of time, before once again stepping within Troy's royal household. The Queen of Troy had been respectfully honoured, and the surviving members of Troy's nobility had nursed their injuries. The old woman had been surprised that those within the city's walls behaved differently as she passed. Rather than clutching their children close and scurrying away, they bent their heads in solemn respect. It was not friendly by any means, but at least she was not shunned. Kadmos, upon seeing her, stepped aside immediately and nodded.

"The king is in the private royal garden. I am sure that he will be pleased to see you, Maeja."

"Ha! I doubt that. Will you not be escorting me?"

"The king has ordered that you have complete freedom within Troy." The guard paused as if unsure what to say next, and surprised Maeja by looking her directly in the eyes. "The people of Troy will be eternally grateful to you for bringing back King Priam and the young prince."

Slightly taken aback by the guard's words, she raised an old, withered hand, and laid it on his shoulder. "They are good men and good men are in short supply. The gardens you say?"

"Yes," he replied.

Without another word she turned away from the guard and walked into the interior of the palace. The gardens were a private place where the royal family could enjoy the breeze upon their face without having to interact with the populace. It was not an area created out of a desire to remain aloof from the people of Troy. Hecuba herself had designed the area to be a place of escape. She recognised that, with power came responsibilities, and they often weighed heaviest on the shoulders of the youngest of the family members. Because of this, it was one of the few places that Maeja felt reluctant to enter. However, she was not one to shy away from her responsibility or fail to collect a debt.

Passing through an arched doorway, Maeja was immediately warmed by the plentiful sun that left its glow around the enclosure. At the far end of the garden, the young princesses were playing. Then Priam rose from a small shrine that was dedicated to the father of gods, she could not help giving a derisive snort at the deity's presence. It was not a loud snort, but it was enough to attract the king's attention.

"Maeja, I had expected to see you at Hecuba's ceremony," Priam announced.

"No, I prefer to deal with the living rather than the dead." Realising that this sounded harsh even for her she added, "She will always live within my heart, Priam, make no mistake."

The king nodded at her kind words.

"And now to the cost. For isn't there always a price to be paid?"

"There is," she replied.

"My kingdom, my firstborn, the blood of an enemy. I gave my word, and it shall be honoured." He gave a wry smile.

Maeja returned the smile. "Nothing so grand. I wish for the small gift of preparation."

"Preparation?" Priam did not hide his confusion.

"As we battled the Mormo in the caverns what can

you remember?" she asked.

"Darkness, blood and fear mostly. And..." he faltered.

"And what else?" she pressed.

"I could smell a sea breeze. I did not concern myself with it at the time. But when I think on that night, I can almost taste the salt upon my lips."

"If we had continued just a few hundred paces beyond the great cavern, then we would have emerged onto a small coastal path. From there, it is a brief walk that leads to a hidden cove. A place that few alive know exist," she explained.

"But how does this concern my debt to you?"

"I kept three men alive that night. A king, a prince and young warrior. I want a ship for each life. They must be strong vessels, with a loyal crew to sail and defend. Supplies ready to be loaded for a substantial journey."

"And who or what do these ships carry?" he asked.

"That will be for you to decide. But may I suggest that Hector and Aetes look to training those that will protect their timbers."

"Hector is nought but a boy and knows little of sailing," Priam argued.

"Hector is no more a boy than you are, besides, we have time. But we must prepare, Priam King of Troy."

"Why do you ask for such things? I have wealth. You could buy ships and crew."

"A debt is debt, Priam. I have told you the price. Not

one item more or one item less."

Priam eyed Maeja. Finally, however, he nodded his head.

"Three ships, men and supplies," he announced.

"And remember only the crews need to know of the ships existence. There is little point in a secret cove if its existence is talked about by every drunken palace guard." Her eyes left Priam and settled on the children.

Priam must have noticed. "Will you stay and take refreshment?" he asked of her.

Maeja did not reply, her attention drawn by the children.

"Have you no children, Maeja?"

The question brought her attention back to the King.

"No, it was not my fate to be blessed with a child. I would have liked..." She stopped talking abruptly and turned from Priam. "I have tasks to perform." She strode away without another word.

PART TWO

'DECEIT'

*"Hateful to me as the gates of Hades is
that man who hides one thing*

in his heart and speaks another."

— Homer, The Iliad

Chapter 12

'Blood Stone'

Tegea was a thriving state and controlled much of the area in the region of Arcadia. A strong military provided the security for trade to blossom. However, all was not how it seemed. Within its borders stood a great woodland. It should have provided Tegea with valuable resources, but the populace avoided it at all costs. Rumours of ferocious beasts were perhaps to be expected in a terrain thick with imposing trees, but these rumours were accompanied by reports of missing people or worse the remains of mutilated villagers.

Many years ago, soldiers were dispatched to clear the forest of any dangerous creatures. The soldiers never returned. Many nights and tears were spent by those loved ones left behind watching the various tracks that led to the forest. As the years passed, the woodland was simply ignored and alternative routes found to the border villages. Only visitors, ignorant of the danger facing them, entered the oppressive landscape.

A dark clad figure crept amongst the trees. He was tall with strong, powerful, square shoulders. His hair was white, unusual for a man not too advanced in years. A solid jaw, and piercing blue eyes complimented a handsome face. He was confident in his task. Years previously, he had added to his ranks. Two princes in dire need to escape the clutches of their uncle had fallen under his protection. Those princes had grown into strong, intelligent men. A fact that would not have gone unnoticed by Thyestes. The figure gave a wry smile, he had every intention of using the conflict between Thyestes and his nephews to his own advantage. Now he must encourage others to follow in their footsteps and be in his debt. The warriors at his side were the most trusted at his disposal. They had been allowed to see his features and know his name.

At his rear, at least a hundred men nervously watched the shadows. Eight of them, however, were not afforded the luxury of watching for possible danger. Their efforts involved carrying a litter that housed an individual that not one of them had laid eyes on. Suddenly, a man emerged from the trees to their front. Breathing heavily, he dropped to one knee.

"Thanatos, I have found them," he announced.

The dark clad figure stepped forward and helped the man to his feet. "I would have thought they would have found us by now, Agapetos," he replied.

"Their attention is drawn elsewhere. They seem to be celebrating some kind of festival. I suggest we proceed with care, they're powerful creatures."

"We would not be here if they were not. But I agree, we should act with caution." Thanatos waved a hand to indicate to his men that they should press forward. As they walked, he pulled a water skin from his belt. "Here, rid your thirst."

"Gratitude, I thought these creatures worshipped no gods. So why the festival?" Agapetos asked.

"There must be more to be thankful for in this world, than those that sit in Olympus. However, their joyful mood may be short lived if they realise that they have uninvited visitors. Our guest will come with me, but you and the men find a suitable place to make camp. I would advise you to remain vigilant."

"Thanatos, is it wise to go into their lair unprotected?"

"I am never without protection. I doubt that I will come to any harm." He gave the shoulder of his scout a pat. "Now send the litter to the front."

Thanatos waited for the litter to move closer, before he once again began to move amongst the trees. The men carrying the litter found the going tough and voiced all manner of curses. It was some time before Thanatos called for them to halt and not to make a sound. As they fell silent, he was aware of another sound. He could make out the eerie notes of the aulos, a piped musical instrument used throughout the known world. He listened more closely, and could also discern the use of other instruments, such as the chelys and crotalum. He turned to the men that carried the litter.

"From this point on you are to remain silent. You must not talk or voice your discomfort. Those that we are about to encounter are easily offended. It would be wise not to give them an excuse to separate your heads from your bodies." Without waiting for a reply, he set off through the trees. As he pressed on, he became aware of shapes moving in the distance.

It wasn't long before an enormous clearing became apparent. Within it, at least five hundred centaurs stood, their attention drawn to its centre.

"Make way, I would speak to your leader!" Thanatos called out.

The nearest centaur to him turned. The beast gave a snort of derision and then reverted its gaze back to the centre of the clearing.

"I said make way!" Thanatos waved his arms as if parting the water as he swam.

Centaurs were sent crashing to the ground, creating a pathway to his intended target. He turned and waved the litter onward. He calmly stepped forward without looking at the distraught centaurs, who could not find the strength to rise. Those centaurs that remained upright started calling for blood, but Thanatos simply gave a broad grin in reply. However, his attention was on the large centaur that raced towards him. It skidded to a halt just to his front. Its flanks rippled with muscles.

"Who are you?" the centaur growled.

"I am merely a tired traveller in need of safe shelter for the night," he said, his honeyed smile never slipping.

"Since when do those seeking aid attack their would-be hosts?"

"You are centaurs. What would have been your response if I had begged for aid? Centaurs loathe displays of weakness," Thanatos replied.

"And how do you know what centaurs loathe?" His hand moved toward the blade slung at its waist.

Thanatos moved a hand before his own face. The human features dissolved and were replaced by what could only be described as a leather, black as night, mask. He stepped closer to the warrior centaur.

"I am Thanatos. I am the point of death in all creatures. I have walked side by side with your kind for many years. They have whispered their hopes and regrets into my ears," he whispered.

"But we are not dead!"

Thanatos gave a wry smile.

"The day is not over yet," he replied.

"Is that a threat?" The centaur rose up on its hind legs, his anger obvious to all.

Thanatos raised a hand and clenched his fingers. As if gripped by an invisible force, the centaur crashed to the earth, its hands scrabbling at its own throat.

"I am sorry I did not intend my words to threaten," Thanatos spoke calmly. "My humour can sometimes be misunderstood. This, however, is a threat. I suggest that you keep your chest beating for your mating rituals." Thanatos waved his hand, and the centaur was released from his discomfort.

"And I suggest that if you wish your men to survive, you will keep your hands at your side." The words did not come from the centaur to his front. Another centaur had pushed his way through the crowd.

Thanatos did not reply in haste; he took his time observing the newcomer. The centaur seemed younger than most and his build was slender. However, Thanatos noticed how the other centaurs watched the youngster. They seemed to hang on his every word, as a subject would to a member of royalty.

"My men seem safe enough," Thanatos replied.

"I was not talking about these men." The young centaur nodded his head. In the distance a war horn blew and was quickly followed by the screams.

Thanatos gave another smile.

"I can always find more warriors. Tell me." he paused, "what is your name?"

"Dromicus."

"Tell me, Dromicus. How will you replace your centaurs?" He matched the stare of the young centaur. The smile never slipping. Finally, Dromicus raised his hand and the war horn sounded. It was not long before the screaming died down.

"What do you want?" Dromicus asked through gritted teeth.

Thanatos pointed over the centaur's shoulder. "I want that."

"That is the Mother Staff. Without it we cannot see our mother, Nephele. She would be unable to visit our lands."

"Nephele, comes to you? I confess I was unaware of that fact. When does she arrive?" Thanatos asked.

"The ceremony takes place over three days, and this is the last of those days. She should be here before nightfall. We mourn her true love and our father together. Be warned. She is not without power and not easily threatened. You would be wise to leave this place rather than risk her wrath."

The esteem Dromicus held for Nephele was etched on the young centaur's face.

"I have said it before, I have no wish to threaten anyone. I believe our paths are entwined. But first I must speak with Nephele." He paused for a moment as he considered his next move. "We should cease our hostilities. I am sure that we can control our aggression until I have had the opportunity to speak with Nephele."

The young centaur nodded an acceptance of Thanatos' terms. Then he bent forward and helped the felled centaur to his feet. "Are you injured, Alcus?"

"Only my pride, but it's not the first time I've taken a beating. I doubt it will be the last," the powerful centaur replied.

"Escort the rest of our visitor's men to a place where they may camp with more comfort. Post guards. We do not want any misunderstanding to result in violence."

"Yes, Dromicus."

"And it might be wise to let Airlea tend their wounded. She has more knowledge than most."

"It will be done." Alcus moved away without looking at Thanatos.

*****

The light of the day had begun to fade. Airlea and several other centaurs moved through-out the newly constructed human camp tending the wounded. Now and then she would cast a glance in the direction of the man that the other warriors seemed to regard as their leader in the absence of Thanatos. At least twenty of their number were dead and many more had suffered a range of injuries. The leader, however, refused treatment for his own wound to the upper thigh. She wondered how a man coped with the loss of so many of his comrades.

Airlea approached him carefully, unsure how she would be received. As the young centaur neared, she raised a water skin. The man studied the offer for a moment, and then nodded his gratitude.

"Your wound needs tending."

He nodded again his agreement.

Taking that as permission to begin treatment. Airlea carefully wiped the dried blood from the deep gash to his thigh.

"Thank you for attending to the needs of my men," he finally spoke.

"It is the least I can do. It was my people that inflicted..." Airlea's words failed, but to her surprise the man gently placed a hand on her shoulder.

"We are warriors. We fight and all too often we end up bleeding in the dirt. Any kindness we experience is both rare and gratefully received.

"What is your name?" she asked.

"Agapetos, and yours?"

"I am called Airlea. I wonder, if so many men will end up bleeding in the dirt, would it not be better to stop fighting?"

"My people have little choice. The men you see around you have no land to call their own. Either we fight and take what we need, or our families starve."

"Did you lose your lands in war?" she asked.

"Not in war," Agapetos replied. He winced as she cleaned the laceration.

"How then?"

"I only know what our elders have told me. It was no war between men that took all that we possessed. Perhaps we displeased the gods in some way, or we were caught between the wrath of two deities. The reason is lost to my people. We were an island race. Few even remember we once existed. Our home was a beautiful island known as Thera. We held a deep respect for the waters that gave us nourishment and wealth. However, it was those waters that tore our lands apart. First, the mountain belched fire into the sky and made the ground shake. Over the years my people grew used to its grumblings. No matter how angry the mountain became, it always calmed eventually. But this time, part of it broke away and tumbled into the sea, taking homes and their owners to watery graves. Then a great wave struck, and most of our warships and fishing vessels were broken on our coastline. It was terrible, but nothing that our people had not faced many times before. However, the waters always receded, but this time they continued to rise. It took too long for my people to realise that the lands were sinking. It took three days for the highest point of our beloved land to slip beneath the waves. My grandmother, a small child at the time, found herself clinging to her mother in open water. Their only company were the dead, swollen to the point of bursting as they bobbed upon the waves. They managed to clamber aboard a damaged fishing vessel. I am sorry this is not a joyful tale. I should not burden you with my people's woes."

Airlea encouraged him to distract him from the pain. "No, please continue. Besides, it will give me the opportunity to attend your wound."

"But my men…"

"They're receiving the best care that we can give," she interrupted. "Please go on with the tale of your people."

"Very well. They were alone for most of the first day, at least my grandmother thought that they were alone. The events of the day had sapped their energy, and both had slipped into slumber. However, as the day moved on and they forced themselves to wake, cries for help began to reach their ears. Despite their exhaustion, they managed to drag several people aboard the battered craft. Some of the people soon succumbed to exhaustion and injuries and were gently lowered back into the water. My grandmother told me of the shame that she would carry for the rest of her life, even though she knew that it was the only option.

"As time passed, the vessel became too small to give

refuge, so the survivors worked together. They found rope and lashed driftwood and other wreckage to their own. As the days passed, more and more survivors were found, and were pulled, grateful for their lives, from the waters. Rich and poor now sat next to one another. Wealth meant nothing with so much lost.

On the fourth day after our lands had completely vanished beneath the waves, two of our war ships were spotted on the horizon. Grandmother told me that waiting for them to come was agonising, especially as the waves had become rough. She expected a huge column of water to smash their broken transport to pieces before any possible rescue. However, she did find herself on the overcrowded deck of a warship. The cramped conditions made her feel safe, as though she were receiving an embrace from her entire people.

"They did not linger once the survivors had boarded the new transport. Lack of food, water and warm clothing was putting the rescued at risk, and so, they went in search of a safe harbour. It would have been impossible to land within the boundaries of a foreign state without an invitation. There was nought to offer a potential host. Few states would have been prepared to feed so many mouths. They knew they had to find a place that was uninhabited and offered shelter from both the ravages of nature and possible attack. Two days later, my grandmother found herself deposited with the rest of her people, on the largest uninhabited island that sat in a cluster of small islands. It offered very little except inland caves for shelter and animals to hunt. But it did offer one important thing that meant everything to my grandmother and her people. It offered the opportunity to stay together and rebuild." Agapetos took another drink.

"But how? Your people had lost everything."

"That is a story for another time. I must see to my men, but I would like to thank you for all that you have done." He handed the water skin back to Airlea.

"I hope your stay will be for more than this night. I would like to hear more about your people," she replied and gave a smile.

Chapter 13

'An Uneasy Alliance'

Thanatos instructed the litter bearers to carry their cargo into a large rectangular timber building. He guessed that if Nephele was to appear, then it would be within its walls. It was the only permanent structure he had observed since he had entered the lands of the centaurs. His men set their unseen travelling companion at the far end of the construction.

"Good. Now go to our camp. I will call you, if needed," Thanatos instructed.

One of the litter bearers began to ask. "You are staying alone with these…"

"We have given our word to cease hostilities." The reply came from Dromicus who stood in the open doorway. "Centaurs do not break their word. Can you say the same?"

The bearer dropped his gaze to the ground, mumbling a feeble apology as he did so.

Thanatos gave a bark of laughter. "I am sure that my man meant no disrespect." He smiled at the thought of the litter bearer being protective. Especially, as the man and the rest of the warriors were nothing to him. He would happily see them all consigned to the care of

Hades. He turned to face the embarrassed man. "You have your orders." His men moved with haste to the doorway, but each of them passed Dromicus with more caution and not one met his eyes. Thanatos watched them leave and noticed that the centaur held the Mother Staff "I will endeavour not to delay your meeting with Nephele."

"I imagine she will dictate such things," Dromicus replied.

"Indeed." Thanatos gave a wry smile. "Loyalty to family should be commended."

"Our loyalty should never be questioned or underestimated. There is not one centaur that would not willingly lay down their life to ensure her protection."

"Let us hope that such a grand gesture is never required." Thanatos replied, amused by the centaur's deep loathing.

Dromicus crossed the room and placed the Mother Staff in a bracket secured on the wall. He turned to look at Thanatos.

"I will be outside should assistance be required."

Thanatos almost laughed at the poorly veiled threat. "It is most kind of you to remain so close."

The centaur gave a curt nod and then left the room.

Thanatos moved to the litter. He glanced briefly to the door and then whispered, "We are alone,"

"I'm surprised that Nephele dares to visit her children. It seems they hold her in high regard," a female voice whispered. "And even if she does agree, it may be all for nought if you cannot convince the Spartans that war threatens their lands."

"Their land is threatened! Thyestes may or may not have sought out an alliance with other states yet, but he will. He will march on Sparta and the now grown princes will have no option but to wage war. So, I must convince them to form their own alliance."

"Then much relies on our hostess. The question is how much esteem does she still possess for Ixion?"

"She loved him once. I cannot imagine that her new husband knows that she visits the children from a former lover. It will be a secret she is desperate to keep." Thanatos smiled. The upcoming meeting with Nephele may go in his favour.

"Then you must convince her that our interests and her own are one of the same."

"Do you mean that we both must convince her?" Thanatos asked.

"I must for the time being remain in the shadows. I will not be present when she arrives."

"But…" Thanatos guessed that his words were seeking out absent ears. He pulled back the fabric that concealed the interior of the litter from the outside world. The interior was devoid of life. "I wish that you would not keep taking your leave. Besides, if I am to play this dangerous game then I would prefer my allies to take the same risk." He allowed the cloth to drop back into place, bored with talking to himself.

*****

Thanatos did not like being idle; waiting for Nephele was frustrating. He waved a hand before his face, and the human disguise reappeared. He thought Nephele might prefer a handsome face. She had after all, fallen in love with a demi-god. Did she enjoy being in the presence of impurity? Suddenly, the Mother Staff began to emit a high-pitched humming sound. The crimson jewel at the top of the staff began to slowly rotate. With each turn, red beams of light shot into the room. The jewel began to gather pace. As it did, more of the light filled the surrounding area. Thanatos realised that this was no act of nature, the jewel contained power not of the world of men. Even though he was a god, he was forced to lift a hand in front of his eyes to guard against the overwhelming light. For a moment, he wondered if the jewel would stop, fearing it would explode and consume all around. The humming stopped as abruptly just as it had begun. Slowly, he allowed his hand to drop from his eyes.

The red light had vanished. In its place stood one of the most beautiful of female forms he had ever witnessed. A white gown flowed over a sumptuous figure. A face that bore an unmistakable resemblance to Hera, Olympian and wife of Zeus, but there were marked differences. The skin was paler, resembling polished marble. Framing the beautiful features of the face was cascading hair the colour of unspoiled snow. Hera's hair was a deep, burning red, which suited her tendency to rage.

"I presume that you are Nephele." Thanatos gave a

broad, welcoming smile.

"I see that we both know who I am, but who are you?" The woman asked. Her voice was soft and smooth.

"I..." he tried to reply, but Nephele interrupted.

"Why do you try to deceive me?" She waved a hand. Thanatos could offer no resistance as his disguise melted away, revealing his true self.

"No deceit was intended. I merely wished to put you at ease," Thanatos replied. He had not made a good first impression.

"I am rarely put at ease by lies," she replied sternly.

"Then I beg your forgiveness. Besides, I offer you an opportunity."

"Opportunity? I doubt I would be interested in anything that a minor god could offer."

"I thought you did not know who I was?" he asked.

"It seems we both deal in deceit. Tell me Thanatos, what brings you among my children?"

"It is simple. The world of men and gods is about to change. Those that choose the right side will gain much, those that pick poorly will lose all. I come to you because I can give you all that you crave."

"And what do you know of my desires?" She replied dismissively.

"That can be answered with one name... Ixion."

For the first time, Nephele's cool exterior showed uncertainty. "Ixion is gone. Banished to Tartarus never to return."

"Even among the gods, the love between Ixion and Nephele is legendary. What started as deceit by Zeus turned into a great love. Its briefness was only matched by its intensity."

"And what good did that love bring? The gods stole it from us when they cast Ixion into Tartarus." A tear rolled down her cheek. Thanatos noticed that it reflected the light, like the most perfect of diamonds. Indeed, when it landed upon the floor it was a flawless jewel.

"Did that adoration fade away like the dying embers of a fire?" He stepped closer and lowered his voice. "Or do the flames of that love still rage like an inferno?"

"I have given my hand to another," she replied. The tremble in her voice was undeniable.

"A coupling forced by the gods. They stole your love and replaced it with a guard dog. Someone to ensure that you remained quiet and didn't question their actions. Tell me, Nephele, does anyone know that you visit this place?"

"They do not know I possess the staff or the jewel to which it plays host."

"And do you know its power?" Thanatos asked.

"I only know it grants me the opportunity to be among my children."

"It is capable of so much more. With that jewel," he pointed to the top of the staff, "I can bring Ixion back to you."

For a moment Nephele was speechless; her eyes welling up with tears. Regaining her emotions, she said, "Tell me Thanatos, what payment would you require?"

"I merely wish to bring balance where there is none. To do that we must break the hold that the Olympians have on us all."

"You cannot defeat Zeus!" Her response dismissive of his words.

"I do not have to defeat Zeus, only a fool would challenge him. Nonetheless, I will take all that he holds dear. To do that I will take away the source of his power, piece by piece."

"And you can do this?"

"Not alone, but I have powerful allies, we gather more followers with every passing day. Some are lesser gods and others are men with great influence. The Olympians will taste defeat before they even know they're at war."

"I admire your confidence, but you still haven't told me what payment."

"I can free Ixion, but for him to remain free the Olympians must fall. You and your children must join our ranks and march under our banner."

"You ask too much. What mother would place her children in harm's way?" She shook her head as she spoke.

"How can a mother deny her children the opportunity to know their father? Besides, you can always make more children." Nephele slapped him across the face, but Thanatos noticed that there was no rage on her features. He smiled. "Look around at what your children have become. Powerful warriors reduced to hiding in the trees. Each one of them fearful what the next man to cross their border will bring. It is truly a slow death. They could possess far more and know the caress of true freedom. I offer you the chance to give them life. A home free from interference from both man and god."

"Will they be safe?"

"Are they now? Freedom does not come without cost. All I can promise is that I will stand at their side."

Nephele did not look convinced, but she reluctantly nodded her head as a sign of acceptance. "What do you have in mind?" she asked.

"The Tegeans are preparing for war. They will be forced into an alliance with Thyestes, he plans to launch an attack on Sparta. "

"Why would they wish war with Sparta?"

"The Spartan king, Tyndareus, is not long for this world and his throne will pass to either Menelaus or Agamemnon. Thyestes will not allow his nephews the power to reclaim his own throne. If we prevent that attack, then the Spartans will be in your debt. They can be trusted and have land to spare. "

"Trusted? I have heard such a claim many times before. It seems deceit lives in the hearts of men," she replied.

"Then let me bring them here to you. Look into the

eyes of those that offer their word."

Nephele considered the proposal. She paced within the lodge, now and then stopping to glance at Thanatos, and then continued. Finally, she turned and fixed him with an icy stare, her pale blue eyes unblinking.

"Very well, I will meet your Spartans. But be warned if I sense betrayal then they will never leave this place. Until then, I will tell my people that you are both friend and ally. Do not make me regret such action."

Thanatos gave a smile and bowed his head in respect.

Chapter 14

'War Horns Blow'

Thanatos and Nephele emerged from the building side by side. The centaurs who had waited patiently, were clearly anticipating a speech from their mother. Nephele took a step to her front.

"Children! I bring wondrous news. Our new friends," she gave a brief nod towards Thanatos, "have given us a great gift. A kindness that we could never repay. It is what my heart," she paused for a moment, "it is what all our hearts desire. If we join with Thanatos and his followers, then we can bring my love and your father home."

There was excited murmuring through the centaur ranks. She allowed them to continue, permitting their exuberance to build. When she felt the time was right, she took another step forward.

"Tell me, how many of you respect the gods?" she asked.

An almost instant change spread through-out the crowd as angry growls and shouts of 'never' could be heard.

"Should we bow to their rule?" Nephele asked.

The same angry reply came from the ranks.

"Should we continue to skulk in the shadows of this forest or seek out our own nation with your father at my side?" Again, she waited as their fervour grew. "I am not saying that the path will be easy or without danger. It is not a simple task to risk the wrath of the Olympians. But there is not much more that we can lose that we have not lost already. The Olympians have exiled us all. They sent your father to Tartarus, forced me to marry another, and banished you all, no land to call your own. The time has come for us to cry no more."

The centaurs called out their war cry.

Nephele glanced sidewards, and then whispered to Thanatos.

"Bring your Spartan and if I sense that I can trust the man, then my children will show you how centaurs were born to battle."

*****

Airlea watched Nephele's speech from the side lines and shook her head in dismay. She turned, feeling the need for solitude, heading for a place that few others of her kind rarely ventured. Her progress, however, was brought to an abrupt halt as her name was called out.

"Where are you going, Airlea?"

"I cannot share the excitement at the possibility of war, brother."

"We do not know that there will be conflict. Besides, our mother wishes it," he replied.

"Dromicus, our mother speaks of challenging the gods. How can you think that our people will survive?"

"She would not place us in danger without good reason. How can you question our mother?" He shook his head.

"Since I was a child, each time that Nephele visited our people she told us to remain within the forest. Do not venture into the world of men, but as soon as Thanatos arrives, we find ourselves doing precisely what she warned against. What do we even know of Thanatos?"

"I share your distrust of our guest, but our mother is no fool."

"That is true, but none of us are perfect. Even our mother can make mistakes. If this is an error, then we will pay a hefty price. The gods are not known to reward rebellion."

"What choice do we have, Airlea? Look around you, we are the only centaurs born in recent memory. If we do not venture beyond our borders, then our people will cease to exist."

"Then we should offer friendship, not the blade."

"Perhaps that is all we will need?" he replied.

"Dromicus, Thanatos does not want peace. I feel he has spent too much time in the presence of death. I would not be surprised if he seeks it out. He does not care about his men, did not even visit the injured. Are we foolish enough to believe that he will value a centaur's life any higher?"

"You always search for ill omens, Airlea. Why can't you see the opportunity?"

"Opportunity! The chance to die to rescue a man that no centaur has ever met."

"He is our father!" Dromicus replied, his temper beginning to rise.

"Our father? My father was Agmea the centaur. He was yours too, do not forget that when you race to embrace another in his stead."

"I do not forget. Nor do I forget his love for a woman or how he offered the hand of friendship to those beyond our borders. I remember his screams as he lay tethered to the ground as they released their hounds to tear at his flesh. I remember the love I had for a fool."

"Your hatred blinds you. Tell me Dromicus, is it the love of your people that forces you onto this path. Or is it the desire for a reckoning? How many of our people have to die until your craving for vengeance is quenched?"

Dromicus struck out; the back of his hand catching her squarely on the jaw. It threw her sideways, but somehow, she managed to keep upright. She threw him a look filled with defiance. She turned and ran.

"Airlea, I'm sorry."

She was not prepared to stop. The pain in her jaw and heart drove her on, crashing through the undergrowth and low hanging branches, driving her to leave all the hurt far behind. It was not long before she broke through the last of the trees and the river that marked the edge of the centaur's boundary. She did not slow her pace and raced headlong towards the water. It wasn't until she could feel the water at her torso that she was forced to stop. For a moment, she stood perfectly still, her eyes clamped shut. The cool waters calmed her fury but did little to wash away the concern she felt for her people. Without opening her eyes, she plunged the top half of her body into the water. The soothing liquid washed away the pain in her jaw, but she did not rush to rise into the daylight.

When finally, she did emerge, her eyes were still clamped shut. As they began to open, she noticed movement on the opposite riverbank. Forcing her eyes open; she ignored the glare from the sun. Before she could make out the cause of the movement, a burning sensation stung at her neck. She attempted to back away, but the water and slippery riverbed slowed her progress.

She grasped at the thick rope as the breath was squeezed from her throat. Airlea reached up as she felt a sharp blow to the top of her head. The warm, trickle of blood ran down her forehead. She attempted to wipe the blood away, but her hand was caught with another loathsome rope. Summoning the last of her strength she yanked her arm across her torso. The rope went limp, and in the distance, she heard a man call out, followed by a sizable splash. However, any sense of victory was short lived, the rope around her neck began to tighten. Struggling to breathe, she stumbled as the rope pulled her away from the lands of the centaur. She had no strength left to give and slowly her world began to turn to darkness. Just as she began to lose all hope, she felt strong arms around her waist, and knew she was being pulled back toward the centaur boundary. She willed herself to stay conscious and observed a familiar face.

"Dromicus," she gasped.

"Calm yourself. Let's get you back to firmer ground," he replied.

As she felt the solid ground beneath her hooves, she allowed herself to fall. Exhaustion would not let her take another step.

"How did you know I was in trouble?" she asked

"I didn't. One of the men under the command of Thanatos sent word. By the time I reached you, your attackers had either been killed or forced to flee."

"Then who?"

"Try to rest. Your questions can wait. You must sleep."

She made to protest, but waves of tiredness and pain washed over her entire body. Closing her eyes, she was only partially aware of the world. She sensed the presence of another person but could not summon the will to open her eyelids. She heard her brother speak.

"You have my gratitude."

"Airlea, showed my men a great deal of kindness. I will not see her harmed in any way."

She thought that she recognised the voice but could not resist her exhaustion any longer. Slowly, she drifted into an enforced sleep.

*****

A cold cloth dabbed against Airlea's forehead. She could smell the acrid smoke of a nearby fire. Opening her eyes slowly, she observed her brother, concern etched on his face.

"I thought I might lose you," he whispered.

"If you hadn't come to my rescue, you may well have. My strength was all but gone."

"It was not by my hand that you were delivered from harm," he replied.

Her brow crinkled, confused at his reply.

"But I felt your arms around me?"

"I pulled you from the water and steered you safely to the bank, but it would not have been possible had your attackers not been slain. Those that didn't die, ran for fear that they would be next."

"Who saved me?"

"I told you at the river. It was one of Thanatos's men," he replied.

Airlea wondered if her brother was being purposely secretive. She eyed him suspiciously but chose not to pursue the matter.

"Will you offer the man, my gratitude."

"That is a task for you. He has waited patiently for you to wake." Dromicus placed a hand upon her cheek. "Airlea, forgive me? My rage sometimes consumes me, but I feel nought but shame for raising my hand to you."

She placed a hand around his and gave it a gentle

squeeze. "It is already forgotten, brother."

Dromicus managed a smile. "Then I shall bring your man, so you can show gratitude."

"My man?" She raised an eyebrow. "Do not tease me, brother."

"He seems overly concerned for a stranger's well-being."

"I don't even know who this man is," she replied. Her cheeks regaining their colour a little too quickly.

"Are you sure?" His smile turned to a broad grin as he moved away.

*****

Airlea had closed her eyes, the pain in her head had lessened, but remained constant

"I can come back later if you require sleep?"

The voice startled her, and she jumped and opened her eyes. "Agapetos, you were the man that saved me?"

"It was the least I could do, after you treated my men." He glanced around the enclosure.

"What is it?" she asked.

"We have journeyed through much of this forest and visited your camp, but this is the first shelter that I have encountered."

"You think we live outdoors, chewing on grass like cattle?"

"I meant no disrespect," he replied quickly.

She laughed at his discomfort. "There was no disrespect. At this time of year, we spend most our time in open shelters like this one. As the weather worsens, we move deeper into the forest. There we have homes that would not be out of place in your world. Centaurs tend to like their own area in which to live, village life would feel too oppressive. I suppose that seems strange to you."

"Not at all. Our islands are small and each year our population grows. To be honest, sometimes it feels as though you don't have room to breathe. It would be enjoyable, to be free to step away."

"It helps to be alone with your thoughts. Especially, when great changes are coming," she replied, unable to hide her concern.

"You seem troubled."

"May I ask you a question? You do not have to answer."

"You may ask. I cannot tell if I will answer or not until I hear the question." He gave a smile.

"Thanatos, do you trust him?"

Agapetos briefly glanced over his shoulder, clearly concerned if anyone was nearby. "Although I have not witnessed him speaking a falsehood or acting without honour. I cannot deny that I would have preferred it, if he had not visited my people."

She nodded her head, unable to stop the tears welling. "I cannot shake the feeling that he will bring doom upon my people. We are too few to risk going to war."

Agapetos placed his hand on hers. "I will defend your people as I do my own."

"They talk about warring with the gods. What can centaur or man do against such power?" she asked.

"I have never had the need for those in Olympus and certainly have no love for their actions. That does not mean that we should choose to inflame their rage. Like you, I must follow the lead of my elders, and so, we must look to protect each other as best as we can."

"It seems when the war horn blows, warriors become deaf to reason."

Sadness seemed to wash over him. "That they do, at least, for a time. They soon tire of the cost."

"Cost?"

"Watching friends die or even the enemy, takes the lustre out of war. That is not the only cost."

"There's more?" she pressed.

"My people began to raid trade routes to survive. They did that so we may have a home where our families could grow and never know hardship, but what home does a warrior obtain? Sooner or later, even the best feels a blade in their flesh, they rarely know the joys of a true home."

"It seems we are both trapped by our lives. I have the home but am forbidden from going beyond its borders. You have freedom, but no real home."

"May I ask you a question?" Agapetos asked timidly.

"Of course," she replied.

"I do not see any little ones within your people, are they kept from strangers?"

Airlea blushed. "We have no little ones."

"But why?"

Airlea gathered her strength to reply. "Centaurs can fall in love with centaurs, but to produce a child they must mate with a human. My father was the last centaur to fall in love with a human and it resulted in Dromicus and I. However, if the centaurs cannot leave their borders, they cannot continue to exist."

"Forgive me, I did not mean to pry."

"Perhaps, the arrival of Thanatos will provide my people with the opportunity to meet potential mates." She looked directly into Agapetos' brown eyes.

"It would be a shame to miss out on an opportunity." He smiled, returning her gaze. A slight colouring appeared within his cheeks.

Chapter 15

'Crown of Thorns'
(10 years since the princes arrived in Sparta)

A man was dying. Outside his royal quarters several people waited for the news that they dreaded. King Tyndareus had led the people of Sparta to unprecedented prosperity. Sparta's influence had grown on both land and sea. He had always tempered his wish to expand Sparta's influence with the need to avoid war. He was wise enough to know that even the victorious, weakened by conflict, could in turn become prey.

The door to the royal chamber opened. Those gathered in the corridor looked up, anxiety etched in all their faces.

Iphitus, one of the king's advisors, held up his hands in a clear attempt to calm their fears. "I have been speaking to the king. Agamemnon, Menelaus he would like to talk with the two of you. He is very weak. I don't think we have long."

The two princes nodded solemnly and walked into the royal chambers. A healer busied himself attending to Tyndareus. They moved closer, both visibly shocked to see a man that they had both come to love looking so ill.

"Leave us," croaked the king.

"But..." The healer tried to protest.

"Haemon, you have carried out your duties with skill and care. Now let your king carry out his duties, while he still can." He raised a hand to wave the healer away, it shook slightly, betraying the effort needed to carry out the act. He signalled that the two men should move closer. "Agamemnon, Menelaus, I hope that you know that I have grown to regard you as my blood. The boys that entered my household have grown into fine men."

"That love is returned, my king," Menelaus replied.

Agamemnon did not speak but moved to Tyndareus' side and grasped his hand.

"I must tell you of my decision," said the dying man, his eyes never leaving Agamemnon, "and the reason why." Tyndareus spoke through deep rasping breaths.

"You will name Menelaus, as your heir," Agamemnon interrupted.

"I will, but you must know that I do so to protect Sparta. You are a fine man Agamemnon, but I know that your heart yearns for vengeance, and that will place my people in danger. I hope in time you forgive me."

"No forgiveness is necessary. Menelaus will make a fine king and will not disgrace your household. It is true that I seek vengeance. I love Sparta and its people, but there is only one throne that I crave. That throne I will not be given, I shall rip it away from Thyestes," Agamemnon replied.

Menelaus stepped forward. "It will be a honour to rule Sparta and I promise to keep your people safe."

"I know and..." Tyndareus struggled for breath, "Helen... try to forgive her actions. She was young when marriage was forced upon her, but she was always a rebellious child. Her mistakes were of my doing."

"I hold no ill will towards Helen. She will always have a place at my side."

The last of Menelaus's words fell on ears that could no longer listen. Tyndareus was dead. Menelaus, son of Atreus, Prince of Mycenae, was now King of Sparta.

*****

Thyestes watched as the men beneath his command preparing to carry out military manoeuvres. It was going to be a show of force, designed to play on the minds of the visitors that were soon to arrive.

He had overseen the doubling of his army and added a third to his naval strength. If his spies were to be believed, then Menelaus was or will soon be, the king of Sparta. He had no intention of allowing this. He must wage war against the sons of Atreus and not give them the luxury of knowing when and where the battle was to take place. He had no doubt he would beat them regardless, but he would not risk his throne on a game of chance. He would take the war to the lands of his enemy, but to do that he needed allies. The lands of Argos and Tegea lay between Mycenae and Sparta. If war was to come, it would be prudent for those two states to march beneath the Mycenae banner.

Cineas approached and gave the briefest of head bows. "The Argoans and Tegeans have arrived."

"Then show them to my side. I think they will be most interested to see my troops in action."

"They may see the show of strength as intimidation," Cineas replied.

"Oh, I do hope so. It would be a shame to waste all this effort," Thyestes replied, giving a wry smile.

Cineas gave another curt nod. "I will bring them to you."

Thyestes watched Cineas go. He knew that the man would like nothing more than to draw his weapon and end his king's life. But Cineas was a man of honour, and he would never break a promise made to his beloved Atreus. Not that it stopped Thyestes having the man placed under constant watch. He knew that even honourable men can break their word, given the right motivation. He loathed Cineas, it was hard to respect a man who allowed himself to be at the mercy of a code that others do not obey. Further thoughts of his commander's foolishness were interrupted with the arrival of the Argoan and Tegean delegations.

Introductions were made and Thyestes invited his guests to watch his military in action. A silence settled on the group. For some time, the guests watched with respectful interest. However, the Argoan king seemed to lose patience.

"What is this, Thyestes? Are we supposed to scared into joining an alliance?" he asked, his tone defiant.

The reply came from a Tegean. "Calm yourself, Abderos. I am sure that was not the intention."

"I am calm, Iamus," Abderos replied. "I want to know if Thyestes sought to place fear in our hearts?"

"The simple answer is 'yes'," Thyestes paused allowing his words to gain weight. "It was my intention, but not in the way you believed, Abderos. I have ruled Mycenae for many years, ever since I reclaimed my right to sit upon its throne. In all that time have I ever threatened your lands? Or sought to claim what was not mine? I show you these warriors to make you aware of a danger. War is coming, whether I wish it or not. If my throne falls, then both of you will find your lands between the forces of Mycenae and Sparta. The question that you should ask yourselves is not, should you join an alliance, but can you afford not to? Two brothers, two armies and the means to plunder the entire region."

"We do not fear any enemy," Abderos replied.

"One enemy of course not, but two? I have heard of your exploits on the battlefield, Abderos. I do not doubt your bravery. But your foe would be too many." Thyestes placed a hand on the Argoan's shoulder.

"What would you have us do?" Iamus asked.

"My spies inform me that Sparta already builds its forces. By the gods they have been doing so since Tyndareus was taken ill. Time is short. We should take up our spears and hunt the bear within its cave. Drag the sons of Atreus, screaming if need be, to peace talks. I do not wish my nephews' death, only that they sit content on the throne of Sparta and leave our lands in peace."

"This is a grave undertaking that you ask, Thyestes. I may be king, but my advisors must be consulted. I should leave in all haste," Abderos announced.

"I too will need to return to my lands. In truth, I am reluctant to rush headlong into war. But I will consider your words," Iamus added.

"Then I wish you a good journey and hope that our lands will join together and rid us of this plague upon our peaceful and prosperous lives."

*****

Iamus was deeply concerned. Both his Tegean and the Argoan delegations had left Mycenae the moment that the meeting with Thyestes ended. He realised that this had not been an invitation to join an alliance for the good of all. The show of strength by Thyestes sent a clear message, and that message was, 'join me in warring against the sons of Atreus or when I am done with them, I shall look to your lands.'

The Mycenaean army was not easily dismissed. They would be free to choose the time and location to invade his lands, and he knew he could not rely on past alliances. The various cities had been in a constant preparedness for war with one another. Loose agreements prevented all-out war, every day. He raised his hand to call a halt to his troops. Abderos was nearby. Iamus knew that he needed to speak to the Argoan king without Thyestes or his spies too nearby.

Abderos approached on horseback. The face set like stone, evidence that he too felt the heavy burden of responsibility. "I doubted that you were ever going to stop," the Argoan king announced.

"We have little choice but to discuss the offer made by Thyestes," Iamus replied. He dismounted and allowed one of his men to take the mount. "Will you walk with me?"

Iamus ensured-they had gone far enough away from anyone that could hear their discussion, before turning to face Abderos. "We have been left no alternative but to agree to Thyestes's demands. But we shouldn't fool ourselves that they're anything other than demands."

"I concur," Abderos replied. "In truth, I have no concern over taking the blade to the Spartans. Our people have warred those bastards since before I suckled my mother's teat. But I admit, I have no hunger for adding to that whore, Thyestes' power. But Agamemnon is no better and Menelaus seems to follow his brother's lead, even if it is true that it is the younger of the brothers that now sits on the Spartan throne. Thyestes and Agamemnon are two sides of the same coin. It wouldn't surprise me if Thyestes slipped inside more than just Atreus's crown. Agamemnon must be his bastard."

Iamus hid his dislike for Abderos. He knew that Abderos's loathing for the Spartans came from his own father falling to a Spartan blade and his hatred of Agamemnon was more than likely from some imagined insult. His rage came too quickly and when it did, clear thought was vanquished.

"If we follow the plan placed before us by Thyestes, then our forces will pay a heavy price as his own will steal into Sparta and claim the reward. I doubt he will relinquish his hold on another throne."

"Then what must we do?" Abderos asked.

"We must war with Sparta, but we must take its lands before Thyestes launches his attack. If we hold Sparta, then we will have the advantage. At the very least, Thyestes will be dissuaded from attacking our lands, but he still retains face by destroying the last of the line of Atreus. I can see no other route out of this quagmire not of our making."

"I agree, but these plans must remain secret," Abderos replied. "I swear that bastard, Thyestes, knows my mind before I do."

"Indeed," Iamus replied, but inwardly noted that the reason Thyestes knew Abderos's mind was because the Argoan was ruled by his emotion. "I suggest that we move our forces as quickly as possible. Both armies will press the Spartans with relentless vigour. When we take city, I suggest a royal marriage to ensure it remains under our influence. But that is for another day. First, we must defeat Sparta."

Chapter 16

'Hunter or Prey'

Tyndareus had been laid to rest within a family vault. Spartans rarely attached pomp and ceremony to death, but Menelaus insisted that the life of the former king be celebrated. Most Spartans had no markers to announce their resting place. Tyndareus, however, was placed in the vault. Once inside, there were no clues to announce which form was his body.

The royal household had fallen into melancholy. Menelaus performed his kingly duties, but the weight of Tyndareus' death was bearing down on him. It had been Agamemnon that suggested that the entire household visit his hunting lodge in the south. Within a day of that suggestion, preparations had been made and the journey embarked on. It took two days to reach the luxurious hunting lodge that was commissioned by Agamemnon, in memory of his father. As part of the royal entourage, only the most loyal were allowed to carry weapons. Apart from Pallas, three others that had courageously helped the young princes flee Mycenae. Aetolos, Gelo and Maeon had proved themselves both loyal and brave in the years since the fall of Atreus. Each led six men, handpicked by the former king, Tyndareus. They may well be Spartans, but each had given their word to their former king to protect Menelaus and Agamemnon. It was these men that secured the perimeter of the lodge as the royal household began to take advantage of its comfort.

Menelaus had bathed and now walked without haste to his quarters. He had discarded his travelling clothes and now wore a simple tunic. As he walked the corridors, he massaged the aching scar that adorned his left shoulder. It was evidence of his uncle's treachery and reach. Thyestes had sent a skilled assassin. It had not been the only attempt on his life, but this killer had shown great skill at avoiding the palace guards and finding his way into the royal quarters. Menelaus guessed that the man had waited patiently for quite some time, hidden from view and ready to strike. Fortunately, Helen had arrived within moments of his own arrival at the quarters. She had screamed as the would-be killer emerged from his hiding place. Menelaus remembered her scream and the burning pain in his shoulder as he twisted away from his assassin. Menelaus silently thanked the combat training he had received, initially from his father, and then by Pallas. It was due to the endless training that he had been able to disarm his attacker, and then use his foe's own weapon to run him through. Helen had saved his life and attended his wound until the healer had arrived. It had proved to Menelaus that, although his wife may not love him, at least she did'nt want him dead. In truth, his feelings were much the same. He did not love her and found it hard to forgive her betrayal of infidelity. However, he could not ignore the stirrings of his passion whenever she was near him.

He'd not spent a night in her presence since that humiliation, but there would be little option over the coming nights. The lodge was opulent but did not offer the room of a royal palace. As he reached his quarters, he could not help feeling trepidation that his and Helen's relationship could only worsen when forced into such proximity. He raised a hand to knock, but it hung in the air. He realised that he was king, and kings did not wait for permission to gain entrance to their own quarters. He took a deep breath and moved forward, sweeping the door aside as he entered.

The effort to present a confident exterior faded away as soon as he saw a naked Helen. His face burned crimson and he spun around, presenting his back to the disrobed queen. "I... I am sorry," he stammered.

She giggled. "You have seen me naked many times, Menelaus. Or do you not find my body pleasing to behold?" she asked.

Menelaus was shocked by her question, but then wondered if she was merely teasing him. She was a beautiful woman, one that knew the power she held over men. He turned, refusing to be cowed by her womanly wiles.

"Finding you attractive has never been difficult, but it has been some time since we shared the same quarters."

"Or the same bed?" She pointed toward the only bed in the room.

"Yes," he replied. He felt the heat of embarrassment on his face.

Without bothering to cover her body, she moved slowly towards him. She did not stop until the heat of her breasts rested upon his chest. She held his gaze with her piercing green eyes.

"My father asked me to fulfil my duties as a queen," she announced.

"I do not expect you to honour the wishes of a dying man, if they go against your own."

She raised a hand to his cheek. "You should know by now that I rarely go against my own wishes. I want to say," she paused as though the words caused her physical pain, "I am sorry, Menelaus. I was a young girl forced to marry a boy that I did not know. It planted a seed of anger within me. That seed took root and spread through me. I ignored that you may well have felt the same, and you had also just lost your family and home. I cannot say that I love you as a wife should love her husband, but I respect you as both man and king." She leaned forward and kissed him.

"But what of Paris?" He asked. He wanted nothing more than to return her kiss, but part of him wondered if this was just a cruel deceit on Helen's part.

"I admit that Paris is easy to admire, but my actions were born out of anger, not love. I brought shame on myself and to our household. I do not deserve forgiveness, but perhaps you may one day understand?"

Menelaus was surprised to see the tears well in Helen's eyes, he was far more used to observing anger in those piercing, emerald-like apertures to the soul.

He placed his hand over hers. "If you truly wish to place the past behind us, then I am willing. Besides, Sparta deserves a royal household that is at peace."

She leaned forward and kissed him, but this time her act of affection was reciprocated. Menelaus returned her kiss with passion. Love may have been absent, but lust was a constant companion for Helen. Reaching down, her hand explored the interior of his tunic. It was not long before the measure of his passion was pronounced. She gave a smile as he moaned at her touch. He lifted her into the air, her legs wrapped around his waist. The bed was too far for their cravings, and so, the table that played host to a vessel of fruit, became the target. Menelaus brought her panting down on its surface, the fruit bowl clattering to the floor in her excitement. Menelaus thrust forward into her, and she cried out in her pleasure. Each of his downward movements were met by Helen's hips moving up to meet his body, eager to take as much of him as possible. Menelaus knew that this was not love making, it was pure sexual lust being acted on. His hands explored each part of her body. As her sharp nails dragged on the flesh of his back her body stiffened. Her eyes grew wider. Her head moved forward, and she bit into his chest. Helen began to shudder. He did not slow or give her time to recover. A groan escaped her, as once again she began to stiffen. Menelaus could feel his own pressure growing and increased his pace. Helen grasped at him again. He couldn't hold on any longer.

Menelaus lifted his exhausted body from Helen and slumped down onto the timbers, at her side. He started to laugh.

"What is it?" she asked.

"I wish all peace treaties were as enjoyable," Menelaus

replied.

"I doubt many kings possess these." She cupped her breasts to emphasise the point.

"On that, you have no argument from me." He rose from the table and lifted Helen into his arms. As he carried her towards the bed, she nestled her head into his shoulder. He could not help being surprised. All these years and this was the first time that his wife had shown him what seemed to be genuine affection.

*****

The following morning, as the sun began to rise in the sky, Menelaus rose and dressed for the hunt. He crept from the quarters, determined not to wake the sleeping, Helen. It wasn't long before he found himself once more travelling through the corridors of the lodge. Despite the early start to the day, he found himself smiling.

As he approached the main door to the lodge, Gelo entered. Menelaus forced the smile from his face and adopted a more royal mask.

"The horses are ready, my king. It's a little cutting this morning, but will soon brighten," Gelo announced.

"A good day for the hunt. Artemis smiles on us," Menelaus replied.

"I'm just going for a few more supplies. The others are waiting on your arrival." Gelo gave a respectful nod and hurried away.

Menelaus left the lodge, walked across the small courtyard to where the stables stood. Agamemnon held up a hand in greeting. "Most unlike you to be late for hunting, brother."

"The journey must have taken its toll on my limbs, they seemed reluctant to rise this morning," Menelaus lied. He tried his best to hide his face that felt warm under his brother's gaze. "But we have not missed too much of the day."

Agamemnon's stare lingered on Menelaus before a small, wry grin appeared on his face.

"Then we should make haste. All warriors should grasp their spear when the opportunity presents itself." Without dropping his smile, Agamemnon urged his mount forward.

Menelaus glanced around at the other men, but they busied themselves with their own duties. He mounted his horse and gave a small shake of his head. He knew that Agamemnon had guessed the reason for his lateness and was sure that when the right moment arose, his brother would take the opportunity to tease.

Agamemnon took the lead as he made his way to a location that he had visited many times. It was a clearing that lay just within the boundaries of a substantial forest. The place was made for hunting with all manner of beasts. Wild boar and wolves were two of the more aggressive creatures that tested the skill and bravery of any warrior.

Upon reaching the clearing the horses were tethered to nearby trees, the terrain unsuitable to hunt from horseback. This suited both Agamemnon and Menelaus, as they preferred to match their wits with their prey, and the danger of being on foot added to the thrill. For the first foray into the forest, Gelo and his six men were left in the clearing. They would prepare a camp. A fire would be ready for the returning hunters and the horses would be guarded against any creatures that prowled too close. Aetolos and his Spartans had remained at the lodge to provide protection for the queen and others. The remainder of the party picked up their spears and shields and walked into the forest.

Pallas took the lead without permission from king or prince. Menelaus smiled; he knew that the old warrior would not listen to his protestations. Pallas took his duties to safeguard his royal charges with the utmost seriousness and placed them above his duty to do as ordered. It was for this reason Pallas did not carry a spear. It was slung across his back and in its place a sword was held. Menelaus knew that to Pallas, the hunt was an opportunity for their enemies to strike. The young king could not help admiring Pallas' unswerving dedication to duty, even if it sometimes brought a cloud to where sunshine should reign. He had hoped that the veteran could find enjoyment in the hunt, but it seemed that Pallas' mind was focused on the task of protection.

The thick canopy formed by the trees cut out much of the daylight making visibility poor. However, now and then thick beams of light breached the forest's defences and bathed them in its warm embrace. It would be a short hunt. Unless Menelaus gave the order to return to camp and collect torches, then they would need to pick up the tracks of potential prey in all haste. If the light weakened further still, then the prey may well become the hunter.

Pallas spotted a small stream up ahead and pointed

it out to Menelaus. No matter the strength or size of a creature, every beast had to drink. The stream would be an excellent place to search for tracks. He nodded to inform Pallas to venture forward. Each of them moved with caution, boars were well known for never straying too far from a source of water. It was always better to see a vicious creature long before it saw you.

Pallas dropped into the stream, the water settling halfway between ankle and knee. Menelaus and the others remained on the near bank searching for signs of prey.

Agamemnon called out. "Menelaus, over here!"

The king moved to his brother's side. "Boar shit," he announced. Menelaus crouched down lower, as he did so, he pushed Agamemnon to the side, to allow more light to show on the tracks. He could see steam rising from the excrement. "It's close."

Menelaus instinctively switched his attention to the far side of the stream. Pallas was cursing as he struggled to climb the far bank. It wasn't that high, but the dark, glutinous mud made obtaining a foothold almost impossible. Pallas sheathed his sword then tossed his shield to flatter ground. With his hands free he was able to crawl up the slippery slope. Menelaus was about to laugh at the state of his old comrade, but movement in the shadows caught his attention. In the undergrowth beyond a dark shape loomed.

"Pallas!" Menelaus called, just as the largest boar he had ever witnessed emerged from the shadows. The beast's skin was dark as night, short black hairs raised upon its back. Its huge head seemed to take up at least a third of its body length, but it was the long, wickedly curved tusks that drew the attention. It gave a deep, rumbling grunt and burst into a charge. Menelaus watched helplessly as Pallas plucked the shield from the mud. He crouched low and braced behind his protection, waiting for the impact. As the boar crashed into him, Pallas was thrown backwards, clearing the bank that had proved so difficult to climb. The water shot into the air as his body landed in the stream. As the surface of the stream calmed, Pallas' body seemed to float but then gently slipped out of sight.

Menelaus raced forwards. He dropped his shield and spear before he landed in the cold waters of the stream. Ignoring any danger posed by the boar, he focused on saving Pallas. Reaching the point where his friend had disappeared, he plunged his hands forward, searching the stream's murky depths. It was with joyous relief that his hand snagged on a tunic. Using all his strength he pulled the body from the water, dragging his friend from the water. As Pallas was slammed onto the slope, he spluttered into life. Pallas, still dazed, raised his left arm. The bone had been broken and had pierced the flesh.

"Stay still," Menelaus ordered.

"Piss to me. Where is that big bastard?" Pallas replied.

There was a splashing to Menelaus' rear. For a moment, he expected to feel boar tusks ripping into his own flesh. He turned and breathed a sigh of relief. Agamemnon and the other men had entered the stream. They formed a defensive line between beast and Pallas.

"Agamemnon, we need to get Pallas back to the

camp," Menelaus announced.

"Maeon, help your king with Pallas," Agamemnon replied.

Menelaus watched his brother start forward. "What are you going to do?"

"I intend to kill the bastard and taste his flesh before nightfall." Agamemnon drove his spear into the far bank. As the other men used their spears to keep the boar from coming too close, Agamemnon used his spear as an anchor and hoisted himself from the stream. Immediately, he drew his sword and began to move from side to side, making the beast unsure when to attack. The manoeuvre only served as a delaying action. The boar charged but checked its headlong rush when Agamemnon's sword swept down and took the tip of its ear.

It squealed with what sounded to Menelaus a mixture of pain and rage. He watched as Agamemnon seemed to be manoeuvring the beast into a more favourable position. With the help of Maeon, Menelaus pulled Pallas free of the bank. He observed the warrior's arm.

"Maeon, I need your belt." He looked up into the face of Pallas. "This is going to hurt old friend."

"Get it done," Pallas replied through gritted teeth.

Menelaus pulled the damaged limb down to straighten the bones. Then, ignoring the groans of pain from Pallas, he used Maeon's belt to secure the arm to the body. He felt Pallas go limp and for a moment feared the worst.

"Do not concern yourself, my king. He just enjoys enforced sleep," Maeon reassured.

The relief showed on Menelaus' face. "Good. Cut branches, so that we can carry him back to camp." Menelaus turned away from Pallas, his concern now for his brother.

Agamemnon was nursing a small cut to his thigh and the boar was bleeding from its left flank. As he continued to watch, his brother suddenly stopped moving. The boar seized its opportunity and raced forward. A moment later, Agamemnon was also rushing forward. Menelaus thought that his brother had allowed anger to overwhelm his common sense, but at the last moment Agamemnon leapt into the air. Using a nearby tree stump the prince was able to rotate himself in the middle of his jump, without losing height. This gave him the angle to strike downward as the creature charged beneath. The blade swept down onto the boar's spine. The beast crashed to the earth, the high-pitched squealing stinging the ears of all those nearby. It tried to rise, but its rear legs were useless, and it slumped on to its chest. A filthy Agamemnon rose from the ground. He wiped the mud from his face as the forlorn boar tried once more to rise. As he moved closer, the boar tried to move away. Agamemnon circled round so that he faced the beast. Without speaking he raised his blade, and with both hands on the hilt, he thrust it downward. The sword took the beast between the eyes. After one violent jerk of its body, it was dead.

Chapter 17

'An Old Friend Returns'

It was some time before the small band had made it back to the camp. Travelling through such dense woodland with an injured man and the magnificent boar had been no easy task. Menelaus rarely allowed his eyes to leave Pallas. The old warrior seemed to grow paler with every step. It was with some relief that the smell of the campfire met his nostrils. He had decided that Pallas should return to the lodge. It took some time for Agamemnon and Pallas to convince Menelaus not to call a halt to the hunt. In the end it was decided that Maeon and one of the Spartans would transport Pallas. Besides, the old warrior had regained some of his colour once he had been given time to rest by the fire.

Several furs were stretched out over a framework of branches attached to a horse. These provided a soft platform to lay the injured Pallas on and afford him as much comfort as possible on the journey. Agamemnon took it on himself to prepare the boar for roasting. Menelaus observed his brother rip the tusks from the beast and place them within his tunic. Menelaus understood the reason behind it. The boar had been a worthy adversary, it seemed right to honour the memory of the creature by keeping a trophy of the battle.

Pallas had fallen asleep within moments of being laid on the makeshift litter. Menelaus picked up the old warrior's sword and laid it next to him. He still wondered whether he should return to the lodge with his old friend but knew that Pallas would be in good hands. He nodded to Maeon to show that he should begin his journey. Menelaus watched until Pallas disappeared. He turned to see Agamemnon poking at the fire, allowing the flames to leap up and lick at cuts of boar on the spit. Menelaus could resist no longer. He strode over to the fire; his mouth filling with saliva in anticipation of tasting the boar's flesh. As he neared, Agamemnon turned and smiled, as he raised a small shallow bowl filled to the brim with wine.

"I think we have earned our drink this night," Agamemnon announced.

Menelaus took the wine from his brother. "I have never witnessed a boar of that size. It seemed to be waiting for the first man to cross the stream."

"We have enough enemies in this world without seeing them where there is none. It waited because it was used to being the biggest bastard around. This was its land, now it is ours." Agamemnon leaned forward and poked the roasting animal's flesh with a dagger. Juices escaped the beast and sizzled as they landed in the flames.

Menelaus thought deeply as he watched the fat bubble and burst upon the embers. One moment the beast ruled its kingdom, the next it was nought but flesh on a spit. His father's image swam into his mind. A strong man and a good king, yet his rule and life was cut short. Menelaus had met many of those from royal households in his time as a Spartan prince. Many had gained their thrones through violence and more than one, had lost them in the same way. The despair that had lifted since his coupling with Helen, returned. He tried to shake himself free of its oppressive embrace and drained the last of the wine from his bowl, Menelaus then handed it back to Agamemnon. "My bowl is empty, brother. It is not proper to drink if your king cannot." Menelaus forced a smile.

"Oh! Forgive me great and powerful King Menelaus. A plague upon my cock," Agamemnon replied in mock submission. Agamemnon poured some wine into the bowl and handed it to Menelaus. He took a drink from his own bowl and looked to the stars. "It may have been a hunt that brought both joy and sadness, but it is a beautiful night. I sit here with wine and a beast on the spit. At my side are the men that I choose for company," he nodded to the men that had gathered about the fire, "Only the inside of a woman's thighs offers better enticement. What say you, Menelaus?"

Menelaus knew exactly to what Agamemnon was referring. However, the night hid the slight blush in his cheeks. "I say you should drink more and talk less."

Agamemnon barked with laughter, then leaned forward and carved a slice from the boar. He stabbed his dagger into the flesh, and then handed the weapon to Menelaus. He eagerly accepted the offering. He wasted no time before sinking his teeth into the beast. The juices from the meat rolled down his chin as he savoured the sumptuous meal. Bread, wine and the boar were consumed in vast quantities. As Menelaus took his last bite, he could not hide his satisfaction. A large smile spread across his face.

"What is it?" Agamemnon asked.

"Pallas, will be furious," Menelaus replied.

"Why?" Agamemnon's brow

"Because when I tell him that we consumed the most delightful of boar flesh, as he lay nursing his broken arm, an injury inflicted by that same beast, he will not be pleased."

Agamemnon laughed. "I am sure the old bastard will grumble. He likes nothing more than an opportunity to voice his displeasure at the world."

"Have you ever seen him smile?" Menelaus asked.

"I don't think he can. He's been that way since he was sucking his mother's tit."

Both men laughed. Menelaus moved closer to his brother and poured more wine.

"But what fate would have befallen us, if it wasn't for him?" Agamemnon picked at the stubborn boar flesh within his teeth.

"I would still be sat here feasting on this boar, but you dear brother, would most likely be dead." Menelaus smiled.

"Really? I am the eldest and have the advantage with a blade."

"But you're too quick to temper. You could start a war in an empty room."

Agamemnon tossed a lump of meat at his brother.

Menelaus burst into laughter. "I think you have proved my point."

The night wore on, and as Menelaus and Agamemnon continued to drink, eat and talk, they were joined by the other men. Heads began to nod as the exertions of the day and the supply of wine took effect. The crackle of the burning timbers and dancing flames accompanied each man as they journeyed to the land of dreams.

*****

A figure walked through the camp. The guard remained unmoving, as he rested upon his spear, ignorant of the camp's visitor. The stranger made no sound nor cast a shadow as the fire's flames caressed his form. When finally, he came to a stop, he reached out to touch the sleeping Menelaus. However, his progress was brought to a halt as he felt the cold blade at his throat.

"Be warned! My brother sleeps and I'm dedicated to keeping him that way. My uncle's assassin will not profit by his slumber," a voice whispered in his ear.

"I do not bring death. My hand is empty of any weapon, Agamemnon, son of Atreus."

Agamemnon applied further pressure to his blade. "My hand, however, is not. If you do not wish harm, then declare your purpose. Be warned before you speak, my dagger and I have little patience for deceit."

"Oh, I have witnessed your impatience, but that was many years ago. I remember a prince that was all too eager to bestow punishment on sleeping traitors. I wondered if a boy now grown had learnt to calm his rashness."

"Who are you?"

The reply to Agamemnon's question did not come from the stranger, but from Menelaus. "Do you not recognise a friend, brother? I never saw his face, but his voice cut through the oppressive darkness in Artemis' mine and saw us safely from our uncle's wrath. It seems our secretive guide has returned to us."

Agamemnon allowed his blade to drop away. "Then I would ask why he has done so?".

"I once helped guide you from danger. I would provide you with similar service this night. Your uncle is on the move, he conspires to rid this world of the sons of Atreus," the stranger replied.

"He has been trying to kill us since we left Mycenae," Menelaus announced.

"He has a small force that moves against your hunting lodge." The stranger held up his hand as both Menelaus and Agamemnon jumped to their feet. "We have time, but there is a danger looming in the future that could tear Sparta apart."

"Danger that prowls but is not ready to strike can wait…" Menelaus realised that he still did not know the stranger's name.

"It seems that I only come to you when death is near. It is perhaps proper that you call me Thanatos." He raised his hands and lowered his hood.

"Thanatos is as good as any other name, but as I was saying, future threats must take their turn. If the lodge is in danger, then further talk must wait."

Thanatos nodded his agreement, as Agamemnon roused the men.

*****

The journey to the lodge, perilous because of the lack of light, discouraged any conversation regarding upcoming dangers. Each man's horsemanship was tasked to its fullest. Speed was sacrificed more than once, as the terrain threatened to send both rider and mount sprawling to the earth.

However, the journey, despite its risk, was completed without calamity. A new day had not yet started as Menelaus and his men entered the hunting lodge's courtyard. It was not long before Menelaus and Agamemnon were bellowing orders, preparing the household for attack. Helen and Clytemnestra, roused from their sleep by the commotion, emerged from the building's interior.

"Agamemnon, what is happening?" Clytemnestra asked. The anxiety and confusion of what was taking place evident upon her face. Helen, without uttering a word, clearly shared her sister's concern.

"We have received word that Thyestes may have dispatched men toward the lodge," he paused as if noticing for the first time, the distress in his love's features. He gave a comforting smile and placed a hand on her shoulder. "We merely take precautions." Behind him, Menelaus slapped the rump of a horse that carried one of his men. He turned and walked closer to Helen.

"I have sent word. It will not be long before reinforcements reach us," he announced. Helen did not speak but moved without warning and threw her arms around him. He lifted her chin and cupped her face. "Helen, do you trust me?"

She looked into his eyes and eventually whispered, "Yes."

"You have my word that I shall not let any misfortune befall you. But we must prepare."

She seemed to find some inner strength, her body straightened, and she lifted her head high. "What would you have us do?"

"Look to the lodge's interior and those within." Suddenly he remembered that they already had an injured man. "Pallas, how is he?"

"The man does not enjoy being ordered to his bed or being attended by women. It was a struggle, but he rests now. I think it best to allow him his ignorance and the chance to heal." She stopped talking, her eyes lingered on a stranger in the courtyard. "Who is that man, Menelaus?"

Menelaus turned to witness Thanatos striding in their direction. "It is Thanatos, the man who guided me and Agamemnon to safety when we were boys. He has come once more, bringing us warning of the possible attack."

"Come Clytemnestra, we should leave the men to their duties and see to our own," she replied. She

grasped her sister's hand and pulled her away from Agamemnon.

Menelaus watched her go. "It seems you have unsettled my queen, Thanatos."

"I assure you, that was not my intent."

Menelaus smiled. "No need for an apology. I am sure
it is nothing more than the possibility of battle that has
caused unrest in her spirit. I doubt that it will last."

*****

The darkness of the night began to lift, and a new
day began to illuminate the lodge and the surrounding
countryside. Six men had arrived with the morning but
declared themselves to be in the employ of Thanatos.
Without ceremony, they reported to their master. They
had spied at least seventy men that sought to bring
death to Menelaus and Agamemnon. Those in the employ of Thanatos had delayed the would-be assassins
in several ways. The enemy had seen its mounts break
free of their tethers in the night, leaving many of their
number to travel by foot. A large tree had fallen across
a narrow track, with no alternative route, time had to
be spent hauling the timber away so that their supply wagon could pass. Then, good fortune had struck.
The same transport smashed a wheel, its cargo painstakingly loaded on to horses, forcing even more men to
travel by foot.

"So, when will they arrive?" Menelaus asked.

Sophus, the most talkative of Thanatos' men stepped
to the front. "They will be here before the sun has
reached its full height. However, they have endured

upon their journey. I would be surprised if they chose to rush to battle."

"I think I need to see these men with my own eyes," Agamemnon announced.

"It would not be wise to split our forces," Menelaus replied.

"Two men is all that I will need. I do not intend to give battle, only see the measure of those that wish to remove my head."

"You will need more than two men for such a task."

"I don't understand," Agamemnon replied.

"Those that wish to remove your head are too numerous, dear brother." Menelaus could not keep the grin from his face.

"Becoming king has swelled both your head and your bravery," Agamemnon retorted and aimed a playful punch at his brother's shoulder.

Menelaus' smile faltered. "Do not take unnecessary risk and do not idle in your return to the lodge." He grasped Agamemnon by the forearm. "You may take that as command from your king."

Agamemnon nodded his agreement, turned and called Gelo to his side. "Choose one other, we must see this enemy for ourselves."

Menelaus watched until his brother had left the grounds of the lodge. After ensuring that his men had made all preparations, he made for the interior. He could feel the tiredness in his limbs but knew that he could not afford the luxury of closing his eyes. Thanatos' man, Sophus, may be wrong. The enemy could storm the lodge the moment it entered their view.

The door to the lodge opened as Menelaus turned. To his surprise Clytemnestra stood unmoving, her arms crossed about her breast. "Where is my husband, Menelaus?" she asked.

Knowing that she must have seen Agamemnon ride from the lodge, he felt danger in her question. "He wishes to scout the enemy."

"He wishes? Is my husband's life less important than his brother's?"

"Clytemnestra, have I ever been able to make Agamemnon go against his own wishes?"

"You have not always been king."

"King or not, Agamemnon is his own man. Besides, there is no kingship between us, we are brothers."

"And yet he is the one riding into the darkness of the forest, where only those that wish him ill dwell." Her anger showed no signs of abating.

"Clytemnestra!" A voice sounded from within the lodge. Helen strode into view; she fixed her sister with a stare. "Do you know so little of your husband that you think Menelaus could dissuade him from heading toward danger?"

"Is Menelaus king or not?" Clytemnestra asked.

"Is Agamemnon a man? Tell me, could you have stopped Agamemnon? Forced him to turn away from the shadows?" Helen fixed her sister with a defiant stare.

Clytemnestra wilted. "But what if he falls, all alone in the darkness." The last of her words were accompanied with sobs.

Helen moved in close and embraced her sister. Menelaus wanted to reassure Clytemnestra but felt that he was somehow intruding upon her misery. He turned slowly and walked away. The only sound to break the sombre mood of the lodge, was a woman's sobs.

Chapter 18

'Blood and Fire'

The call went up, three men approached the main gate. Menelaus strode into the courtyard as the three riders were permitted entrance. Despite each of the arrivals being caked in heavy, glutinous mud, Menelaus recognised the infectious grin, of the lead rider, it could be no other than Agamemnon.

"I thank the gods for your safe return, brother."

"Thank the enemy's idleness. They did not even bother posting guards," Agamemnon replied.

"The next world loves the overconfident and idle. What did you make of our guests?"

Agamemnon dismounted as he replied. "They wore no insignia of their master. No banners displayed their allegiance. They do not march as soldiers or resemble trained men in any way."

"Then we have..." Menelaus began

Agamemnon cut in, "I said that they were not soldiers. But there is an edge to their ill fashioned blade. They do not look like they have simply been swept from the streets and given a weapon. These men are brawlers, men used to the fight. They may not know the life of a soldier, but I would wager that they know how to kill."

"Fortunately, so do we," Menelaus replied defiantly. "But we must show our enemy respect before we show him the next world. Now, Agamemnon why don't you reveal to me what weapons you have hidden away."

"What makes you think I have weapons?" Agamemnon could not hide his smile.

Menelaus gave a playful slap to Agamemnon's back. "Brother, you built this lodge. It will be made to withstand attack and have plentiful supplies."

"You know me better than I know myself. Come, I will show you what surprises we have for our unwanted guests." He turned and moved toward the steps that led to the upper tier.

"You store weapons in the heavens?"

"When Tyndareus gave me permission to build this lodge, and the wealth to meet my plans, I decided that the very timber and stone would aid our survival." He came to a stop as he entered a walkway that looked down onto the courtyard. "Our best weapon, is the lodge itself." He grasped one of three levers that resembled the tillers you would find on a substantial vessel. He smiled, then using no little strength, pulled it downward.

For a moment, nothing happened but then a scraping began to invade Menelaus' ears. He watched as a heavy bronze shield rose from the flooring and did not stop until it matched the height of the rail that prevented any unfortunate soul from slipping from the walkway into the courtyard below. The king watched as between each section of the walkway a similar shield rose and formed an impressive defence against attack from below. Agamemnon walked to each section and slid a large bolt into place, securing the shield. He then motioned that Menelaus should approach. "Look into the courtyard. If you observe closely enough you will see another surprise."

Menelaus looked. For a moment he could not see anything that would cause havoc in the enemy's ranks. But then he saw an outline running around the perimeter of the courtyard's floor. "Is it some kind of trench?"

"A trench with more than one unpleasant surprise. It will be hard for an attacker to break down the doors that lead to the upper floors, if they cannot reach the door."

"You have not been idle, brother," Menelaus announced, not bothering to hide the fact that he was impressed.

"If we are forced from the main gate, then the courtyard will become a trap for our foe. This shield will stand against any arrow or spear, no matter the power of the man wishing us harm. We will thin their ranks long before they're within sword's reach." Without waiting for a response, Agamemnon gestured for Menelaus to follow him. He led the way to a heavily timbered door, three bolts held it secure. Once opened, the door allowed entrance to a room that contained a plethora of weapons. "There are bows with a good supply of arrows, plus spear and sword. I cannot say they will not reach us, but they will bleed in the attempt."

"And what if our enemy decides to burn this place about our ears?" Menelaus asked.

"There is a way for us to leave, but I would rather not be out in the open with the enemy free to choose their place of attack. Let them come to us and will shall ensure a warm embrace."

"Then I suggest that you bathe and eat. It may be some time before the opportunity arises again."

"You will not join me in a meal?" Agamemnon asked.

"I wish to walk the defences again and ensure that the men are ready. Besides, I believe that there is someone that is keen to know that you have returned." Agamemnon gave a look of confusion. Menelaus shook his head with dismay. "Clytemnestra was not best pleased with me allowing you to leave the lodge. You should attempt to soothe her sorrow."

"Ermm - yes of course. I will go now."

Menelaus watched his brother leave. He wondered how the most strong and unyielding of men could be brought to jabbering, bashful children when it came to women.

*****

The day moved on; Menelaus noticed that those within were beginning to feel anxious waiting for the enemy to show themselves. The sun rose high into the sky and then began to dip beyond the horizon. Agamemnon, usually so calm under pressure barked unnecessary orders at his men.

Menelaus strode over to his brother. "The night will embrace us soon," he announced.

Agamemnon span around, an expression of irritation on his features. However, seeing Menelaus, Agamemnon drew back his anger. "What makes them wait? They already have the advantage of numbers."

"Perhaps they saw our scouts and know that they have lost any chance of a surprise attack?"

"Or the man that leads them prizes caution over boldness," Agamemnon replied.

"Whatever the reason we must keep the men ready, but they must also rest."

"We have too few warriors to draw from the defences." As Agamemnon talked, his attention seemed drawn by a warrior crossing the courtyard. "Have the women and non-combatants been moved to the upper level?" he asked.

"Yes, you know they have."

Agamemnon did not reply. Menelaus was surprised as his brother pushed passed him, and suddenly burst into a run.

"What is it?" Menelaus shouted.

"Stop that man!" Agamemnon called out, pointing to a warrior approaching the main gate.

Menelaus watched with horror as the two guards at the main gate fell to the blade of the unknown warrior. The man then closed on gate and began to lift the securing plank from the lodge's main entrance. Agamemnon grasped a spear from one of his men and without breaking his stride, cast the lethal missile. A moment later, its tip struck flesh, pinning the enemy to the timbers of the gate. It was an act of violence honed on the training ground from youth. However, Menelaus continued to watch as the dying man, with the last of his strength, levered the securing plank from its housing. As it thudded to the ground, a war cry could be heard from beyond the lodge's defences.

"Get everyone to the upper level!" Menelaus screamed.

As the defenders began to run to safety the attackers were entering the courtyard. Menelaus drew his sword, refusing to leave until the last of his men had made it to safety. The last to reach him was Agamemnon, who for some reason seemed to be smiling. "This is not a time for joy, Agamemnon."

"Thyestes sends his hounds. They have the scent of our blood, Menelaus. They may snarl and bare their teeth, but the sons of Atreus are not easy prey. Yes, I feel joy, dear brother. This night I will whip the dogs of Thyestes and send them yelping to the next world."

"Then we had best move or the dogs will be tearing at our flesh." Menelaus placed his hand on his brother's shoulder and guided him to the doorway that led to the upper level. Once they had cleared its threshold Agamemnon turned and closed the door. Both men raced up the steps to where the levers were placed.

"Observe, brother." He grasped a lever that Menelaus had not seen in action and pulled it downward. All around the perimeter of the courtyard a large trench appeared, spilling many of the attackers downward. The screaming had already begun by the time Agamemnon pulled down on the last lever.

At the main gate a large bronze wall slid downward, separating those enemy within the lodge from those that still clamoured for entrance. Agamemnon raised his arm in a signal to his bowmen to be ready.

"Now!" He dropped his arm and all around the upper balcony, the twang of bows replied.

Menelaus guessed that at least forty of the enemy had entered the courtyard. Men that had worn masks of pure rage, clearly intent on slaughter, now they scrabbled around like trapped rats. Only fear could be seen upon their faces, as they pitifully tried to hide from the missiles that rained down. He was tempted to call a halt to the slaughter. Wondering if these men were content to die for Thyestes, Menelaus doubted that his uncle could command such loyalty in men. His thoughts of pity, however, were driven from his mind as Gelo approached.

"My King, the enemy that could not enter the courtyard are retreating."

Menelaus could not hide his shock. What kind of men would leave their fellow warriors to be slaughtered without any rescue attempt.

"Are they simply running away?" he asked.

"We cannot allow them to slip into the shadows," Agamemnon replied.

"Then we must cease being the prey and become the hunter. But we cannot leave this place defenceless. I wish Pallas was here," Menelaus replied.

"And where else would I be?" A deep, growling voice caught the king by surprise.

"This fight is not yours, you need to rest," Menelaus replied.

"Call this fighting." He pointed to the dead and dying within the courtyard. "I will look to the defence of the lodge, while you hunt these bastards down. You cannot allow them to choose when and where to strike."

Menelaus beheld the old warrior. His friend's face a mask of determination. His friend's jaw was set stone-like, the eyes remained unblinking. Menelaus knew that Pallas had spoken the truth. Menelaus glanced into the courtyard. Broken and twisted bodies lay strewn about the lodge's inner wall. The trench filled with all manner of traps, had left its victims impaled and smashed. Those that hadn't reached the trench were left to withstand the archers. Menelaus saw the strained, agonised features of men that died as the deadly shafts broke bones and ripped apart their flesh. Many of the dead displayed multiple injuries, the arrow shafts changing their form from men, to resemble a demonic creature rising from the underworld.

"We will clear away the dead before we give chase. I will not have our women witness such a sight. The prisoners..." he faltered, unsure how to deal with an enemy that was living.

"We will not be taking prisoners." Agamemnon announced.

"What?" Menelaus asked, shocked by his brother.

"If we are to take most of our men to hunt, then we cannot leave those left behind to guard prisoners," Agamemnon replied.

"Your brother speaks the truth," Pallas declared. "Now is not the time for mercy, it is a time to ensure that loved ones are safe and remain so. These men were not asked into our lands, they came with murder in their hearts. If they had taken the lodge, then we would not be afforded mercy."

Menelaus walked over to the levers.

"Gelo, take ten men into the courtyard." He pulled the perimeter trench lever upward. "It is to be cleared," he paused, and then added, "Gelo, ensure that only the dead leave the courtyard."

"It will be done." Gelo's solemn expression showed that he understood his order.

"Wait! I should not ask a man to carry out a task that I would not be willing to do myself." He drew his sword, are you with me, Agamemnon."

"Lead the way, brother."

Menelaus moved sombrely past his men. Gelo and Agamemnon fell in behind him, as they moved toward the steps, Gelo tapped other warriors on the shoulder and made them aware that they should follow. The door to the courtyard was flung open, but Menelaus only took one step, before stamping on the cover that now hid the trench. Agamemnon stepped to his brother's side.

"There is little chance that any live beneath our feet,"

he announced.

"That may be so, but do we really want the dead looking up at us from beneath our feet?" Menelaus replied.

"I will have them removed after we track the rest of the bastards down. They pose no threat where they lay."

Menelaus nodded his agreement and moved further into the courtyard. He picked his way through the dead. The first living enemy he neared groaned and attempted to crawl toward the main gate. A long black shaft had buried deep into the base of his spine, slowing any progress. Menelaus was thankful that he could not look into the injured man's eyes as he raised his own blade. The sword was driven powerfully downward and struck, point first, puncturing the back of the neck. It did not stop until it struck the ground beneath the body. The enemy twitched briefly, as a gasp escaped his mouth, and then he lay still.

Menelaus took a step back. He felt the warmth of blood, as it splashed across his sandalled feet. For a moment, he closed his eyes and tried to calm the bile rising in his throat. He had killed men before, but the slaughtering of the injured did not sit easy on his mind. He rallied, knowing that he could not show weakness before his men. Glancing to his right, he observed Agamemnon dispatching another poor soul. His brother's face showed no such horror at the act. Agamemnon was clearly enjoying himself.

Menelaus pressed on, he tried to separate his mind from his actions. It was his lack of focus that allowed an enemy to draw a blade unseen. As the figure arose from the dead, it called out a scream of defiance. Caught unaware, Menelaus tried to evade the attack, but stumbled across the legs of a corpse. The attacker let out a triumphant growl, his weapon ready to strike. A broad grin broke out on the man's face, yellowed teeth coated with spittle on show. Expecting nothing but death, Menelaus closed his eyes as he awaited his end.

Moments passed. Menelaus allowed his eyes to open. His would-be killer was no longer looming over him. He glanced to his left, unable to see his enemy, he looked to his right. The yellow teeth were still on show, the spittle now mixed with blood. The reason was obvious. Some of those teeth were now broken, smashed apart by the blade of a dagger that stood upright from its victim.

"Take my hand, brother," a voice sounded.

A hand appeared in Menelaus' view.

"Thank you, Agamemnon. I thought my time in this world was at an end."

"And so, it would have been, but you do not owe me gratitude." Agamemnon hoisted Menelaus to his feet. "It is our guest that has once again proved invaluable." He pointed toward an approaching figure.

"Thanatos, I thought you were a man of thought and not violence?"

"You are most fortunate that my blade found this wretch, rather than your flesh." He bent and retrieved his dagger. "In truth, I had my eyes closed as I threw." He gave a wry smile.

Menelaus could not tell if Thanatos spoke in jest. "Erm... I still give you my thanks," he finally managed to reply.

"No need for gratitude, but I would like the opportunity to speak with you and your brother," Thanatos replied.

"Then join us as we hunt down those beyond the wall. It will take time and your company is always a welcome distraction. Besides, I have not met a person that matches your ability to cook a rabbit."

"Then I shall gather my things."

*****

The scouts had returned with the movements of the enemy. They had split into two groups and were attempting to flee to safer lands. Menelaus decided that mounted men would have ample time to engage each group before they could escape Sparta. It did, however, pose a problem. The stables within the lodge only contained sixteen horses. It would mean that Menelaus could not bring all his troops to bear against the enemy. Leaving the lodge on foot would mean that their foe may evade punishment.

"We must make a decision, brother. If we delay for much longer then it will not matter whether we travel by foot or horseback," Agamemnon announced.

"We will take the horses. Two scouts will keep track of the second group as we put blade to the first. It will at least leave more men to guard the lodge," Menelaus replied. It was a strange feeling to be giving his brother orders in military matters. Agamemnon, being older, had always taken the lead when it came to blood being spilled.

Agamemnon nodded, the sweat pouring off his dark hair. "Agreed. With the mounts we should be able to choose when to give battle."

"Then say your farewells. We leave with all haste. The time has come to rid our lands of these bastards."

Thanatos exited the lodge a long blade hanging from his waist. Before he could speak, the visitor held up a hand. "I realise that you have too few mounts. But I will not be found wanting when you call upon my sword. It is important that I speak with you at length."

Menelaus could not ignore that Thanatos had just saved his life. He would rather have had one of his own warriors at his side but could not deny the talents of the stranger.

"Very well, Thanatos, but you will not be an observer. There is no doubt that your blade will be needed," Menelaus replied. For a moment, he wondered how Thanatos had travelled so far without his own mount. He was clearly a man of means, and yet he seemed content to travel by foot. "You can ride?"

"I have both experience and skill. I simply prefer to feel the ground beneath my feet," Thanatos replied.

"Then get a mount from the stables," Menelaus stumbled over his words. He could hide a feeling of discomfort deep within his guts, when dealing with the mysterious Thanatos.

Chapter 19

'The Hunt'

The pace had been frantic until the trail of the first group of assassins was located. An attempt to hide their movements had been made, but few hunters possessed the skill of Agamemnon. A broken branch, an upturned stone within a running stream were all the signs he needed. He had tracked some of the most skilful prey that nature had to offer. A handful of killers desperate to escape would not overly test his ability. Agamemnon took the lead, the various signs left by their prey led them eventually to a small clearing in a wooded area. In its centre, the burnt patch upon the ground revealed that men keen to avoid the blade of an enemy, also needed to avoid the cold of the night. Agamemnon placed his hand into the ashes of the extinguished fire.

"We will need to proceed with more caution. It is not long since they left this place. Remember that these men are dangerous. They will not be trapped like their comrades. We will need to get our hands bloodied." He rose from the fire, brushing the ash from his hands. He strode around the deserted camp, and occasionally dropped into a crouch and examined the ground.

"What have you found?" Menelaus asked. He was

keen to continue the hunt, fearing that the second group of assassins would gain their freedom.

"They haven't tried too hard to hide their path. It seems they have chosen speed over caution. At least, that is how it seems,"

Menelaus sensed his brother's unease. "You are not convinced?"

"Our uncle is a bastard, but I have never considered him to be a fool. Why would he choose such incapable killers?"

"We have slaughtered many of his assassins, perhaps it is no easy task finding those willing to undertake murder." Menelaus suggested.

Agamemnon raised an eyebrow. "If the prize is of substantial worth, then there's always someone willing to commit slaughter."

"Then what do you think these killers have planned?" Menelaus asked.

"We sent for reinforcements the moment that we knew our borders had been crossed by those we hunt. I would have expected our messengers to have returned, even if those reinforcements were still far behind. The enemy broke with little more than a whimper when they attacked the lodge."

"Surely that is because of the defences that you put in place?"

"I thought so, but now I have seen the movements of the enemy I am not so sure." Agamemnon crouched once more to the ground. He picked up a piece of grass.

He seemed deep in thought as he twisted it between thumb and fingers.

"What is it, brother?"

"Those we chase do not take the shortest route from our lands. They do not take a path that makes it difficult for mounted men to follow. In truth, they seem to be moving to a point that does not aid their escape." He picked up a stick and began to trace a line in the dirt. "This is the enemy we seek," he made a groove in the earth, "they have hardly made any progress toward our border."

Menelaus thought that he understood but felt that he needed to hear his brother speak the words. "Tell me, Agamemnon," he pressed.

"I believe our messengers have been killed. I would also wager that our scouts tasked with watching the second group of assassins have also met their end. These killers lead us toward their comrades and hope to fall on as their forces combine."

"Then what should we do?" It was Thanatos that asked the question.

"What we always do," Menelaus replied. "We haven't turned our backs since we left our father to his fate. We will not dishonour his name by doing so again."

"Then it is time that I share with you the purpose of my visit," Thanatos announced.

"I doubt you bring joyful news," Agamemnon replied.

"I wish that was within my power. I believe that these men in your lands are nothing more than a mist to hide his true intention. Thyestes has gathered allies in his desire to destroy the sons of Atreus."

"Who would dare move against Sparta?" Menelaus asked.

"No one state would dare, but Thyestes has convinced Tegea and Argos that you pose a threat to their lands. He would have them believe that Agamemnon seeks the throne of Mycenae, and that once he holds that power, the two sons of Atreus will seek to expand their borders. Thyestes has poured honey into their ears and fear down their spines."

"And their plans?" Menelaus asked as he took a knee next to his brother. He traced the path of the men that they hunted with his dagger.

"Within Tegea and Argos the warriors are preparing for war. They will come by land, entering Sparta at two separate points. They will try not to engage in all-out war. Once all of Sparta's troops are engaged, Thyestes will set sail and land behind your forces. I doubt he will be merciful or content to leave you to rule Sparta." Thanatos shook his head, as though the war could not be won.

Agamemnon, however, gave a broad grin. "It was inevitable. It would be easier to hold back the waves than stop war coming to Sparta. What say you, brother?"

"I say that it is fortunate that we knew that war approached and have prepared. The warriors from Argos and Tegea must wait to test our blades, we have prey to hunt."

Thanatos could not hide his surprise. "I admit I expected more concern,"

Agamemnon slapped him on the back and gave a great barking laugh. "Do not doubt our understanding of the danger, but we have had time to study our uncle. We know his deceitful ways, and with good fortune, we can give him a surprise or two."

"Enough of future battles," Menelaus interrupted. "It is time we gave chase."

"I have more to share, but perhaps it should wait until our thoughts can be focused upon future dangers, rather than those close by," Thanatos replied.

Menelaus nodded solemnly. "You have my word that you shall have your audience."

*****

Menelaus and Agamemnon looked down from a small ridge. Below them, the enemy they pursued seemed to have ceased their attempt to escape. No more than ten men were chopping down a large tree, in an attempt to bring it down across a small track.

Agamemnon spat on the ground. "Busy little bees, aren't they?"

"They choose their ground well, Agamemnon. A small track that gives mounted men no room to manoeuvre. The tree laid across the track will help them slow our progress or perhaps they plan to lay a trap,"

"They still face trained men with shield and spear. They are too lightly armed and too few to drive home an ambush."

"Only if their numbers do not swell and we fail to form up in time. I doubt they will attack if we march down the track in formation."

"But we must draw them out," Agamemnon announced.

"Then we will need to ride into their trap?"

As they conversed, Thanatos dropped down alongside them.

"I found the second group," he announced.

"Are they close?" Menelaus asked.

"They have become bogged down in the forest to the east. It may be half a day before they can join with this force."

"Then it would be wise if we ensured that our friends down there," Menelaus pointed to the enemy, "were dead long before their reinforcements can arrive."

Thanatos stroked his neatly trimmed beard. "Unless we dispatch the reinforcements first,"

"What is it you have in mind?" Menelaus asked.

"I am no military commander, but I would wager that the moment we proceed along that track our enemy would melt away. They could not hope to launch an attack without their reinforcements. If we could avoid those men and defeat the second force, then we could fall upon these men from the rear without fear that they will move from the track."

"Agamemnon, do you know this land well enough to allow us to slip away unseen?" Menelaus asked.

"We would need to retrace our steps, but it could be done."

"Then we should move out with all haste." Menelaus rose and gave Thanatos a grateful pat upon the shoulder as he did so.

They descended the slope with care, ensuring they were not seen or heard by the enemy. Gathering the men together, Menelaus gave a brief outline of the intended mission. Each man mounted and followed Agamemnon, as he led the small band away from the enemy. They would need to keep plenty of distance between themselves and the men at the track but could not afford to dawdle. The countryside opened occasionally, allowing the mounts to flex their powerful muscles, but that burst of euphoria was tempered all too soon, as a steep climb or stream bank had to be traversed. Finally, Thanatos moved to Agamemnon's shoulder as the horses were allowed to drink from a narrow, but rapidly, flowing river.

Thanatos kept his voice low. "We near our prey. I fear if we proceed much further on horseback then our position will become known."

"I know this land. Our enemy must cross the river at this point. It is the only place within a day's march that a man can hope to keep his footing, and not be dragged beneath the waters."

*****

Menelaus surveyed the surrounding countryside, before approaching the water's edge. He pulled his dagger from his belt, and without using much force, pushed it into the river's bank. The blade encountered little resistance. "The enemy will struggle gaining a foothold on this bank, despite its lack of height. The land chooses our place of battle for us." He turned around and pointed. "We will take up position in those trees, with the horses out of sight and ear shot. We will move on the enemy as they reach this side of the river."

"Agreed, brother. They cannot fight and climb at the same time," Agamemnon added, a smile spreading on his features.

Menelaus gave the order that the men should make ready, but his eyes never left Agamemnon. He was always uneasy at his brother's obvious delight at upcoming slaughter. Menelaus may have killed, but he had never found it an enjoyable task. Agamemnon, however, relished not only the fight, but the kill. In truth, his brother seemed to prefer the kill. The death of his father and mother could not even be used as an excuse, Menelaus had seen the glint in his brother's eyes from an early age. Menelaus wondered if he would ever be on the receiving end of that stare, a stare that all too often resulted in blood. Finally, he turned from the riverbank and walked towards the trees, his brother's disturbing bloodlust still haunting his thoughts.

*****

The sun had just begun to drop in the sky as the first man-made noise emanated from the far side of the river. Menelaus and his men dropped lower in the undergrowth to ensure they could not be seen. Menelaus couldn't yet see the source of the noise but estimated its maker couldn't be more than one hundred paces from their position. The damp coldness of the ground made his hiding place uncomfortable. However, giving the signal to attack too soon would give the enemy the opportunity to slip away into the trees. It seemed an age before a figure emerged and cautiously moved toward the riverbank. It bent low once it reached the water's edge, as if searching for signs of an enemy. Menelaus silently thanked Agamemnon for ensuring that none of the men crossed the fast-moving waters. The distance and lack of light would ensure any tracks on the near bank would remain concealed.

Finally, the figure, obviously a scout, rose from his crouching position and made a signal toward the far trees. Menelaus watched as further shapes emerged from the tree line. He counted each as they came into view. The scouts had made an error. This group's numbers had been slightly underestimated. He counted fifteen figures breaking cover, making sixteen in all. It gave the enemy a slight advantage in terms of numbers, but Menelaus was confident that if he chose the right moment to attack, then his men would carry the day. He continued to observe; for a moment it looked as though the enemy would make camp, but then they cautiously plunged into the cold waters of the river.

Menelaus glanced to his right; he expected to see Agamemnon at his side. To his surprise, it was the face of Thanatos that stared back.

"Where is my brother?" he whispered.

"He slipped away just before we heard the sound of the enemy approaching," Thanatos replied.

Menelaus wanted to go and find Agamemnon, he

always felt reassured with his brother at his side but knew that was not an option. He forced himself to look to his front. Some of the enemy had already crossed the river and were scrabbling their way up the bank. The rest were bunching together, waiting for their turn to make their climb.

"Get ready," he whispered to his men.

He plucked his spear from the ground, feeling the comforting strength of its unyielding shaft. He remained crouched, watching and waiting. A third of the enemy had cleared the river now. Most had their backs to Menelaus as they helped their comrades traverse the thick mud that coated the bank. Suddenly, it dawned on Menelaus that the time had arrived.

"Now!" As he called out his order; he raced clear of the trees. His powerful arm drew back his trusted weapon. Body turning as he took aim, then with all his might sent the deadly missile soaring toward the unsuspecting enemy. Before his spear struck home, it was joined in the air by a further five. Each thrown by his warriors as they too, emerged from the tree line.

Menelaus raced forward, drawing his sword. His missile met its aim and the target fell, screaming into the river, clutching at his back. More fell to the onslaught before they realised that they were under attack. They tried to form a defensive line, Menelaus and his warriors leapt amongst them, swords drawn. He brought his shield up; the rim caught in the throat of the fighter in front. A powerful thrust from Menelaus and the man's unprotected gut spilled open. With no time to celebrate, Menelaus kicked the man from his blade and sought out another victim, but only the dead and dying seemed to occupy the solid ground. Those that remained alive raced back to the opposite bank. Some slipped beneath the fast-flowing water, their cries for rescue ignored by comrades concerned only with their own survival.

Menelaus and his men retrieved their spears and used them, first to impale the enemy close to the bank and then with careful aim those attempting escape.

Menelaus watched his men enter the river dispatching the wounded with brutal efficiency, ignoring any pleas for mercy. Four of the enemy almost reached safety, when beyond them Agamemnon appeared.

Although, Menelaus could not make out the detail on his brother's face, he knew a menacing smile adorned it. His brother allowed the men to scramble upright, their features and shape obscured by the bank's foul glutinous mud. Two vaguely human-like shapes moved towards Agamemnon. He remained perfectly still; his blade remained undrawn. Four men against one would have seemed impossible odds, but few could match Agamemnon's speed or brutality in close quarter battle. Menelaus could not help feeling a little sorry for the enemy who were about to die. Menelaus knew that Agamemnon would want to draw out the kill, a quick death served as poor entertainment. As the first of the two made an attack, Agamemnon stepped to the side, his sword appearing suddenly in his hand. Menelaus watched as his brother sliced his attacker's thigh, causing the man to scream and collapse. Menelaus marvelled at his brother's skill. The man's show of agony was rewarded with a kick to the jaw.

The second man had clearly decided that he needed to close the distance to his prey and raced forward. It was a reckless act that made Menelaus winced, as his brother merely reversed his blade and pinned the man's foot to the ground. Agamemnon grasped the man's head and used his thumbs to blind his attacker. He calmly retrieved his blade from the mangled foot and moved toward the two that had stayed clear of the fight.

The third attacker did not rush to meet Agamemnon. He pulled a small axe from his belt. In his other hand he carried a short sword. Menelaus watched the man closely, he seemed to hold himself with confidence or at least showed no outward signs of fear. Agamemnon advanced, he moved slightly from side to side. Menelaus had observed the snake-like movements employed by his brother many times. It helped him conceal the moment of his attack and placed uncertainty in an enemy's mind. This enemy, however, did not seem distracted and remained perfectly still. That was until, he exploded with fury. Menelaus gasped as Agamemnon was forced backwards. Axe and sword moved with precision and speed seeking out his brother's flesh.

Menelaus dropped down into the river and felt the water attempt to drag him away. Ignoring its grasping, icy touch he pressed onward, without taking his eyes from the battle being waged on the opposite bank.

Finally, the two men broke apart., Menelaus drew a deep breath when Agamemnon reached up to touch his bloodied shoulder. But then noticed that his opponent trying to hold in his guts. His brother's attacker then turned to the fourth man and called out that he should run, but the figure remained motionless. Menelaus clambered up the bank, to face the other man who was no more than a boy. As Menelaus stood upright, he used his blade to tap the transfixed boy on the shoulder. The frightened lad reached for a small blade within his belt.

"That would be a mistake," Menelaus announced. "My brother," Menelaus nodded toward the battle that still raged, "will be finished soon. It would be wise for you not to be here."

"My father!" Tears rolled down the boy's face, mixing with dark thick mud that smeared his cheeks.

Menelaus knew how it felt to lose a father far too soon in life. "Your father has brought you time. Do not waste his sacrifice." The boy remained rooted to the spot. "Run! You foolish bastard!" Menelaus raised his sword above his head, as if ready to deliver a devastating blow. The lad jumped backwards, regained his footing and spun to race toward the nearest tree line. Menelaus put away his sword and turned his attention to his brother just in time to see a blade pierce a torso. A figure dropped to his knees, his axe slipping from his hand. An obviously triumphant Agamemnon pulled back his blade and in one powerful blow, hacked the unfortunate warrior's head from his body.

Agamemnon looked from his fallen enemy; the smile faltered.

Menelaus guessed that his brother sought a fourth victim. "He was only a child," Menelaus announced.

"Children grow into men that seek vengeance," Agamemnon replied. "As you well know."

"That may be, but I will not slaughter children."

Agamemnon was clearly enraged by the act of mercy. "Then you are a fool."

Menelaus bristled at the insult. "A fool possibly, but King definitely." His arm instinctively moved toward the blade at his waist.

The movement was not lost on Agamemnon. The anger upon his face turned slowly to a smile. "Forgive me, brother. I spoke in haste. The taste of battle too often leaves me hungry for blood."

"Then we should move out. More men await our blades."

Chapter 20

'A Warrior's Mercy'

T he boy had never felt such fear, shame, and anger as he did at that moment. He knew that if the man caught him, then he was sure to die. Never had he witnessed such brutal skill. However, that fear was matched by the shame of running from battle and accepting mercy from the enemy for which he felt nought but a deep burning hatred. He ran until his chest heaved to breaking point. His limbs felt as heavy as Sisyphus's rock. Dropping down at the foot of a huge tree, he curled into a ball. Thoughts of his father brought tears to his eyes; his woes did not stop until exhaustion brought a disturbed sleep.

His rest did not last long. He opened his eyes, half expecting the warrior to be standing above him with murderous intent. However, the noise that had woken him from his sleep was in the distance. He knew that he should run and place as much ground between himself and those responsible for the death of his father and the men he had come to respect as brothers. It came as a shock as he found himself dragging his weary body to his feet, when all he wanted was to close his eyes. He picked his way through the foliage back toward the slaughter that he had been so keen to leave. He questioned his own actions, but still he moved forward.

When at last he came to the site of the battle, he saw that only the dead now occupied his side of the river, but on the far side men were clambering onto their mounts. He watched as they rode away. He already knew that he would follow them and when the time was right, there would be a reckoning, but first he must say farewell to his father.

The body was heavy; it took time to drag from the mud of the riverbank. The exertion did not cease until his father was laid at the foot of an impressive tree. His father had been a man of many talents. He had a particular skill for working with wood. It seemed right that he should be laid next to what he loved. The boy straightened his father's tunic and then rose for a far more solemn duty. He walked back to where his father had been killed and retrieved the head. However, he could not bring himself to stare at the eyes. He crossed back to the body and keeping his gaze averted, he returned the head to its proper place. Finally, he allowed himself to gaze into the face of his father.

"Forgive me, I ran when I should have been at your side," he sobbed as he spoke. "It would have been better that we both pay our fee to Charon and take the journey together across the Styx." He forced the sobbing to stop and wiped the tears from his face. Reaching down he took hold of the brooch that his father always wore. His trembling hands made removing the jewellery cumbersome, but finally it came free. "I promise that fear will no longer have a home in my heart. The men responsible for your death will hear your name bellowed in their ears, before they die. They will know that Bakchos, son of Gregorios, seeks vengeance. Not only those that left you within the mud, but those who sent you on this fool's errand. We were sent to the slaughter. No more thought was given to our lives than if we had been the lowest of vermin." He rose from the side of his father's body, attached the brooch to his own attire. Suddenly, he felt another presence. He turned, his hand instinctively dropping to the sword at his hip.

A dark clad figure gave a slight bow. "Calm yourself. This place has seen enough death on this night," it announced.

"Do you serve Menelaus?" Bakchos asked without removing his hand from the hilt of his blade.

"Serve? No, I do not serve any man, but I have walked by Menelaus' side many times. But it is your path that intrigues me."

"My path? I seek bloody vengeance," Bakchos replied. His jaw clenched as he held back his emotions.

"But to whom do you direct your fury?"

"Those responsible for my father's death."

"The royal house of Sparta? Surely, all they have done is dispatch a paid assassin." The figure held up a hand to prevent Bakchos from speaking. "Your father looked to profit from the death of another. He may have been a good father, but that does not mean he was a good man."

"I tire of you!" Bakchos' face flushed with growing anger.

"Many people do. I do not dismiss your right to vengeance for a lost father. I merely wish to point out that your wrath needs a worthy target. One that is deserving the fate that you have in mind."

"You talk of Thyestes. I know that he sent us to be slaughtered. With his spies, he must have known what awaited us."

"I agree. If you pursue Menelaus and Agamemnon now, I doubt you will ever leave these lands. Thyestes will not answer for his ill deeds. Return to Mycenae and from the shadows you may be able to strike at the beast within his lair."

Slowly Bakchos nodded his head. "I do not know how, but I will see Thyestes bleeding before I leave this world."

"Then do not allow fury to replace reason. Do not announce your return, but seek out Cineas, he commands the men that look to Thyestes' safety." The stranger held out his hand, offering him a purse.

"Surely, he will simply slit my throat?"

"Cineas has no love for Thyestes. Tell him what has happened on this day and whisper into his ear, that the birds that flew south to escape the winter shall soon return."

"I... I don't understand." Bakchos' face contorted with confusion.

"There is no reason that you should. But deliver that message and Cineas will be sure to keep you safe. Perhaps even find you employment within the palace."

Bakchos understood that he was being given an opportunity to get close to Thyestes. He took the purse, the weight of which surprised him. He looked inside. It contained more coin than he had ever seen, let alone held within his own hands.

"M... My gratitude," he stuttered.

"No gratitude is necessary. Deliver the message and do not let the need for blood blind you to danger. I am sure that your father would not like you to join him in the next world so soon." Without another word the stranger turned from Bakchos and strode away.

Bakchos watched him leave. He realised that he did not know that the name of the man that had brought him an opportunity to see Thyestes dead. He placed the purse within his tunic, said farewell to his father and set off on a journey that would lead him away from the lands of Sparta.

*****

The second band of assassins fared no better than the first. Menelaus and his men had fallen upon them from the rear. Many died without having time to draw their weapons. No mercy was offered as each man was cut down and those that lay wounded were dispatched with cruel efficiency. When finally, the killing was at an end, Menelaus and his men felt the exertions of the hunt. Many wanted to simply slump to the ground among the dead, but the young king forced them to gather the last of their strength.

"I feel as you do, men. But this is not the place to lay our heads," he announced.

"But the lodge is too far, brother," Agamemnon

pointed out.

Menelaus wanted nothing more than to hold Helen within his arms, but he could not deny that the long ride to that simple comfort was a task that required more strength than he possessed.

"I agree. You know this area. Find us a suitable place to camp before we are forced to sleep amongst the slaughter."

Tired warriors climbed aboard their mounts. Fortunately, the small clearing chosen by Agamemnon was only a short ride. It was not long before aching limbs were being warmed by the campfire and only Menelaus and Agamemnon remained alert to the dangers of the forest. They chewed on bread as they watched for a possible attack. Even Agamemnon seemed too tired for conversation. The silence, however, was short lived as another figure was highlighted within the flames, as he rose and approached the two royal watchmen.

"Thanatos, do you not need sleep?" Menelaus asked.

"My mind is filled with our future journeys. Paths that seem intertwined," Thanatos replied.

"I promised that we would talk. I see no better use of our time. Sentry duty saps the energy, of which I have little." Menelaus sat down on a fallen tree. He rolled his head around, forcing the ache from the neck below, it cracked its discontent. "What troubles your mind, Thanatos?"

"I told you of your uncle's plans. Of how he had persuaded other states to wage war against you."

Agamemnon interrupted. "They will not find us trembling in our beds as they approach."

"Of course not. Your bravery or skill is not in question. But it would be wise to know all that I have learnt and all I can offer. Thyestes waits for your army to be spent, exhausted by a war that he does not care if you win or lose. You will be forced to fight on two fronts and keep men within Sparta for defence. Even if you bring Argos and Tegea to their knees with relative ease, your troops will be depleted and facing Thyestes when he lands with his substantial forces. Not only that, but Thyestes has been recruiting mercenaries to bolster his ranks. He will field an army not yet seen in these lands."

Silence followed. Menelaus would place a hefty wager that his men would gain victory against any enemy on equal terms, but the odds seemed too great.

"Tell us more, Thanatos. I pray that you bring words that not only point to our doom."

"I have a force of warriors. The skills they possess with the bow will cause panic in the ranks of our enemies."

Menelaus did not miss the fact that Thanatos claimed that he shared the same foe. But it was Agamemnon that posed the next question.

"Who are these men and what number can they commit to battle?"

"I did not say they were men, and their force would be no more than a few hundred."

"A few hundred," Agamemnon snorted, "you're a

trader in favours, Thanatos. Perhaps, you should leave war to us." Agamemnon walked away, his head shaking from side to side.

"Forgive my brother, Thanatos. He means no disrespect. Tell me more of these warriors."

"Tell me what you know of centaurs?" Thanatos asked.

Menelaus's brow crinkled. "Creatures of myth. My grandfather told me that he saw one once, but he claimed many things once the rhyton had been raised to his lips too often."

"I cannot say whether you grandfather was being honest, but I can tell you that centaurs are far more than myth. Their famed skill as warriors, especially with the bow, has not been exaggerated."

"And this is the force of which you speak?" An intrigued Menelaus asked.

"It is."

"Then what would they require as payment for their service?"

"Two things. Firstly, they're honourable beasts and would not offer their allegiance without meeting the king that they would serve. Secondly, the centaurs require a new home. A place where they can live unmolested. But, be warned, they do not trust easily. They have paid dearly for the lies told by man."

"If they are as accomplished as you say, then it would be a mistake not to have them within our ranks. I will meet with your centaurs, Thanatos."

Chapter 21

'Fear the Gods'

*"Like the generations of leaves, the lives of mortal men.
Now the wind scatters the old leaves across the earth, now
the living timber bursts with the new buds and spring
comes round again. And so with men: as one generation
comes to life, another dies away." Homer - The Iliad*

TROY

10 years after the death of the Mormo queen.

Priam stepped into the brilliant sunshine of a new day. As he raised a hand to guard his eyes against the light, he nearly lost his balance. Cursing beneath his breath as he steadied his footing, filling his lungs with air he summoned the strength to begin his walk. It had been more than twenty days since he had ventured beyond the palace's gate. Breathing heavily, he felt the ravages of time on both his body and soul. He had reigned for nearly three decades in his beloved city, but now he stumbled like a new-born child, powerless against the relentless ravages of time.

As a prince, he was forced to carry a blade to Troy's enemies many times. Violence had been the all too frequent answer in the past. As king, he had forged alliances and succeeded in avoiding major conflicts that would have threatened his people and his beloved Troy. With the Hittite empire to the east and warrior Hellene states to the west, he had performed a delicate balancing act to remain neutral. Even at a cost to his honour, he briefly remembered the son of a dear friend that he was forced to refuse a home. But he did give a home to people from around the known world. Providing they offered friendship and did not bring dark clouds of misfortune to the city. His own warriors honed their skills by aiding Troy's friends to defend their own lands. But only ever in defence.

The urge to rest overcame his thoughts as he placed a hand against a nearby wall to aid his balance. Closing his eyes, he allowed the warmth of the day to caress his weary body. Then as he opened them again, his gaze was drawn to the feeble, skeletal hand upon the stonework. The skin had lost its lustre and the strength that fingers, hand, and arms once possessed had all but evaporated with the passing of time. Only the scars, plentiful in their number, stood as testament to a departed power. The realisation that his grasp on this world was weak evoked visions of a disturbed sleep the previous night.

He had found himself climbing the steps that led to Olympus.. No other soul could be seen, and it seemed to Priam that the home of the gods had been deserted. The climb had been exhausting but he had to know if the deities had gone. It wasn't until he placed a foot on the final step that the sound of voices met his ears. He pressed on until he reached a mighty door, as tall as any earthly tower. He raised a hand but hesitated before rapping his knuckles against the timbers. He was suddenly aware that he was just a man. The beings beyond this door could crush him beneath their heel with no more effort than it took him to crush a bug. He thought about fleeing back down the steps, but the distant voices grew louder, and his curiosity drove the fear from his mind. He took a deep breath and went to knock upon the door. However, as he ventured forward, the mighty doors silently parted and allowed him access. Timidly, he stepped across the threshold, wondering to himself how the timbers moved without a sound.

He forced himself to explore deeper into Olympus. His hand instinctively moved toward the blade that sat, ever willing at his side. He caught himself in the action and gave a nervous laugh at his own stupidity. What mortal blade could strike at those who dwelled within this place? It seemed to Priam that, with each step he took, the voices became more enraged. He wondered if his trespass would calm or further antagonise those within. Tales of their unmerciful wrath were legendary. Thoughts of his impending doom evaporated as the corridor merged into a vast hall. Columns ringed the hall stretching up to where the ceiling should have been. But these structures supported only the very heavens. In the hall itself, at least thirty deities were engaged in an angry meeting. Priam noticed that when a god raised his voice in anger, the clouds above darkened and a deep rumble of thunder made the ground beneath Priam's feet shudder.

"Silence!" A voice called out.

Its owner was hidden from Priam by the other gods. To his surprise the other deities ceased their bickering with little or no protest and began to move towards the columns. Priam's eyes widened as he observed each column contort, changing shape as a god approached. Moments later, magnificent thrones stood where the columns once did. The hall had fallen to an awkward silence as each god took their place upon their thrones and left one figure standing in the centre of the hall. Priam had never seen a god before this day but knew the identity of the speaker. Statues and temples had been created to honour the father of the gods throughout the known world. Priam himself had commissioned the building of a small private temple within his own palace walls. There was no mistaking the impressive form of Zeus. Some of the other deities were larger, some had physical attributes that would put any human hero to shame. Zeus, however, was of a slender frame, with a long silver beard. His eyes were a deep green and Priam could swear he saw the flicker of lightening each time the god blinked. The hall had fallen to complete silence, as Priam and deities all waited to hear what the mighty Zeus had to say.

"War is coming. Tensions within our ranks have been building for some time. I would say only this, if gods go to war, then all living creatures will perish." He waved a hand and the centre of the hall burst into life. An image showing Troy came into view and then many more states. After that, the images of men were shown. Then the many beasts that occupy land, sea, and air, filled the vista. "It is clear that some here want more than they have."

"I do not disagree, Zeus." A deity had risen from his throne and took several steps towards the centre of the hall. Priam thought he recognised the god who interrupted Zeus as Tarhun, the Hittite storm god. "However, if those that seek power are intent on gaining it, then what can we do until they reveal themselves? My own temples have been desecrated and the priests murdered, but I cannot find which god influences the perpetrators' actions. If we find those that…"

"There is only one of us that we can be sure does not seek power," a female deity interrupted. Her beauty and confidence held Priam's gaze.

"And that is?" Tarhun snapped. Clearly frustrated at being interrupted.

She gave a patronising smile. "Zeus, of course. You do not seek what you already possess."

"That may be, but I would not destroy my own temples, Athena." Tarhun looked further agitated.

"You would if you wanted to appear innocent," Athena replied.

"How dare you?" Tarhun's hand moved around his back to where a double headed axe hung. Priam guessed that the weapon was as long as the tallest of men, doubting even a god would survive a blow from such an axe.

Zeus laughed, "Athena, your wisdom and charm bring light to Olympus. Tarhun, calm yourself, Athena was not making an accusation but merely stating what those that seek power would be prepared to do." Zeus's tone was friendly, but his eyes burned with a threat that made Tarhun remove his hand from the axe. Tarhun dropped his hand to his side, then returned to his throne. "If there is war," Zeus said, addressing the whole room, "between the gods, then all the humans will perish, as will many in this room. If there is war between humans, then the loss will not be as great. It is obvious that one or more of the gods are carrying out plots of which we have no knowledge." Zeus suddenly looked sad. He waved a hand, and the city of Troy once again came into view. "One city is the bridge between the Hellene states and the Hittite empire, soon it will be without the steadying hand of Priam." A figure appeared as Zeus once again waved his hand, shocking Priam as he observed his own image. "It seems that Troy must perish with my loyal servant Priam, and I am powerless to stop its downfall."

Priam could not believe what he had just heard. He had always honoured the gods. Even when disease and hunger descended on the city, he had not forsaken them. Why was Zeus turning away when his beloved city needed his protection?

Priam was so lost in his own desperate thoughts that he missed much of what followed. It was not until a deity that Priam did not recognise rose up abruptly and stormed toward Zeus.

"You are not my master," the god bellowed. "I will not agree to your demands!"

A moment later, serpent like strands burst from Zeus's fingertips. They slivered through the air with tremendous speed and wrapped around the lesser deity. The calm exterior that Zeus had previously shown had disappeared. He was now filled with ominous rage; his frame swelled to twice its size and his eyes glowed with fire.

"Do you think I make a request? I am supreme here - my will is absolute." The golden strands that had curled around the unknown deity were tightening. Despite the captive being a god, he was powerless to resist.

"Zeus!" Athena shouted clearly trying to calm the situation.

"Sit down!" Zeus to her as his eyes glowed with further intensity. The strands tightened and the lesser god screamed his agony. The armour he was wearing provided no protection as it crumbled beneath the power of Zeus. Bones broke and skin fell away. Then silence filled the room as the golden strands simply vanished, leaving only a patch of fleshy pulp on the polished marble floor of Olympus.

Priam looked from the gruesome remains to Zeus and suddenly realised that his gaze was being returned. Without saying a word Priam forced his elderly legs to take flight. Panic motivated ancient limbs beyond their natural ability. He raced down the long corridor that he had so timidly journeyed earlier. He slipped through the enormous doorway and did not look back, as he took the steps that led from Olympus.

He had travelled about half the length of the steps when he observed an elderly man, a crooked back and head bent, slowly making his way in the opposite direction.

"Go back! It's dangerous, the gods are warring." Despite Priam's warning, the man continued his slow climb. As Priam closed on the figure he tried again. "Did you not hear me, leave this place."

"Have I ever given you reason to fear me, Priam?" The elderly man for the first time raised his head.

"Zeus, but..." Priam looked toward Olympus and then back to the old man.

"I would be a poor excuse for a god if I could not manage to be in two places at the same time. Besides, the gathering is at an end. They have decided to follow my instructions."

"Which were?" Priam realised that his tone was not one that he should use to a god. "What were your instructions?" He asked more meekly.

"The gods will refrain from interfering in the lives of men. With the one exception. Each of them will be permitted to choose one champion."

Priam stared at Zeus wondering if he should point out the fatal flaw in the deity's plan. But before he had the chance to speak, Zeus gave a snort of laughter.

"You wonder if those that seek power will simply agree in my presence and then carry out their treacherous plans." Zeus paused as he plucked a wineskin from his belt. He took a long thirst-quenching drink, and then offered the skin to Priam. "I cannot be certain that they will honour their word, but at least they are certain of their fate should I learn of their betrayal. I have made them aware that I will destroy them on nothing more than a suspicion. That should make them take great care and slow their plans at the very least."

The wine was sumptuous, Priam had never tasted its like before, but even the delightful taste could not dispel the bitterness in his heart.

"And what of Troy?"

"Priam, you know that all things come to an end. Troy – at least the Troy as you and I know it, cannot survive." Zeus looked at Priam and in a softer tone added, "A city may cease to exist but they never truly die. They live on because of great men such as you, Priam. Besides, it is your actions that have brought about its downfall."

"My actions! I have always tried to better the lives of those within my city."

"I did not say that your actions were contrived through malice. On the contrary, you have increased the influence and prosperity of Troy. You control the Hellespont and through that trade route, the city has become so wealthy that other states look on with envy. A god or gods looking to create mischief would find it easy to seduce men with the promise of Troy's riches. Your success Priam, is your greatest failure."

"My legacy to my people and my sons is destruction?" Priam shook his head with dismay.

"You have been a wise and generous king... that is your legacy. It will be known down the ages."

"But Hector..."

"I have looked into Hector's heart. He will not take the crown willingly."

"Make him your champion. With your guidance I am sure..."

"Hector must choose his own path," Zeus replied, his

tone becoming gentler. "A crown rarely sits well when forced upon a head. Besides, Hector has no love for me or any god. I would find it difficult to guide such an independent man."

"Then make me your champion," pleaded Priam.

"Men like cities do not last forever, Priam. Your body is too weak for the battles that lie ahead. Violence, sacrifice and heroic deeds dwell in the realm of the young."

The king shook his head. "Then all is lost."

"Despite what you think, Priam, I do not know the future. I see shapes of things that may come to pass. However, be warned. It is certain that danger nears, so do what you can to safeguard both family and city. I shall do what I can, but I must obey my own rules. I can have only one champion and he shall look to save all men of worth, not just those within Troy. Go now my friend, you will have time enough to prepare."

Priam did not reply. He nodded and then reluctantly moved away, his mind and heart filled with despair.

*****

Priam's thoughts of the previous night's vision had robbed him of senses. When finally his mind drifted back to the realm of men, he realised that he had walked a fair distance from the palace. He wondered for a moment how he had managed to stray so far. Then he glanced around at his surroundings. It was some time before it dawned on him that he had inadvertently stumbled into the Shadows. He knew that despite his many successes as king, he had failed to rid the city of the thieves that preyed on the weak. He also knew that many of those thieves called the Shadows home. It was a rabbit warren of tight alleys and hidden escape routes, which provided its populace with ample opportunity to avoid any attempts to place them in bonds.

He wished that he had worn a sword but realised that he would be too weak to brandish the weapon. He glanced around, hoping to see a way out of the foul place, but each direction offered no obvious route. He decided to simply turn and walk back the way he hoped he had come. He thought that the Shadows was well named; the tall buildings threw the narrow alleys into an eerie, light starved breeding ground for the corrupt. He felt the walls begin to close in around him as weariness overtook his body.

"Are you lost, old man?" A voice sounded from the darkness.

"Now, now Alfio, that is no way to address royalty," another man's voice replied.

"Royalty?"

A man stepped from the shadows. He took a bite from an apple and casually tossed the core aside. He gave a mocking bow towards Priam. "Do you not recognise our mighty King Priam?"

"He's a long way from the safety of his palace," the second man replied, as he too stepped from darkness.

Priam had stayed alive for many years by weighing up his opponents, both military and political. The man he assumed to be Alfio, was a huge beast of a man. The blade at his waist was far longer than most men could hope to wield in battle. However, it was the smaller man that Priam knew was the real danger. Alfio was a brute, and brutes do as they are told. The man to his front, may be of smaller stature, but was clearly used to giving orders.

"Do I know you?" Priam asked, forcing himself to focus through the weariness.

"A king, who knows a lowly subject? No, you do not know me, but you knew my brother. Strung him up and left him for the birds. I was away when your guards took him. By the time I returned the crows had stripped the flesh from his bones. They even took his eyes. How is a man supposed to see his way in the next world without his eyes?"

Priam searched his memory. He had only given the sentence of death to three men in recent years. One had been an old man, and he had managed to take poison before the sentence was carried out. Another had been a Hittite who had killed several citizens. Priam had contacted the Hittites, and they had washed their hands of the man. The only other death sentence carried out was…"

"Arkadios, your brother was Arkadios? He was a bastard and deserved nothing but death," Priam announced defiantly.

"Oh, I didn't say he didn't deserve to die, but he was my brother. I'm a man of honour Priam, despite my low standing in this city. Honour demands that I seek out justice." He pulled a blade from his tunic. His lips turned up into a devilish grin displaying a mouth almost devoid of teeth. "What say you, King Priam? An eye for an eye?"

Priam wondered how a man with so few teeth could bite so easily into an apple. The bewilderment made him smile. "May I be permitted to know my killer's name?" He asked holding back a chuckle.

"Arius, I am king in the Shadows."

"Well, King of the Shadows," Priam gave a snort of laughter, with no attempt to hide his amusement. "It seems you have an uninvited guest."

Both Arius and Alfio turned, the larger of the two reaching for the weapon at his side. The action was slow and predictable, a figure emerged from the shadows and smashed a fist into his jaw before the blade could be drawn free of its scabbard.

"For a big man, he falls over far too easily," the owner of the fist announced.

"King of the shadows – I would like to introduce you to the Prince of Troy, my son, Hector."

"He will be prince of nought after I've gutted him," Arius warned, as he moved toward Hector, his blade at the ready.

Hector circled around Arius placing himself between his father and his would-be killer. Despite, the dangerous situation his own sword remained firmly in its scabbard. A fact not lost on the fury-filled Arius.

"Draw your weapon and fight!' he screamed.

"My son does not require a weapon to defeat the likes of you," Priam replied.

"Keep crowing, old man, when I have finished with

him, I will take my time skinning you."

"Enough talking, I grow weary of your boasting," Hector goaded.

Arius lunged. He didn't come close to hitting Hector. Time and time again he tried to land a blow, but each failed attempt was met with ridicule. On the seventh attempt, rather than meeting nought but air, his arm was caught and held fast.

"My turn," Hector teased. He drove a fist into Arius's face, but held the man firm so he could not fall. The powerful fist was delivered another three times causing a senseless Arius to drop his weapon. It was at this point that Hector allowed his enemy to topple into the dirt. The Prince of Troy strolled to where Arius's weapon lay and plucked it from the ground. He crossed over to Arius who was attempting to rise only to be knocked flat on his back by a casual kick from Hector.

"The Shadows is going to need another king," announced Hector as he pulled back Arius's head and placed the blade against the soft flesh of his throat.

"Wait!" Priam called out. The old king wearily moved closer so that he could look into the eyes of the man that hated him. "You told me that you were a man of honour, Arius."

Arius spat a mouthful of blood into the dirt. "I am, so don't expect me to beg for my life."

"I don't have to kill you, Arius. Both you and I observe the old ways, honour has meaning in our lives. I shall spare your life, and so, you owe my family a great debt."

"Father, I would not trust this man," announced Hector.

"Arius is without doubt guilty of every crime we have witnessed, and probably some we haven't, but his word is his bond. "What say you, Arius? Die here in the dirt or serve my family until you are released from your debt?"

Hector applied a little more pressure to the blade to aid the man's decision.

Arius closed his eyes as though the decision took all his concentration to think through. Finally, his body slumped as though resigned to a terrible fate. "Very well Priam, I am your man. That big bastard gets thrown in for free," he nodded to the unconscious Alfio as he replied.

"Good, visit me at the palace tomorrow. We shall discuss your duties."

Chapter 22

'A father's Wish'

P riam had allowed Hector to lead him by the arm until they had walked clear of the Shadows. He knew that Hector would have plenty to say about what had happened just moments earlier, but Priam wanted to observe the city. Time, or the lack of it was suddenly an oppressive master. Matters must be discussed even though it would not be easy to talk of death and the crown with a son that had no wish to hear of either. He waited until the Shadows and Arius were left far behind.

Hector broke the silence, "Father, you cannot honestly hope to trust that man?"

"His word will hold him captive as securely as any rope. Come tell me how that boy of yours fares." Priam changed the subject.

"He becomes more stubborn with the passing of each day."

"Ha!" Priam laughed knowing that Hector was referring to both his child and his father with the comment. However, the joy was short-lived, and he was assailed by a deep rasping cough.

"Come, Father, you must rest." Hector gently took

his father by the elbow, but the old man would not be steered.

"I shall rest in the next world. Come let us walk our way home."

Priam and Hector always took the same path about the city. Firstly, they would inspect the great walls of the citadel. Standing the height of six men and the width of four, the walls were formidable. Watchtowers added to its impressive defensive capabilities; an enemy wishing to enter Troy by force would require the gods' help to breach the inner defences. Priam was more concerned over the defences that surrounded most of the city. A substantial wooden fortification skirted around Troy. Before an attacker reached the timbered defence, they would have to navigate a ditch that encircled the entire city. A man-made lake obstructed an attacking force on the eastern side. Priam, however, still felt concerned that most of the populace did not have the protection of solid stone. "When you are king, turn timber into stone. Protect those within the city, Hector." The statement caused his son to stop in his tracks.

"You can undertake that task for yourself, Father."

Priam placed his hands on the muscular shoulders of his first born. "The plans are in place. Work will begin in the next coming days." Priam paused, reluctant to speak the words that he knew must be spoken. "I am dying, Hector. You must realise that the time is approaching that you must decide to wear the crown or not."

"I am no king. The crown would not sit well upon my head. Besides, I am a soldier I only know how to solve problems with a blade. I have no skill or interest in the politics required to be king."

"Being a king is like living with a woman. It takes time to grow into the role, and hopefully you don't get your balls cut off in the process," Priam laughed.

"Paris craves the crown. Besides, he could convince the gods to give him the key to Olympus."

"Your brother is a capable man. His failings, however, could put the city in danger. He is quick to temper and thinks too much with his cock." Priam did not like to speak ill of his second eldest son, but the boy had nearly caused a bloody war. "If King Tyndareus had not soothed the wrath of Prince Menelaus, then conflict would have ravaged our home."

"He seems to have calmed his spirit. Besides, Menelaus has no real love for Helen. They were little more than children when the marriage was forced upon them. He was never serious about going to war over a woman he does not love. I think Paris has learnt from his mistakes, at least his wondering eye rarely falls on other men's wives anymore."

"That is because I threatened to remove his favourite weapon from his body. I fear placing a crown on his head will put an end to his newly discovered control."

"I understand, but a man should not seek the crown if he does not want to wear its responsibility. Leading men in battle has been more than enough weight for me. I have no wish to add further to my burden. Is there no other that could take the crown?"

"Paris could not feel aggrieved if you became king, you are my oldest son. I doubt that his temper would hold if he was overlooked in favour of someone not of my blood."

"There is Polydorus," Hector announced.

"Paris would never serve under Polydorus. Besides, I love Polydorus, but we both know that he does not have the mind for kingship." Priam thought of his youngest son; a smile emerged on his face. He was a man in all but mind. It wasn't that he was slow or dim witted, but he took delight in the things that warriors shunned. He would rather walk amongst the flowers of the palace gardens than test his strength in more manly pursuits. Priam wondered why the gods had bestowed the boy with uncommon strength.

"I am sorry, Father. I just don't believe that I am a suitable choice for king. You could break with tradition. You have a number of daughters that have more than enough guile to run the city."

Priam could not hide his disappointment. "Troy is not ready to embrace that kind of change. We may not be a warrior race, but the people still want one on the throne. All I ask is that you consider becoming king. Leave these shores and think about the matter. Let your mind be free of your princely duties and unclouded by those within this city. Besides, I have received a message from Ithaca."

"Have there been more raids on their lands?"

"Yes, Odysseus believes that he knows when the next attack will take place. He has a plan."

"Doesn't he always?"

Priam stopped and rested for a moment. "That he does," he wheezed.

"A curse on the gods for your weakness, Father."

"They have not shown me disloyalty for my service, Hector. Time sits heavily on all men and precious few live to experience the years that I have seen. I have few complaints. Although more time with your mother would be one. Now, be gone with you. Let an old man enjoy a walk in peace."

"Yes, Father. But please stay clear of the Shadows."

*****

As Hector walked away, he felt sadness weigh heavily on his heart. The time was approaching that this world would no longer be graced by Priam. Hector knew that Troy would always find another king, but he could not replace his father. The prince felt a lump rise in his throat; he thought of more joyful times. A straight backed, powerfully built father had been a far more splendid vision to behold. Hector remembered how they had spent hours in mock battle as his father taught him the ways of the spear and blade. The training taught Hector to kill without hesitation. That friendship and compassion were luxuries a warrior could not afford when the horns of war sounded their battle cry. When a day's training came to an end they would walk beyond the city's gates.

The destination would always be the same point overlooking the city and surrounding countryside. His father would use the vista to impress upon the young Hector the importance of a world that lay beyond the walls of Troy, and the need to care for the souls within them. It had been a valuable experience, one that Hector now repeated with his own son, Skamandrios. The thoughts of his son brought even more sadness to his heart. If his father was right, then Troy could soon face upheaval and without the steadying hand of Priam.

Hector was lost in his thoughts and without realising it, found himself at the point that he used to look down on the city with his father. He placed a hand against the tree on which he had leaned so many times.

"What preys on the hero of Troy's mind?" a woman's voice asked.

Hector looked up and smiled. "Hero? You listen to the ramblings of old warriors too much, dear wife of mine," he replied.

"I think not. I have seen your heroic deeds with my own eyes," Andromache replied.

Hector pulled her close. "And when did you witness such deeds?"

"Only last night, your prowess with a weapon is without equal."

Chapter 23

'Band of Brothers'

H ector spent the remainder of the day preparing for his journey to Ithaca. Refusing to risk too many Trojan lives in another man's land, he had decided to take only one vessel. That said, he'd bring his best and most loyal warriors. The wish to keep his men alive could not be used as an excuse to allow the House of Priam to lose face by suffering a humiliating defeat.

His first stop came at the docks. Many nation states looked at Troy's trading prowess with envy. It stood perfectly positioned between the Hellene states and the influential Hittite empire, to take advantage of the plentiful trading opportunities. His father, King Priam, had nurtured good relations with Hellene and Hittite alike. He had gone further and ensured that his people embraced neutrality. Travellers from other lands were treated with respect. Residents of Troy found to be treating foreigners with anything but the highest regard were punished severely. At the same time, Priam had ensured that his warriors were skilled and armed with the finest weaponry. The king knew that an open city would also play host to foreign agents, gathering information for various city states. Priam ensured that they would take the news to their masters that Troy had an impressive military capability. All this wisdom he passed onto his son, Hector. He, in turn, had done his best to follow his father's example. Hector had forged friendships throughout the many kingdoms; he counted many kings and princes amongst his closest friends. However, he ensured that each of them understood that he was a son of Troy and was prepared to defend the city to the last drop of his blood.

It was to the defence of Troy that Hector dedicated much of his time. He helped train those that would take up arms in times of peril. Creating a specialist group, paid for from his own funds, these were men that had proved themselves in battle many times. They were set apart from the ordinary ranks. Their lives were dedicated to the craft of war, taught not just to follow orders but to be able to work as individuals. Their numbers varied because war is chaotic and even the finest warrior can be felled by a boy with a sling. His most loyal man was Huzziya, descendent of a prominent Hittite family that had established themselves in Troy over three decades previously. However, to Hector and the rest of the men he was known as Clops due to his ample size, and the loss of an eye during his first battle. Clops was busying himself on one of the Trojan warships. Hector knew that the man had no children and the ships benefited from the love he would have given to any offspring.

"Is the lady ready to sail, Clops?" Hector asked.

Clops stood from cleaning the deck, his hands on his lower back as he rubbed it with a sigh. He growled, his face a picture of discomfort as he stretched his back.

"She is always ready. I see to that." He took a piece of rag from his tunic and gave the timber of the rail a gentle polish.

Hector watched Clops and wondered if the man had ever spent the night with a woman. The man wasn't ugly, and the missing eye may have proved an attractive element. Some women liked their lovers to look dangerous, but few adored one that looked like he slept with pigs.

"That's good. She will be needed tomorrow."

"How far?"

"Ithaca, thirty men - enough supplies for the journey and no more than three days on the island."

"I will get the provisions aboard."

"Thank you, Clops. I will need him – where is he?"

"How would I know, Hector?"

"By the gods, Clops, don't mess me about or I will throw you over the rail."

Clops looked beyond Hector and then shook his head.

"No matter how hard I look, I cannot see your men."

"What are you talking about?" Hector asked.

"The men you would need to throw me over the side."

Hector laughed, "Is that the proper way to talk to your prince?"

"It is." Clops gave a crooked smile. "I think he was planning to go and see *her*."

Hector raised a hand to his eyes. The news struck a blow as powerful as any fist. He took a moment before gaining the composure to speak. "Why does he do it to himself? They will probably kill him this time."

"I will get my sword," Clops replied.

"No stay here and prepare the vessel. Let's hope he got too drunk to find his way."

*****

Hector left Clops aboard the ship as he made his way back through the city. He cursed under his breath as outwardly he smiled at the populace. He reached the city stables and ordered one of the grooms to fetch him a horse and left the city, heading east. He journeyed to the only property that sat on the banks of the lake. Hector had no real wish to visit the residence of his uncle, Kallinicus. However, he knew that his cousin, Elene, was more than likely there, which meant Aetes, would not be far away. Hector smiled when he thought of his friend, but that humour soon turned to frustration. Why had he gone there? It would be the end of him this time. Kallinicus was never going to let him wed Elene. Not even Hector's intervention had helped. It had not come as a surprise to Hector. He had always found Kallinicus to be the most disagreeable of men.

Hector knew that he had arrived before the building came into view by the sound of shouts and cursing. He dismounted and tethered his mount to the nearest tree, then stole through a small orchard in the direction of the commotion. As he broke through the trees, he could see a dozen men in front of the main gate, three were face down in the dirt. The remainder were raining blows on an unseen individual. Although Hector could not see the features of the unfortunate person, he knew that it was Aetes.

He stepped into the open. "Stop! I am Prince Hector, step away from that man."

The men stopped and turned to glare at Hector.

Elene's brother, Copreus, stormed toward him. "You have no say here Hector. This is my father's land."

"I agree. But I would see it as a favour to me if you would release my man. He is needed for an important mission. Troy needs him."

"Then Troy had best look for another. He has trespassed on our land for the last time."

Hector remained calm, not wanting to cause tempers to rise further. "I give you my word that he will not visit this place again."

"I do not want or need your word. Now leave before we forget that you're a prince of Troy."

"You leave me no option. Either you step away from Aetes and allow him to leave, or I will gather my men and burn this place to the ground."

"You would not dare!"

"Why not? There would be no witness left alive to complain." It was a threat Hector knew he could not carry out, but the expression on his cousin's face showed uncertainty. "Come, Copreus, let this madness end."

"You talk of witnesses. But what does it matter if we throw two bodies in a ditch, rather than one?"

"You would kill a prince of Troy?" Hector asked.

"If forced to do so, now leave and let us have our sport."

Hector strolled up to Copreus. "I suppose you leave me no choice. Aetes is a good man, but I cannot deny that he has made a nuisance of himself." Copreus smiled, he obviously enjoyed the thought of Hector slinking away like a whipped dog. "There is just one issue."

"And what is that?" Copreus snarled.

"I think you and your father are a pair of bastards." Hector punched Copreus on the jaw, sending him crashing into his men. He charged forward and began beating any of the men that attempted to rise. Those that weren't knocked over by Copreus seemed uncertain as to what action to take. Copreus may have been their master but to attack a prince would have meant certain death. They backed away as Hector picked the beaten body of Aetes from the ground.

"Hector, what are you doing here?" Aetes asked, gaining consciousness.

"Stopping a fool from getting himself killed."

"I was just getting warmed up." Aetes smiled revealing bloodied teeth.

"Would you prefer me to leave you here?"

"No, I think I am ready for another drink."

"No time for a drink. We have a task, if we get away from here alive, that is." Hector helped Aetes back through the orchard, and then to mount his horse.

"I will not ride while my prince walks." Aetes made to dismount.

"Stay where I put you, and for once do as you are ordered. You are not to visit this place again."

Hector was irritated. He knew that his father would not be pleased that he had used violence to rescue Aetes from the household of Kallinicus.

"I am not afraid of a little beating."

Hector stopped the mount and looked at Aetes. "I have given my word. Would you make me lose my honour for the sake of this woman?"

"No – no of course not. I am sorry," Aetes muttered.

Hector was suddenly filled with sympathy for his friend. Aetes was orphaned at an early age and had no siblings. Finding love that would lead to a family had always been a deep desire for his friend. Hector patted him on the shoulder. "Put the household of Kallinicus from your mind. We have a task to complete, if your wounds are not too severe?"

"They will mend soon enough."

"Good, but you had best visit your sorceress. We leave as the sun rises and I would have you at least looking like a warrior."

*****

Aetes waved his temporary goodbyes to Hector. Thankfully, the prince had left him the mount. Beginning to sober up, the pain of his beating intensified. Walking to Maeja's lair with his injuries would have proved difficult. It was a journey that did not take long, even if he did feel every step made by the beast beneath him. With some effort, he dismounted and tied the horse to a near tree. Turning, he looked down the narrow path that led to his destination. The track was narrow and overgrown. The ground was heavy with water and would make walking treacherous. He reluctantly took a step and slipped. He grasped one of the branches, but it gave way with an unhealthy crack. He toppled forward pulling the branch with him. Waves of pain seared through his body. Cursing, he used the branch to support his weight as he struggled to regain his feet. He pressed on, his makeshift crutch providing much needed stability.

The journey was slow and tortuous, but finally he stood still, looking towards the open door of Maeja's home. He had visited the old sorceress many times, but each time he could not escape the fact that he was in the presence of a being that could extinguish his life within a heartbeat. He had faith in his skills as a warrior and had never been found wanting in battle. Maeja's power, however, was undeniable and caused him amazement and fear in equal measure. He summoned his courage and proceeded through the doorway. He raised a hand to his nose on his face. Its swollen and crooked form explained why he was unable to smell the scents that usually invaded his senses.

He reached the inner chamber. Pots bubbled, carcasses of strange unfamiliar beasts, hung from the wall. All was as he expected except for the absence of Maeja.

However, a sleeping area, not usually present in the chamber, had been created. At its side a vessel containing a liquid that seemed to shimmer a multitude of colours in the lamp light. From its surface, a smoke containing those same colours, rose into the air. He crossed the room and lowered his aching form onto the bed. He took a piece of fabric that lay next to the vessel and made to submerge it within the liquid.

"Since when have you been a healer?" A voice sounded. It made him jump, an action that he instantly regretted.

"Maeja, I did not think you were here?"

She crossed to him and relieved him of the fabric. "Where else would I be? Tending your wounds is becoming a constant task."

"I am sorry. I..."

She held up a finger to prevent his words. "Look at me," she demanded. "Eyes straight forward." He stared into to her eyes. Her hands moved faster than he could have believed possible. Her fingers clasped about his nose and gave it a short sharp twist. The loud crack was followed by his agonised scream. "Your face is a thing to behold. You should take care with it." She raised the fabric causing him to pull back from the possibility of further agony. "Calm yourself, this will soothe your pain," she announced with a gentler tone.

As she dabbed at his injured flesh, a sensation danced on his skin, the pain fading away.

"Thank you, Maeja."

"I suppose these wounds are a result of that girl."

"Elene has uncommon beauty," he replied.

"With a mind as sharp as a rock. Have you bedded this woman yet?"

If his face wasn't so bloodied and swollen, she would have seen him blush.

"Yes," he reluctantly replied.

"Then she has no more to offer. Seek a woman that will excite your mind and not just your cock, Aetes." She pulled his hand close and examined the twisted fingers. "I suggest you grit your teeth," But before he had chance, she snapped the fingers into place."

He grunted with pain.

"A little more warning would be nice."

"Perhaps the pain will serve as a warning." She wiped the hand with the cloth and then rose and collected another vessel from the table. "Drink it." She handed it to Aetes."

"Ugh," was all he could manage.

"I know its foul, but it will mend and soothe the injuries within. Now, rest." She placed her hands over his eyes and his world turned to darkness.

Aetes was oblivious to Maeja's potion repairing his damaged body as he slept. It wasn't until he woke that he was aware that the cuts and bruises had all but disappeared. So too, had his clothes and the blood that had decorated his body. He pulled a fur around his waist to hide his embarrassment. He glanced over to Maeja, who was busying herself next to the large table. Without turning to face him, she spoke.

"How are you feeling?"

He rose from the bed, and stretched out his limbs, keeping a firm grasp on the fur.

"Surprisingly good. In fact, I feel strong. But where are my clothes?"

"They were fit for nought. I have others that will suffice. I also have another gift for you."

"You have done enough," Aetes replied.

"That I have. But you will need this gift for a future that is uncertain."

"You have always told me that the future is always uncertain."

Maeja turned to look at him. "That is because I have an uncommon intelligence. You would be wise to listen to me." She smiled and returned to her task at the table.

"What is going to happen, Maeja?"

"That I cannot say."

"Can't or won't?" Aetes replied.

"Seeing into the future is beyond me, Aetes. But I can read the signs."

"Signs?"

"Armies marching in distant lands. Kings and cities will fall. Troy will not be immune to the engulfing chaos. A dark cloud moves in the world of men. It bends all to its will." Her eyes focussed on a far-off point, that

Aetes could not see.

"What can we do?"

"Perhaps nothing, perhaps everything. But we must prepare, no matter the outcome." She threw him a tunic. "Put that on."

Aetes caught the garment. The cloth was different to any other he had laid his hands on. It was impossible to see the weave. He gave it a tug, it somehow felt strong but had so little weight. Slipping the garment on; it caressed his flesh. It was almost as though it was a second skin.

"I have never known the like," he announced.

"You are so easily impressed." She walked to what Aetes had thought a wall, raised a hand and grasped an unseen cloth. The darkness of the cloth had hidden the contents beyond.

Aetes could not hide his wonder. "Are those for me?"

"Shield and armour. Alas, I think you will need both."

Aetes walked over to the armour. Tentatively, he ran a hand over the shield, its face adorned with the head of Medusa. Plucking it from the ground he felt its weight.

"Let us hope the enemy feel the same fear as they face you, as they did when Medusa was nearby. It will not slow your movement, but do not concern yourself because of its lack of weight, for no mortal weapon could penetrate its surface. Try on the rest."

Aetes picked up the body armour. Once again, Aetes was surprised by how light the thorax felt. He wondered how it could prevent a sword from opening his flesh. Nonetheless, he slipped it on. He gasped as the armour began to change shape. Like water washing over rocks, the material flowed around the form of his torso. A moment later, it had solidified and perfectly mirrored his body. The greaves followed the action of the thorax and moulded to his legs. The helmet was like no other that he had witnessed. The best helmets he had seen had bone or tusk to protect from sword or missile, but this was one single piece of metal, of a kind that Aetes had never seen. He placed it on his head. He wouldn't have even known he was wearing it if it had not been for the cheek guards. His amazement, however, was nought compared to when Maeja presented him with a sword. The handle was made from bone. The rest, however, resembled the material that had been used in both shield and armour. He gave the air a swipe.

"It is perfectly balanced," he announced.

"Of course. And it will never lose its edge."

"Thank you, Maeja. How can I ever repay you?"

"By staying alive. Now bugger off and allow an old woman to sleep."

Chapter 24

'Peer into the Abyss'

The following morning, Priam, sat on the balcony attached to his private quarters. Despite a slight chill in the air, the sun bathed the city buildings in its cleansing light. His sleep had been disturbed by a vision of an impressive, beautiful, white stallion charging through a meadow, only to scream a woeful cry before it fell to the ground. Moments later, the animal's stomach burst open and a great snake with eyes the colour of blood, slithered from the carcass. Priam felt a shiver down his spine as he remembered the scene.

A rapping at the door shook him free of the image.

"Enter!" Priam called out. A familiar faced appeared around the door.

"Forgive me for disturbing you, Father. Two men have called on the palace and claim that you have summoned them. They do not look the kind of men that usually visit our home."

"Polydorus, it is a man's character that we should judge not their outward appearance."

"Yes, Father." The young man bowed his head to show his shame.

"Polydorus, take them to the gardens and provide

them with refreshment. And Polydorus..."

"Yes, Father?"

"Chest out and speak clearly. You are a Prince of Troy, be proud of that fact. As I am proud to have you as a son." Polydorus' face erupted into a huge smile, as he straightened his back.

"Yes, Father." The young prince slipped back through the door and raced away.

*****

Priam could not move with speed and so it took time before he could join Polydorus in the gardens. When he finally arrived, he spied an animated Polydorus talking as Arius and Alfio looked on. Priam approached them. The two men were utterly dismayed at their young host. The king pressed on, advancing with as much stealth as he could manage.

"Polydorus, I am not sure our guests have an interest in the gardens." To Priam's surprise, Arius and Alfio stood up to pay their respect. "Run along, I have more serious matters to discuss."

Polydorus looked at Priam and then at the two men.

"Are you sure, Father? I could fetch the guard," he replied.

Arius laughed. "King Priam, has nought to fear from us." Arius announced. "Not any longer, that is." Arius gave a sickly-sweet grin.

"I will not be in any danger." Priam placed a hand around his son's waist and guided him away from his guests. "Look to your training."

"But…" Polydorus began.

"I realise that you have no love of the blade, but if not for your king - then do it for your father."

"Of course." Polydorus embraced Priam and kissed him on the cheek before leaving.

Priam watched Polydorus go and raised a hand to his cheek. The kiss was not out of the ordinary for his son. The boy was no warrior, but Priam did not care. The passions that stirred the young prince may well have been different to those of Hector and Paris, but it did not diminish his love for his son. In many ways, he admired Polydorus for being brave enough to be different. It would have been all too easy to pick up a blade or bow. The prince had his own mind. Priam sighed, he wondered if Polydorus would survive the hardships he knew would befall Troy.

King Priam felt the eyes of his guests upon him. He wiped a tear from his eye and turned to greet them.

"Arius, Alfio I am delighted that you have come," he announced in an overly pleasant way.

"You ordered it," Arius replied.

Priam gave a broad smile. "Yes, I did - didn't I?"

"I will need time to close down my… my interests before entering your service," Arius said.

"Interests? What a delightful way to describe your activities. No – I don't think you need time." Priam locked Arius in a stare.

"I have family. If I do not make certain arrangements, they will be in danger. "

Priam held up a hand to stop Arius's protestations. "I simply mean that I do not wish for you to cease your 'interests'." Priam looked at Alfio who was enjoying the refreshments provided by Polydorus. "Come Arius, walk with me." Priam led the way with Arius following close behind. When they had travelled far enough not to be overheard, Priam decided to rest, taking a seat on one of the small walls, which snaked through the gardens. "In your world within the Shadows do you watch for signs of danger?"

"Of course, in the Shadows danger is never more than a step away," Arius replied.

"And do you sometimes feel that danger without seeing the evidence?"

"I feel it. Feels like rats gnawing at my guts. But taking a blade to my enemies usually brings me calm."

"Being King of Troy is no different, with one difference, the blade is not always an option no matter how tempting."

"Why?" Arius asked.

"Because despite our wealth we do not possess a large army. Or even the populace to fill its ranks. The battles that we fight are ones of diplomacy. I had thought that I had won the battles, but recently it feels as though I have been outflanked."

"What is this to do with me?"

"See those walls, Arius? When the enemy swarm over them bringing the blade and fire, they will not come to just kill those belonging to the royal family. Men, women, and children will fall to the slaughter. Wealthy or poor, it will make no difference. Blood is the same colour no matter the owner."

"But who is the enemy, and what would you have me do?" Arius asked.

"Firstly, I would like you to confirm that the Shadows hide secret tunnels that lead toward the coast." Arius' expression was one of disdain. Priam continued, "Arius, if I wished to remove the criminals from this city then I could simply wipe the Shadows from the world of men. This is not the time to play games."

"Very well. I know of such tunnels."

"Then we have a task to complete before it is too late. I would like you to take a journey to meet with someone. After that task is completed, I will ask you to care for my family should disaster strike the city. You will be provided with ships, men and gold."

"Why ask? I am in your debt. All you have to do is command."

"No, Arius. If you're to do this task, it must be of your free will. If my family is forced to leave this place, they will be hunted. They will need a man that is used to hiding in the shadows, a man that knows how to survive. Do not answer now. We have a woman to meet."

A voice sounded from the far side of the gardens. "Father! Who are these men and where is your guard?"

Priam leaned in towards Arius.

"Not a word to the prince. All that we discuss and the preparations that we take are to be in secret," Priam whispered. Arius nodded as Priam turned to greet his son.

"I thought that you had gone hunting for the day, Paris?"

"I did not feel compelled to do so. Who are these people, Father?"

"This is Arius, and the larger man is Alfio," Priam replied.

"And?" Paris pressed.

"And what?"

"What are they doing here?" Paris asked, exasperated.

"The last time I looked Paris, the crown still sat firmly on my head. I am not used to being questioned in such a manner."

His son blushed. "Forgive me, I only show concern that you're here without a guard with men that I do not know."

"If you must know, they are from the Shadows." Priam had learned at an early age that if you were going to tell an untruth, then you had best sail as close to the truth as possible. "I seek to rid the city of its darker elements."

Paris looked from Arius to Alfio and then turned to his father. "Why not hang them from the nearest tree.

Give me fifty men and I would cleanse The Shadows."

"Your men would be dead before you had taken twenty paces," Arius snapped.

Paris's hand moved towards the sword on his hip. He stepped toward Arius. Priam placed himself between the two men.

"I have much to discuss with these men. I am sure that you have more pressing matters."

"Erm – Yes, Father." The prince's hand dropped from his blade. Without another word he turned and strode away.

"I think I prefer Prince Polydorus," Arius announced.

"Most men do. Although, females seem drawn to Paris." Priam's eyes continued to watch Paris until he walked away. "I think we should go."

*****

The walk was slow. Priam was unable to maintain a steady pace. Arius was forced to place a steadying hand on the king's arm on more than one occasion. The act of kindness did not go unnoticed by Priam and for the first time he felt comfortable in trusting his decision not to leave Arius bleeding in the dirt. He didn't discuss his thoughts with Arius but did ask the man about his family. Priam knew that no matter the standing of a man, rich or poor they all had the same look on their face as they talked of their children. Alfio walked five paces behind and seemed content in the role as protector of Arius.

They passed through the small, but heavily guarded

gatehouse on the east side of the city. They walked towards the man-made lake. Turning northward they proceeded along a small dirt track.

"Are you sure that you should be doing this, sire?" Arius asked.

"It isn't much further. There is still life in this old dog, at least, for the time being." Priam raised a hand and pointed to a small doorway cut into the hillside. "Let's hope she will see us."

"But you are the king!"

"I am not sure Maeja is too concerned by a man's position," Priam replied.

"Maeja!" Arius repeated the name, shock on his face.

"Yes, have you met her?"

"No – but I hear she speaks to the gods."

"She may speak '*at*' the gods. She has little time for man or deities. But she sees things that others don't." A noise to their rear made all three men turn. They saw a figure slip down a small incline and give out a curse. "Paris, I thought I told you to go about your duties?"

"This is my duty, Father. I must ensure that you face no danger," Paris replied.

Priam stood perfectly still for a moment, looking at his son. "Very well. You may accompany me, but you must remain silent. That is an order from your king." Priam gave an unflinching stare, so that his son knew that it was a command not to be disobeyed. Without waiting for a reply, he turned from Paris.

The four men continued until finally coming to a stop before a small doorway carved into the side of a hillside.

"Should I knock?" Arius asked.

"No point, she will not answer. We must press on." Priam opened the door and moved forward. As his eyes adjusted to the dimness, which was lit by a torch, he could see a long tunnel stretching before him. He had faced many battles in his time, but his heart thudded anxiously. He could not decide what he feared the most, the oppressive darkness or the person they travelled to meet.

As the group moved deeper into the hillside, strange fragrances invaded Priam's nostrils and stung his eyes. Through blurred vision he could see a figure moving in the distance. The tunnel opened out into a large room and on the opposite side, a small figure, features covered by a black cloak, moved between various pots. Every now and then an almost skeletal hand would reach out and drop an unknown item into one of the vessels.

"Maeja, may I speak with you?" Priam plucked a purse from his belt and placed it in one of the few places not taken up by a vessel. Maeja ceased brewing and moved toward him. She raised her head. To his shock, Maeja seemed little more than a skeleton whose skin had taken on an almost transparent quality. The old woman had lost most of her hair with just the odd silver strand falling onto the sharp, jutting cheek bones Her eyes were pools of clouded milk, and the only eye to be seen, was the one made up from a series of dots, applied to the old woman's forehead.

"How very noble, a virtuous king visits a poor, and weak old woman. I am truly himbled." Her voice was high, bordering on a screech, but the poorly hidden sarcasm was clear. "He brings coin and other guests." Maeja's head moved serpent-like, as she studied the other men. "Hmm – a poor selection, thieves and liars."

"You should not talk that way about my father's companions," Paris announced.

"Who said I was talking about them, Prince of Troy?" Maeja replied. A large grin spread across her face. The prince went for his sword, but his action was stopped almost before it begun. Maeja had closed the distance between her and the visitors in a blink of an eye. Paris suddenly found that the crone held his sword arm with one hand; the other was at his throat, the inch long thumb nail cutting into his flesh. "What a shame it would be if your pretty head left its shoulders."

"Maeja," Priam knew that this was not the time to give a royal command, "I have need of your services, I would be grateful, if you would release my son."

"The fool should learn to hold his tongue, unless he wants me to remove it," Maeja replied.

"Paris, will say no more."

"Very well." Maeja released the prince and retired to safe distance. "What would the great King Priam need the services of an old woman for? You have vast wealth to buy what is for sale and an army to take what is not."

"You have the sight. I need to know what my people

face."

"But you know. Have you not seen the gods as they play their games of power?"

"Then all is lost?" Priam replied, hoping that Maeja may speak some words of comfort.

"All that is worth having is attained through hardship. The fate of Troy and its people may lie on different paths, but you and I will not see their journey's end." She dropped what looked like herbs into one of the vessels. A burst of flame, followed by a heavy green cloud of dust erupted into the room. "I see misery and death, cracked walls and broken hearts." She gave a shrug. "Isn't that always the way of man."

"Is there nothing that I can do?"

"I cannot see clearly into the future. Too many deceitful souls, both deity and man, are manoeuvring for power. So, you must do what you can, and stop wasting time talking to old women. I will say only this – the household of Priam will have its champion and when he beats his shield, even the columns of Olympus will crack and fall."

*****

The sun had already begun to fall in the sky by the time Priam and the others returned to Troy. Judging by his sullen downturned mouth, his son was still feeling humiliated. Paris left without saying a word, and Priam waited until he was out of sight and then turned to face Arius. "I hope I have convinced you that my ramblings are not that of an old man close to losing his sanity?"

"Can it be true?" Arius shook his head in obvious dismay. "Who would bring the sword to our city?"

"That I cannot say. All we can do is prepare for an uncertain future. We must work in secret. Our enemies will be watching. More importantly," he paused as he stared into the Aruis' eyes, "can I trust a man that recently wanted me dead?"

"I gave you an oath. I will not break it. Besides, if Troy is in danger, I would have my family as far from this place as possible." Arius turned and looked across the city. "What of all the others that inhabit Troy?"

"I have given this a great deal of thought. I cannot warn a people of impending doom without the answer to the questions that would surely follow. They would think me suffering from a madness. But if an enemy attack the city, and finds the royal family has fled, then the need for slaughter may be reduced. They can simply take their place upon the throne. We shall try and give the people a way of escape if the time comes. So, Arius King of the Shadows are you with me?"

"I am your man, King Priam."

Chapter 25

'Bring forth the Cursed'

There are few beings, whether it is man or deity, that could walk unhindered in the underworld. Hades kept a tight grip of his land. He may have loathed being forced to tend the land of the dead, but it was still his land. He employed various means to detect those that transgressed. One such method was the deployment of Cerberus, a fearsome three headed hound that stood far higher than any creature in the underworld. It was blessed with savage fangs and a temperament to match. Even Hades was reluctant to get too near to the beast. Persephone, wife of Hades, was the only being that could quell the beast's fury. This made the image of a solitary figure walking towards Cerberus, all the stranger. Although the being's features were completely hidden by cloak and hood, it was clear that its form was not female. There was no hesitation in its approach, despite the ferocity of Cerberus.

The hound growled its discontent, baring his teeth to add menace to its warning.

"Calm yourself. I mean you no harm."

The beast ignored the stranger's words and burst into a charge, clearly eager to sink its teeth into flesh.

Without any visible fear, the stranger continued his path, and as he did so, he reached within his robe. A moment later, he held aloft a sphere, which rotated within his hand and emitted crimson beams of light.

"Do you recognise this, beast?" The great hound skidded to a halt. "Your former master, Cronos, created it. He feared that his subjects kept dark secrets and so he wanted admittance to any door or lock. It is rumoured that the sphere contains his left eye." Cerberus backed away, whimpering like a whipped dog. All three heads displayed fear. "In truth, I find that hard to believe but I do know that it will grant me access to all, and that includes Tartarus." The figure pushed the sphere toward Cerberus and the last of the beast's resistance vanished. Turning on its heels, it raced away. "Time to see what powers this Blood Stone truly possesses." He allowed his arm to drop away; the sphere remained floating in the air. It matched his movements. It moved forward when he did and came to a halt the moment he paused, never more than an arm's length away.

He strode forward until his progress was brought to an abrupt halt by a huge bronze wall. There was no doorway that would allow access to the world beyond. The hooded figure smiled and took a step to his front. The Blood Stone began to spin at a greater pace, emitting beams that darted forward and danced upon the wall's surface. Like boiling water on ice, the bronze began to melt away. He stepped through the barrier; once on the other side, he glanced back and watched as the bronze wall began to reform and gain its previous condition. He pressed on, only slowing as his journey was interrupted by a further two magnificent walls. Nonetheless, the Blood Stone cleared a path for its master. As the final wall gave way, he plucked the spinning sphere from the air and tucked it within his robe. Stepping through the , he found himself on a causeway, a single road that ran through a vista that could not have been more different to the underworld. The dark caverns gave way to beauty. On either side of the causeway lay before him, beautiful green valleys, hills and impressive mountains. He peered over the edge of the causeway; no structure supported the road on which he travelled. It stood like a bridge over the surrounding countryside with no obvious route to the terrain below. He moved onward; his only option to proceed along a set path.

It was some time before he came to a door. It was perched precariously on the edge of the road. Its reverse side pointed towards the oblivion that awaited anyone foolish enough to step over the edge. As he neared, the carving on the timbers became apparent. His hands traced the etchings, painstakingly crafted of giant beasts ripping up trees and smashing them down on helpless victims.

"Giants," the figure whispered to himself. "Now that would be interesting. But I think it is too early to release your wrath upon the world." He gave the door a playful tap and continued his journey along the road.

He passed a further two doors without much delay before finally coming to a complete halt at the next. This entrance also contained intricate carvings, with the main character pushing a large rock up a mountain. The hooded figure placed his hand on the carving and pressed, A small click sounded, and the door swung open. However, the opening timbers revealed nought but the vista beyond the causeway. An audible gulp escaped from the stranger. He knew that Tartarus did not recognise any difference between human, beast or deity. Death in this place was a final death.

The visitor closed his eyes and stepped forward. Moments later, a breeze whipped at the hood on his robe. He shuffled his feet. The ground was rough, in stark contrast to the smooth stone that paved the causeway. He opened his eyes and found himself standing on a the side of a mountain.

In the distance, a solitary figure struggled to push a large boulder. The hooded visitor casually strode toward the struggling labourer. Then, some ten paces from him, he raised a hand, causing the boulder to come to a halt.

"Sisyphus, rest for a moment. I would have your attention."

The old man slumped to the ground, his back resting against the very rock that caused his eternal exhaustion. "What do you want?" Sisyphus asked through heavy intakes of air.

"Perhaps I just wanted to witness the fate of the great Sisyphus. How the mighty have fallen."

"If I remember correctly, the last time you visited me you ended up my captive."

The visitor pulled the hood closer to his face, clearly concerned that his identity was no longer a secret. "I am not here to dwell on the past."

"The past is all I have," Sisyphus replied.

"Perhaps not. Change is coming to the worlds of gods and men. Even those that dwell in Tartarus feel it upon their flesh."

"Not while Zeus lives." Sisyphus spat out the name as though it were rancid meat.

"All things come to pass, including Zeus."

Sisyphus managed to bark a laugh through his laborious breathing. "You seek to challenge Zeus – father of the Gods. Have your powers grown so much?"

"It is not necessary to chop down the apple tree to pluck its fruit. I admit to being surprised, Sisyphus. I would have thought that you would have been eager to bring Zeus to his knees."

"I loathe him." He slumped forward and slowly shook his head. "But I am broken. The fight has left me."

"Would you not like..."

Sisyphus held up a hand to prevent his visitor from further comment. "I am tired, and not just from pushing this bastard rock. I wish you good fortune, but I am not your man." He paused for a moment as he struggled to his feet. Stretching out his arms he took the weight of the rock. "Zeus will not hear of your plans from me. I am beyond the point that I fear his punishment."

The visitor bowed his head and without another word he left Sisyphus to his eternal damnation. As he walked away, a door appeared, without a backwards glance to Sisyphus he took his exit. Moments later, he was once again on the causeway. He did not dawdle, striding along the route in search of further doors. Now and then he would stop, examining another structure that gave him the opportunity to leave the causeway after examining the carvings on each, he moved on. At the fifth door he studied the carvings in more detail. It featured the murder of a young boy and a thief stealing from the gods in Olympus. The visitor pressed the carved figure of the thief and the timbers opened to allow him entrance.

He found himself walking in long grass, parallel to a riverbank. A soft breeze whipped at the hood of his robe. He allowed his arms to drop to his side, his fingertips caressing the grass as it danced in the gentle wind. His progress matched the winding river until both came to a halt. The waterway formed a small pool that was no more than thirty paces from bank to bank. In its centre a man stood waist deep in the water. The man's frame was painfully thin, his bones giving the impression that the skin was about to split under the pressure. The eye sockets were dark and sunk into the skull. The lips were raw and blistered as though the man had baked relentlessly beneath the burning sun.

The visitor walked to the water's edge, resting his back against a large pear tree. He raised a hand, the breeze dropped, and the branches ceased their movement.

"Tantalus, you look in need of a meal."

"I am not in the mood to be mocked. If my father has sent you, be warned, I will not be captive forever. I will know your name and will hunt you down."

"Mock? No, I'm not here to mock you. Perhaps you should drink."

"You are beginning to become tiresome," Tantalus replied.

"You stand in water and yet, cannot drink." He reached up and took a pear. "You stare at this fruit each day but cannot taste it." He threw the pear towards the condemned man.

Tantalus stared with obvious disbelief at the succulent fruit he had just caught.

"But how?" he asked. Tantalus devoured the pear as he waited for an answer.

"I told you, Tantalus. I am not here to mock you. I am here to grant you both freedom and vengeance." The hooded figure plucked another pear from the tree, but this time held it within his grasp. Tantalus eyed the fruit; his desire was plain to see. "Speak your heart, son of Zeus."

"I want my freedom. I wish to eat and drink until my arms ache with the effort of raising them to my mouth. However, the food would be nought, but dust and any liberty would be short lived while my father sits in Olympus. You ask me what I want - I want to crush the skull of Zeus beneath my heel."

"Then come with me. Together we will make those that sit within Olympus tremble."

"But I cannot leave this place," Tantalus replied.

"Did you not taste the fruit? Reach down, fill your

hand with water and quench your thirst."

Tantalus slowly placed his hand in the water, a task he had done many times, it had always proved a disappointment, the water always drained away before he could drink. As he raised his hand, his eyes widened to see that the water did not escape through his fingers. He drank, allowing the liquid to soothe his raw, cracked lips.

"But how?" Tantalus asked.

The visitor reached within his robe and withdrew the Blood Stone. He held it aloft between thumb and finger. "Do you know what this is?"

"I do. I thought that it was lost," Tantalus replied.

"It was, but now I am its master. It serves me as it once served Cronos. With the stone in my possession, Tartarus yields to my will."

"Even with the Blood Stone, Cronos could not defeat Zeus and the Olympians," Tantalus replied.

"I have no intention of challenging Zeus face to face. Where there is unity, we shall sow discord. We shall unpick the strands of Zeus's power. We are not alone in this struggle and more still will flock to our banner. The Olympians will be overwhelmed by enemies that they have created. Our task is to guide the actions of those wishing to destroy Olympus. When the fires of rebellion finally die down, then we shall be ready to create a new order. So, Tantalus, son of Zeus, are you with me?"

Tantalus walked toward the riverbank. With difficulty he heaved his frail body from the water. As he did so, the visitor held up his free hand, within it a robe appeared, its fabric as dark as night. Tantalus took the garment and nodded his agreement to join the visitor.

"I am with you."

"Then use your hood and cover your features, we must preserve our identity. We have more stops to make, but I promise that once Tartarus is at our back, I will provide you with a feast that will put flesh on your bones."

"Then lead the way," Tantalus replied.

A doorway appeared on the riverbank.

"Come Tantalus, let us expand our following."

*****

The visitor to Tartarus entered many doors, most of which provided him with another follower.

"Are we not lingering too long?" A nervous looking Tantalus asked.

"We will be on our way soon. Besides, I only intend to open two further doors. Both are required to strike at the heart of Zeus."

"Are we sure that we can trust..."

The visitor rounded on Tantalus.

"Trust, Tantalus? What makes you think that I trust any that stand at my side. You dwell in the bowels of Tartarus for good reason. You have an opportunity to leave because I believe that you may be useful." The visitor raised his voice. "We are not yet brothers in a struggle. All of you have joined my ranks because you had little choice and have nought but loathing for those that reside in Olympus. That does not blind me to your past deeds. Or sway me to throw away common sense and place my faith in any of you. Trust like respect must be earned and takes time. Until then you are little more than tools to complete a task. If you do not like the words I speak, then I am happy to return each of you to your eternal torment." The visitor waited for a reply, but his followers fixed their stares on the surface of the causeway. "Good, then remain here. I will enter the next two doors alone."

He strode from his subdued companions without another word or backward glance. Doors came and went but he took little notice of them, with just a brief glance at their carvings. He did, however, come to a halt outside a door that was at least twice the size of any that had preceded it. The figures too that adorned its timbers were different to the rest. There was no central figure that brought together a story of who lay beyond. Instead, all manner of beasts and fantastic creatures were shown in all their glory. He spent some time tracing the fine carvings with his fingertips, and then quite suddenly he left the causeway.

There was no valley, mountainside or riverbank to be seen. The visitor found himself in a room, a room that was lined with nothing but shelves that held hundreds of amphorae. He walked forward taking in the images that adorned the vessels. For the first time he knew that he was alone and pulled at the hood that hid his features. Thanatos raised a hand and stroked the neatly cropped beard that adorned his face.

"Oh, what chaos you will reap in the world of men,"

he whispered to himself.

He reached into his robe and pulled out a black cubed object, no bigger than the pear he had thrown to Tantalus. He crouched and placed the object onto the floor of the room. Taking a step back, he nodded in the object's direction. As if in answer to an unspoken command the object doubled in size, then again and again. When finally, it stopped, it had reached the height equal to the visitor's waist, and as long as the tallest of men. He stepped forward and rapped his fingers upon its surface. Moments later, the surface slid away to reveal compartments ready to be filled. Moving quickly; he selected certain amphora from the shelves and placed them within the object. More than twenty were plucked from the shelves before he took a step backwards again nodded towards the object. The top surface slid back into place, and then the object shrank back down to its original size. He returned the object to his tunic.

He made to leave but then turned as he approached the door.

"Why make a gift to our enemies and let them know what has been taken from this place?" He placed a hand upon the timbers that held the remaining amphora. Immediately, it began to age and splinter. Before long the shelves gave way, spilling the vessels to the floor and smashing them apart. He replaced the hood and gave an unseen smile as he took his leave.

Back on the causeway, he continued his journey. He faced one more final door. Without hesitation he stepped through the doorway. The terrain that faced him was far more like the underworld. A dark and oppressive atmosphere, with flames erupting from the ground. A beast-like groaning could be heard in the distance. He pressed on, keen to find the source of the woeful cry. As if in answer to a trespasser, the terrain released its fury, bellowing smoke and flames into the dark sky. However, the visitor remained true to his path and did not stop until he was confronted by a figure bound to a burning wheel that span, throwing fire into the air.

"Ixion!" the visitor called out. "Son of Ares, King of the Lapiths, I would speak with you." The only reply he received were screams of torment. He reached into his robe and touched the Blood Stone. The ground tremors and fires ceased immediately, but the wheel despite slowing, continued to turn. He took the Blood Stone from his robe and held it aloft. "I will be heard." He pushed the stone towards the wheel. Gradually, the timbers slowed to a stop and the bonds that held Ixion captive slipped away. The visitor held out a hand to the burned flesh of the fallen king, the tormented man screamed out in pain and fell forward.

"Leave me!" Ixion's head was bowed as he knelt upon the ground.

"Forgive me, Ixion. I have come to offer you freedom and the opportunity for a reckoning on those that inflicted such a punishment. Also, your children are anxious to meet you."

Ixion raised his head. His skin blistered and raw like slaughter meat stood as evidence to his torment His eyes, however, burned with a fire born of rage. His jaw clenched like an animal trap against the pain. He spoke through gritted teeth.

"Lead me from this place and my kin and I will show my enemies the meaning of pain," he growled. The madness within his eyes momentarily unsettled his liberator.

Chapter 26

'The Curse of Intelligence'

Ithaca

Odysseus strolled into the large banquet hall. He could hear laughter and felt compelled to investigate. This was no reserved chuckle, but a full uninhibited belly laugh. Not such a strange occurrence in a palace with so many inhabitants. However, Odysseus could tell that the owner of the laugh was his wife, Penelope. He crossed the hall and entered another large room that contained statues depicting members of Odysseus's household. The generations of his family stood in testament to an island state content with its royal family. The usual reverence maintained in this part of the residence was broken completely by Penelope's inability to stop laughing.

"What is so humorous?" Odysseus asked. Her merriment making him smile.

Penelope replied through her obvious amusement. "Oh! Heraclios, he has delivered his latest work for us,"

Odysseus looked to the small, diminutive figure of Heraclios, and then to the covered piece of art. He placed a hand on the sculptor's shoulder.

"Do not take offence, Heraclios. Penelope has always taken amusement in the strangest of things." He reached up and pulled the cloth from the statue. Odysseus looked at the piece, he knew that it had been a challenge for Heraclios. Most statues were motivated by vanity either for an individual or the family. Odysseus had asked for a statue that showed himself with Penelope and their son, Telemachus. "Tell me, Penelope." He gave up trying to see what had caused so much amusement.

"It's nothing really. It is beautiful only..." She started to laugh again.

"Penelope," pleaded Odysseus.

"I just wondered when I had married Achilles," she giggled.

Odysseus looked once more to the statue. Facially, the talented Heraclios had captured his likeness, but the frame of his statue had been enhanced. Odysseus smiled. He understood that an artist would want to flatter his king. In truth, he knew of many kings who would take the head of a sculptor if they had given a true depiction, but he hoped that his subjects did not believe him that conceited.

"Heraclios, you seem to have depicted me as a heroic figure of god-like stature."

"I simply showed what you represent to your people, King Odysseus," Heraclios replied.

"Hmmm – I admire your ability to think on your feet. However, I think living up to such standards would be too great a task. Change it – you will be paid for the extra work."

"Oh, I quite like it," Penelope teased.

"Then I am sure that you will take great delight when Achilles is our guest in the coming days."

"Alas, my love - muscle is all a man like Achilles has to offer and I could never replace his true love," she replied.

"Achilles is not wed," Odysseus replied, a little confused.

"Because Achilles cannot marry himself."

"You are a cruel woman." Odysseus pulled Penelope close and gave her a passionate kiss, only stopping when he realised that Heraclios was looking extremely uncomfortable. Any further conversation was brought to an abrupt end when one of the palace guards burst into the room.

"King Odysseus, black smoke to the east!"

"Show me!" Odysseus ran towards the guard, who in turn made his way back through the door he had previously entered. Once outside, the soldier pointed towards the east, revealing a large, thick plume of thick smoke rising into the air. Odysseus estimated it had come from one of the villages on the coast, his thoughts, however, were interrupted by a woeful cry.

"My village! Boys, quickly!" Heraclios called to his two sons that were seated in the cart used to transport his works of art. "Your mother needs us."

"Eudorus!" Odysseus called for one of his military

commanders. Within moments, a figure was rushing across the courtyard.

"Yes, my King," The man was clearly unaware of the crisis.

"By Poseidon's cock, do you not see what is happening on our soil." Odysseus pointed towards the smoke. Eudorus's mouth gaped as he gazed in the direction of Odysseus' raised arm. "Ithaca's lands are under attack. "I want fifty men mounted and ready to leave in all haste. You will follow with a larger force."

"Surely I should lead…" Eudorus tried to reply.

"See to my orders," Odysseus snapped, knowing that those responsible for the attack would be finished with the village and already heading out to sea. He cursed himself for his own arrogance. He had known that an attack would come but was sure that he had more time. The reports from other attacks and those responsible, suggested at least another seven days. He tapped his forehead, annoyed at his own stupidity.

Penelope moved to his side and placed a hand on his cheek. "You could not have known, my love."

"As king, it is my responsibility to know," he watched as Heraclios and his two sons sped away. "I must make ready. My armour, now!" He called out to the servants within the palace.

*****

Despite the urgency shown by Odysseus, it still took longer than he wished to be travelling the trackways of Ithaca. Indeed, their journey was nearly completed before they managed to overtake the desperate Heraclios. He paused briefly and ordered four of his men to accompany the sculptor. He doubted any enemy was left in his lands, but Heraclios was a good man and deserved protection. Then Odysseus and his men urged their mounts forward once again. Speed was essential, but the track to the village was not designed to play host to so many horsemen and three of the king's men were sent sprawling. Horses screamed out their agony, two of which would never regain their feet. Odysseus did not slow the pace or wait for those unhorsed.

As they neared the village the taste of acrid smoke invaded their nostrils and throats. It was at this point that Odysseus ordered his men to slow their progress. He doubted that he was wrong that the attackers were long gone, but he had been wrong about when the attack would take place. He was not prepared to risk his men's lives without good reason. One hundred paces short of the village, he ordered his men to dismount and to draw their weapons. As they neared, he ordered a group of men to circle around and enter the village from the eastern side.

He saw the first body at the side of the track, just outside the village. He guessed it had once been a boy not much older than his son, Telemachus. A heavy blade had taken the slain boy's features and detached one of the arms, which now lay two paces from the body. Odysseus had always prided himself on the ability to use his head to conquer emotions, but he could not deny the rage that was swelling within his gut. He waved his men forward and witnessed the burnt-out buildings that had once been a home to more than twelve families. He resisted the urge to search each home and decided that ensuring that the village was secure must take priority. He and his men pressed on, and as they moved through the settlement, they encountered more slaughter. Men, women, and children had all shared the same violent fate. He fought the urge to vomit and glanced around at the faces of his men. Most were veterans and had witnessed many horrific scenes, but all wore the same expression of disbelief and building anger. The youngest of his warriors, Duris was clearly trying to hold back the tears. Odysseus was about to speak words of comfort when a cry of despair split the air.

The cry came from behind them and when Odysseus turned, he saw Heraclios emerge from one of the burnt-out homes.

"Meet up with the others," he ordered his men. He walked towards Heraclios wondering what he could tell a man who had just lost his wife and home. The man was on his knees in the dirt. The two young boys clutched at their father. Their tears left white streaks down their smoke-stained masks of woe.

"Heraclios, you must return to the city with me."

Heraclios looked up to his king and then back into the burnt- out ruin that was once his home. "My men will take care of everything. All will be treated with the greatest of respect." Odysseus paused for a moment, wishing that he could remember the name of the sculptor's wife. He also felt that he needed to say something. "Heraclios. I am sorry."

"Sorry, my king?" Heraclios asked between sobs.

"I did not prevent this attack and it was because of me that you were not here to protect your home."

"I am no warrior, King Odysseus. If it were not for you, my boys and I would be dead." Heraclios rose from the ground and grasped his sons. "We will gratefully accept your offer to return to the city."

"Of course," Odysseus replied and spoke quietly to one of his men. "You are to escort Heraclios back the palace, they will be treated with the same respect as you treat me."

"Yes, King Odysseus."

"You will find my wife and inform her of what has taken place and that I wish Heraclios be granted the most comfortable quarters available within the palace walls. You may also meet Eudorus on the road. Tell him to detach one hundred men to aid us here but return the remainder of the men to the city."

"It will be done."

Odysseus needed to think. He moved away from all that were present and tried to understand the attacks. Why assault a lowly fishing village, the gains must have been pitiful? These were a simple people. They scratched a meagre living from the sea. They worked, slept, and prayed that was all. *They prayed...* the words triggered something in his mind. He set off at a brisk pace, passing his men without a word. Thirty paces away he saw what he sought. His father had gifted a magnificent statue to the people of this village. It was intended to protect the fishermen. A shrine to the one God that had mastery of the seas. As he reached the shrine, he began to understand that the attackers had come to the village to carry out an act of discretion. There was nothing in the village to tempt pirates into violence. So why risk the wrath of Poseidon. He studied the impressive statue as it gazed over the open waters. It could have been a beautiful sight, if not for the blood that had been splattered across its features. The statue had brought slaughter to the shores of Ithaca.

"You!" Odysseus called out to his nearest warrior. "Gather the men and tools. I want this statue tipped into the waters."

"My king?" The warrior was clearly not keen on angering a god. Especially, one as powerful as Poseidon.

"It has been desecrated. We will make sacrifice and seek forgiveness later. But I want it down before nightfall. Do you understand?"

"Yes, my king."

*****

The sun had disappeared from the sky by the time Odysseus placed his foot on the steps, meticulously carved from rock, leading to the main gate of his palace. As he expected, Penelope was standing at the entrance, a worried look on her face. He raised a tired hand in greeting. She raced forward and embraced him, caring nought for the filth that adorned his entire frame.

"I have made Heraclios as comfortable as possible, but I fear the spirit has died within him," she announced as she placed a gentle kiss on his cheek.

"Thank you, my love. I made a mistake and others

have paid the price for my arrogance," he replied.

"Arrogance? Odysseus, you cannot see into the future, and you can only act on information that is known, who knows why the raiders broke their pattern."

"Pattern, they broke their pattern," Odysseus said to himself. *Why did they break their pattern? Something has taken place in their own lands forcing an early attack, possibly. Did they know I was planning to lay a trap? That would mean we have a traitor within the city or... one of the allies of Ithaca is the traitor? And finally, why have their attacks become more violent and usually concentrating on religious festivals and temples?*

He had contacted various states asking for help in ridding the world of the raiders. Each of them had suffered similar attacks and he had thought it fitting that they should be present in the raider's destruction. *But which ally is an enemy posing as a friend?*

"I've lost you, haven't I?" Penelope asked.

"Sorry, I'm just thinking," Odysseus replied, his mind still searching for answers that would not come.

"Well, come and bathe. You're filthy and you will not embrace our son in that state."

*****

Four days later, Odysseus held his goblet high, saluted his friend Hector, and then proceeded to salute each of the men that were seated at his table.

"I give thanks to you, my friends. Our coast has been

plagued too long by these vermin of the sea. Many of you have travelled days to stand at our side. I give thanks to Poseidon, for bringing you safely to my humble home."

"I could be tempted to let these sea demons take you if it were not for Penelope. She is far too good for you." The reply came from the warrior to Hector's left.

"But who would warm my bed, Achilles?" Penelope asked.

"The greatest warrior in the entire world is seated before you," he replied.

Penelope rose and approached Achilles. She ran a gentle hand along the warrior's muscular arm, an act that caused murmurings around the table. "You are a fine warrior, but I fear your strength is all in the limb and not in the mind. Besides, I hear that the blade you use in battle is all the length you have to offer."

The room erupted in laughter and Odysseus slapped his friend on the back. "Restrict yourself to combat with swords, Achilles. I believe that when tongues are used, Penelope has the best of all of us." Odysseus held up a goblet in salute to his wife.

The drinking and eating continued late into the night. When Odysseus determined that each of the men were sufficiently at ease, he raised the issue of the marauders.

"I realise that Ithaca has faced more raids than most, but we are not the only ones to have suffered at the hands of these sea dogs. We cannot carry the fight to them because we have no idea from where they sail. For three years I have employed trusted men to travel in many different lands. They have had one task - to gather information on the raids and those responsible. Four days ago, they struck my lands. This attack was far more brutal than previous incursions."

"They are becoming troublesome. We have had attacks near Phthia, an entire village was raised to the ground," Achilles was clearly angry at the atrocities. "They must be fools to attack my lands."

Odysseus had a feeling that Achilles was more concerned about his reputation than the plight of his villagers. "It is worse than you think. I have reports that they are growing in number and becoming more daring. They have attacked the lands of Lokris, which is many days ride from the coast. Whoever leads these men has been blessed by the gods with ability. They hit and slip away without suffering loses." Odysseus replied.

"They have destroyed a number of our trading vessels," Ajax, cousin to Achilles added. "I concur with Achilles, they may be brave, but their actions are foolish. They create enemies of us all."

Odysseus struggled to keep the smile from his face. It was no surprise that Ajax would agree with Achilles. He was a huge, mountain of a man. However, he yapped at the feet of Achilles like an energetic pup.

"Fools, brave, gifted – what does it matter until we can bring them to task? To do that we must know where they call home. We cannot take war with the mist." Hector announced, "My own lands have been relatively unscathed, but it's clear that if these bastards remain free to pick and choose where to attack, then all our lands will suffer."

Odysseus nodded in agreement with his old friend. "There is little that we can do now. I am sorry that you have had a wasted journey, but at least this night can be one of merriment. Despite his guests being unable to help him destroy the raiders, their arrival did allow Odysseus the opportunity to observe those around the table. He was not foolish enough to believe that they were all loyal friends but had hoped that they did not hold treachery within their hearts. To his left Penelope was seated next to Hector, then came Glaucus of the Lyceans. His next guest was an unusual one at such a gathering. Mursilis was a part of the royal Hittite family, but his homeland had been struck by the raiders several times. Odysseus had extended the hand of friendship in the hope of fostering a profitable relationship. He had seen how Troy had benefited from using an open hand rather than the sword. Then came several individuals that Odysseus did not know, with the exception of Aetes, trusted friend of Hector's, and Patroclus who was never far from Achilles. The rest were loyal aids to the other men around the table. Directly to his right sat Achilles and Ajax. Both were mighty warriors, but Odysseus wondered if they could also be devious.

He watched his guests for most of the night, allowing the wine to flow freely in the hope that it might loosen tongues. However, as the hours passed his guests revealed nothing of any consequence and after Penelope had left the men to their drinking, Odysseus decided to take a walk in the gardens. It was not long before Hector was at his side.

"You look troubled my friend," Hector remarked.

"I sense troubles ahead, but by the gods I cannot see from where," Odysseus replied.

"My father agrees with you. He seems determined that his time is nearly at an end, and that Troy will crumble to dust on his passing."

"Does he not say from where the danger comes?" Odysseus asked, his interest stirred.

Hector gave an abrupt laugh. "That would be too easy. My father has always placed too much faith in a disturbed sleep and understanding the ways of the gods. I find it is of little help in the world of men."

"But Priam is concerned?" Odysseus pressed.

"Yes, he has given orders that a great wall be erected around the city. I have never known him so worried. He is not easily panicked, so I must take his concerns seriously. Even if he cannot explain his fears. We have no obvious enemies. My father has fostered good relations with all that could threaten our city."

Odysseus tried to reassure Hector. "You need not fear Ithaca, old friend."

"Do not make a promise you cannot keep, Odysseus. Both our lands are at the will of our larger neighbours. Sometimes, we must take the blade to those we admire to prevent our own lands facing slaughter."

"I cannot deny your argument, Hector. Let us hope

that the turbulent waters calm. I have no wish to bring the sword to my friends. Besides, it may come to nought and other states look far more certain to fall into war."

"You talk of Sparta," Hector replied, his face suddenly looking even more solemn.

"Thyestes fears the sons of Atreus. If one of them ascend the throne of Sparta, then it is only a matter of time before war breaks out."

"Thyestes is not a man to have as an enemy. But I have met Agamemnon when we were not yet men. He has a fire in his belly that I believe will only be quenched with his uncle's death. I agree, there will be war."

"Then let us pray that it does not come to our shores." Odysseus held up his drinking vessel in a salute to peace.

"I will drink to that my friend," Hector replied, raising his own vessel to his lips.

Chapter 27

'Sibling Rivalry'

The old man picked his way along the coastal path. It seemed to him that it had been far too long since he felt the soil beneath his feet. The ragged grey cloak did little to stop the breeze that swept in from the waters, but he felt no chill in his elderly bones. He stopped for a moment to watch the hare no more than ten paces away as it searched for a meal. He wondered if the simple creature knew happiness. Then the animal stopped, suddenly alert to an unseen danger. It burst into a run and disappeared into the thick undergrowth. Moments later, a shadow appeared on the ground where the hare had once been. The old man looked to the sky and observed a bird of prey as it soared on the breeze.

"Is it not always the way. Where there is prey, you will find an eager predator."

He continued his journey. The coastal path carried him along a part of land that jutted out into the see. A large rock marked where it ended, and the cliff edge began. He climbed onto the natural structure and sat taking in the beauty before him. He reached into a small leather bag at his side and took out an apple. The fruit was a deep red, the kind of colour found in rubies of perfect clarity. He rubbed the apple on his tunic, enhancing its brilliance. As he raised the apple to his mouth, his attention switched to movement in the water. A whirlpool had suddenly appeared. The waters circled around and around, with the centre being pulled down towards the seabed. They began to move faster, and faster still. Then, when it seemed impossible for them to further increase their speed, a huge waterspout shot from the centre, reaching into the sky. The spout began to travel along the surface of the water, closing on the cliff edge.

As the spout reached the cliff, the bottom section smashed apart on the rocks. However, the upper section continued to the land and began to take shape. A figure was revealed. Its armour depicted scenes from the ocean and the helmet held the carved image of a hippocampus, rather than a plume. The arms were powerful, one of which held a mighty trident.

"How very theatrical, brother," said the old man.

"I think the least we can do for our followers, is create a sense of wonder, Zeus." His eyebrows raised at Zeus's outwardly appearance.

"Our brother is late," Zeus replied, ignoring his brother's attempt at a sly insult.

"He thinks it adds to his importance. I just think it is arrogance."

"Not arrogance, Poseidon." A figure rose from out of the earth. "My duties are plentiful and pressing. Some of us have more to do than merely swimming with fish."

Hades brushed a speck of dirt from his robe, which

seemed to Zeus darker than the darkest of nights.

"Shall we not bicker, we have important matters to discuss," Zeus suggested. As he did the apple rolled from his lap, it dropped from the rock and picked up pace as it hit the ground. The momentum of the fruit did not cease until Hades trapped it under foot. The god of the underworld bent and retrieved the apple, but as he held it in his hand it began to wither. In the briefest of moments, the fruit crumbled to dust.

"All things turn to dust, Brother. Why should we worry if someone hurries it along?" Hades brushed the dust from his hands as he replied.

"You have dwelled in the darkness for too long, it prevents you seeing beyond your nose," Poseidon replied. "It is not only the humans that are threatened. Someone is moving against Olympus, against the gods themselves. Why are you so sure they won't also look to your domain?"

"An accusation? You may have forgotten but I rule the underworld. The only followers I obtain, have one foot placed firmly in the world of insanity. I have no need of worshippers. The world of men believes in me because they have no choice. The god you seek is full of self- importance, the kind who arrives by whirlpool."

"Enough!" Zeus stepped in before his brothers came to blows. He liked this part of the world and had no wish to see it reduced to ash. "Hades, whether you care about those who die or not, you should care about who is trying to claim power in Olympus. Perhaps, they wish to remove the old order? That would mean that even the great Hades would perish. I suggest that we join forces to hunt down those that threaten our existence. After all, it would not be the first time that we have put our rivalries aside."

"That was before I was abandoned to the underworld. I will hunt these gods, but I will do it alone. I have no need of Zeus or the king of fish. Now forgive me, but I have duties." Without another word Hades sunk back into the earth.

"That went well," Poseidon announced.

"It would have been helpful if you were more welcoming," Zeus suggested.

"He was never going to help. When will you learn? Hades has drifted too far to return to the family embrace. He blames us for his woes, rather than take responsibility for his own actions."

"We are not without blame."

"He tried to kill you and destroy Olympus! When will you see him for what he is?" Poseidon shook his head with obvious dismay. "I will send word if I hear anything of value." Before Zeus could reply Poseidon turned back into a spout of water and disappeared over the cliff's edge.

Zeus shook his head. "It seems gods and men are not so different. No matter the power, affairs of the heart destroy us all."

*****

Hades returned to the underworld, but the journey

had not soothed his rage. His blood boiled at his siblings' arrogance. They had cast him aside, ignoring his very existence, only to call on him again when trouble loomed. He clenched his fists, his body on flame with at his hurt pride. Just as it seemed he would surrender to his fury, a stray strand of thought flickered within his mind. Something was not quite right, although he could not put a name or reason to the imbalance.

A voice sounded from the darkness. "You look troubled, my love."

Hades looked up to see Persephone walking towards him.

"My brothers weigh heavily on my mind," he replied.

"Your brothers always do. I think this is different."

"They claim that a hidden foe challenges our power." He looked around at his surroundings. "Power?" he gave a wry smile. Poseidon seems to think that I am up to mischief."

"And Zeus?" she asked.

"Who knows his mind? Catching his thoughts is like capturing the mist."

"But you are Hades. You can capture the mist," she replied, and gave a brief chuckle.

He grasped her by the waist and pulled her close. "You know what I mean," he replied, in a mock stern tone.

"Then what do you believe?" She placed her hand

over his heart. "Is it the gods jumping at shadows, fearful of losing what they have, or is there a real danger?"

Hades did not reply immediately. He stepped away from her and began to pace up and down.

"Would you take a walk with me?" he finally asked.

"Of course," she replied, "where are we going?"

"For some time, I have felt that there is a breach in my world. I cannot answer for the world of men or Olympus. However, the underworld is mine and even if I haven't witnessed a change, I sense all is not right. I must walk this place."

"Then let us walk." She took him by the hand.

*****

The hairs on the back of Hades neck rose, as it did whenever he became aggravated. The walk with his wife had revealed no answers.

"It seems my senses are at fault."

Persephone squeezed his hand. "I do not doubt your senses, my love."

Hades did not reply, he was looking at the great walls that guarded Tartarus.

Persephone followed his gaze. "Surely, nobody would be foolish enough to enter that place?"

"If that is true, where is Cerberus?" Poseidon asked.

She looked around; confusion etched on her face.

"I do not understand, he never leaves this place."

"Go find Cerberus. The foul tempered beast is never too pleased to see me."

"What do you intend to do?"

"I am master of this place and that includes Tartarus. First ensure the beast is unharmed, and then you may follow me," he placed a hand on her cheek, "but ensure that you remain on the path, even the gods must walk with care within those walls."

"But…" She tried to reply, but Hades was in no mood for conversation. He turned away from her and strode toward the colossal bronze walls that held so many captives.

*****

Hades stood within Tartarus. Before him a man pushed a great boulder up a mountainside.

"Your task seems tiresome," Hades mocked.

"I feel honoured that the master of the underworld sees fit to visit me. Two visitors in such a short time, I am starting to think I am missed."

Hades waved a hand, and the great boulder came to a stop.

"What do you mean two visitors?" Hades demanded.

"Did I say two? Perhaps my exertions have made me see what does not exist," Sisyphus replied.

"Do not play games with me. Who was here?"

"I saw no face to attach a name." Sisyphus replied, a smile appearing on his tired face.

"Tell me what they required of you, or..."

"Or what?" Sisyphus interrupted. "You will punish me? Tell me Hades do you have punishment that will rival my eternal damnation? Or perhaps you will destroy me? Forgive me if I do not tremble with fear."

"You should. I am sure that I could best my brother in ways to increase your torment." Hades scowled as he replied.

"Then do it. Waste your time on me and allow those you seek to place further distance between them and you. I know nothing of any worth, even if I did my lips would remain sealed. Be gone! I have a task to complete."

"You have a task, but it will never be completed." Hades strode away from Sisyphus without a backward glance.

Hades had no further success with other doors. Either the prisoners were absent or unable to shed light on who had infiltrated Tartarus. He was becoming angry. His mind searched for answers. Someone entering his kingdom without permission was annoying, but the individual who had released the captives was playing a very dangerous game. For what reason would they unleash such unpredictable forces?

He stepped through another door; broken pottery scratched at his feet. His unease turned to deep concern. He moved deeper into the room, crouched low and began sifting through the broken amphorae.

"Hades!"

"I thought I told you to stay on the path, Persephone?" he replied.

"I am not a weak mortal without power, Hades." She looked around the room. "What is this place?"

"It has no name. Those that knew of its existence would rather not."

"But why, what did those," she pointed to the amphorae, "contain?"

"The world of men has seen many beasts. Usually created by gods or titans and constrained by the deity that breathed life into them. The creatures that inhabit those vessels proved impossible to control."

"Then why not simply destroy them?"

"You may as well ask why not destroy Cronus. It proved more difficult than you would imagine. Their bodies were mere flesh and perished, like all flesh. But the essence of the creatures lived on and would return to cause chaos. Hephaestus created the vessels that would contain the creatures and prevent them returning to wreak havoc. The essence of each of the creatures was mixed with the clay that made the vessels."

She stared at him with concern. "Are the creatures destroyed if the vessels break?"

"In truth, I do not know. I think we have more pressing matters," Hades replied.

"What could be more pressing?"

"Why enter a room and simply destroy amphorae? It is my belief that the individual responsible for freeing the captives has also taken some of the vessels, the destruction was an attempt to hide which ones."

"We must send word to Olympus."

"Poseidon already thinks I am guilty of plotting against them, this will add weight to his claim." His faced hardened as he imagined the accusations he would face.

"But you cannot remain silent. Sooner or later those creatures will be unleashed." She moved closer and placed a hand on his shoulder. He put his hand on hers, grateful for her comfort.

"As always, you're right, Persephone. I will send word and request a meeting with my brothers." Even as he spoke the words Hades knew that it was a lie. He could not deny that he had on occasion allowed beasts to escape, had set them free in the world of men to cause death and devastation. He did not do it through a hatred of man. He did not deem them worthy of hatred. His actions were to cause irritation to his brothers, nothing more. However, his choice of beast was always part of a plan, one that he could crush within his hand when it suited or ceased to be entertaining. This was different, but he knew that his brothers would place the blame on their troublesome sibling. He gave a wry smile, part of him could hardly blame them. He admitted that he found life in the underworld tiresome. The tormenting of Zeus and Poseidon at least provided some respite from the boredom. He took Persephone by the hand and began the journey back to the giant bronze walls that protected Tartarus, deciding the best action to take was to wait and watch. Sooner or later, the beasts would surface in the world of men.

*****

Zeus returned to Olympus. He could not deny his concern for a future bathed in shadow, but for the father of the gods, concern did not equate to fear. He had vanquished his own father, put paid to the chaotic titans and put an end to countless power struggles with lesser gods. He'd even defeated his brother, Hades, in his attempt to rule more than just the underworld. In truth, he did not blame Hades for his disquiet. When Zeus defeated their father, casting him into the bowels of Tartarus, Hades may have expected a better fate than to be master of the dead. He understood his brother's anger, Zeus however, had made promises to enable him to win the war with Cronos and the titans. The underworld was all he had left to offer Hades, and despite his brother's rage, he was one of the few he would trust to guard Tartarus.

He strode through the magnificent gardens granting only the briefest of interactions to the other deities. Even his wife Hera, received only a raised hand and a polite smile. He moved through the palace, crossed the throne room and entered a long-deserted corridor. Only one other being had ever placed a foot within that place. It was the one thing that Zeus had followed in the path of his father, and like his father had done, Zeus headed toward the plain, heavy timbered door in the distance. As he approached, the timbers creaked into life without feeling the weight of his hand. Slowly, they swung open, the age of the doors announced in the high-pitched complaint at being forced to move. Only darkness lay beyond.

The first step across the threshold was taken reluctantly. Only the most powerful being could enter this room. Zeus may have had the power of the heavens coursing through his every sinew, but if the room, or rather what it contained, sensed weakness then he would be turned to nought but dust. He felt his first step land and gave an audible gasp. He moved forward, and as he did, torches burst into light, illuminating each side of a small causeway that spanned a bottomless chasm. At first, the torch lighting matched his pace, but then began to race ahead. Finally, they split from their parallel path and formed a circle. At its centre a large shape, dark as the deepest chasm, drew his entire focus. He strode forward, eager to close the gap between himself and the object. As he neared, he could see the exquisite architecture of the structure. It was a throne, but unlike any observed by man or God in all the world, or any world for that matter. Skeletal figures of men and beasts flanked the seating area, this was no throne to portray opulence or wisdom. Its reason to exist was power, it declared that those fortunate to take a seat had risen to be the ultimate being.

Zeus turned and lowered himself onto the throne. His fingers curled around the throne's arms that ended in the sculptured form of human skulls. As he did so, a soft humming broke the silence. As it became louder, the bottom of the throne began to emit a brilliant white light. It rose the seat of power and engulfed both throne and Zeus. It was not long before the entire room was bathed in the light, then abruptly the illumination and sound fell away. Zeus remained perfectly still, the throne beneath him was no longer as black as the darkest pit, it shone with the colour of deepest gold. The deity had not released his grip upon the throne. His eyes were closed as he felt the structure's power course through every sinew. His concern for the outer world had gone. No man, deity or beast would dare to challenge his might.

Chapter 28

'War Comes'

I t had made a pleasant change at first. Menelaus and his companions had swapped the salted deck of a sea vessel for the sweat covered backs of mounts. However, with little opportunity to rest and terrain that did nought to aid comfort, the King of Sparta would happily avoid horseback for the rest of his days. His back ached and skin of his inner thighs had been rubbed raw. He was relieved when Thanatos raised a hand and called out that they had reached their destination. Menelaus observed the clearing. It would have made an ideal location for an ambush. However, as he dismounted, the pain he felt drove any anxiety from his mind. He gave a grunt of discomfort and silently declared death preferable to spending any longer on the foul-smelling beast. He gave a stretch, trying to force the aches from his back but only succeeded in making his thighs sing out their pain. He closed his eyes and winced, as he reopened them, he saw a smiling Thanatos approaching.

"We have some time to rest and soothe our backsides," he announced.

"My arse is numb, but that is better than the lack of skin on my thighs. May the gods grant me battle rather than travelling on these creatures," Menelaus replied.

"You will feel better once a fire is lit."

"When can we expect our would-be allies?" Menelaus asked.

"Centaurs are a proud race. As such, they like to make an entrance and will arrive with a new day. But I can assure you that some eyes will already be within those trees. They're proud, not reckless."

"Then we should do nothing to cause them concern." Menelaus motioned to Terakles, one of his personal guards, should come closer.

"My King?"

"Set the guard, your best men that are not easily unsettled. Our allies may already be in those woods. It would be unfortunate if someone is too quick to violence."

"It will be done."

"And Terakles, double the guard. We are being cautious, not reckless." Menelaus smiled at Thanatos who nodded his approval.

"Come Menelaus, let us sit by the fire. We will need rest for the days ahead." Thanatos led the way to the warming embrace of the fire. A rabbit lay just above the flames, its flesh beginning to brown from the heat. Thanatos sat down; he lifted a blade and tested if the animal was ready to consume. He gave a sigh, that coveted his disappointment. Menelaus sat down at his side.

"Tell me, Thanatos," he kept his voice low not wanting

his men to hear. "You're no mere mortal. No man could have achieved or know as much as you. You have taken the name given to the god of death, are you a god? Or perhaps a sorcerer, that is playing a dangerous game?" Menelaus narrowed his stare, ensuring Thanatos was under no illusion that he was serious.

"Does it matter? Have I ever given you reason to mistrust me? God or man is not judged on his name, but on his actions. Tell me Menelaus, what does your name tell me about you?"

"I am Menelaus, son of Atreus and King of Sparta," Menelaus replied.

"Your brother is the son of Atreus, are you the same? There have been many kings of Sparta. I doubt many had your qualities. It is your actions that will set you apart."

Menelaus pondered Thanatos' reply but wasn't entirely satisfied. "And what kind of man would I be if I lead my people to war without knowing those that stood at my shoulder?"

Thanatos stared for some time at Menelaus, and then gave the rabbit another test with his blade. "Very well, Menelaus. I do not come from Olympus, but my home is also not the world of men. I am not without some… *gifts,* but I will not win you battles, blot out the sun, or turn back the waves. However, where I can help I will, and upon my honour I mean you no misfortune."

"But why do you help?" Menelaus pressed.

"I have my reasons. I have lived a long time and seen most with power use it to gain further power or wealth and do little for others. I have grown tired of the injustice. Now, can we forget what fills our minds, and focus on what fills our bellies?" Thanatos tore a leg from the rabbit and tossed it toward Menelaus.

The young king caught the food and resigned himself to the fact that the conversation was at an end. He sank his teeth into the leg, it was sumptuous. He closed his eyes and delighted in the succulent meat. His mind raced back to the first time he met Thanatos, on that day too, he was offered spit roasted rabbit. Menelaus doubted he'd tasted food so delightful in all the days in between.

*****

The night had passed without serious incident. Now and then, word was passed between the sentries that movement had been heard within the trees. Eager eyes watched for possible attack, but as time passed, the grip on spear or sword lessened, and men relaxed. Menelaus was left undisturbed through the night. Despite the length of slumber, he woke to sore muscles. Fresh water had been obtained from a nearby stream, enabling Menelaus to wash some of the tiredness away. It was during his cleansing that the long-awaited allies made their entrance. War horns sounded from within the trees. A startled Menelaus reached out for his sword, but Thanatos caught him by the wrist.

"No cause for concern. Our guests have arrived."

Menelaus nodded and pulled his arm back. "Terakles, pass the word to the men that there is no need for concern. Allow our friends to enter the camp." His guard nodded his compliance and raced off.

"You look anxious," Thanatos announced.

"Strangely, I am not used to speaking to centaurs."

"Speak truth at all times. Besides, it will not be the centaurs that you need to convince."

"What do you mean?" Menelaus asked his face contorting with confusion.

"The centaurs are fearsome warriors, but they will go where ordered," Thanatos replied as he looked into the distance.

"Tell me, Thanatos!"

Thanatos pointed toward the lead figure that approached the camp with at least thirty centaurs to her rear. "You will need to convince, Nephele. But be warned, you cannot hide the truth from her, but if you convince her to join your cause, then where she goes, the centaurs will follow."

"You wait until now to tell me that I must impress a god?"

"Nephele, is no god. Oh, she has power and far too much rage for one so beautiful, but she's no god."

"Wait rage? Why is she..." Menelaus began, but the figure he assumed to be Nephele, was too close for explanations. He decided to meet the danger head on. He strode forward leaving Thanatos behind, stopping a few paces away from the figure.

For a moment his breath-was taken away by her sheer beauty. He forced himself to focus on the task at hand and bowed his head to show respect.

"Nephele," his eyes moved from her piercing blue eyes to the warriors at her rear, "Centaurs, welcome to my camp." The centaurs acknowledged his greeting by giving curt nods, but Nephele remained perfectly upright. She stared directly at Menelaus. It felt as though she were looking into his soul.

"Tell me, son of Atreus, why should my people pledge allegiance to a boy, in a fight that they are unlikely to win?"

Menelaus raged within at being shown such disrespect. However, he dampened the burning fire of his anger and even managed a smile.

"I was warned that your tongue is as sharp as any blade. Shall we walk? I am interested to hear your views at length." Menelaus gestured the way. Initially, she did not move, then finally nodded her acceptance. They moved through the trees before coming to a stop at a small, fast flowing stream. Menelaus took in the scenery before closing his eyes and allowed the cooling breeze to wash over him.

"It's beautiful here," he announced.

"What! Oh yes, it is at the very edge of my children's lands," Nephele replied.

"I have no wish to place the centaurs in danger."

"Then why come?"

"War is coming to these lands whether the centaurs enter the fight or not. I did not choose this conflict. But in answer to your question earlier, the odds may be against us, but we will be victorious."

"One state against three."

"Spartans against three. A Spartan army that has received the best training and equipment. The only thing we lack is numbers, but quick victories can change that," Menelaus spoke with confidence, military matters drew his attention from his guest's beauty.

"The centaurs are great warriors, but not great in number," she replied.

"They do not need to be. I wish only for your archers to slow and disrupt the Tegean forces. If that is achieved, then my army will destroy the Argoans in the south. Once that threat is blunted, my force will march north to engage the Tegeans, and your task will be completed. Whether or not you choose to remain at our side will be for you to decide."

"And why should the centaurs' risk all?"

"Thanatos has told me that your people need a home. One that is protected from the greed and anger of men. I have such a place in mind. Aid me and I will ensure that the centaurs have a land to call their own where the borders will be as open or closed as you permit. No Spartan will raise a fist of anger against your people."

Nephele looked at Menelaus.

He wondered if she was studying him for signs of deceit.

"You speak the truth, at least what you believe to be the truth. But tell me of your brother, Agamemnon. I have heard that he holds honour more loosely than you."

"My brother is his own man, and I will not make a promise in his name. But I am King of Sparta, and my subjects are under my influence, not my brother's. Besides, Agamemnon would not be the reason that my word is broken."

"My people have been given promises by men before. What happens if your army loses? The centaurs will face the wrath of the Tegeans. We may lose what little we have," Nephele replied.

"Then I shall share your fate," he replied.

"What do you mean?" she asked.

"My army will be led by Agamemnon. I shall remain here with you and see the Tegeans put to the sword. If fate is against us, then we shall suffer as one."

For the first time there was something other than scorn etched within Nephele's face. Suddenly, a smile appeared, and she held out her arm.

"I do not know if we will survive this madness but let us return to our people. We will announce that Spartan and centaur will march together."

Menelaus took her arm and guided her back toward the camp.

"May I ask, why the sudden change? I was sure that you would refuse."

"In truth Menelaus, I have little choice. My children are hidden away in the shadows, a slow death for such proud warriors. If they are to die, then it is better to do so with the sound of war horns and alongside those worth dying for." She gave his arm a gentle pat. "Tell me, Menelaus, I will go to war for my children and if that means death then so be it, but who do you risk all for?"

"I would gladly let my uncle keep his stolen throne. Oh, I would like nothing more than pull his cold heart from his chest, but war will cost too much, even in victory. But you see, I have no choice. Thyestes has tried to end my life many times, and I have been content to disappoint him. However, now he hopes to kill my people, the luxury of staying alive is no longer enough. Both I and my brother must go to war and teach Thyestes a lesson that he should have left us alone."

"And who awaits your return?" Nephele seemed to be teasing him.

"Oh, you mean… Helen waits for me, I think."

"You don't seem sure?"

"Our union has been complicated," he replied. Heat rose in his cheeks. He wished the conversation would revert to military matters, once more.

"It may well be complicated, but you smiled as you uttered her name. It seems to me that its far clearer than you think." She laughed.

They came to a stop. Every set of eyes within the camp, whether it belonged to man or centaur, was fixed upon the pair. Just for moment, it seemed that even the creatures of the woodland had stopped to hear Nephele or Menelaus speak. It was the mother of the centaurs that stepped forward.

"My children we have new allies. When we have

shown them how centaurs make war, we will have a home, we will have a family, we will be free." Her words were greeted with cheers by centaurs and men.

Chapter 29

'A Warrior's Fate'

It was three days since Menelaus sent word back to Agamemnon that he had decided to stay with the centaurs. Since that day, the preparation for war had accelerated. First, Menelaus and the few Spartans under his command were led further into centaur land to meet with the main force of centaur warriors and Therans. In all, fewer than five hundred warriors were at his disposal, but he recognised that these were not usual warriors. He had witnessed the centaur exceptional skill with a bow. He doubted that any of his men could even draw the bows they used, let alone shoot with the accuracy and distance that seemed to come so easily to the centaurs. The Therans too, though no match for the centaurs, were no mere farmers with a blade. These men were hardened on the battlefield, and it was clear that killing came easily to them. It was with no little pride that he observed his own men. They may have been small in number, but each had earned the respect of both centaur and Theran. Menelaus felt his confidence growing, despite the number of enemies that he must face.

Two more days marching brought the warrior band far beyond the centaur borders, avoiding any settlements and well-trodden routes. Menelaus hoped the Tegeans would be oblivious of his force until the very last moment. Surprise and speed would be his weapon.

As night fell, small fires were permitted, guards set, and rest embraced. Taking his place next to the fire, Menelaus sensed excitement in the camp. In the distance, he could make out Nephele's slender form as she conversed with a centaur that-Menelaus had come to know as Dromicus. Both looked in his direction and proceeded to walk towards him. He rose from the fire reluctantly, it was a cold night, and the flames had begun to drive the chill from his bones. He moved toward the oncoming Nephele.

"Dromicus, has found them," she announced.

"How far?" Menelaus asked.

"We could use our bows within two days, but there is a problem," Dromicus replied.

"Which is?"

"The Tegean are on the move, but it does not move as one. The main part of the army, including a small, mounted force, move through the eastern marshes as we speak. The second force is with King Iamus, and his best troops. They seem to be avoiding the marshes."

"I know that terrain," a voice came from the dark. Thanatos stepped forward. "It may be called the marshes, but you could march three armies through there without difficulty."

"So why does Iamus avoid it?" Menelaus asked.

Thanatos barked with laughter.

"Trust me, if every beast in the world used the same place to shit, that place would still smell better than the marshes. The stench lingers, even after you have left the cursed place far behind, and flies plague your every step. Tell me, Dromicus, does Iamus take the mountain path?"

"Yes, but he has at least six hundred men. We cannot allow them to fall on our flank as we harass the main force,"

"Come closer to the fire." Thanatos collected a branch from the ground as the others gathered around. "The marshes lie within a long valley." He etched its position in the earth. "On either side, the terrain rises steeply. On this side," he pointed to the far edge of the valley, "only goats move with ease. It is far too treacherous to move an army. Across the valley, there is a path. It is a tight and unyielding terrain, the track winds like a serpent amongst the bracken. To move six hundred men will take time."

"Yes, but move they will. If we are engaged against the Tegean main force, then we risk being flanked. We may have to content ourselves with hit and run tactics, wear them down," Menelaus replied.

"What if I could ensure you more time?" Thanatos asked.

"How much?" Menelaus countered.

Thanatos smiled. "Allow me twenty of my men and

ten centaur archers and I will delay their progress for at least two days."

"But how?"

"I know the terrain and a few tricks. I will slow them down. Every step will cost them. Besides, they march in their own lands and will not expect what I have planned. Trust me, Menelaus. You can begin your assault on the main force."

Menelaus stared at Thanatos. He could not see how thirty men could delay six hundred well trained troops for such a length of time. But he also knew that Thanatos had never failed to carry out a promise.

"Very well, Thanatos. Take the men you need, but be warned if you fail, we all do."

"I will take my leave immediately. We have some distance to travel." Thanatos gave a respectful nod and turned away from the group.

"Dromicus, tell me of the main..." Menelaus began.

"Forgive me Menelaus, Thanatos before you leave, I would have a word with you," Nephele said.

She had disappeared into the night after Thanatos. Menelaus hid his shock by her departure by crouching low and observing the patterns in the earth created by Thanatos.

"Dromicus tell me, does the valley narrow as this suggests?"

"It does, and at this point," he pointed to a section of the make-do map, "provides both higher ground and cover for archers. If the Tegeans do manage to mount a charge, it will be easy to defend or slip away. But also, at this point," he gestured to an area beyond what Thanatos had created, "there is a bridge. In truth, the river is no more than a wide stream, but it has pace and I doubt there will be many willing to wade across while arrows assail them."

"And if the archers are cut off from the bridge?"

"You mean if the centaurs are cut off?" Dromicus corrected him.

"Yes," Menelaus replied without looking up.

"We would simply retreat and find a place to cross in safety. The river would hold few fears for my people."

"Then come closer, for I have a plan that may end the Tegean threat before it has even begun."

*****

Nephele caught up with Thanatos; for once she had shaken off her serene outward appearance. She bit her lip and her hands fidgeted, betraying her nervousness.

"I would have words with you, Thanatos."

"I have pressing matters, Nephele," he replied dismissively.

"You will listen, or I shall leave this place and my children will follow me!"

Thanatos gave a sigh. "How can I serve you?" The sarcasm dripped from his tone.

"My centaurs will go into battle. I have kept my side

of the bargain, Thanatos. But my love still languishes within Tartarus."

"You worry without cause."

"I worry because you have lied," she accused.

"What untruth have I uttered?" He asked calmly.

"You promised to free Ixion."

"And so, I have."

"I do not take deceit well." She paused unsure if she had heard him correctly "Wait what did you say?"

"Your love is free, but the years in Tartarus have taken their toll. He wanted to regain his strength and become once more the man that you knew."

Nephele held her hand to her mouth as the tears began to show. "I doubted I would ever see him again," she announced through sobs.

"I will never knowingly mislead you, Nephele. I am not your enemy. I may not be your friend, but I am your ally. I cannot succeed if you fail, and you cannot have what is in your heart if I fail. Like it or not, our fates are intertwined. But I must leave now, otherwise our preparation and our plan will be of little use."

"Yes of course," she replied, managing to smile through the tears.

*****

Agamemnon had received word that his brother was to remain with the centaurs. He did not fear for his brother's safety, he knew Menelaus possessed far more military intelligence than most. However, it presented Agamemnon with a problem. He knew the Argoan army was at this very moment marching toward Spartan lands. He also assumed that spies were watching for troop movement. They would expect to see the Spartan army split in the face of two armies approaching their lands. Agamemnon would need to create the illusion of a split, while still preserving his forces to face the Argoan threat. He called for a war council, where only the most trustworthy were invited.

He had decided to hold the meeting away from the throne room, he was not king, and would not show his brother disrespect by sitting upon his throne. Instead, he chose to have one of the many rooms within the royal palace turned into a war room. A large table had been man-handled into the room. He sat at the head of the table as he waited for the others to arrive. He wondered how the Spartans felt that war was coming because they had taken in the sons of Atreus. The people had only shown the deepest respect, but would they regret their charity should their own loved ones begin to die on the battlefield? He placed his fingers against his eyes and attempted to rub the lack of sleep from his vision.

"Where is my husband, Agamemnon?" Helen asked, bursting in on him.

"He's in your quarters nursing an injury obtained from hunting," he replied.

"Don't be a bloody fool! Where is Menelaus?"

Agamemnon motioned for her to come closer. Noticing that the door was open he kept his voice at a whisper.

"Sparta is in peril, Helen. Menelaus is recruiting allies to our cause."

"Why has it fallen to him? Could *you* not have recruited these allies. Or Pallas?"

"Menelaus is king. His words have weight that mine do not. I would gladly have gone in his stead." He added with a gentler tone, "He will return. It is important, however, that those beyond these walls believe that he is here within the royal palace. If they learn he has no protection, his life could be in danger."

"And at the moment there is no danger?" She pressed.

"There is always danger, Helen. That is why it is better not to invite more," he replied.

"Perhaps, it would be wise not to reclaim your father's throne." Her tone was bitter.

"The throne was stolen, and my father murdered. Not many would have simply walked away. But even if we did, Thyestes would still look to end our lives."

"All I know is that an enemy threatens my home, and my husband is nowhere to be seen."

"Menelaus does what is needed."

"Needed for Sparta or Agamemnon?" she spat.

"I know that there has never been any love lost between us, but you must know that I hold no ill-will to you or Sparta. I will do all in my power to protect both."

"The only thing that I know is that the great Aga-memnon will ultimately do what is best for himself. No matter the pain he inflicts on others." Without wait-ing for a reply, she spun around and stormed from the room.

He forced his annoyance at his brother's wife down deep as Pallas entered the room. However, he did notice the poorly hidden smile on Pallas's face.

"You find humour in something, Pallas?" he asked.

"It does an old man good to see a young stallion come close to losing his balls." Pallas made no attempt to hide his expanding grin.

Agamemnon sat back in his chair. "She needs to show more respect," he snapped.

"Hmm let me see. She is your brother's wife, which makes her," he stroked his beard as if searching the an-swer, "oh yes, that makes her queen. Besides, even if she stirred shit for a living, that one would still pay you no heed. You might as well try to tame the waves."

"She should still…"

"Don't make an enemy of Helen. At best it will drive a wedge between you and your brother. At worst, she will cut your balls off and feed them to you. Besides, we have more important matters to address."

"I get the feeling that you like her."

"I admire her from afar," Pallas gave a mischievous grin. "As you would a wild animal," Pallas replied.

"Not one to wed then?" Agamemnon chuckled.

"I would last two days. After that, I would either throw her from the city walls or willingly leap to my own death."

Agamemnon burst into laughter.

As they laughed, more men filed into the room. Aetolos, Gelo and Maeon completed the Mycenaean contingent, but Leon and Cleometes, both experienced Spartan commanders, joined the group. The last to arrive was Dorieus, who Menelaus, and the old king before him, trusted to gather information on both friend and foe. Agamemnon had little time for the man, but Menelaus valued his skills.

Agamemnon waited for the men to settle; he wanted their complete attention. He poured himself a drink and allowed the liquid to caress the interior of his throat.

"We know that Sparta faces danger," he began, his voice not more than a whisper. He was delighted to see every man leaning in close to ensure that they heard his words. Tegea and Argos march toward our lands, and Thyestes prepares his forces ready to strike. The enemy watches our every move..."

"As we watch theirs," Dorieus added.

"Of course - of course." Agamemnon hid his annoyance at being interrupted. He gave the man a pleasant smile. "But until now we have hidden our troop movements, we have tried to keep them guessing. If we are to win this war, then we must show them something new.
"

"You want them to know our troop positions?" Pallas

asked.

"I want them to see exactly what they expect to see."

"Which is?" Leon asked.

"They will expect our army to leave the city, leaving only a small defensive force. They know that we will not allow invading armies to run unchecked across our lands. They also know that we will be forced to fight on two fronts, and so, our army must split. We will not disappoint."

"How is this to our advantage?" Leon pressed.

"Because we are carrying out nothing more than a slight of hand. The Argoan army will march toward Sparta in the belief that the Tegean army does likewise. Unfortunately, for our Argoan friends, this will not be. Our army will split, and when the Argoans are committed to battle," Agamemnon pushed his two fists together, "our forces will become one."

"But how will the Tegean army be prevented from joining the attack?" Pallas asked.

"As we speak my brother, your king, has amassed a great force of allies." He embellished the size of the force,. "They, at the very least, will delay the Tegeans. This will give us time to put the enemy facing us to the sword or persuade them to forsake their attack on Sparta. Menelaus believes that our enemies today can become allies tomorrow."

"He wants us to defeat them without killing them," Pallas gave a snort. "That sounds like a boy's wish."

Agamemnon slammed his fist on the table. "That is your king, of which you speak, Pallas. Show some respect! Menelaus knows that this war will not stop until Thyestes or we sons of Atreus is dead. When I defeat the Argoans, the army will not return to Sparta. It will march north and will not stop until it is at my uncle's door. My knuckles will bleed with the ferocity of which I will knock on its timbers. Menelaus knows we will need all the warriors that we can muster. If that is former enemies then so be it." Agamemnon eyes burned with a fury normally reserved for an enemy on the battlefield.

"Forgive me, Agamemnon. I spoke out of turn," Pallas replied, as he lowered his head.

Agamemnon closed his eyes and allowed the rage to subside. He raised a hand and placed it on his old friend's shoulder.

"Pallas, my friend. Forgive my anger. No man has earned the right to speak freely more than you. But know this, Menelaus and I have known this day would come for many years. We have prepared, now is the time to put an end to Thyestes. Either he falls or we will. The time for choosing safety over danger is at an end."

Chapter 30

'Claw, Teeth and Blood'

Cineas walked with haste from the private quarters of Thyestes. A warrior for many years, he knew that even the most honourable were forced to carry out tasks that weighed heavily on the heart. Warriors were born to wallow in filth, but in all his years soldiering he never felt so unclean as when conversing with Thyestes. He wanted nothing more than to bathe and wash the man's influence from his skin.

He turned, making his way to his own quarters, when from the corner of his eye he spotted movement. He turned back and walked as nonchalantly as a man ready for violence could manage. He even pursed his lips together and whistled a tune. As he approached the place where he had seen movement, a large statue of Thyestes, he darted forward, drawing his sword. A figure dived from his blade, hit the floor but a moment later regained its feet. The boy held a long dagger and showed no sign of fear.

"You are out matched. Throw down the dagger and you may yet see another day."

"I will throw down my dagger, after it has opened Thyestes's throat."

"A noble quest, but one that you are ill suited to complete."

"What is all that noise?" a voice sounded from Thyestes' quarters.

Seeing the boy's concentration slip just for a moment, Cineas took his opportunity. Reversing his blade, he caught the lad squarely on the jaw. The boy dropped like a stone as his world turned to darkness.

"It is nothing my king. All is well," Cineas called out. He bent low, removed the dagger from the boy's hand and then lifted him bodily onto his shoulder. He moved quickly through the palace, beyond the courtyard and did not stop until he reached his own quarters. He dropped the body down and fetched water. When he returned, he was glad to see that his young captive had not woken from his enforced sleep. Without ceremony, he threw the water in the boy's face. He sat up with a start.

"I hope you do not wait for gratitude." The boy rubbed his jaw. "If you had not stopped me then Thyestes would already have perished by my blade."

"If I had not stopped you then you would be being tortured at this very moment. You would have given up the names of those who helped you and when you had finally told all you knew, your death would have been no easy matter. You may have so little regard for your own life, at least care for those that you place in danger."

"I made a promise to my father," the boy replied, as the fight seemed to leave him.

"And where is your father?" Cineas asked.

"Dead! Sent to his death by that bastard."

"I'm guessing that your father was sent to kill Menelaus and Agamemnon."

"My father and others. Now they're all dead." The boy could not hold back the tears.

"But you live?"

"I tried to fight, but I was not strong enough. I was told to run."

"And now you find yourself seeking vengeance against the biggest bastard of them all. What makes you think that you have the strength for this task?" Before the boy could answer Cineas was struck with a thought. "What is your name?"

"Bakchos," came the reply.

"How have you managed to return here and gain access to the royal household? Forgive me, but you do not look the sort to have the wealth to convince others to look the other way."

The boy looked ashamed.

"I hid in the trees until my father's killers had gone. I wanted to see my father one last time. As I stood over his body, a figure approached. I was sure that he would kill me, but he gave me coin and asked me to complete a task."

"Which was?"

Bakchos looked reluctant to reply.

"If I was your enemy, I have all manner of ways to loosen your tongue." Cineas pressed.

"I was to pass a message to a man, that is all."

"Which was?"

"I was told to tell a man called Cineas, that the birds that flew south to escape the winter shall soon return. But it seems I have failed to kill Thyestes, and pass on the message."

"Oh, I would not say that."

"What do you mean?" Bakchos asked.

"I am Cineas. You have succeeded in your task and perhaps one day you will use your dagger on that bastard's flesh. But for now, you will contain your rage. I will keep you busy and alive. But you must not move against Thyestes until I say, agreed?"

"Agreed."

*****

Thanatos had not dawdled once leaving Menelaus's camp. Even the centaurs within his small band struggled to maintain his pace. The relief of both centaur and Theran was visible when Thanatos finally raised his hand and called their advance to a stop.

"We have little time. Our enemies' advance guard are nearly upon us and if we are going to slow the column then we must first deal with the guard," Thanatos announced.

"Then we should take advantage of the high ground,"

Dromicus suggested. The centaur turned and looked toward Airlea. "With me, sister. I would keep you safe."

"I am centaur. I am in no need of a protector. I will choose my own ground," she replied.

Dromicus flushed with rage.

"You should try not to anger your brother. Family is too easily lost in times of war," Agapetos suggested.

"He angered me by rushing to a war that we did not want or could afford," she replied sternly. Then in a gentler tone added, "but I will stand at your side, if you will permit it?"

"Of course," Agapetos replied.

"May I suggest that we talk less and move more," Thanatos interrupted.

The last of the small band had just taken cover when the Tegean advance guard came into view. Twenty riders that seemed oblivious of their surroundings, ambled unknowingly into danger. Thanatos had never considered himself knowledgeable in military matters, he usually only had dealings with those that fell in battle. However, he knew that these men placed not only their lives in danger, but the column they were sworn to protect. He watched as they moved without a care into the trap. Already they had journeyed beyond where the first of his men had taken cover. There could be no retreat for these men. He heard Dromicus call out, a moment later, the familiar twang of bows sounded, and shafts of death sought out their target. Screams of men and mounts filled the air, as the Therans swarmed forward. The Tegeans died easily and quickly. Thanatos smiled, not because he took delight in the death of men, but because it was a task that needed to be completed. He walked among the dead, paying them no heed.

Dromicus moved to his side, the young centaur puffed out his chest, as if he had won some great battle.

"Shall we hide the bodies," he asked.

"No need," Thanatos replied.

"But the column will see them and be on their guard. We will have lost our advantage."

"If you want to clear the bodies away then do it. I am going to speak to our Tegean friends."

"What?"

"I am simply going to ask them to turn back."

"They will kill you!" Dromicus blurted.

Thanatos smiled. "That would be an interesting adventure. I suggest you fall back and make camp." Without waiting for a reply, he strode forward, leaving a clearly bemused Dromicus behind.

*****

All centaurs are warriors. The females at least a match at warfare as their male counterparts. Airlea, however, was not impressed with the slaughter as she stepped among the dead.

"Is this what we have become, Dromicus?" she called out.

"We fight to survive," her brother answered.

"By committing slaughter. We are no better than those who hunt our people."

Dromicus looked around at those listening. "Now is not the time." He stepped closer to his sister and whispered. "Not now Airlea, please."

"I agree, Dromicus. Not now. Not ever." She began to walk away but heard groaning coming from one of the bodies. Dropping down at its side, she flipped the man onto his back. The wounded soldier mouthed words, but no recognisable word escaped his blooded lips. Airlea placed a hand on his cheek, but as the act of kindness was carried out, the man's breathing slowed, his eyes showed the fear of death and then he was gone. "I am sorry," she whispered.

She was only partly aware of a figure placing an arm upon her shoulder.

"Come Airlea, let's leave this place."

She wiped her eyes and rose from the dead man's side.

"Will you walk with me, Agapetos?" she asked quietly.

"I will not leave your side," he replied.

His words raced along every part of her, their steps upon her skin, dancing across her breast until and they rested upon her heart. For the first time she looked up into Agapetos' eyes. Amongst the dead of an enemy that she did not hate, she suddenly felt a happiness that she had never experience before.

*****

Thanatos too felt delight. He had come to a halt when out of sight of all. He reached within his robe and pulled out the small black cube. He placed it on the ground in the centre of the track. He waved his hand, and the cube began to grow. Dirt and stone were cast aside as every few moments, the cube doubled in size.

When finally, it ceased expanding, and changing shape, Thanatos took the Blood Stone from his robe and held it aloft and called out, "You are summoned!"

The cube was now rectangular in shape. It began to shake. A crack appeared down the centre, a bright light emanating from the flaw in its surface. As the fracture widened, the light intensified to such an extent that any observer might think it would surely explode. Suddenly, the light and shaking had ceased, the crack was gone, the object's surface once again flawless. Except for a single amphora sitting innocently on its pristine top. Thanatos crossed to the vessel and plucked it from its former home. Within a moment, the magical housing of the beasts of Tartarus had returned to its former shape and size. Thanatos cast the amphora at the ground and stepped back, as he did so, he held the Blood Stone aloft.

The pottery smashed apart, releasing a thick black smoke gathering to form a shape. A torso, powerful limbs, and a head. This was no man. The hands and feet developed dark, curved claws, the head, elongated, and the mouth, and nose jutted forward. Within that mouth, were long yellow teeth, capable of tearing a man in half. The smoke cleared to reveal a wolf-like creature, focusing its attention on Thanatos. It sprang forward, ready to rip out the throat of its prey, but Thanatos held his ground. The Blood Stone began to rotate, causing the beast to halt its attack.

"Agriopas, how long as it been since you smelt fresh blood or sank your teeth into flesh?" Thanatos asked.

The beast did not reply, it merely growled its discontent at not being able to feast.

"Agriopas, tasted the flesh of a child and as punishment was forced to live as a foul creature for ten years. You were allowed to return to the world of men, but you had already tasted the delight of human flesh. It called to you, didn't it? Your beast-like form returned, without the intervention of the gods. You spilled the blood of countless people to satisfy your hunger." Thanatos moved closer, unconcerned by the beast's power or inherent fury. "You cannot kill me, Agriopas. But if you wish to run among the hills once more, to taste the flesh of man, then you had best calm your anger and listen to my words. Serve me and do as I wish, and I shall grant you freedom. Do as I command, and I shall use this," he held the Blood Stone higher, "to hide your bloodletting from the gods." Agriopas continued to growl his annoyance, spittle dripping from his fangs. "No? You wish to return to Tartarus. Very well." Immediately, Agriopas slunk back, whimpering pathetically as would a whipped dog. "Good, now listen."

*****

The Tegean column moved snake-like along the mountainous track. The width of the route only permitted four men to march abreast, and even that was tested on the sharp turns. It sapped both energy and patience. It was as they rounded a turn and entered one of the few lengthy straights, they spied a singular figure standing in the centre of the track. The column ground to a halt. Two men detached themselves from the front and walked toward Thanatos.

Thanatos raised a hand in greeting. "I offer greetings to the magnificent Tegean army," he spoke in a honeyed tone.

"Stick your greeting up your arse and move out of the way," the elder of the two warriors replied.

Thanatos chuckled. "I expect that usually works. Tell me, what is your name?"

"Iason," the warrior replied. Clearly a little unsettled that this lone man stood in front of an entire column showing no fear. "I said, move." His hand journeyed to the hilt of a sword at his hip.

"I imagine that you have fought many battles." Thanatos looked to the column at his rear, "unlike many of those in your ranks. Too many boys too eager to throw their lives away. But not you Iason, you're hardened by war. Battle has nothing new to show a man such as you."

"Enough!" Iason bellowed.

Thanatos held up his hands to calm the man.

"No need for anger. I offer you an opportunity."

"What opportunity could you offer me?" Iason asked.

Thanatos's face suddenly turned serious.

"I offer you the chance to live. Speak to your king, tell him to retreat and leave this place." Iason did not rely. He drew his sword. "That is disappointing," Thanatos announced.

A large, dark figure emerged from the rocks. The monstrous form leapt at Iason. Its tooth-filled mouth clamped tight around his throat, his scream was cut short as the powerful jaw slammed shut, biting off the warrior's head. The younger warrior at his side stood frozen. A massive hand, tipped with dagger-like claws grasped him by the face and smashed him to the ground, crushing helmet, skull and brain to pulp. Men in the ranks cried out as they formed a defensive line against the onrushing Agriopas. Like stalks of grass standing against the sickle, they were felled all too easily. Agriopas, rushed forward like a tornado whirling with rage. He tore limb from limb, as he closed upon his victims. Spears flew at him, increasing his rage, but caused little damage. This was no battle, it was slaughter. Before long the warriors turned and ran. At this point Thanatos called out to the monster.

"Stop! Stop Agriopas!" The beast reluctantly ceased its rampage and soothed its annoyance by feasting on a nearby fallen warrior.

Thanatos picked his way through the carnage, watching as the last of the Tegean warriors disappeared. It was unlikely they would return.

Thanatos counted the bodies. Thirty men lay dead, but he took no pleasure in their deaths. He looked at Agriopas as the beast dined on yet another warrior.

Thanatos felt nothing but revulsion for the creature. He stepped in close to the beast, which paid him no attention. Thanatos held up a hand. A long-handled sickle appeared, its blade curved and wickedly sharp. Without hesitation the weapon swept forward and took the foul beast's head. Thanatos tapped the small box shaped object that lay within his robe.

"I cannot kill you, Agriopas. But your fury is too much for this world. For the time being at least, you must remain within my control." The beast would not hear his words. It had been consigned back to his amphora, which, like the cube, had returned to its pristine condition.

Chapter 31

'Hearts and Minds'

Thanatos had returned to his small band's camp. The men's eyes were on him. He afforded himself a small smile as they sat around the fire and then crouched down to warm his hands on the flames.

"It will be a cold night. The track is perilous we had best remain here until the morning," he announced.

"Where are the Tegeans?" Dromicus finally asked.

Thanatos ripped some flesh from the creature that roasted over the firepit.

"I won't deny I feel ravenous," but as he spoke, he was reminded of Agriopas and the carnage along the track, "well, perhaps not." He threw the flesh into the fire. "Oh! Sorry Dromicus, the Tegeans are moving in all haste," he pointed over Dromicus's shoulder, "in that direction."

"But how?"

"I asked them politely to retreat. That was not warmly received, so then I asked them less politely."

"One man stopped an entire column?"

"You seem to forget that I am no ordinary mortal,

Dromicus. I have certain skills. In this instance, those skills persuaded the Tegeans to retreat. I doubt it will change their mind regarding the upcoming war, but they will not venture up this track again. We set out to give Menelaus time, we have achieved that."

"But..."

"Dromicus, I need rest. Besides, we leave as the sun rises. May I suggest that we take the chance to sleep. We don't know when the next opportunity will present itself."

*****

Agapetos did not enjoy the conversation at the fire. His distrust of Thanatos had grown each passing day. He rose from the warming flames and went in search of a place to lay his head. However, he observed a figure standing alone beneath one of the few trees that blessed the terrain. He strode over, not sure of what to say. As he got within a few strides a voice sounded.

"What news does Thanatos bring, Agapetos?"

"The Tegeans are in retreat. How did you know it was me?"

"Centaurs are excellent hunters. Mostly because we can pluck scents from the breeze," she replied.

"So, you're saying that I stink?"

Airlea laughed.

"No more than any other man."

"Why are you out here on your own?" he asked.

"Just using the silence to think," she replied.

"Oh, forgive me. I shall leave you to your thoughts." He turned to leave.

"No please Agapetos, stay. The noise comes from those that beat their chest, and cheer for war. My brother is the worst of them."

"He does seem to have a hungry desire for slaughter."

"And Thanatos feeds it. You asked me why I stand alone…-it is because I do not belong here. I want to run, put distance between myself and this madness. Better to be alone than watch my people die."

"You don't have to be alone." Agapetos stepped in close and placed his hand to her cheek.

"I could not ask you to leave your people," she whispered, but did not pull away from his touch.

"You didn't ask. Besides, I fear the same fate that awaits my people, awaits yours. They too are blinded by Thanatos' promises. Better to leave and spare ourselves the horrors of bearing witness to the conclusion of such foolishness. I have wanted to leave many times but had no vision of what life could be like away from my people. You have given me that. I will no longer kill for a promise of a homeland, for wealth, for Thanatos or a king of a foreign land. But for you Airlea, I would tear down Olympus with my bare hands." He moved forward and kissed her.

*****

Menelaus stood halfway between the centaur archers

on the high ground and the Therans guarding the bridge. He observed the lay of the land. He tried to picture how the battle would play out in his mind. He doubted that the Tegeans were aware that an enemy was close. That would mean an army racing to get clear of the wretched landscape would be tired and slow to react to any threat. They would lose plenty of men to the first couple of volleys from the centaurs. It was at that point a decision will be made. Would they press on and ignore the centaur hailstorm, or would they mount an attack on the high ground? If Dromicus had been correct in his report, this Tegean army was made up of farmers and boys. Most states had few experienced warriors, calling on their citizens to train and fight in times of need. However, there was always a strong base of men that knew what it was to fight a battle. If those warriors are in the second column that Thanatos intended to delay, Menelaus knew that this column would suffer this day.

The day was ending before he received a signal from the high ground, which meant that the enemy were drawing near. Slowly, he began to move back toward the bridge. Every few paces he turned to see if he could see the Tegeans, but he heard them before his eyes bore witness. Hundreds, perhaps thousands of them, the exact number unknown, marched as one. When just twenty paces short of the bridge he turned to see the enemy come into view. His eyes moved from column to the high ground, which if he didn't know to the contrary, seemed devoid of life. The column pressed on. Many in the ranks would have little or no protection. Even a basic shield would be slung on the back to make it easier to carry. Warrior or farmer, it made no difference when they did not fear their terrain. Suddenly, Menelaus observed what looked like a flock of birds erupting from the high ground. It rose into the air and then dived toward the column. Before it could land amongst the Tegeans, another flock flew into the air. Then it came, the undeniable sound of men dying. The front of the column that looked so uniformed, dissolved into chaos. They did not have time to organise before the second volley from the centaurs struck. More screams rent the air, but battle is not the place for mercy. It wasn't until after the fifth volley had landed, ripping cloth and piercing bone and flesh, that the Tegeans managed to form a wall of shields. It slowed the kill rate, but the centaurs were the finest archers that Menelaus had ever witnessed. Their power and accuracy were still taking its toll, so much so, that the Tegeans decided to launch an attack on the high ground. It was a pitiful affair. Around thirty men gathered behind the shield wall, and when ordered they burst forward. The slope of the land killed their pace almost immediately. Then shafts began to pluck them from their feet. Before long the attack was in full retreat, but the centaurs continued their slaughter. Tegeans that tried to reach their own shield wall felt the power of the centaurs, as long, dark shafts took them in the back. Tegean archers tried to answer the deadly missiles with their own but did not possess the range to trouble the centaurs. Finally, an unseen Tegean must have taken charge of the chaos. Two ranks of warriors with shield and helmet formed. To their rear, the Tegean bowmen and slingers filed into place. Slowly, the three ranks moved up the slope, the only purpose of the warriors was to keep the archers safe, so that they could unleash their own missiles.

This was finally the right tactic, Menleaus thought. The centaurs would be forced to give up their high ground. It was always going to be that way, but the centaurs had proved themselves a deadly tool on the field of battle. Now Menelaus wanted to see how well they held their nerve. It would be easy for them to see their position was in danger and take flight. It would also be easy to allow blood lust to overwhelm the senses and stay too long, allowing the enemy to inflict a heavy toll on their own ranks. Menelaus did not enjoy war, but he took delight in observing those that knew how to battle. The Tegeans slowly moved on, their ranks coming under constant missile fire. They were losing men but not enough to stop the advance. At the Tegean rear, archers and slingers would occasionally test the range to their target. Finally, as Menelaus continued to study the skirmish, a Tegean archer manged to drop his missile exactly on the centaur's position. The archer was unable to celebrate his feat, as two centaur shafts struck him in the chest and sent him crashing down the slope.

Menelaus whispered to himself. *Now is the time. Leave that place.* He turned, knowing that the battle for the high ground was over, and strode toward the bridge.

As he passed over the unsubstantial crossing, he observed the preparations made by the Therans and his own men. On their side of the bank, sharpened stakes had been driven into the earth. It was possible that the Tegeans, realising that the bridge restricted their movement would try a cross the narrow stretch of water. The stakes would make climbing from the fast-moving water troublesome. It also provided cover from the enemy's slingers and archers. On the bridge itself, two barricades had been erected. It was a simple plan. Force the Tegeans to use the bridge, slow their progress and restrict their movement. Make their numbers count for nought.

As he clambered over the second barricade he looked to the sky. The light was beginning to fail, he wondered if the Tegeans would try to take the bridge or wait for a new day. *So much had been left to chance. Had Thanatos been successful or had the Tegean second column been victorious? Would that column fall upon their exposed flank?*

He didn't have the men to fight an enemy to his front and on the flank. He wasn't even sure he had enough men to fight those across the bridge. *What he would give for a few ranks of Spartans at the head of the bridge.* He tried to drive negativity from his mind. His Spartans and the more heavily armoured of the Therans had taken up position behind the two barricades. He exchanged pleasantries with some of the men. One asked if the centaurs had succeeded in their task, to which, Menelaus gave an emphatic '*yes*'. He left the bridge and walked down the riverbank. The Therans had done well. One row of wooden spikes jutted out toward the opposite bank, while a secondary row acted as a barrier. He was pleased, it was an extra duty that he hadn't asked for but showed that these men could see danger and acting upon it, without the need for orders.

"When will they come, King Menelaus?" a voice

sounded.

Menelaus turned to see a relatively young Theran staring directly at him.

"What is your name?"

"Damaris," he replied.

"In battle, you may call me Menelaus. It is not a time to stand on ceremony." He looked to the sky. "I had hoped that the failing light would make the enemy set up camp for the night. But there is light enough to continue their march. Once they're certain our friends, the centaurs, have left the high ground never to return, then they will press on. So, Damaris, be ready. Keep your head low, there is no need to gift them an easy target."

"Yes Ki... Menelaus," Damaris replied, correcting himself.

"Just remember, if we deny them the riverbank then they will be broken on the bridge." Menelaus tapped the boy on the shoulder and moved on.

Any further interaction with other warriors was ended as the call went up. The enemy was coming. He made his way to the bridge, climbed the first barricade and then took his place amongst his men at the second.

"You should not be here, my king. It would be safer in the rear," the nearest warrior suggested.

"Gelo, when have you ever known me to look to safety when my men face danger?" Menelaus replied.

"But that was before you were king. Your brother will have my balls if you were to fall."

"Surely not, Agamemnon is such a kind and understanding man."

Gelo gave a bark of laughter. "Well, we shall see." Gelo pointed beyond the far riverbank. "It seems the Tegeans are eager we move off this bloody bridge."

"The bridge I don't mind, but I would gladly leave the stink of this place behind," Menelaus replied.

Gelo nodded. "I would rather not die with that rancid smelling shit in my nostrils."

"No dying today, Gelo. That's an order from your king." But his eyes were not on his friend. He was watching a lone figure approaching the bridge. "It would seem the enemy would rather talk than cross swords."

"Perhaps the bastards wish to surrender?"

Menelaus gave a wry smile. "I had best listen to what he has to say."

Concern spread across Gelo's face. "Menelaus, let me go."

"Fear not, old friend." Menelaus clambered over the barricade and trying his best to look at ease, strode toward the advancing Tegean.

He stopped when he was no more than a few paces apart and observed the sheer size of the man. It was not just the man's height, the limbs on the beast reminded him of a tree trunk. His overshot jaw jutted out giving him the appearance of a fierce boar. The man spoke with a great booming voice that matched the man's frame.

"Your feeble force is blocking a bridge that the Tegean

army wishes to cross. I demand that you remove your rabble without hesitation."

"Who makes these demands?"

"I am Androx, commander of the Tegean forces."

Menelaus had heard of Androx, his deeds on the battlefield a thing of legend.

"Tell me Androx, why does the Tegean army move in such force?"

"Merely training. Too many young warriors not long from sucking their mother's tit," Androx replied.

"That is a shame. I thought this was a coming together of two men with honesty in their hearts. You march to war against a foe that deserves no such attack. Two columns intent on reaching the lands of Sparta."

"Who are you?" Androx asked, clearly unnerved by the reply.

"I am King Menelaus of Sparta."

Androx raised his hands to show that they held no weapon. He stepped in closer to Menelaus and whispered.

"Look to Sparta, Menelaus. Leave the bridge and I will not harass you or your men as they return to their homeland. We are not the only army that marches this day."

"You speak of the Argoans. Their fate I fear will soon be settled. I give thanks for your generous offer, but I think we will stay."

"You cannot win, Menelaus."

"I have no need to win, Androx. I simply give my brother time, when he has put the Argoans to the sword he will march north. If that is to avenge my death, then so be it."

"You will not be swayed from this madness?" Androx's tone was almost pleading.

"We will stay," Menelaus replied.

Androx offered his hand. "Then may the gods grant you sanity before misfortune."

Menelaus took the giant's hand and then returned to the bridge. When he dropped down from the barricade, he glanced toward Gelo.

"Alas, he did not wish to surrender." Menelaus announced.

Gelo turned and called out. "Archers and slingers, make ready!"

Menelaus watched as the Tegeans neared. It was clear that they intended to use weight of numbers on the bridge, with their own archers and slinger attempting to thin the ranks of the defenders from the riverbank. As the enemy neared the river, Menelaus gave the order. The twang of bow strings was accompanied by the whir of the slings as they unleashed their deadly missiles.

"Concentrate on their archers!" Menelaus called out.

The Therans were trading missile blows with the Tegeans, the latter suffering far worse because they were exposed with no cover. Menelaus, however, watched the main Tegean attack approach the bridge. He needed to get his timing right. An arrow struck the barricade just to the left of his face but did not break his concentration. The enemy were being squeezed, as a throng of men tried desperately to gain access to the narrow bridge entrance.

"Now! Switch to the bridge."

The Therans did as ordered. Arrow shaft and sling landed amongst the Tegeans. Unable to move forward or retreat because of their own men trying to advance behind them, the Tegeans began to die. Even those that possessed shield could not raise them above their heads because they were too tightly packed together. But those that had managed to navigate the front of the bridge were now streaming toward the first barrier. Menelaus had insisted that his men travel with two spears. One was long and designed to kill while keeping the enemy at a safe distance, the second was shorter, and its purpose was to be hurled at an advancing enemy. The time had come to test his men in battle.

"Spartans! Make ready." He held his arm aloft and waited for the precise moment. "Now!"

They answered his order immediately. Only twelve men defended the first barrier and each of them used every bit of their strength as they hefted the spears toward the enemy. Men screamed out their agony as the missiles struck home. At least seven men were sent sprawling to the ground. As they fell, others were brought down, unable to avoid the dying and injured men.

As the Tegeans, pressed on the Spartans took up their defensive position. The first rank of four knelt with their spears pointing toward the top of the barricade. The second stood, ready to strike at anyone trying to climb over the formidable obstacle. The third and last rank waited to take the place of any comrade that fell.

Menelaus and Gelo took up a position between the second and third rank. The Tegeans reached the barricade, but were arriving as individuals, the charge had lost all its momentum. As the Tegeans climbed the barrier they were all too easily struck by the defenders. Some were run through, the spears tips ripping through bone and flesh. Others were knocked sideways, tipping them from the bridge into the fast-flowing river below. If they scrambled from the water toward the Theran side, they were quickly dispatched. It was becoming too easy for the defenders on the bridge. The Tegeans seemed incapable of mounting a proper charge and all the time, they faced a devastating barrage from the Theran archers. Before long, a horn sounded out, and the pressure on the barricade suddenly disappeared. Menelaus watched as the enemy streamed away from the bridge. Therans and Spartans cheered at their fleeing enemy.

"Gelo, how many men did we lose?" Menelaus asked, thankful that apart from a few minor injuries, all his men at the barricade remained alive.

"I will find out." Gelo headed toward the second barricade.

Menelaus knew the enemy would come again. They must have lost at least sixty men, but the numbers were still vastly in their favour. He doubted that they would make the same mistakes as they had in the first attack. The light was failing, if he could just hold them back for a little longer, he doubted they would risk a river crossing when the night shrouded their advance. It took a brave commander to risk a night attack where you could not see the foe or your own troops.

"Just a little longer," he whispered to himself, knowing that every day he slowed the Tegean's march would give Agamemnon the time he needed to defeat the Argoan threat. He looked to the distance; the Tegeans were already beginning to form up. Rather than just a single column they had an extended front line and the column itself was far narrower. Inwardly, he praised Androx, it was the tactic that he himself would have used. He could do nothing to counter the opposition's tactics, his position was fixed with no excess troops to disrupt the enemy. Gelo interrupted his thoughts.

"Four dead, two won't see another day and a further twelve injured, but they can fight," he announced through deep intakes of breath.

"They will need to," Menelaus replied, pointing in the distance.

"The Tegean learns quickly," Gelo announced.

"Unfortunately. We will just have to face the storm."

"Let the bastards come. My blade will cut ten as easily as one," Gelo replied.

Chapter 32

'Bring forth the Slaughter'

Agamemnon had been receiving reports about the enemy all day. As he listened to the latest of those reports he spied the edge of his blade. It seemed that the Argoans had been keen to grasp most of the glory for themselves. They had covered far more distance than would have been expected by the Tegeans. Although a testament to their marching prowess; it was no way to fight a war. Allies needed to trust each other. What surprised Agamemnon was that the Argoan command had neglected to inform either the Tegeans or Thyestes of their movements. No messengers had left their ranks. Agamemnon was as sure as he could be that the Argoans were intent on winning this war before their allies had wiped the sleep from their eyes. It meant that they had more than likely fallen for his ruse. The enemy believed they faced only a fraction of the Spartan army.

His scouts had brought no word of the Tegean approach. He wondered if Menelaus had been successful in slowing their advance or had his brother fallen in the attempt. He tried to drive the image of his brother lying dead from his mind. Now was not the time for such thoughts. His plan had been set for some time and the scout reports had given no reason to change it. His army would face the Argoans in two days. He rose from the rock that he had chosen as a seat. He hung his sword at his side.

"Break camp, we march!" he called out.

*****

Menelaus licked his dry lips. He glanced at the men around him, he knew each of them by name. Despite not being Spartan by birth, each of these men had only ever shown him respect. The old king had asked them to accept a young prince from Mycenae, and they had done so without hesitation. Now they faced death to defend their land because of a family feud that started many years before, in another land.

Switching his attention to the enemy that approached, Menelaus saw that the bridge was still laden with their dead; that at least would slow their advance. The enemy would attempt to attack the bridge and the riverbank, which would mean the Theran warriors would be dealing with the threat to their front rather than concentrating their missiles on the crossing. Menelaus crouched lower as Tegean missiles began to fall. He looked along the riverbank, the Therans were already replying with their missiles.

The Spartan in front of him suddenly jerked backward and landed at his feet, grasping at the arrow buried deep in his throat, eyes bulged as blood poured from the wound. The warm liquid ran into Menelaus' sandals. He bent lower and held the man's hand. At first the grip from the warrior was tight, making Menelaus' hand turn white, but then it loosened and with a long rattling exhale of breath, he was gone. A Spartan stepped past and took the dead man's place. Gelo grasped Menelaus by the shoulder and lifted him to his feet.

"We can mourn our dead after the battle. The bastards are upon us, with all due respect Menelaus, get off your bloody arse."

Menelaus drew his sword and nodded at Gelo.

"Spartans! You will hold your ground. Do not yield. If they want this bridge then they will lose blood with every step." His men growled their approval at his words as the first of the Tegeans attempted to climb the barricade. Spears rose to meet the attackers. Screams of pain and rage split the air. Menelaus glanced sidewards and saw Tegean men entering the river. Many of those fortunate enough to have a shield discarded them at the water's edge so as to not be slowed or dragged down.

Hundreds of men were now part wading, part swimming across the narrow river. A deep, growling war cry brought his attention back to the barricade. An enormous warrior clambered on top of the barrier, swinging a great axe that brushed aside two spears, and then swept down splitting a Spartan's skull in two. Obviously, encouraged by their comrade, the wave of enemy warriors seemed to intensify as more of them swarmed up the barrier. As the enormous enemy warrior lifted his axe once more, Menelaus swooped down, snatched up a spear and drove it forward. It took the warrior in the thigh. He screamed with rage and used the axe to break the shaft. The warrior dived toward Menelaus, but the young king was ready. He brought his blade up as the powerful warrior landed on top of him. Both men hit the timbers of the bridge, the breath driven from Menelaus's body. For a moment, the strength left him as he struggled to lift the enemy's weight from his body. Finally, he managed to roll the dead man away, but as he did so, another warrior appeared above him. Menelaus was helpless, his blade was still buried deep in the dead man's chest. His new enemy smiled at the easy kill, but the smile turned to shock as his throat opened from ear to ear.

"I can't keep picking you up. We are in the middle of a bloody battle," Gelo announced as he grasped Menelaus and lifted him to his feet. Gelo sliced the arm off an enemy warrior, but as the he fell, Menelaus saw the amount of Tegeans swarming over the barricade.

"We are going to fall back to the next barrier. Get a defensive line set to cover the retreat."

Gelo nodded and disappeared to the rear. Menelaus called out to his men to ready themselves to withdraw. He waited, giving Gelo time to complete his task, then killed an enemy to his front. "Back! He screamed. Dreading turning his back to the enemy, he forced him run behind the defensive line. He ordered his men to keep going and seek safety beyond the second barrier.

"You must go too, my king," Gelo called out, wincing in pain.

Menelaus reached out to prevent his friend from falling from the bridge. Looking down he saw a long black arrow shaft buried deep in Gelo's thigh.

Gelo cursed, then said urgently, "Go Menelaus, I will hold them here as long as the gods permit."

"The gods have better things to do than look to an old dog like you." Menelaus called to another Spartan. "Cripos, take Gelo to safety." Menelaus took the shield from the man as he supported Gelo's weight. "I shall return it to you, now go."

The enemy seem to have been momentarily surprised by the Spartans withdrawing, it had caused them to delay their advance. However, they soon regained the urge to move forward. Menelaus stepped behind the last two remaining Spartans that were not running for the second barricade.

"Lenaes, Ochylus, we will give our friends the chance to reach safety. Fall back but face the enemy. Are you with me?"

"Yes, my king," both replied. They threw their spears at the onrushing Tegeans and drew their swords.

Menelaus doubted that he would see another day, but if he must die then he would do so taking as many of the enemy with him to the next world. "Come on, you bastards!" he screamed. Glancing back, he saw Gelo had reached the second barricade. Turning he saw Lenaes take two Tegeans out with one sweep of his blade. Ochylus sliced the hand from an attacker, who fell past the Spartan, only for Menelaus to drive a blade into the enemy's chest.

The three fought in close proximity to one another, not only defending themselves but each other. Therans who had noticed Menelaus's plight had ignored the danger to their front and used their bows to thin the attack on the Spartan king. The Tegeans kept moving in for the kill, but time and again they would fall to a Spartan blade or Theran arrow. Fifteen paces short of the second barrier, Lenaes was speared, his shin bone smashed apart. It brought him to his knees, despite the agony he must have felt, he killed the owner of the spear. Menelaus was helpless as he observed the brave Spartan overwhelmed by the enemy. Menelaus and Ochylus now backed away, fearing that the enemy could out flank them. The Tegeans, however, did not seem overly keen on engaging the Spartans that were proving so difficult to kill. Then Menelaus heard a familiar voice.

"Make ready. Kill the bastards," Gelo screamed.

Suddenly, Tegeans were dying as a volley of short throwing spears struck home.

"Run you fools," Gelo's voice sounded again.

Menelaus and Ochylus did not need to be told a second time. Both turned and raced to the barrier. They clambered over the obstacle, Gelo stood grinning at them. Menelaus grasped the man by the arm. "My gratitude, Gelo."

"If I let you die that old bastard Pallas would have the skin from my back. Now if you don't mind, I will find a healer and have this removed." Both men looked down at the broken arrow shaft embedded in his thigh.

"Cripos, you are to go with Gelo. He is not to return to the battle this day. That is an order."

Cripos nodded and helped Gelo away from the bridge.

Menelaus turned to observe the enemy, but as he did, horns blew in the distance. He couldn't understand why the enemy would withdraw after gaining ground. He then looked to the river. So many dead warriors floated on its surface, it made him wonder if the dead could be used as a bridge.

"Will they come again?" Ochylus asked.

"Not this day. I think they have had enough."

"I know how they feel," the Spartan replied.

Menelaus placed a hand on the warrior's shoulder. "You did well today. Eat and rest, for we do not know what tomorrow brings."

Menelaus watched as the last of the Tegeans retreated from the bridge. Across the river, too, their warriors looked forlorn as they moved away from the river. Menelaus suddenly felt the day's exertions weigh heavily on his limbs but knew that this was not the time to rest.

"You have done well today men, but our task for this day has not yet come to an end. When our enemy has retreated, and night has fallen, then we shall once again occupy that barrier. I doubt our guests across the river will be pleased when they wake in the morning to see that their previous day's work was all for nought."

"Why do you think they gave up the position?"

"They were losing too many men to continue the fight. I can only guess, but I think they realise they cannot take the bridge until their second column arrives. Perhaps Androx believes that his men would lose heart and his army would run if compelled to continue fighting and dying for a few timbers across a river."

"That's what warriors do?" A Spartan replied.

"I doubt many of those are warriors. Farmers. traders, fishermen are not warriors unless defending their homes. They rushed to war, whether through choice or enforced. I do not doubt their bravery, but a poorly trained army are ripe for the slaughter."

It was not long before fires began to be seen in the distance as the enemy made camp for the night. Menelaus wiped the tiredness from his eyes. His entire body ached, and he wanted nothing more than to sleep. Glancing around, a mixture of twenty Spartans and Therans stood ready for his orders. He went to speak, but his throat was dry. A warrior offered him water, which he gratefully accepted.

"No torches, we move silently and in darkness. We cannot be sure what awaits us on the other side of the barrier. If we come under attack, do not wait for orders, retreat back to this point and prepare for the enemy."

Menelaus heaved his heavy body up and over the barricade. Within a few paces his feet began to touch those unfortunate warriors that had fallen in the day's fighting. Here and there he would hear an injured man call out, begging for help, but in the darkness, it was impossible to know if it was friend or foe. Despite the body-strewn surface of the bridge it did not take long before they had reached the barricade. Menelaus half expected the enemy to flock over the obstacle, but he could detect no movement on the bridge or riverbank. It wasn't until his men had formed up to make a defensive line that he felt sure that the enemy would not attack. They had missed their opportunity.

"Pattos," Menelaus spoke to the youngest of the Spartans under his command, "I want torches along the length of the bridge. When that is done look to any injured and take them to our healers."

"And the enemy?"

"They will be treated as though they were our own men."

"If we put torches along the bridge, will it not show our position? I am sorry my king, I do not mean to question your orders." The young warrior looked ashamed.

"No apology is necessary. The enemy will more than likely already know. I would like them to see that we care for their injured. If there is to be peace, gestures become important. If war is to continue then perhaps our injured may receive similar treatment."

"Yes, my king."

Menelaus heard rather than saw Pattos carrying out his orders. Menelaus then placed his back against the barrier and slid down the timbers until he was seated on the surface of the bridge. He closed his eyes.

*****

Menelaus felt a hand on his shoulder. Cripos stood over him, offering him food and water.

"I thought I told you to rest until the morning?" Menelaus asked.

"And so I did," Cripos replied.

"What?" Menelaus jumped to his feet. "Why did nobody wake me?"

"I am sure they would have done so, had it been necessary."

"But..."

"This small band of warriors need you, Menelaus. But even kings need to sleep. Besides, the enemy do not look interested in moving off their arses."

Menelaus blushed slightly, he still found compliments difficult to accept. "The centaurs, have they returned?"

"They have, most took up position on the riverbank. But they have also set guards at any fords along the river. We will know if the Tegeans plan to flank our position."

"And Thanatos?"

"No sign, but there is also no sign of the Tegean second column."

"Good. Did Pattos find many injured?"

"Only two of our own men, but we now care for sixteen of the enemy. Our healers say they will not die. What would you have us do with them?"

Menelaus considered the injured men. He wished them no ill will, but in battle the last thing that you need is enemy troops behind your lines.

"Have the men build some litters. We shall carry them

beyond the bridge. Besides, it will take minds from the thought of battle. It is not helpful to dwell on what might happen."

Cripos shrugged. "It never weighed on my mind."

"That is because you're a bloody fool," Menelaus replied. He could not keep the smile from his face.

Cripos crumbled up his face. "Hmm - I never thought of that." His face broke into huge smile, highlighting the lack of teeth within his mouth.

*****

Airlea avoided her brother on the journey back to the main camp. She'd even kept away from the other centaurs, her thoughts of leaving weighed heavily on her mind. As the small group neared their destination, her thoughts turned from concern to horror. As they headed toward the bridge, evidence of the previous night's battle showed its ugly reality. The dead, far too many to count, were floating in the free-flowing river.

As she observed the twisted forms as they moved involuntarily on the water's surface, she paled as she imagined those forms to be centaurs. Her eyes reddened, and tears welled as she fought to hold onto her emotions. Just when she felt she would lose control, a warm, strong hand grasped hers.

"I am here, Airlea."

She turned her head and looked into the eyes of Agapetos. "So many dead," she replied, her words broken with emotion.

Agapetos pointed to a group of centaurs in the distance. "Keep your eyes from the fallen. Look to your people. They have survived the fighting and seem in good humour."

As she looked toward the group, they held up a welcoming hand. Her face remained sullen, without the merest hint of a smile. "For how long, Agapetos?" she asked.

He clearly could not think of the words to soothe her misery. He gave her hand a reassuring squeeze, but a moment later, Agapetos was thrown into the air.

"My sister is not part of this alliance!" Dromicus raged.

Immediately, the centaurs and Therans turned on one another, blades drawn.

"Stop it!" Airlea yelled.

Agapetos regained his feet. "Out of respect for your sister Dromicus, I will refrain from gutting you. I offer comfort only and my intentions are honourable. Perhaps you should show Airlea more respect."

Dromicus growled his discontent. He moved forward, his hand dropping to the blade at his waist. His fury and movement, however, was brought to an abrupt end, as he felt the cold surface of a blade at his throat. Airlea held the blade, and she showed no sign of reluctance at the act.

"Do you like slaughter, Dromicus?" she demanded.

"Airlea, don't," Agapetos pleaded.

"But this is what he wants. The chance to spill blood, to gain a glorious death. No matter the cost."

"But it's not your way – or your cost to pay," Agapetos replied. He raised a hand and placed his palm against the blade, forcing it from Dromicus's flesh. "We should continue to the camp."

Airlea turned and without a word, left Dromicus far behind.

Chapter 33

'Make Allies from an Enemy'

The news of Thanatos' arrival had been broken to Menelaus. Despite his eagerness to learn news of the Tegean second column, it would not be proper to chase after him. He would wait for his mysterious friend to venture to the bridge. He turned back to observing the Tegean camp. They seemed unwilling to continue the fight.

"What are you waiting for?" he whispered to himself.

"They probably think that their second column is about to smash into the rear of our small force," a voice sounded from nowhere.

Menelaus jumped. He turned to see Thanatos smiling.

"How... But...You-" Menelaus's words failed him.

"For a man of my age I can still move with haste."

"And silently it seems," Menelaus replied, regaining his composure.

"Yes, that too. But enough of my skills, I bring favourable news."

"You managed to delay the second column. I am surprised that you have returned so soon. I only expected a messenger."

"There was no need for us to remain in the mountains. The Tegean column has not only been delayed, but it has also been turned back. I imagine those Tegeans," he pointed over Menelaus's shoulder, "will receive word soon enough."

"How could you turn back an entire column with so few men?"

"In truth we encountered very few. Their numbers counted for nought on such a narrow track."

"But even so.?"

"We had surprise on our side. They were not expecting to be attacked in their own lands. Panic swept through their ranks long before they could organise themselves. But we should not question our good fortune, we should embrace it." Thanatos closed in on Menelaus and dropped his voice to a whisper. "We both know that I have skills. I have brought the centaurs to fight under your banner. I have convinced the Therans that your paths are the same. I also have creatures that will serve only me. They are dark, violent beasts use only when absolutely necessary."

"And you used one of these beasts?" Menelaus asked.

"I did."

"Where is it now?" Menelaus glanced around at his surroundings half expecting a dark form to leap from the shadows.

"It is gone. It can neither harm friend nor foe."

"I am grateful to you, Thanatos. Both I and my brother owe you more than we could ever repay, but I do need to know what those I go to war with are planning. What I, my men or my allies do, reflects upon my family's name."

"I understand," Thanatos replied.

Menelaus was more than aware that Thanatos's answer was not one of a willingness to comply with his wishes, merely an acceptance that those wishes exist. He was about to press Thanatos further, when Cripos called out.

"Movement in the Tegean camp!"

Eight mounted Tegeans were moving away from their camp and headed toward the bridge.

"Cripos, Pattos you are with me. Thanatos are you..." Menelaus realised that Thanatos had disappeared as quietly and silently as he had arrived. He shook his head. He was beginning to feel unsettled by Thanatos. However, he had more important concerns. He clambered over the barricade and waited for Cripos and Pattos to join him. As they landed with a thud on the bridge's timbers, he began a slow walk toward the oncoming Tegeans.

"Is this wise, Menelaus?" Cripos asked.

"Probably not. If we must fight, then we will. But if there is a chance of turning the Tegeans away from our lands without bloodshed, then I will take it."

He watched as the mounted Tegeans brought their horses to a stop, dismounted, and began walking towards him. He recognised Androx, but the Tegean commander was not the man leading the small band.

Both groups came to a stop with only few paces apart.

"Tell me, Menelaus. Why is the King of Sparta so far from home?"

"I would have a name before matters are discussed," Menelaus replied.

"I am King Iamus, and I demand an answer."

The king's words were severe, but Menelaus sensed that the Tegean king was far from confident in his position.

"Be warned Iamus, you may ask, but never demand. I am willing to discuss a better future than what is currently promised. But you should not see my willingness to talk as being fearful to fight. Now, speak your mind."

"Why have you brought an army to my lands?"

"Because you sought to wage war against Sparta. With the Argoans and my bastard uncle you have hatched a treacherous plan. One that displeased me and brought dishonour to your household."

"The plan was not mine and you talk as though we had a choice," Iamus replied.

"You always have a choice. You could have sent word to Sparta. My forces would have fought at your side. Thyestes is not a man to be trusted. To be his ally is no better than being his enemy."

"That may be, but what are your intentions now?"

"I have already achieved what I intended. I merely wanted to slow your army. Both columns are bloodied, and despite your presence, I guess that your second column is at least a day, perhaps two behind your mounts. It will take time for you to organise an attack on the bridge. By then, my brother will have crushed the Argoan threat with the entire Spartan army at his command. He will then march north. So, the question should be, what do *you* intend now, Iamus?"

"If the Spartan army stands against Argos, who fights here?"

"You already know that I have more than just men serving my banner. No men in the world could have rained down arrows on your column at the distance that we did yesterday and the creature that struck at you in the mountains is just one of many at my command. You cannot win this war, Iamus. That is unless," Menelaus paused to add weight to words, "you stand at my side. We could take care of your dead. All warriors deserve respect."

"My King Iamus, Menelaus cared for our injured and returned them to our lines," Androx announced and then added. "He has acted with honour."

Iamus raised his hands to his eyes. His obvious exhaustion preventing him from clear thought.

Menelaus leaned in close to Iamus and whispered.

"I have no wish to war with the Tegeans. But you leave me a problem. The Spartan forces will march on my uncle. We cannot leave his allies free to attack us from the rear. You have a simple choice. You must choose a side. Join me, Iamus. I cannot promise you victory, but I can promise that Sparta will not abandon Tegea, no matter the price."

Iamus looked into Menelaus's eyes, he then turned to Androx who gave a small nod.

"Very well, Menelaus. Tegea will march under the same banner as Sparta."

*****

To the south two armies faced one another across a narrow valley. The Argoans were in good voice as they screamed curses at the much smaller Spartan force. Agamemnon, however, was oblivious to the noise as he strode into the centre ground. He walked alone; his personal guard left behind.

Abderos, King of Argos, was not so reckless. Six men stood ready to defend him. Agamemnon, however, paid them no mind. He walked right up to Abderos, a broad grin on his face.

"Abderos, it has been too long since we hunted together," he announced.

"Stand your army down. Surrender Sparta to my forces and perhaps we will hunt again one day."

"I am sure that Thyestes has other plans for me."

"If I take Sparta then I will be in a position to demand your life as payment."

"You really need to know your allies better. Thyestes will most likely take your head and your crown."

"Enough!" Abderos became enraged. "Surrender the field or you will die this day."

Agamemnon made no attempt to hide his amusement. "You are too easily angered. Too easily lured to battle and too easily defeated. Retreat now and if I feel generous, I will not hunt Argoan warriors for sport."

"Kill him!" Abderos shouted.

The personal guard were not expecting the order; that delay in reaction was more than enough to give Agamemnon the edge. Before their weapons had been drawn, a dagger was thrown and took down the guard to the left of Abderos, through the left eye. Agamemnon's sword was drawn and took the throat from one man and crippled another as it sliced through his right knee cap. Abderos backed away as his remaining men protected their king. One managed a slight cut to Agamemnon's shoulder, but his victory was short lived as he received a kick to the groin. Bent double from the pain, Agamemnon's blade was brought down and through the exposed flesh of his neck. As another guard rushed in, Agamemnon ripped his sword free of the dead man and used its hilt to break the on-rusher's nose. Then the blade was swung around and emptied the man's stomach onto the earth below. The last guard did not rush in.

"You can leave now. There is no need for you to die for this whore," suggested Agamemnon.

"He is my king," the man replied.

"Loyalty should be rewarded. I will kill you quickly."

The guard lunged forward. Agamemnon side stepped the blade and with one blow removed the guard's head. Abderos had not waited to see the fate of his loyal guard, both armies witnessed him run like a whipped dog, back to his own lines. The Argoan lines had fallen silent. Agamemnon smiled, wiped his blade upon the grass, and strolled leisurely back to the Spartan lines.

As he reached his own ranks, Maeon offered him a water skin.

"He's not going to be able to calm his rage. Angry men make poor choices," Maeon announced,

"That is the plan. Are our forces in position?"

"Yes, our fall-back position is ready. Aetolos has already set out on his mission, he will be ready to move when the time is right."

"I cannot see why Menelaus wants these Argoans for allies. They lack the skill for battle." Agamemnon shook his head with disgust.

"Perhaps, what they lack is a leader," Maeon suggested. "But we will test their quality soon enough,"

"It won't be long now." Agamemnon handed the water skin back. He turned just as the entire Argoan army began to move forward. This was no thoughtful strategy by Abderos, he had ordered his army forward. Obviously, the fool was keen to eradicate his shame, but Agamemnon knew that his opponent was just making one mistake after another. "Fall back!" he shouted.

*****

Abderos was clearly beyond rage. It seemed to his son that the king's every sinew craved the destruction of the Spartan army, he would not rest until he held Agamemnon's severed head in his hands. The army moved forward, but Diomedes placed a hand upon his father's shoulder trying to stop him from following.

"Father! We must call back our forces. The Spartans are retreating for a reason."

"They're retreating because we are advancing and they are outnumbered," Abderos replied, as he shrugged off his son's restraining hand.

"When have you ever known Spartans to run from battle?"

"If you're afraid, Diomedes, stay with the women."

"Father!" Diomedes tried to grasp Abderos's arm again, but the king brought his hand across his son's face, leaving the flesh red as evidence to his anger.

"Fight or run, but never lay a hand on your king again." Abderos turned and strode after his men. Diomedes followed but kept his distance. He watched as in the distance the Spartans began to disappear over a slight rise in the terrain. He knew that the attack was madness, his father had lost all reason. The ground beneath his feet began to rise; he could not help wondering what lay beyond the summit to his front. With each step the crest of the small hill came nearer and yet, he could not hear any sound of battle. Perhaps his father had been fortunate; maybe the Spartans were merely running away. For a moment, as he reached the summit of the hill, his eyes were blinded by the brilliant sunshine. He felt its warmth on his skin and allowed that warmth to wash over him.

He forced himself to open his eyes. The horror that met his vision brought his forward movement to an abrupt end. To his front, the entire Argoan army had also come to a stop. The Spartans had occupied the high ground to their fore and on the flanks. Their numbers had swelled threefold and now they had no intention of retreating. Diomedes tried to see his father among the ranks of his own men. Before he located the king, enemy missiles began to land. Archers poured their deadly fire into a disorganised rabble, Spartan light troops raced forward, using javelin and slingshot with devastating effect.

Diomedes forced himself forward; calling for his men to move aside. He needed to find his father. He called out his name, but no reply was heard. He pressed on through the men, who huddled together trying desperately to avoid the enemy missiles. Suddenly, he felt a burning sensation on the side of his face, and then the warm, unmistakable trickle of blood run down his cheek and onto his neck. It was not the time to tend to minor wounds. Ignoring the stinging pain, he forced himself through the front ranks of the Argoan army. His father stood five paces further forward, seemingly oblivious to the enemy's deadly fire. Diomedes observed his father screaming at the men to press the attack.

"Father! We must retreat before all is lost."

Abderos spun around a mask of pure hatred on his face. "You sniffling coward! I might have known that whore of a woman could only birth a useless coward.

Go, you are no son of mine."

"We must fall..." Diomedes words were caught short as he was forced to avoid a blade cutting his throat. There was no mistaking that his father had intended to kill him. "Don't father, I do not want to fight you." Diomedes took two paces back and became aware that the enemy missiles had ceased to land. His mind was brought back to his father who was advancing intent on violence. "I am not your enemy, father." Diomedes, however, drew his sword.

"If you won't fight, you're the enemy, a worthless dog not worthy of your bloodline." Abderos raised his blade and charged.

"No!" Diomedes screamed and brought his own blade up. Abderos stopped abruptly, the rage still etched on his face. Blood bubbled at his mouth.

"I will claw at you from the next world," Abderos announced, spitting blood into the face of Diomedes. His eyes rolled backwards and then he slipped to the ground, dying without another word.

Diomedes stared at his father. He wanted to scream his sorrow, to walk from the battlefield, never to raise a blade again. He looked to his men and then to the multitude of Spartans that stood ready to commit slaughter. He plunged his blade into the soft earth and then walked toward the Spartan lines. He half expected a spear or arrow to strike him down, but his only thought was to save Argoan lives. Perhaps then his people may forgive him, because he would never forgive himself.

A lone figure detached itself from the Spartan lines

and advanced on his position. Diomedes's concerns were raised when the same figure drew a blade, but then it too was driven into the ground. As the figure neared, Diomedes recognised it as Agamemnon, the renown prince of Mycenae.

"You are Agamemnon?"

"I am and who are you?" came the reply.

"I am Diomedes. I suppose I am now King of Argos," he replied reluctantly.

"You either are or are not. There would little point to us talking if you do not speak for your men."

"I am king," Diomedes replied more assuredly. "Whether that honour is deserved or not is another matter. Killing both father and king, is hardly an honourable act."

"You talk as though you had a choice. Tell me Diomedes, how do you want this day to end?" Agamemnon asked.

"I just want my men to be allowed to go back to their lands."

"That cannot happen."

"They played no part in the decision to invade Sparta. Each one is guilty of nothing more than loyalty to their king. They do not deserve death."

"I have no wish for their death. Besides, I would save as many as my warriors as possible. I doubt that even with our numbers and superior position that we could leave the field unscathed."

"You are welcome to the throne and my life. All I ask is that my men keep their freedom."

"I have no wish to sit upon the throne of Argos and if I wanted you dead, then you would already be so."

"Then what do you want?" Diomedes asked.

Agamemnon walked forward, placed an arm on Diomedes' shoulder and spun him around.

"My father lies within the ground. His eyes do not see the beauty of the day. My mother suffered the same fate, all because one man's greed. That man is also the reason your father lies bleeding in the dirt. I want vengeance on Thyestes. Join with Sparta and your men will walk from this land unhindered."

Chapter 34

'Freedom'

For seven days, Menelaus and his new allies remained at the bridge. It almost developed into a celebration. Tegean, Theran, centaur and Spartan, so intent on killing one another only a few days earlier, now shared meals and stories of their homeland. This change, however, did not sit well with Airlea. Although happy that the slaughter and screaming had stopped, she recognised that it could all so easily return to the bloodletting. She also noticed that much of the talking from all sides was on war with Mycenae. She missed Agapetos, away on a scouting mission, suspecting that it was her brother's influence that ensured that the Theran was absent from the camp. Becoming more distant from her people as each day passed, finally she strode away from the camp seeking solitude.

Leaving the campfires far behind, she walked at the edge of the riverbank, the full moon at least providing a little light. Her mind was tormented, she wanted to leave, but feared for her people. Nephele seemed to have fallen beneath the spell of Thanatos and her brother, the latter heart turning blacker with each day. She doubted that her voice would be heard; reason had left her people.

"Be careful, the bank can be treacherous under foot," a voice sounded from the dark.

Airlea was startled, but quickly recovered. She drew her sword and held it in the direction that the voice emanated.

"Be warned I am armed!" she called out into the darkness.

"You need not fear me. I am Menelaus, King of Sparta. I shall leave you to your thoughts," he replied.

"No wait! I would speak with you," she put the blade away.

"You are the sister of Dromicus." His voice betrayed the fact that he was moving closer. "You seem less..." He stopped speaking as if searching for the proper word.

"Of a bloody fool," she finished his sentence.

His laughter rang out and then his face appeared as the moonlight caught its features. "I was going to say reckless. Brothers can be very troublesome."

Menelaus had a pleasant face. Airlea detected no malice behind his eyes.

"Why do you seek out war?" she asked bluntly.

"I have never sought war. As a boy, my family was torn apart, and I had to leave all that I loved to stay alive. I found a new place to call home. A new people I could call family. In truth, that was enough for me, but the man that killed my parents, would not let me live in peace. I have lost count of the times he sent assassins to kill my brother and me. Now he sends armies and I must do battle, but I admit I would happily leave my uncle to his stolen throne, if only he would leave me in peace."

"And he would never do that?"

"No, he thinks that everyone seeks the throne as he did. Therefore, we are a constant threat until dead."

"And what of my people?"

"What do you mean?" Menelaus asked.

"Will you keep your word, provide a land they can call home and let them live in peace?"

"I can only give you my word again. I cannot prove to you that my heart is not filled with deceit. If I am still king when this war is over the centaurs will have a home within my lands, and the Spartans will safeguard it."

"But you have to stay alive."

"Even dead men can keep no promise. But I will say that your people are free to leave at any time. I will not hold them against their will, and they would go with my gratitude for the service that they have already given. But it is Nephele and Thanatos that you must convince to break camp, not to mention your brother."

"I would have more chance of convincing the rain not to fall." She was reluctant to ask the next question but pressed on. "Do you trust, Thanatos?"

"Thanatos saved my life," he replied.

"That is not what I asked," Airlea pressed.

"Both my brother and I owe a great deal to Thanatos.

However, I feel that his actions are part of a great game that he is playing. I do not know what that game entails, but more and more I feel that we are all just part of a scheme, of which we are only an insignificant part. So, the answer is no, I do not trust Thanatos, but kings rarely have the luxury of being able to trust. We have what others want."

"I wish I knew what path I must take."

"I think you should speak to Nephele. I have not known her long, but I do know that she has love for your people. Now I must return to the camp." He gave a respectful nod and disappeared into the night.

*****

Nephele was one of the few within the camp afforded the luxury of a shelter. The centaurs had erected a part branch, part animal skin structure. It was crude, but afforded Nephele protection from the elements and some privacy. She turned towards the equally crude entrance, when a rather timid sounding voice called out her name. Without seeing the owner of the voice, she replied.

"You may enter, Airlea."

The thick animal skin acting as a door was pulled back and a nervous Airlea, entered.

"Forgive me, Nephele. But could I speak with you?"

"Of course, my child. I had hoped that you would come to see me sooner, it has been too long since we last spoke. What troubles you?"

"I want to leave," Airlea had not been certain of that desire until she spoke it out loud. "I fear for our people, but I cannot...-will not wage war. There has to be a better way." She recoiled slightly, expecting wrath from Nephele. But the mother of centaurs raised a hand to Airlea's face and gave a comforting smile.

"I understand your concerns. I cannot in all honesty say that the path we are on is just or correct. I may have chosen poorly and that may lead to our destruction. I do not doubt your words, you were always determined, but tell me how you expect to survive all alone?" Nephele noticed a slight flushing in Airlea's face. "Ah, you will not be alone. Is it that handsome Theran?"

"He is kind and understands my heart," Airlea replied.

"But does he understand what the world is like for centaurs beyond the borders of their forest?"

"He does, but Agapetos is not daunted." Airlea could not help smiling as she mentioned his name.

Nephele did not reply immediately. She looked at Airlea as she fingered a bejewelled object about her neck.

"Have I ever told you of how I came into existence?"

"No," Airlea replied.

"Zeus wanted to play a trick on the father of our people, my beloved Ixion. Zeus believed Ixion to be in love with Hera. He used his great power, far more power than I could summon, to create me from the clouds. I was to be made in the same image as Hera and prove Ixion's disloyal intentions. But Ixion and I fell in love, even when he knew that I was not Hera, he offered me his heart. Even though our time was short, our love had become unbreakable. Come." Nephele held out a hand and walked Airlea to some furs that lay on the ground. After she had instructed Airlea to lie down, she fetched a small drinking bowl that contained water. "Do you love Agapetos?"

"I do."

Nephele took the jewel from around her neck. She held it above the bowl and squeezed. To Airlea's surprise the jewel seemed soft within Nephele's fingers. As she squeezed faint wisps of white smoke escaped from the jewel and mixed with the water.

"The jewel contains the last of the cloud from which I was created. It is not as potent as when it was first used, but we do not intend to create a deity and love can add powerful potency. But true love is sacrifice. If you flee this place, then both you and Agapetos would face dangers, I doubt that you would survive. The world of men is no place for a centaur. But as I was transformed from the clouds above Olympus, you can transform from centaur to human. "So, I ask again. Do you love this man?"

"I do, I truly do."

"Then drink." Nephele offered the bowl to Airlea. The young centaur took one last deep breath, and then drained every drop from the vessel. She closed her eyes; not knowing what to expect.

"Nothing has happened," Airlea announced, her disappointment etched on her face.

"I am not Zeus. You have three days. You and your

man must leave this camp and find a safe place. Be warned, Airlea, the transformation will not be a pleasant experience. You will need time to recover, but by the end the centaur in you will be no more."

Airlea raised her hand to her mouth.

"Agapetos is not here. Dromicus has sent him away."

"Your love approaches the camp as we speak. He is tired, but do not let him rest. Dromicus will seek to send him away again. Do not concern yourself with your brother. I will keep his mind on other things. At least, long enough for you to make your escape."

"Thank you." Airlea rushed forward and threw her arms about Nephele.

"Go, you must leave with all haste. One last thing," Nephele took the jewel from around her neck and placed it over Airlea's head. "Should you decide one day to return to your people, the jewel contains just enough cloud to return you to centaur form."

*****

Agapetos walked from the rest of the scouting party. He wanted to wash the filth of the day from his tired limbs. Removing both his weapons and clothes before beginning to wade into the river. The cold water made him shiver, but he was determined. As he made ready to fully submerge beneath the surface, a form burst from the bushes.

"Agapetos! Quickly we must leave."

"Airlea! I am naked." He turned away from her, "and

this water is very cold," he added quickly.

"Oh, I will turn my back," she replied, but allowed her eyes to linger on his muscular frame. "But we must leave. I will explain all, on the way."

"Could we not eat first?" Agapetos replied, as he struggled back to the bank. He hurriedly dressed, not an easy task in poor light and with hands that now felt like ice.

"We must leave. Nephele has given us an opportunity."

"Very well, but I cannot promise to match your speed."

As he neared, she moved closer to him.

"Are you tired?" she asked.

"Your brother has kept me busy. Yes, I am tired."

"Then climb on my back. I have strength enough for both of us."

"I will not," he replied sternly.

"Why not?"

"You are not a beast to be ridden. You are..."

"I am what?"

"You are..." He struggled to say what he yearned to say. "A proud centaur, deserving of my respect."

"You're a fool, Agapetos. Do you love me?" Her eyes widened as she waited for his reply.

"What? I don't think now is the..." He dropped his

gaze to the ground.

"Do you love me?" she asked again.

He slowly raised his head and looked directly into her eyes. "I have loved you since the first time that I laid eyes on you," he replied.

She took him by the hand.

"And I love you. Now please, my love, let me carry you, at least a little way."

He reluctantly did as he was requested.

"I'm not too heavy, am I?"

"For now, I am still a centaur and carrying you is no hardship." Agapetos wrapped his arms around her torso. "Oh, and Agapetos?"

"Yes."

"The water was not that cold." She laughed and took off without waiting for a reply.

*****

Agapetos felt the sun on his shoulders. The realisation that he was moving took time. Suddenly, he sat upright and immediately jumped from Airlea's back.

"You carried me through the night?"

"I wanted to put distance between us and my brother. It wouldn't surprise me if he tried to force me to return," she replied.

"Are you sure that you don't want to?"

"That is not possible. Let us rest and I shall tell you why. If you don't mind, I will let you gather the wood for the fire. I shall prepare some food."

"Of course." Agapetos could tell she was exhausted. He felt ashamed in his own frailty. He moved away quickly, determined to get a fire lit and Airlea fed, so she could rest.

It was not long before the fire was licking at a small pot that Airlea had the foresight to bring. Within, a mixture of chopped meat, roots and herbs that Agapetos did not recognise. The meal was mostly spent in silence as both hungrily devoured the food.

"What did you mean that it was impossible for you to return?" Agapetos asked. He was no longer able to dispel his curiosity.

"Last night I thought I was unsure whether to leave my people behind. But the moment I began to speak to Nephele, I knew that I must. Rather than be angry, she used this," Airlea fingered the jewel about her neck. Nephele told me that in three days I would no longer be centaur."

"How is that possible?" he asked.

"It is beyond my understanding of this world. But I believe in Nephele. She would not mislead me. When it happens, it is likely to be painful and I will need time to recover. That is why we must place distance between us and those that may follow."

Agapetos rose from the ground crossed to Airlea. He bent and kissed her.

"First, you must rest. Sleep at least for a little while. I shall watch for any that pursue us."

*****

It was a full day before Dromicus realised that Airlea was missing. His rage built with every step as he searched. It took a request by a messenger from Nephele to call a halt to the quest to find his sister. Reluctantly, he abandoned the search and complied with the summons. Though he visited Nephele in body, his mind still lingered on the whereabouts of Airlea.

"How fare my children?" Nephele asked.

"Fine," he replied.

"Any injured in the battle?"

"No." Dromicus knew that she would be with Agapetos. Perhaps some of his men would know where they would be.

"Dromicus! I am not used to one-sided conversations," she snapped.

"Forgive me, Nephele. My sister has gone missing."

"In my opinion your sister has always been more than able to look after herself."

"Yes, but…"

"There is no but, Dromicus. Your mind should be on the fate of our people not one individual."

"Of course, Nephele. Forgive…"

"I do not want apologies, Dromicus. I want you to

carry out a task for me."

"Is there no one else that could…"

Nephele's eyes burned with fire.

"How dare you!" she growled.

Dromicus backed away, terrified.

"Please, give me the task and I will see that it carried out."

"You will take five of our best men and seek out the Spartan army. I want to know if they were victorious and if they march to join Menelaus. We must know if our allies are capable of delivering on their promises." As she finished speaking, the fire in her eyes died. In a gentler tone she added, "complete this task for me and I will ensure that your sister is safe. You must apply your mind to the task in hand. The lives of many may rely on it."

"Yes, Nephele. I shall leave immediately." He turned and walked away.

Once outside he looked around the camp searching for one person. His eyes came to rest on a figure that sat next to a campfire. He moved forward quickly, knowing that he did not have much time.

"Thanatos, I would have a word with you," he announced. He loathed Thanatos, but knew he had little choice if he wished to bring Airlea back.

"How can I be of service?" Thanatos replied through a broad grin.

"Not here." Dromicus turned and walked away, leaving Thanatos no alternative but to leave the caressing warmth of the fire.

When far enough from anyone that could hear the conversation, Dromicus came to a halt. He waited for Thanatos to come close.

"My sister has left the camp with that bastard Agapetos. I need her to return."

"Forgive me, Dromicus. But what has this to do with me?"

"I have been forbidden from giving chase. Nephele has given me a task that cannot wait."

"And so, I ask again. What has this to do with me?" Thanatos's smile never faltered.

"You want the centaurs to continue aiding Menelaus. But my people are not happy fighting alongside the Tegeans. They have mistreated centaurs for many years. It would not take many words to convince them to leave, even if Nephele wants us to stay. They may even find employ with another king. Tell me Thanatos, would Menelaus enjoy seeing centaur archers defending Mycenae walls?"

"Be careful young centaur. You overreach, Dromicus."

He stepped closer to Thanatos. "I do not trust you. I do not like you. But bring my sister back and I will be in your debt. I have the ear of my people, which would mean you will also."

Thanatos stroked the neatly trimmed beard that

adorned his chin as he thought over Dromicus's offer. "I have men capable of bringing your sister back. But what of Agapetos?"

"I don't want him to return forced or otherwise. In fact, it would be best if he could not return at all."

"And if your sister will not return?"

Dromicus stared at Thanatos for a moment. "Then better that she was dead than living as a whore for a human."

"You have a great anger for one so young. But I will do this task. Although, I do so with a heavy heart. I have always liked Agapetos. But I will send men that like you, have no love for him and are skilful hunters."

Dromicus did not reply, but did offer a courteous nod, before taking his leave.

*****

Thanatos watched the centaur leave. He wondered if it would be easier for all if the hate-filled warrior met with an unfortunate accident. However, he had said that he would help and unless forced to, he would comply with Dromicus' request. He was about to leave when a voice sounded from the trees.

"I am becoming concerned. You are too easily distracted." A voice sounded from the trees.

"And you arrive uninvited and leave before the conversation is finished. It seems neither of us are perfect," Thanatos replied.

"First, you try to destroy the Trojan royal household,

then you send the Therans raiding lands, destroying festivals and statues. Now you are rescuing centaurs from themselves. Tell me Thanatos, how does this help our cause?"

"The raids were simply to show man that the gods to not care enough to watch over them. If they don't watch their own temples, how much can they protect a farmer's crops or ensure a full fishing net. As for the centaur, I have no concerns one way or the other, but I want his people beneath Menelaus's banner. What matters now is that Thyestes is destroyed, and Agamemnon sits upon the Mycenae throne."

"Be careful, Thanatos. We risk all."

"It seems to me that I am the one taking the risk."

"For now, but these things change." The voice seemed to trail off.

"And she's gone." Thanatos shook his head.

Chapter 35

'Different Paths'

More than one group had undertaken a journey. The Spartan and Argoan armies were marching to join the forces that were holding the bridge. A reluctant Dromicus and a small band of centaurs had set off to find the exact location of the Spartan force, under the command of Agamemnon. Airlea and Agapetos were attempting to place distance between themselves and the camp and hoped to find a safe refuge for Airlea's upcoming transformation.

Another group had left the camp. They did so in secret, with a very specific task to complete. Thanatos had been explicit in his command. If possible Airlea was to be brought back to her brother's embrace, however, if that was not possible both she and Agapetos were to die. The men were Therans, but that is where the similarity with Agapetos came to an end. These Therans had not fought for a new homeland for their people. Their reason to kill was to gain wealth and the excitement of battle. Other Therans avoided the group, only when a task required their *special* gifts, were they called upon. They were skilful hunters but were known for their savagery. If an enemy needed to be reminded to pay a debt or to stay clear, then the group would be employed to carry out the task. They slaughtered without mercy and revelled in the distaste that others held them in.

Krinos was their leader and believed in leading by example. It would be hard to find another man so lacking honour and empathy in the world of men. No act was beneath him. Taking another's life often weighed on a man's conscience, but Krinos delighted in both the act and the misery it caused. He also had nothing but pure hatred for Agapetos, who had taken the killer's left eye in a brawl that had left both men beaten and half dead. He would of course accept the payment offered by Thanatos for the task, but he would gladly have killed Agapetos for free.

The group had picked up on their prey's trail relatively quickly, but by the end of the first day it had gone cold. Krinos cursed and spat on the ground. It was more for show. He didn't want the hunt for Agapetos to be easy. He needed it to be hard, which would make killing the bastard all the more enjoyable. As for the centaur, Thanatos knew perfectly well that he didn't take prisoners. This was no more than being paid to murder, and that was fine by him. Krinos brought his men in close.

"That bastard Agapetos is no fool. He knows how to hide his tracks. We will split into four groups. We will spread out, one of us will pick up on his trail. But be warned, Agapetos will die at my hand. If you find him, bring him to me."

"What about the centaur?" The largest of the Therans asked.

"Gut her for all I care. You've all eaten horse flesh in

your time. I expect she will taste just as fine. Now go! Ampelio I will have a word."

The huge man nodded and waited for the other men to move away. "I know what you are going to say, Krinos. I am not to kill Agapetos."

"He gutted your brother, but your brother was a fool. If it wasn't Agapetos, then some other warrior would have done the deed. Having a quick mouth, but a slow blade is no way to live a long life." Krinos fingered the eye patch that stood instead of his left eye. "Agapetos, is mine, or you will answer to me."

Ampelio stiffened at the words but remained calm. "It will be enough to see his fate in your hands," he replied.

*****

Agapetos had started to become worried. The three days were coming to an end, and he was yet to find a safe place for Airlea. He wondered if he had made a mistake choosing higher, less travelled ground. Dromicus would expect his sister to choose woodland or plains to aid her escape. Centaurs were not best suited to mountainous terrain, though so far, she had coped well. After reaching the summit of a steep climb, the terrain fell away to reveal a hidden valley with a small stream that snaked between the rocks. There sat in one of the bends of the stream, a small hut made from rock and timber. He saw no signs of life and decided that it would have to suffice. To confirm his decision, Airlea let out a gasp of pain. He raced to her side.

"Look," he pointed to the hut, "just a little further and then you can rest."

Airlea seemed to be in too much pain to reply, offering only the slightest of nods. He supported her weight as much as possible, not an easy task, centaurs were powerful creatures. More than once he doubted whether they would reach the hut. As he neared, it became obvious that the dwelling had been abandoned for quite some time. Much of the timber was in disrepair and the roof would offer little shelter should the rains come. He forced the door open and peered inside. Only gloom and dust met his vision. He steered Airlea inside and laid her upon the ground. He bent down and gave her a gentle kiss.

"I will find something to make you more comfortable and get a fire lit." In reply she raised a hand and stroked his cheek. "I will not dawdle," he added.

Once outside, Agapetos spied the surrounding area. A fire pit lay just a few paces from the hut. He gathered some wood and began a fire. Once the kindling had taken, he took his dagger and cut into the grass and earth. He gathered enough for his task and carried them to the hut. Airlea had fallen asleep. Either exhaustion had overpowered the pain, or the pain had lessened, he had no intention of waking her to ask. He laid the sods of earth on to the ground and covered them with both his and Airlea's cloak. He examined the supplies that Airlea had packed. A small oil lamp would at least provide the hut with a little light. There was some food and small vessels. The ability to prepare a meal had never been one of his strengths. He glanced over at Airlea's bow. Knowing that they both needed a substantial meal, he picked up the weapon. Running his hand over its sublime form, he tried to draw the bow. His arms shook with the strength needed; he knew that hitting any prey would be almost impossible. He returned the bow to its resting place and took out his dagger. With a last look at the sleeping Airlea, he left the hut and found a suitable tree with which to fashion hunting a spear. When done, he left the hut, knowing that the fire would keep possible prey away. Staying close to the stream he searched for a suitable vantage point.

A small deer paid the price for venturing to quench its thirst. Agapetos flung the animal over his shoulder and moved quickly, fearing that he had left Airlea alone for far too long. Upon entering the hut, he could see his love beginning to stir, and by the expression on her face, the pains had returned to interrupt her slumber. He raced to the stream and filled a vessel, so that she would have fresh water. After placing the vessel at her side, he butchered the animal and placed it above the fire pit. As he watched the flames lick at the unfortunate beast, Airlea let out a terrible scream. He hurried to her side. The pain was so great that she sobbed. He wiped her eyes and offered her some of the water. She struggled to move to the makeshift bed, the strength seemed to have left those powerful muscles. In a moment of relative calm, she raised a hand to his cheek.

"My love, I do not want you to see me like this," she whispered.

"I will not leave your side," he replied. As he did so, for the first time he noticed that the floor on which she had previously laid, was covered in hair. He looked down to see the flesh was now exposed on Airlea's back and flanks.

She said in a weak voice, "You will not hear danger if I fill your ears with my screaming. Please my love, I will call if I need you."

"Are you sure?"

"I am."

"I will be just beyond the door." Reluctantly, Agapetos rose and left Airlea to her misery.

For a time, he remained standing on his side of the door. Each cry from Airlea made his heart feel heavy within his chest. He was a warrior; pain was a constant companion. He would give all he had to suffer rather than Airlea. As the night moved on, Agapetos crossed to the fire pit. He tapped at the rocks about the fire with his sword. The deer smelled divine but was merely sustenance offering little enjoyment. Staring at the fire, he became lost in the flames. The snapping of a branch upon the ground brought his mind into focus. He dived over the fire, feeling a sharp pain in his side as he did so. As he rose, he drew his sword. Four figures were highlighted by the flames. He pulled a dagger with his free hand and readied to battle.

The four men split and began to walk around the pit, the flames of which danced on the edges of their blades. Agapetos, however, was watching another, more impressive form, emerge from the darkness.

"Ampelio, how's your brother?"

"He will rest better after I have gutted you," the big man snarled.

One of the Therans darted forward, keen to register

a second hit on Agapetos's flesh. Agapetos blocked his lunge with his sword, into the man's left eye, twisting it before he pulled it free. The dying man grunted as he sank-to the ground with a thud.

"You should have brought more men."

"Arrogant bastard!" Ampelio reached behind his back and pulled a weapon out that most men would have struggled to lift, let alone wield in battle. It would have been more at home in the hands of a cyclops. It was a hammer capable of inflicting extraordinary damage.

Agapetos ignored the strutting giant. He took the throat of another Theran and then reversed the blade, plunging it into another's chest. As the fourth Theran swung his blade, Agapetos moved his impaled enemy into path of the oncoming sword. The offending blade lodged in the already dying Theran. Without hesitation Agapetos released his hold on his sword and darted forward. His dagger slashed at the fourth Theran's knees, causing him to scream with agony. Agapetos rose and, bringing the blade up and took the man beneath the ribs. Agapetos twisted the blade free and kicked the man into the fire. He retrieved his sword.

"Shall we stop playing now?" Ampelio asked. His vast bulk moved forward.

"You should have stuck to killing old men and children. You will find me a far greater foe," Agapetos replied, although he knew his opponent to be a skilled warrior. Perhaps, too skilled. His enemy did not possess speed, but his reach and power made up for that failing. Close enough now for Agapetos to observe food scraps within Ampelio' long unkept beard.

"Just two deaths tonight. One arrogant bastard and a centaur whore." He began to swing the great hammer above his head, and then swept it forward towards Agapetos' skull.

Doubting he could stop such a blow, Agapetos backed away.–Ampelio moved forward, but Agapetos maintained his distance, dancing around the big man, waiting patiently for an opportunity to attack. At all times Agapetos ensured that he could block the path to the hut, should Ampelio choose to change targets. His enemy brought his hammer down hard. The blow would have destroyed any warrior in its way, but Agapetos side stepped it and flicked out his blade. It slid up the handle of the hammer and removed two fingers, causing the beast to howl in both rage and agony. Ampelio, however, caught Agapetos by surprise as he dropped his weapon and grasped Agapetos before he could escape the bear-like hands. Ampelio used his head as he would his hammer and smashed it into Agapetos's jaw. Airlea's lover found himself dazed, lying across the hammer on the ground. He tried to rise, but Ampelio aimed a kick to his ribs. There was a loud crack as Agapetos flew into the air and then crashed back down again. Ampelio retrieved his hammer and then advanced. Agapetos reached out for his blade but found none. The hammer rose, Ampelio smiled as victory was assured. Agapetos could do nothing. He closed his eyes, expecting death.

A loud thud sounded. Agapetos opened his eyes. Above him Ampelio stood, the smile still in place. However, just below the nose a black shaft stood proud. He could see that most of the shaft had gone through Ampelio's head. Blood and brain adorned the dark shaft and tip. The hammer fell, landing between the legs of Agapetos. He blew out his cheeks at the near miss and was then forced to roll sideways as the huge frame of Ampelio came crashing down. Agapetos felt the pain of the broken ribs, and the sword cut to his side, but neither were enough to keep him from regaining his feet.

He looked to the open door of the hut where Airlea lay across its threshold. The bow was next to her form. He could hardly believe that she had summoned the strength to kill Ampelio. He crossed to her, pushing the door wider. To his surprise, his eyes no longer beheld a centaur. Airlea was completely human in shape and completely naked. Wincing at his injuries, he crouched low and grasped her within his arms, with no little effort, he carried her back to the makeshift bed. He laid her down on one cloak and covered her with the other. He was about to leave when she spoke.

"I think the worst of it is over," she announced weakly.

"I will get you some food and we will need to find you something to wear."

"I can make something from my cloak, as it will be far too big now." Her eyes welled with tears.

"How do you feel?" he asked.

"I have always been centaur. I... I don't know how I feel."

"Let us eat and rest, at least until morning." He stroked her arm and then rose, making sure that his face did not betray his wounds to Airlea. She had enough on her mind without concern for him. He hoped that Ampelio had been alone. Agapetos knew he would not have the strength to fight another enemy and fleeing was not an option.

Chapter 36

'New Beginnings'

A new day had brought the warmth of the sun. It invaded the hut like an invading army and fell across the rested bodies of Agapetos and Airlea. The former centaur slipped from beneath the arm of her love. Rising, Airlea took in her new form. Her torso, although a slimmer, hadn't altered drastically. Her gaze lowered to her legs or rather the lack of legs. Nakedness made her feel vulnerable. She crossed back to Agapetos and with some relief noted that he was still asleep. Picking up her cloak, she wrapped it about her body.

She eyed the bow against wall of the hut. She had used the weapon since a child, biting her lip nervously, she crossed to it and grasped its familiar form. She gathered several arrows and walked into the light of a new day. The ground beneath her bare feet was bumpy with stones and twigs. She felt a sharp stabbing pain as one of the stones dug deep into the base of her foot. Cursing loudly, she wondered how humans coped with such fragility.

Across the stream a withered tree rose from the ground. A bare patch on its trunk, no more than the width of a hand, made an ideal target. Taking a deep breath, she swivelled the bow in her palm and whipped the bow up. Moments later, a dark shaft stood proud from the centre of the trunk. She made a noise that was somewhere between laughter and sobbing.

"Thank you, Nephele."

She had chosen to become human, but to hold onto one thing that was undeniably centaur, caused her heart to soar. After shooting two further shafts in quick succession, both nestling next to the first, she gave a whoop of joy. Only the sound of footsteps made her turn, a shaft notched, and bow raised in the same movement. Agapetos held up his hands, but the smile on his face revealed he understood her delight.

"I couldn't even draw the bow," he announced.

Airlea, however, felt her cheeks flush. Agapetos had emerged from the hut stripped to the waist. As he spoke, she was distracted by his muscular frame and could not deny the strong feelings that raced through her.

"You can lower the bow," Agapetos suggested.

"Oh yes, apologies." She turned away to hide her embarrassment. "We should move out soon."

"Indeed, if these men are hunting us, then Krinos will not be far behind," he replied.

"Krinos?" Airlea turned back to face Agapetos.

"Krinos is a Theran, who has no love for me. He leads men that only bring shame to my people."

"Then why are they allowed to be part of your camp?" Her eyes dropped to his chest and followed the flow of his body down to the fabric that covered his manhood. She gave a cough. "I mean to say, why not banish them."

"Firstly, Krinos comes from a powerful family within Theran people, but it's more than that. We have become a warrior people and war dictates the need for men like Krinos. He's a bastard, but he is our bastard. So, we deserve the shame."

"Why does he want you dead?"

"One of his men forced himself on a young prisoner. One of my men tried to stop him and in the chaos my man was killed. I demanded that the killer face justice, but Krinos refused. I had expected him to do just that, and I prepared. My archers dropped half of his men before they could draw their weapons. I called on Krinos to surrender, but he demanded that I face him in battle. He knew that I could not refuse with so many Therans looking on. We fought until we were both bloodied and exhausted, but Thanatos put a stop to the fight. He threatened to leave the Therans to their own fate should the fight continue. Our elders feared that without the help of Thanatos we would never gain a homeland. They demanded that we stop or face execution. The fight was brought to a halt, but the hatred lives on."

"And now he hunts us?"

"The man you killed last night; he was Krinos's second in command. Where he goes, Krinos is never far behind. But in this instance, I believe that we may have a little time."

"How so?" she asked.

"Krinos wants me dead by his own hand. Ampelio," he pointed at the corpse of the man, "also wanted me dead. I imagine Krinos would have sent his second in command on the least likely trail. Which means we should have a meal before we move out. We also need to find you some better garments and covering for your feet. This terrain will tear your skin apart."

"You seem to have a lot of people that want you dead."

Agapetos laughed.

"I have a habit of finding trouble. Come, let us prepare."

*****

Agamemnon did not allow the two armies marching beneath his banner to slow their pace. He was yet to receive word that Menelaus was safe. It was hard for Agamemnon to admit to himself that he had a weakness. Menelaus had always more focused on honour than he was, if it had been his choice, the Spartan army would have marched on Thyestes, the moment the old Spartan king died. Menelaus, however, just had to allow their uncle one last attempt on their lives. Despite his brother's failing he could not help loving him. Besides, Menelaus was skilled in the tactics of war and warriors found it easy to show him loyalty. Agamemnon's unease had been further intensified when the scouts reported seeing centaurs in the distance. The creatures made no attempt at contact and after they observed the moving armies disappeared over the horizon. Agamemnon was full of questions, *had the centaurs switched sides? Did they now scout for the Tegean army? Was Menelaus dead?*

It would be two days before he received answers to those questions. Cripos and two other riders rode into the Spartan camp. Agamemnon, upon hearing that a messenger had arrived from the north, did not wait to be approached. He raced through the camp; calling out to Cripos before he was able to dismount.

"My brother, is he safe?"

"King Menelaus sends you warm welcome Prince Agamemnon," Cripos replied. Seeing the relief in Agamemnon's face, then added, "The Tegeans were fought to a standstill and were convinced to switch sides. His words were met by cheers as Spartans gathered around them.

"Welcome news indeed, Cripos," said Agamamenon happily. "Will you take a meal with us before you return?"

"King Menelaus instructed me to return immediately. He would have word on your progress and his camp is less than two days ride."

Agamemnon grasped Cripos by the hand. "Instruct my brother that the Spartan and Argoan army marches as one. The sons of Atreus are returning home."

Cripos broke into a beaming smile. "It will be done." He turned his mount and both he and his two riders left the camp.

*****

Agapetos and Airlea stood upon a small summit. He scanned the scenery, the beauty of the countryside was not lost on him, but he searched for signs of an enemy.

"Will Krinos follow?" Airlea asked.

"He will follow us to the underworld itself," Agapetos paused, "unless, we…"

"Unless we what?"

Agapetos turned and placed a hand on her shoulder. With his free hand he pointed into the distance.

"Do you see that range of hills and mountains? They jut from the world like the spine of a great beast."

"I see them." she replied.

"The terrain is not easy and as we get higher, it's cold enough to freeze piss." He paused, concerned that he might have offended her. "I am sorry, I have spent too long in the presence of men."

"I was a centaur, living among hundreds of other centaurs. Trust me, Agapetos you don't know what piss is," she laughed.

He grinned.

"Let's just say it gets cold, very cold. But there are passes that we can use that lead to the coast. If we were to get passage to Troy, there are lands beyond that Krinos has no knowledge or influence in. He would be blind in foreign lands and if they catch up with us in the mountain passes, then we would see them long before they are close enough to be a problem. We could pick our ground and with your skill with a bow, I would wage fortune would be in our favour."

"Then what are we waiting for?"

"It will not be easy, Airlea," he replied, his face showing that it was a grave undertaking.

She held his hand and gave it a loving squeeze. "We will take one step at a time, together."

Chapter 37

'The Sons of Atreus'

Thyestes felt a cold chill race down his spine. His plans to rid the world of the only threat to his throne had failed utterly. The scout that informed him of the approaching armies nervously took a step back from his king. Thyestes stood on the walls of the city in silence as he contemplated his misfortune. His hand grasped the blade at his waist. Anger coursed through his veins, he wanted nothing more than to sink that blade into the flesh of his nephews. He spat over the walls as he thought of the Argoans and Tegean forces. Taking a deep breath, he forced himself calm his spirit and think clearly. He needed time to fortify the city. An army made up of allies only stays united if victories come quickly. If he could delay and frustrate the enemy, then their ranks would soon thin.

The scout gave a cough and then timidly spoke.

"Any further orders, my king, or may I leave?"

Thyestes did not like having his train of thought interrupted, but he managed a smile. He reached over and placed an arm around the man's shoulder. "You have done well today. I know how daunting it can be to deliver bad news to a king. You have done enough, you may go." He struck the man in the stomach, then without hesitation threw him bodily from the city walls. The scream seemed to last an age, and then ended abruptly with a thud. "Bring my son and Cineas here now!" He returned his gaze beyond the city walls, oblivious to those scrabbling to follow his orders and put distance between themselves and the king. *"You will find my grip on the throne is tighter than your father's,"* he whispered to himself.

Rapid footsteps sounded to his rear; he turned to see Cineas and Kleitos both breathing heavily.

Thyestes stroked the hilt of his sword as he spoke. "It seems that the sons of Atreus have returned. This may fill your heart with joy, Cineas. But I would remind you that you have sworn an oath not only to me but to your dead king, you must serve me loyally."

"I have and will always do my duty," Cineas replied. "No matter how distasteful."

Thyestes laughed.

"Honour can be the bonds that tie our hands. But we have more pressing matters. Kleitos, I want you to take our forces and slow down the enemy. Hit and run only, do not engage. I need time to strengthen our defences. Their army is large and cumbersome, use that to your advantage."

"It will be done, father."

"Then don't waste time talking to me. Go!" Thyestes waited until Kleitos had gone and then turned his attention to Cineas. "I realise that you are commander of my forces in my absence, but I thought it best not to test your honour. But I will have tasks for you."

"I am here to serve, my king."

"Yes, of course. Your first task is to send a messenger to those mercenary bastards that we paid to invade Sparta. They can defend rather than attack. They're to march here directly. After that I want extra men at the gates and on the walls. Any male that is strong enough to lift a weapon is to defend the city. Send out troops to gather supplies, we may need to wait out the rabble that approaches." Cineas nodded and made to leave. "And Cineas, ask Erasio to call out my personal guard. We wouldn't want people confused to where their loyalty lies."

"Yes, King Thyestes." Without waiting to be dismissed, Cineas turned and left.

Thyestes smiled. He had bent people like Cineas to his will all his life. They were slaves to their honour. The fool would rather die than break a vow.

*****

Cineas cursed Thyestes with every step that he took. His anger grew as he passed the message to Erasio. It grew even further as he ordered troops to go out into the nearby lands to collect supplies. He walked into the main courtyard within the city walls. He had spent many joyful moments in that courtyard, but that seemed like a different world. Atreus would throw lavish celebrations, where people would come from every corner of Mycenae land. King, farmer, warrior, and fisherman would walk shoulder to shoulder, they would laugh, drink, and eat until fit to burst, and all at the king's expense. That world had come to an end; only those that found favour with Thyestes tended to smile at the world now. Others walked with eyes fixed firmly to the ground beneath their feet, eager to avoid the attention of Thyestes or his personal guard under the leadership of that bastard, Erasio.

At the far end of the courtyard stood a small building that housed the royal messengers. It hadn't existed when Atreus was king, he would simply send a man that he could trust. Thyestes, however, was constantly sending messages to other royal households, usually demands or veiled threats. The complex web of spies also needed to be directed, as Thyestes loved to play his little games. The result was at least twelve messengers that awaited orders at any given time. As Cineas made his way toward the building, a figure emerged. He recognised the young man to be Galenos, a reputable horseman. Cineas knew him as the grandson of a dear friend and could not stop the images of the young father and grandfather, who lost their lives the night Thyestes stole the crown.

"Galenos!" Cineas called out. "I have a task for you."

Galenos smiled upon seeing Cineas.

"What would you have me do?" he replied.

"In truth, the task comes from King Thyestes." Cineas observed the young man's smile falter just slightly, but not enough to raise the concerns of those with unswerving loyalty to Thyestes.

"You are to take a message to our paid friends on the coast." Cineas made sure his words carried to all those that may want to hear. "They are to march will all haste to this city. You had best take a spare mount and provisions. The king says that this is most important."

"What is happening, Cineas?"

"An army led by Agamemnon and Menelaus approaches." Although his words sounded alarm, is face remained—emotionless. "I must impress upon you, Galenos. Without reinforcements it is likely the city will fall."

"Then I will leave immediately."

"I will go with you," a voice sounded from the rear. Cineas turned to see Timaeus, a man dedicated to his king, already placing his sword at his waist.

"Yes, two are more likely to succeed than one." Cineas turned back to Galenos. "Remember, the hills are a dangerous place. Return safely, your mother wouldn't forgive me if you were to fall." Cineas did not break eye contact with the young messenger.

"I understand," the young messenger replied. "Come Timaeus, let us set about this task."

*****

Menelaus had been more than satisfied with his army's first test. To reach Mycenae they had to cross the lands of Argos. It would have been all too easy for the warriors to slip away in the night and return to their farms and loved ones. Menelaus had been impressed with the young King, Diomedes. The man himself seemed to be dealing with an inner turmoil. Agamemnon had told Menelaus what had taken place between Diomedes and his father, and it was clear to Menelaus that the young king was plagued with both grief and guilt. Despite the misery within, Diomedes proved to be a capable leader.

Menelaus spoke quietly. "Agamemnon, journey to our allies and speak with Diomedes and Iamus. Ask them if they would join us at the head of the column."

"And if they refuse? They may be reluctant to leave their own troops."

"Then they refuse. I offer a hand of friendship; it is up to them whether or not they grasp it."

It was not long before all four were moving forward as a group. Androx had also moved to the head of the column. Iamus plucked a wine skin from his mount and offered it to the group.

"I will wager that none of you have ever tasted its like. It comes from my private stores, most Tegeans have never had it caress their lips."

Menelaus eagerly accepted the skin. He allowed the liquid to roll down his throat. "That is wonderful. I have never tasted a wine so smooth. It's almost like honey."

"It is, isn't it?" Iamus replied proudly. "Agamemnon you must try it. When you sit upon your father's throne. I will have some presented to you."

"I will drink to that, Iamus." Agamemnon took his turn to drink. A wide smile appeared as he lowered the skin.

Diomedes took his turn. "I have been to your household many times. Why have I never been offered this wine before."

Iamus held up his hands in apology. "Forgive me, Diomedes. The wine is supposed to be consumed only by the Tegean royal household. But today is a day for breaking down barriers. I can think of no greater gift the land of Tegea can offer its friends. From this day it will be known as the Wine of Kings."

"You are most kind, Iamus. But I am not yet a king," Agamemnon replied.

Menelaus took another drink. "You are a king amongst men, brother."

Androx, Menelaus, Iamus and Diomedes held up imaginary goblets.

"To Agamemnon, king of men!" They called out in turn.

Agamemnon gave a mock bow and nearly fell from his mount.

"It has a power that few wines can match," Iamus announced and to groans of disappointment he stoppered the skin. "Another time, my friends, we need our senses to serve us well."

As if to reinforce the words of Iamus, two scouts could be seen moving at great speed toward the column. Menelaus was concerned. He had expected more time before encountering the enemy. The scouts obviously brought news to the contrary. The scout did not take long to cover the ground between themselves and the column. The riders' mounts came to an abrupt halt, the flanks of the beasts thick with sweat.

"King Menelaus! The enemy is gathered less than half a day's march, across the Alfeios River."

"I did not know the waters of the Alfeios came this far into Mycenae land," Iamus interrupted.

"It is hardly a river. It's no more than a finger from the hand that is all," Menelaus replied. "My father used to make camp on its bank when hunting. I find it hard to believe that Thyestes would meet us out in the open."

"Arrogant bastard," Agamemnon announced.

"No, brother. This is something different." Menelaus stared into the distance and asked a simple question to himself. *What would he do, faced with the same advancing army?* "He's buying himself more time."

"What do you mean?" Diomedes asked.

"Thyestes has no doubt learnt that his great plan has failed completely. He is not used to failure; this will make him shrink back into his lair. I would wager my throne that Thyestes does not lead that army across the Alfeios," Menelaus replied.

"Then who, Cineas?" Agamemnon asked.

Menelaus shook his head. "Cineas is a fine commander, but that would be too great a risk for Thyestes. No, it will be someone that he trusts," Menelaus suggested.

"There can't be many that bastard trusts," added Agamemnon.

"It doesn't really matter because I doubt that whoever is in charge has orders to engage us in battle." Menelaus pondered his next action. "We need to increase our scouts."

"Then how will they delay us?" Diomedes asked.

"By sending out small groups to harass the column. My concern is not what lies directly to our front, but what Thyestes hopes to gain from a delaying tactic," Menelaus replied.

"The mercenaries on the coast. Thyestes spared no expense in preparing his army to attack Sparta. More than enough men to defend a city," Iamus announced.

"Do we carry on?" Diomedes asked.

Agamemnon barked with laughter. "Of course, Diomedes. It doesn't matter how many men Thyestes calls to his banner, I will have his head. Besides, many within his ranks were loyal to my father. He does not just face an oncoming army. He faces an enemy from within." Agamemnon paused and then added. "We must increase the pace."

"It is difficult to move such a large army at pace, Agamemnon. Besides, we must deal with the threat to our front, before we deal with Thyestes. Diomedes, you will take control of the column. Agamemnon, Iamus, we will take all of our mounted troops and the centaurs and meet the man that commands the Mycenaean army."

*****

The tracks that led to the coast took in many different terrains. Mostly plains and low valleys to begin with then they snaked through high ground before sweeping down toward the various coastal settlements. The two messengers had cleared the valleys with efficient ease, but the higher ground was treacherous for their mounts. Loose rocks could cause a horse to fall or throw its rider, and so the pace slowed. The slower pace, however, did not make the task easy only manageable. The ground gradually became steeper parts of the track were replaced with all manner of debris and obstacles from the winter rains. Both men and beasts were exhausted.

Galenos called his mount to a halt. He walked the animal and his spare to a clump of trees.

"Why have we stopped?" Timaeus asked.

"If we continue at this pace, then the beasts will die beneath us," he replied.

"But we must reach the coast in all haste."

"Which of us knows horse flesh, Timaeus? If we do not allow them time to rest, then we shall never reach the coast and will fail our king. A short rest and feed and they will carry us swiftly to our destination. Besides, I have some bread and a little wine, the rest will not be wasted." Galenos knew that Timaeus rarely refused wine. Reluctantly, the scout dismounted and began to wipe the sweat from his mount's coat. Galenos turned from the man and looked into the distance. He was sure that he could see dust rising. He guessed that it must be the army that Cineas spoke about. He and many of his people had hoped for many years that the sons of Atreus would one day return and inflict a terrible revenge on

Thyestes. Timaeus stepped to his side.

"What is it?" the messenger asked.

"Dust in the distance. Whether it is the enemy or our own army, I do not know." He broke his bread and handed half to Timaeus.

"It's better that we are here. I do not regret missing out on the slaughter. You mentioned wine."

"I will fetch it." Galenos walked to his mount and collected a wine skin that had been tied to its back. He reached within a small bundle and drew a blade. Before returning to Timaeus he slipped it into his belt. "You are right. It is better to be here." He took a drink from the skin, then offered it to Timaeus. Without hesitation Timaeus snatched up the skin and threw his head back. Closing his eyes, the wine glugged into his mouth. Galenos gave a resigned sigh, took out the blade from his belt and drew it across the throat of Timaeus. The man's eyes opened wide as he dropped the wine skin and grasped at his killer's tunic. Galenos desperately pulled himself free of the dying man's grasp but could not release himself of the awful look in Timaeus' eyes. "Forgive me, but Thyestes must lose his throne. Galenos drove his blade into the man's heart, determined to end the scout's suffering. Timaeus fell to the ground, his blood mixing with the earth.

Galenos placed a foot beneath the body and tipped it from the track. Without ceremony, Timaeus rolled down the slope and came to rest within a small ravine. The eyes, still wide with shock, burned into the young messenger's mind. He had never taken a life before and hoped he would never do so again. He plucked the wine skin from the earth and used its contents to wash the blood from the hand that had held the dagger.

He glanced around at the various paths that lay before him. Returning to the city would mean certain death, the coast would lead to questions that he wasn't sure he could answer. He spied the dust rising in the distance; he doubted that he could reach the invading army without coming across men loyal to Thyestes. He gave a sigh as he realised his only options were to remain where he was or cross the mountainous terrain and head towards Nemea beyond the lands of Mycenae. He had little to keep him tied to the only city he had ever known. Cineas had given him a mission to complete, and he had done it without hesitation. The message may have been given in code, but he understood. Cineas had laboured the point that the order was from Thyestes and failure to carry it out would lead to the city falling. He had also talked about his mother, as though she still lived. Galenos was certain he'd done as his grandfather's friend, Cineas, had wished. Now he must look to his own future, he could do no more for the future of Mycenae.

Chapter 38

'The True King'

The combined mounted force of Spartans, Tegeans, Argoans and centaurs moved with haste. Menelaus knew it was a dangerous move. Should the enemy move forward in numbers then it could spell disaster. He wanted to close on the enemy before they could prepare and lay traps for the main column. If Menelaus had guessed correctly then Thyestes would have very few men truly loyal to him. The tales of his cruelty since seizing the throne had spread to many lands, including Sparta. Most of the influential families that had thrived when Atreus once held the throne were eyed with suspicion by Thyestes. Many lost their lives or land. Only those that provided Thyestes with a route to the throne seemed to flourish. Menelaus wasn't sure what he planned to do; all he knew was he wanted to give the warriors of Mycenae an opportunity to see Agamemnon. Let them know that slaughter is not why the sons of Atreus came home. A message that might be best delivered without an enormous army.

Menelaus raised a hand to slow the advance.

"What is it, brother?" Agamemnon asked.

"If you wanted to slow an army, how many times could you have struck at our force with a few well-placed men?" Menelaus asked.

"Five or six times at least. A narrow valley, high ground, two streams and a few more ideal places."

"Have I got this wrong, Agamemnon? Why haven't they taken advantage of the terrain? They could have reduced our number by at least a third."

"Poorly led, perhaps?" Agamemnon suggested.

"Thyestes is a bastard, but he is no fool. He would have ensured the those able to fight are trained. We will slow our approach. If this is a trap, our main force should not be far behind."

"We will find out soon enough. If my memory serves me well, we shall soon reach the Alfeios."

"It has been too long since we were on Mycenae soil," Menelaus announced.

"As long as we don't end up in it." Agamemnon pointed to his front. The track up ahead took a sharp turn. Both sides of the track were flanked by higher ground and covered in trees. A few expertly placed archers on either side could rain destruction upon his force. "Perhaps Thyestes is so tired of kingship, he welcomes us with open arms."

"I think you need to leave Iamus's wine alone. They will need to rip the crown from his head. He would wear it to meet Hades."

"He would have to have a head." Agamemnon smiled.

"Not willing to show him mercy then," Menelaus replied wryly.

"All but him, brother."

The force pressed on, nervously looking to the trees on each side of the track. Menelaus spied two men break cover on the high ground to his left. He was relieved to see they did not raise a weapon. Then to his surprise both men bowed their heads.

"Ermm that was unusual," Menelaus noted.

As they cleared the sharp turn a group of six Mycenae scouts sat in the long grass their weapons piled before them. As Menelaus and his riders passed, they rose from the ground, but made no effort to retrieve their spears or swords. They, like the first two men, simply stood with their head bowed.

"Do you want me to question them?" Agamemnon asked.

"No, we will press on," Menelaus replied, his brow wrinkled with confusion.

The terrain began to flatten. Rock was replaced with more and more long grass and the ground became softer for the mounts. In the distance, the ranks of the Mycenae army stood, although the Alfeios was not visible, Menelaus knew that it flowed between his position and the enemy. As they neared it became apparent that around thirty of the enemy were not with the rest of their army. Menelaus wondered why they stood on his side of the river. He glanced to his flank, worried that the enemy would emerge on either side. "Agamemnon, I think it best if we ride alone."

"You cannot go alone," Iamus interrupted.

"Alone or not, if they decide to attack, we will be dead. If you remain here, you at least will be able to return to the column," Menelaus replied.

"But…" Iamus began.

"There is no point arguing with him, Iamus. He will not throw your lives away." Agamemnon spat on the ground. "Come Menelaus, let's see what the fates have planned for us." Agamemnon moved his mount forward without waiting for a reply.

Menelaus could not think of anything to say to Iamus, so he merely nodded. He urged his mount to close the distance with Agamemnon. He kept his eyes fixed on those to his front. The time for worrying about a trap was at an end. Twenty of those to his front were for some reason kneeling, leaving around ten others standing around them. One man stood much closer, his arms held behind his back. With about twenty paces to go, Menelaus and Agamemnon brought their mounts to a halt and dismounted. They strode towards the man standing by himself, he seemed to be smiling, which did not help Menelaus's unease.

The man took a step to his front and bowed his head. "King Agamemnon, King Menelaus your army awaits."

Menelaus looked at the man. He was greying in both hair and beard. Despite his advancing years, his limbs were muscular, chest broad, and straight backed. Just below the left eye a long scar raced down towards his mouth.

"I know you." Menelaus moved forward, keen to place a name to the face. "Doras is it?"

"Yes, King Menelaus."

"You served in my father's personal guard."

Agamemnon stepped forward and grasped the man by the shoulders.

"I remember you. You used to show me how to use a blade in the palace garden."

"I did, but your talent far outstretched mine even as a boy," Doras replied.

Agamemnon pulled him into an embrace, which clearly took the man by surprise.

"Tell me, Doras. What is happening here?" Menelaus asked.

"Cineas received word that you were returning. He has ensured that we were ready to act. Few have love for Thyestes. These," he pointed to the men on their knees, "are some of those that cannot be trusted." Doras walked to the centre of the prisoners and grasped a man by the hair. "This is Kleitos, son of Thyestes."

"And what of the city?" Menelaus asked. His eyes never leaving the kneeling Kleitos.

"Thyestes has kept his most loyal warriors close, but we have men at the gates. When we move on the city, she will open her arms to us."

Agamemnon had stopped listening. He walked to Kleitos. Agamemnon whispered so only those close by could hear. "The son of Thyestes on his knees. You should be thankful that we do not behave like your father. Your head would already be in your lap."

"Enjoy this small victory because it will be fleeting," Kleitos spat.

"Oh! The son of Thyestes is a warrior," Agamemnon mocked.

"Give me a sword and I will gut you, like my Thyestes gutted your father."

"I believe that is a challenge," Agamemnon announced to all.

Doras stepped in close to Agamemnon. "Careful my king, Kleitos may not be much more than a boy, but he is a murderous bastard who few can match with a blade."

Agamemnon smiled. "Come Kleitos. Let us play this game. The winner takes everything. The loser... well the loser dies."

Doras approached Menelaus. "Is this wise?" he whispered. "I have never known a man enjoy killing like Kleitos."

"Then you should prepare for a new experience. This will be slow and painful," Menelaus replied.

The bonds were cut from the wrists of Kleitos, a blade thrown at his feet. He did not rush to pick it up, rubbing where the bonds had cut into his flesh, he smiled at Agamemnon.

"I once asked my father, how he so easily took the throne from Atreus. Do you know what he replied, Agamemnon?"

"Please enlighten me," Agamemnon replied, as he drew his sword.

"He said your father was an intelligent man, who claimed his honour was a beacon for good men to follow. But it was all a falsehood. Atreus was a coward. My father took all he had because he was too frightened to keep it. He stood by as his wife was slaughtered, his sons driven from their home, his city turned to ash. Yes, the great Atreus was nought but a snivelling coward," Kleitos sneered as he spoke.

"Is that really the best that you have to offer for an insult? I was going to kill you quickly, you are after all, no more than a boy, but your taunts are pathetic. I think I will take you a piece at a time. Not out of rage, but as a warning to others. If you are going insult an enemy, then it best not to sound like a naughty child."

Kleitos retrieved the sword from the ground. "Enough talk!"

He moved quickly using his sword without much back swing. Agamemnon parried each swing and thrust without much difficulty.

"You move well in attack," Agamemnon spoke as the two broke from each other. "How is your defence?" Agamemnon darted forward, his blows more powerful than his younger opponent. The last move of his attack was only just blocked by a desperate Kleitos. He had little time to celebrate his fortunate escape as Agamemnon brought around his free hand and delivered a punch to the bridge of his nose. Blood and mucus sprayed Kleitos's tunic and armour as he backed away with a yelp of pain. "Come now, you can't taste victory without first experiencing the exquisite sting of pain."

Agamemnon attacked again, his blade slicing the upper thigh of his enemy. Kleitos, swung wildly, but Agamemnon dipped below the blade, reversed his own and drove it through the top of Kleitos' foot. Agamemnon rose quickly, the top of his head smashing Kleitos's nose once again. Thyestes' son staggered backward, trying desperately to keep Agamemnon at distance.

"If you have a weak stomach, Doras, then I suggest that you do not watch this," Menelaus suggested.

"I find it impossible to look away," Doras replied.

His words were met with a howl of agony as Kleitos' right hand still holding his weapon, was severed from his wrist, dropping onto the blood-strewn grass. Kleitos, now severely wounded and without a weapon to defend himself, began to whimper.

"Stay back," he screamed. His tears mix with the blood from his nose, creating a grotesque panic strewn mask.

Agamemnon laughed. "Pick up your sword, Kleitos son of Thyestes, you still have one good hand. Do not die a coward." Kleitos bent to retrieve his sword, he struggled to pull his own severed hand from the hilt. His sobs intensified as he rose, and Agamemnon moved forward. "You shouldn't have insulted my father, Kleitos. I would have sent you back to yours in one piece had you been more respectful. It would have allowed your mother to recognise her son." Agamemnon darted forward, Kleitos raised his sword too slow. Agamemnon's blade swept down removing his opponent's arm just below the elbow. A reverse thrust punctured Kleitos' gut, for good measure Agamemnon brought the blade around to smash the kneecaps. Kleitos dropped to the ground.

He didn't seem in pain anymore. Menelaus guessed that his mind had been unable to cope with his imminent death.

Agamemnon bent in close to Kleitos and whispered. "I will present your head to your father, but your body will have no home. No marker will pay testament to you ever walking this world." Agamemnon allowed his blade to sweep down one final time. The head came away easily. What was left fell without a sound.

Menelaus watched as the head bounced once, rolled and came to rest.

"Doras, if you would have the body removed," Menelaus requested.

"No!" Agamemnon interrupted. "Burn it where it lays and find something in which to put the head."

"Agamemnon, is that necessary?" Menelaus asked.

"To defeat a creature like Thyestes, we must become more terrifying than him. At least until this war is at an end. And the enemies are no more."

Menelaus did not press the matter, but he wondered if Agamemnon would ever be free of enemies.

Chapter 39

'Tyrant'

Warriors stood ready, like hunting dogs straining at the leash. Never had these lands witnessed such an army. Mycenaean, Argoan, Tegean, Theran, Spartan, and Centaur, standing shoulder to shoulder, all prepared to march against the Tyrant of Mycenae. One figure, however, did not prepare for battle. He sat by a campfire, warming the souls of his feet.

"Will you not march with us, Thanatos?" Menelaus asked.

"I have told you before, Menelaus. I am no warrior. Besides, with such an army at your side, I doubt that my skills will be required."

"There are no certainties in battle. If our friends within the city fail to open the main gate, then this night will be bloody indeed."

"Anything of true worth is rarely obtained without cost," Thanatos replied. "But I think you and your brother have paid enough and this night will deliver your reward."

"I hope you are right."

"How often am I wrong?" Thanatos smiled.

"I admit it is rare. I must take my place at the head of the column."

"Safe return my friend," Thanatos replied.

Menelaus strode through the ranks of warriors to reach the head of the column. He spied Agamemnon in deep conversation with Doras.

"How goes preparations?" he asked.

"Doras will send a messenger to the city. The messenger will inform those within that their army returns. As we reach striking distance, we shall shoot a burning arrow into the air. This will give the signal for those loyal within, they will take the main gate by force. With good fortune, we should be able to pour our troops into the city and Thyestes will be helpless to stop us. Are you in agreement?" Agamemnon asked.

"It's a good plan," Menelaus replied.

"And yet you seem less than enthusiastic."

"Not at all, brother. I just remember our father saying that war was too dependent on good fortune rather than good preparation." Menelaus looked to the failing light. "I wish that the night was not so clear, those on the city walls will see our approach from some distance. Perhaps, most of our forces should stay back from the Mycenae army?"

"Agreed," Agamemnon replied. "But once we have secured the main gate, we do not proceed until the rest of the army reaches the city. Menelaus, will you join me at the head of the column? I think we should be the first to enter our city."

"I would be honoured," Menelaus answered and grasped his brother by the arm.

"Then let's move out. With the coming of a new day, the sons of Atreus shall have reclaimed what was stolen from them."

*****

Thyestes stood upon his city walls. He stared into the distance as the shroud of night began to fall. The messengers arriving throughout the day gave pleasing reports. His son Kleitos had succeeded in halting the advance of the enemy. Before long, the mercenary army would flock to his call for aid and would fill his city with defenders. Cineas had carried out his orders and supplied the city. He allowed himself a small smile. He could hold back an army, no matter its size, for years if need be. He knew that no attacking army far from home kept its cohesion. The warriors, thinking of home, their crops dying in the field would begin to slip away. A slight trickle would turn to a torrent of desertion. Then, just when the attacking army retreats, Thyestes and his forces would erupt from the city and show those that dared to raise a blade against him, the error of their ways. He would bring Tegea, Argos and Sparta to their knees.

He was suddenly aware of his hunger. Taking one last look at the preparations, he decided to return to the great hall. He required sustenance for the days that lay ahead. Leaving Cineas to oversee that work on the defences continued, he and his personal guard left the city walls.

The great hall had been prepared in advance. The servants had learnt not to keep Thyestes waiting. Except for two that stood either side of his throne, his personal guards lounged nonchalantly on couches. Small tables nearby housed various vessels: fresh fruit, cheese, bread and cuts of meat. A larger table housed much of the same, a large boar, Thyestes's favourite meat, at its centre. Servants stood waiting to serve the king's every wish. A young servant brought a mix of dishes to Thyestes.

"Who are you?" Thyestes asked, taken aback by the handsome youth that he had not seen before.

"Bakchos," he replied. The boy kept his eyes on the food.

Thyestes ran his hands up the boy's thigh. "I will need some more boar." Thyestes's tone was sickly sweet.

"Immediately, my king." Bakchos pulled away from the king's grasp. Returning to the large table, he took a blade and began to carve the impressive beast. When he had cut enough, he placed the blade next to the carved meat. He strode to Thyestes and even managed a slight smile.

"That is more like it! Tell me why I have not seen you before?"

"I have only been here a short time," Bakchos replied.

"Who brought you into our embrace?" Thyestes asked, his hand once again feeling the inner flesh of

Bakchos's thigh.

"My father died and Cineas took pity on me."

"Oh, that is a shame." Thyestes's lecherous smile did not falter, "What did your father do. A farmer, fisherman, trader perhaps?"

"He was an assassin!" Bakchos dropped the food as he snatched up the blade.

Thyestes saw the blade coming and recoiled in his throne, crying out as his cheek was torn open.

Bakchos pulled back the blade to strike again, but a far longer weapon struck him in the shoulder, breaking bone as it passed through his body. Thyestes kicked out at Bakchos, knocking him backwards. Thyestes' personal guards rose, their swords drawn.

"Wait!" Thyestes screamed. He raised a hand to his face, then looked at the blood soaking his fingers. He kicked a small couch out of his way and strode to Bakchos. "Who sent you?"

"Nobody sent me. You killed my father, you bastard!"

"That is quite possible, but who helped you?"

"Nobody helped me," Bakchos replied defiantly.

"Take his hand," Thyestes ordered.

The personal guard forced Bakchos to his knees and stretched his arm out on a couch. Erasio stepped forward laughing. The blade swept down, cutting the hand free of the arm. Bakchos screamed his agony. Thyestes ignored his captive's pain.

"I will ask again, but be warned, you only have so many parts to remove, and some are more precious than others. Who helped you?"

"I span Cineas a tale. Made him feel sorry for me," Bakchos replied through gritted teeth.

"Remove his cock!"

Erasio dropped his word and drew a dagger. Bakchos struggled, as he was forced upright but his strength had left him. Erasio grasped his genitals and placed the cold blade against the skin.

"No, please. I swear on my love for my father. I received no help or orders to kill you. The path I took, I took for my own vengeance," Bakchos blurted.

Thyestes looked at Bakchos and then nodded to Erasio who dragged his blade upwards. Bakchos screamed and was allowed to drop to his knees. His missing body part was dropped onto the couch in front of him.

"Such a shame," Thyestes commented on the dismembered part. "But a king must be sure that it is the truth that reaches his ears." He nodded once again to Erasio who thrust his dagger into the throat of Bakchos. The youth jerked violently, and then dropped to the floor, dead.

"And Cineas?" Erasio asked.

"It seems that he was fooled by this wretch, it is not surprising, the boy did have uncommon beauty. But I suppose that we should speak to Cineas. If only to ensure that his judgement is not determined by his cock in future. Send word that he should join us. And I will need another plate of boar."

*****

Thanatos had taken a walk down to the riverbank of the Alfeios. After ensuring he was alone, he placed the black cube on the ground. Moments later, it had grown and opened to reveal its contents. He pulled out the Blood Stone and called on Ketos. The black object closed, but perched upon its flawless surface, a vessel stood. Thanatos plucked up the vessel and then brought it crashing down on the black object. The vessel splintered and cracked apart. A thick black smoke arose from the broken pieces, then darted toward the Alfeios.

For a moment, the waters remained calm. However, as Thanatos watched its still surface, a strong breeze began to blow, then the waters began to bubble. It was reasonably gentle to begin with, then the water raged, like liquid on a fearsome fire. A creature broke the surface, its giant snake-like neck swaying back and forth. Its elongated head played host to a long snout and yellow eyes that fixed their stare on Thanatos.

"Why have you ssssummoned me," it hissed.

"I have a task. Complete it and you shall go free, Ketos" Thanatos replied.

"Trusssst a god to keep itssss word. I think not. Return me to my ressssting place."

"I will have no need of you once the task is complete. As long as you return home beneath the waves, then the gods will have no reason to trouble you. And it is such a simple task."

"What issss it you would have me do?"

"Breathe your mist. Cover the advance of the young sons of Atreus."

"And I sssshall be free?"

"You shall," Thanatos replied.

The creature threw its head back and when it came forward again, its great mouth had opened wide. A thick, grey mist flowed outward. It quickly covered the riverbank and raced along the terrain beyond. In the distance, Thanatos could hear those in the camp call out as the mist enveloped all that it touched. Finally, the great beast snapped its mouth shut. It began to sway back and forth once again.

"It issss done, little god. Issss thissss god trusss-worthy."

"He is. Go home, Ketos."

*****

Cineas watched the mist as it rolled toward the city.

"Light extra torches!" he called out. As he did so a messenger emerged from out of the mist. "Open the gate!" The huge timbers of the main gate were slowly pulled back and the messenger was allowed entry. He dismounted and raced to Cineas.

"I have great tidings, Cineas. It is more than we have hoped for. The enemy have been stopped in their tracks. The glorious Mycenaean army is returning to the welcoming bosom of the city. They will fire a burning arrow into the air, to avoid confusion in the heavy mist."

Cineas gave a smile, knowing all too well of which enemy the messenger spoke. "That is welcome news indeed. Take care of your mount and take nourishment."

One of the king's personal guards approached. For a moment, Cineas was concerned that the messenger's words had aroused suspicion.

"The King would have a word with you, Cineas." Without waiting for a reply, the guard turned and left.

Cineas hoped that his relief did not show to those that manned the wall. "I must see the king. Watch for the signal from our troops as they return and don't act rashly, those men have done our city a great service and deserve better than receiving a spear tip on their return home. He strode away reluctantly. He had hoped to see Agamemnon and Menelaus.

As he moved through the city, he noted how the populace seemed unconcerned over possible attack. He crossed the courtyard that had seen the death of Atreus. He missed the man that was both king and friend. Cineas may well have betrayed his own honour to restore the throne to its rightful place, but he had done so gladly, no matter the cost.

Moving through the corridors of the royal palace Cineas contemplated turning around. What did it matter if he ignored an order from Thyestes? Even as he thought it, he knew that he must comply. Refusal might bring Thyestes to the city walls, and that could spell disaster.

He reached the heavy timbers that stood at the entrance to the great hall. Without hesitation he pushed the door aside and marched inside.

Almost immediately his eyes came to rest on the unfortunate form of Bakchos that lay in a bloody heap on the floor.

"What... w-why?" he stammered.

"Young Bakchos here attempted to cut my throat," Thyestes announced. "Thankfully, my personal guard dissuaded him."

Cineas could not take his eyes from the bloodied pulp that was once Bakchos. "He was just a boy," Cineas replied meekly. Bile rising in his throat.

"He was a murderous bastard deserving of his fate," Erasio announced.

Cineas made no attempt to hide his loathing. "Erasio, perhaps you should be careful in what you wish for. Your fate would not be pleasant,"

"Perhaps, we should discuss it at length." Erasio's hand moved towards the blade at his waist.

"Be warned, Erasio. If you draw that sword, I will gut you like swine." Cineas spat at his hatred for the man.

"Silence!" Thyestes raged. "Bakchos gave your name as the man that brought him into the royal palace."

"He told me that his father was dead. I thought he could be put to use." Cineas kept his tone neutral.

"Perhaps Cineas should give up his weapon and face

further questions, my king?" Erasio suggested. His voice was threatening.

Cineas turned to face him. "Perhaps you should try and take it?" Two of the guards took a step closer. "So, after keeping my word to you, Thyestes. This is how I'm to be treated? Tortured by your hired fools because I took pity on a young boy. Well fuck you, Thyestes. If I am to die, I will die with my sword in hand."

The personal guards rushed forward, swords at the ready. Cineas brought his sword up and took the throat from one of them. With little room to manoeuvre he could only attempt to block the second's sword with his free arm. The blade was forced down and cut into his thigh. Cineas growled, allowing his anger to overcome the pain. He threw his head forward and broke the man's nose and then plunged his blade into his enemy's gut. More guards were rushing forward. Cineas managed to take the weapon from one of the fallen and threw it at the advancing men. It stuck deep in the thigh of an attacker. The remaining men rushed forward their blades pierced Cineas, pinning him to the heavy-timbered doors. Erasio stepped through his men, grasped Cineas by the hair.

"I was always going to kill you, Cineas."

"Fuck..."

A dagger was drawn across Cineas' throat, cutting off his reply.

Thyestes raged at Erasio. "Did I say I wanted Cineas dead. You have robbed me of my commander."

"Forgive me. I thought that he posed a danger to you."

Upon the door, Cineas could do no more to help the sons of his friend. His sight turned to darkness, his chest ceased to rise, and his journey to reunite with Atreus had begun.

Chapter 40

'Vengeance'

Menelaus marched at Agamemnon's side as the burning arrow was fired into the air. They could see the torches on the city wall and heard the heavy timbers of the main gate being drawn back.

"Are you with me, brother?" Agamemnon asked.

"Till the end," Menelaus replied.

As the massive walls of the city began to appear, Menelaus knew that the moment for success or failure was at hand. If the plan had worked then friends within the city controlled the main gate and once that had been secured, victory was assured. If it wasn't and this was an elaborate ruse by his uncle, then it was likely that neither he nor Agamemnon would live to see another day. He heard Agamemnon drawing his sword and followed in kind.

"Now, Agamemnon. This is your time."

"Attack!" Agamemnon screamed. "Take the city!" His troops answered with their war cry.

Menelaus began to run. He could see the main gates and with some relief, realised that they were staying open. He screamed as he burst through the gate. As he continued through the gateway, he spied a few men lying dead upon the ground and those that remained standing, bowed their head to show that they meant no harm.

Doras came to his shoulder. "These men are with us!" Doras called out.

"Secure the gate and start cleansing the walls of any filth that is loyal to Thyestes," Menelaus replied.

"And find out where the bastard skulks," Agamemnon added.

An arrow whipped just a hand's width from Menelaus's head. But he did not shrink from the danger. He stepped to his front and dragged a line within the earth.

"I want a shieldwall here, now. Doras, take men, clear those bloody walls."

To the left of the main gate a tower filled with archers was raining down arrows upon Menelaus and his men. The shieldwall was limiting the damage caused, but some of the deadly shafts were finding their targets. Menelaus looked for Doras's progress, but it would clearly take time for him to fight his way to the tower. He cursed, but then the men within the tower started to die, black shafts striking them down.

Agamemnon whooped with joy, and slapped Menelaus on the back. "By the gods, it seems the centaurs have entered the battle."

Menelaus looked to his rear. "They're not the only ones. Agamemnon, lead your army. My Spartans stand at your side."

Agamemnon ordered the shieldwall to move forward. The enemy melted away, far too few to offer resistance. Menelaus took his place at the head of the Spartans and prepared to give the order to move forward. He glanced to the walls, on both sides on the gatehouse, the men led by Doras were making steady progress with only small pockets of resistance coming from those loyal to Thyestes.

"Spartans! You will treat the people of this city with respect. You are here to liberate, not to enslave. Do you understand?" The Spartans hammered their shields in response. "Forward!"

*****

Thyestes sat upon his throne; his eyes drawn to the body pinned to the great hall's doors. He wondered why Cineas had gone to his death so easily. Why take offence at the words of Erasio? The two men have loathed one another since the day they met. Every conversation since that point, had been filled with poorly disguised threat. Cineas must have known that torture was never an option. Thyestes took a drink of wine, a good portion of which missed his mouth and ran into his neatly trimmed beard. What reason could there be to throw away his life? Cineas denied knowing the true intentions of the traitor, Bakchos, but also seemed genuinely grief stricken at the sight of the boy's body. Had Cineas, fallen in love with the boy, that would have been a side to Cineas he'd never witnessed. A side Thyestes's spies had never observed.

He decided, this was something different. Cineas picked a fight, but why? He looked at the body again. The body resembled a figure on guard, barring entrance or rather barring exit. Thyestes's eyes widened as he realised Cineas was buying time. He'd sacrificed himself to keep attention within the great hall rather than outside it. He rose from his throne, his mouth opened, ready to bellow orders, however, the doors swung open, the body of Cineas swept aside with them.

A frightened warrior ran inside. "My king, the city is lost. Our forces have been over run!"

Thyestes did not reply. He slumped into his throne, raising the wine to his mouth and drank.

Erasio stepped forward. "My king?" No reply was forthcoming. "Thyestes what would you have us do?"

Thyestes looked up and stared at Erasio. "Fight."

"But we are outmatched, surely we could flee?"

"Flee? You shrunk behind your men when Cineas had blade in hand. Now is the time for you to test your metal against real men, Erasio. Leave or stay it makes no difference, who will aid your escape from the city? You have delighted in cruelty, the people will tear you limb from limb."

"But Thyestes?" Erasio protested.

"Out!"

"My king?"

"Get out! Leave me," Thyestes demanded.

The personal guard filtered from the room. Thyestes looked to the body of Cineas, who once more stood guard at the door. He raised his wine in salute.

"You traded your honour to return the sons of Atreus to the throne. I salute you, Cineas."

*****

The men under the command of Menelaus and Agamemnon surrounded the courtyard that lay in front of the royal palace. The walls seemed deserted of any defenders.

"Do you think Thyestes has left the city?" Agamemnon asked.

"I am not sure that he would leave his throne. Besides, what allies has he left that would be willing to provide him with protection?" Menelaus replied.

"Then why are the doors to the palace not guarded?" Agamemnon pressed.

"I can only assume that his men have deserted him. Would you lay down your life for a man like Thyestes?"

"I suppose to find our answers we must enter the beast's lair."

Menelaus continued to look to the upper walls, but they remained devoid of any life.

"Do we go with speed or caution?" Menelaus asked, already certain of which option Agamemnon would choose.

"Let's just get in there and drag the bastard out. Besides, I have a gift for our uncle." He tapped the sack at his waist. Twenty men were selected from the each of the two armies. Each man chosen for his skill with a blade. The plan was simple. Menelaus and Agamemnon would storm the gate, if they met resistance then the remainder of the army would follow. If not, then they would search the palace for Thyestes. Too many warriors within the palace corridors would only create chaos as men became too enclosed to wield their blades.

Menelaus took a deep breath. The city was taken, but now they must take the throne. He heard his brother call out for the attack to begin. He forced his tired legs into a run, keen to cross the open ground as quickly as possible. It was only a few hundred paces, but with each step he expected enemy archers to appear on the walls. But no missiles whipped through the air to deliver pain and death. The ground was covered quickly and the gateway to the palace opened without being forced. The group moved with more caution now, the palace gardens showed no evidence of an enemy lying in wait. However, the corridors beyond showed that the enemy had taken the time to loot all they could before fleeing. Menelaus began to think that Thyestes had fled the city, but as they entered the next corridor, they came face to face with seven men that showed more resolve.

"Step aside," Agamemnon ordered.

"I think not," came a reply.

"Step aside and lay down your weapons or you will die," Agamemnon demanded.

Two dropped their swords and raced in the opposite

direction. The five that stayed readied themselves for battle.

"Our king does not want to be disturbed," the same voice announced.

"What is your name?" Menelaus asked.

"Erasio, I answer only to the king."

"He's a murderous whore," one of Agamemnon's men called out. "Thyestes's guard dog."

"In that case, there will be no stepping aside for you Erasio. You die this night." Menelaus announced.

Agamemnon burst forward, his speed taking Menelaus by surprise, who, after regaining his senses, rushed after him. Two of the enemy fell quickly, the remainder were forced to defend as both Agamemnon and Menelaus rained down blow upon blow. Menelaus sliced the opponent to his front just below the knee, crouching low, ducking below his brother's sword and driving his blade forward taking another between groin and gut, ending his resistance.

Menelaus rose and kicked the man nursing his injured knee hard in the chest. The man's blade slid from his hand. Without the means to fight back, he raised his hands in surrender and pleaded for mercy. Menelaus stepped back and accepted the plea for mercy. Agamemnon was grappling with Erasio, who could only block Agamemnon's blows. Finally, blade cut deep into Erasio's forearm, slicing through muscle and sinew. Erasio was beaten and dropped to his knees, begging for mercy. Agamemnon raised his blade and then brought it smashing down. Erasio's scream was cut short as his skull was smashed apart.

His foot against the corpse of Erasio, Agamemnon freed his blade. He wiped the blood and brain matter on the dead man's tunic, then turned to see Menelaus waiting to enter the great hall.

"Is the pace too much for you, Agamemnon?" Menelaus grinned.

"Is that any way to talk to your king?" He gave a wink.

"Not a king yet, brother. One last task is before us." The smile faltered as Menelaus considered what could lay beyond the doors. Both he and Agamemnon pushed the timbers and then stepped aside, just in case their welcome was a spear or sword tip. However, there was no enemy racing forward; no spear, no arrow or other missile sent in their direction. The room was silent. Menelaus spied the dead body on the floor and wondered what the crime could have been to deserve such a punishment. However, his focus was soon taken by the figure that sat, wine in hand, upon a throne.

"Ah, the sons of my brother have returned. Come... come join us." Thyestes motioned that they should come closer.

"Us?" Menelaus asked.

"Cineas and I. I know that he has been most anxious for your return." He pointed behind them.

Menelaus felt a rage burn within when his eyes rested on the tragic form of Cineas. He had been no more than a boy the last time that he seen the old warrior. But he remembered the man with fondness.

"Your time for such acts of cruelty, are at an end, Thyestes," Menelaus spat out the words.

"Let me guess. You are going to kill me. I killed your father, and the sons claim their vengeance. You kill me and my son claims his vengeance, and so, it continues."

"I think not," Agamemnon replied. He took the sack from his waist and removed its contents. He threw the object to the feet of Thyestes. It bounced twice and then came to rest, its open eyes blind to the world of the living.

For a moment, Thyestes did not reply. His eyes widened at-the sight of his son's severed head.

"And so, it ends," he whispered, then looked up at them and said, "Well, nephews, do not dawdle." He reached up and plucked the crown from his head and cast it down on to the floor.

"Not here," Menelaus responded. "You die before the people of this city. Your death will take place at the same place that you murdered our father."

"Very well. I am ready." Thyestes raised the wine to his mouth.

Agamemnon strode forward.

"I don't give a fuck if you're ready or not." He drove a fist into his uncle's face. Wine, blood and several teeth were sent flying across the floor. He grasped the king by the hair and lifted him bodily from the throne. He threw him across the hall, sending him sprawling onto the remains of Bakchos. "Take this piece of shit to the courtyard," he ordered. Two Mycenaean warriors entered the hall and wrestled Thyestes from the ground. One delivered a blow to his gut to make him cease struggling.

The warriors of the Spartan and Mycenaean armies had remained on the perimeter of the courtyard. Murmuring began as they saw several their comrades exit the palace gate. Then cheers arose from the crowd as a bloodied Thyestes was marched into the centre of the courtyard. The cheers grew even louder as Agamemnon and Menelaus came into view. Both ignored the crowd, their attention on Thyestes.

Menelaus spoke to Thyestes. "Do you regret your treachery?" For some reason, Menelaus wanted to see what his father would have wanted to see: the desire that Thyestes show remorse.

"Regret?" Thyestes smiled. "I only regret that I failed to kill his sons.

Menelaus delivered a punch that broke the king's nose. But still Thyestes' smile remained. Menelaus drew his sword and growled with rage, for some reason he could not strike.

"Not so easy to kill a king, is it?" Thyestes laughed.

Agamemnon placed his hand on Menelaus's shoulder and moved him to the side. He walked up to Thyestes.

"Oh, another one of Atreus's bast…"

The blade split his gut. "I am king here, killing you is no more troubling than swatting a fly." He twisted the blade and then dragged it sideways, spilling Thyestes's intestines to the courtyard surface. Agamemnon leaned forward. "It will be as though you never existed," he whispered.

Thyestes toppled forward. His eyes remained on Agamemnon until his last breath escaped his body.

Chapter 41

'Horizon'

Agapetos and Airlea had increased their pace. Their pursuers had gained ground over the last day and were dangerously close.

"We cannot outrun them, Agapetos."

"If we can reach that rise," he pointed into the distance, "I have an idea to slow their progress."

"Then we better increase our pace," she suggested.

"You may be able to, but I doubt that I can," he replied.

"Then I shall slow them down." She stopped and pulled the bow from her back.

"No, I can't leave you," Agapetos protested.

"This is no time to allow your pride to get in the way. I can strike at them long before they can be a danger to me. And if I'm honest, Agapetos, the pace has been little more than a vigorous stroll for me."

"But..."

"Get to the summit and make your plans. I will simply force them to keep their heads down."

"Do not delay too long. Watch out for Krinos. He is no

fool."

"Go, Agapetos you waste valuable time," she insisted.

He leaned forward and kissed Airlea on the lips. "Be careful," he whispered. Without waiting for a reply, he turned and strode away.

Airlea turned her attention to the figures in the distance. She could only make out eight or nine of them, but that didn't mean that more of them were not hidden within the broken terrain. She closed her eyes and felt the breeze upon her face. It was no more than a whisper of a wind; it would not trouble her aim too much. The distance, however, was at her very limit. Notching an arrow, she raised the bow. In her secondary vision, she could see a figure moving in the distance. She let the arrow take flight. The missile shot into the sky, when it looked as if it was about to hide among the clouds, it suddenly levelled, then began to fall, picking up speed as it raced towards its target.

Airlea winced as it struck her target in the groin.

"Ouch! Forgive me, I was aiming for your chest." She did not rush to fire another arrow. They were after all in limited supply. Figures dived behind any surface that they thought would protect them. A warrior hid behind a large rock, his footing must have been unsure as he held himself in position by pressing his hand against a nearby tree. Airlea brought out another arrow. The target was a challenge that could not be refused. She slowed her breathing. Imagined the arrow sailing through the air and striking home. She loosed the missile. Moments later, flesh and bone were driven apart as the dark shaft pinned the man to the trunk of the tree. Whooping with joy at the shot, but that delight ended abruptly as her vision spied a figure that Agapetos had once described. A patch covered one eye, as he tried to force his fellow killers to continue the pursuit. Wondering if she could end this hunt with one well-placed shot, Airlea drew back the bow and slowed her breathing, she was just about to fire when the breeze brought with it another scent.

Turning quickly, she saw three men burst from the undergrowth. Adjusting her aim she let loose at the first of the three. The shaft thudded into his chest; he threw his hands in the hair as the power of shot struck him. Instinct took over, in a fraction of time she slung the bow over her back and caught the falling attacker's blade. She found herself making the centaur battle cry, racing towards the remaining two enemy. The first slashed at her, but Airlea leapt in the air clearing both man and blade. Stabbing to her rear, her newly acquired weapon took the man in the centre of his shoulder blades. The third man was armed with a spear and kept his distance.

Excitement coursed through her body. Realising that she had kept the power of a centaur, but with a much lighter frame. This enabled her to do things that were not only beyond a human, but also a centaur. The attacker thrust the spear forward, and Airlea slipped beneath the thrust. She grasped the shaft halfway along and drove it backwards. It smashed into the man's gut. As he reeled, she rose and cut the spear in two. She reversed the half she retained and plunged it into the man's throat. He was dead long before his body hit the earth. She turned her attention back to the figures in the distance, but they had gone to ground. Placing the sword, she had taken from the attacker in within belt, she turned and strode without haste toward the summit. Now and then she would turn, but the pursuers remained hidden from view.

As she finally reached the summit, Agapetos could not be seen. She glanced around. A sudden fear washed over her as she thought that he may have left, his fear of Krinos greater than his love. A whistle made her turn her head and she could not hide her joy at seeing Agapetos standing on a ledge, a large branch beneath a mighty bolder.

"What are you doing?" she asked.

"If we can block," he heaved on the branch, but his efforts were in vain, "the path. Then they would have no alternative, but retreat and find another path. That will take days. "If only I could move this bastard rock, it should cause a rockslide."

"I will help," she announced.

"Careful, it's quite awkward to..." he began, but his words fell away as Airlea raced forward and with ease scaled the ridge face.

"You were saying?"

"Erm nothing."

Both grasped the heavy branch and used all their strength. Initially, the bolder stood steadfast, but then it started to shift. Agapetos moved from the branch and braced his back against the bolder. His thighs bulged with the effort, the great bolder toppled and took with it all manner of debris. Tired and aching they climbed down from the ridge, just in time to witness Krinos waving his men back.

"I saw you kill those men," Agapetos spoke quietly.

"I am not proud of the fact, but it seems that my transformation has left me a formidable warrior. It seems strange that someone who does not seek violence, can be so accomplished at it."

"Is it not better that way? A warrior that kills out of necessity is surely better than one that kills for enjoyment."

"Yes, I suppose so." She rested her head on his shoulder, but a noise to their rear made both turn and draw their blades.

A figure on horseback with three spare mounts, held his hands up to show that he meant no harm. He looked into the valley, now blocked by the rockslide.

"Bandits?" he asked.

"Bastards," Agapetos replied.

"Do you have food?" the stranger asked.

"We will once I have hunted," Airlea replied.

"I've never mastered hunting. But I know riding is better than walking. A mount for each of you for a decent meal."

"What's your name?" Agapetos asked.

"Galenos, I ride towards Nemea. After that who

knows what the gods have in store for me. And you?"

"We hope to get passage to Troy," Agapetos replied.

"Then Nemea would serve you just as well as me." He dismounted and held at a hand of friendship.

*****

It had been two days since the death of Thyestes. The bodies had been cleared away and a great celebration thrown for the victory and forging of friendships. As silence fell across Mycenae, two men sat alone in the great hall.

"I will take my Spartans home when a new day comes. The families of my men deserve to know that they are safe," Menelaus announced.

"I will send an escort with you. My wife needs to see her new home," Agamemnon replied.

Their attention was drawn to the doors of the great hall. Thanatos bowed his head to them and strode across the hall.

"We missed you at the celebrations, Thanatos." Menelaus announced.

"I prefer a quiet life, Menelaus."

"But you are here now. Come take a drink with us. If it was not for you, I doubt this moment would ever have come." Agamemnon poured wine into a goblet as he spoke.

"I am sure that it would. But it is of the debt that I wish to speak."

"A debt? I think we all know that we owe more than one," Menelaus replied.

"It is just the one that I ask to be repaid this day."

"Ask Thanatos, if it is within my power then I will gladly pay it," Agamemnon replied enthusiastically.

"It is nothing that is beyond your power, nor or yours Menelaus. All I ask is that the honouring of the Olympians within your lands stop. No temples, statues or festivals. What your people do within their own homes is for them to decide, but elsewhere it is to stop."

"Will this not enrage the gods?" Menelaus asked.

"Only if you replace them with other Olympians. If you replace them with lesser gods or not at all, those in Olympus will think nothing to the loss. They take little notice of what happens in the world of men. Besides, neither of you have ever placed your faith in deities, preferring to achieve your ambitions through your own deeds."

"I cannot think what purpose this serves and doubt that you would tell me if I asked for a reason. But a debt is a debt. It will be done," Agamemnon declared.

Both he and Thanatos turned to look at Menelaus.

"I will do as you ask because I gave my word. But I cannot deny I don't have misgivings," Menelaus drained the last of his wine and rose to his feet. "I would bid you goodnight. I leave for Sparta in the morning and will need my rest."

Both Agamemnon and Thanatos watched a troubled

Menelaus depart.

"My brother thinks too deeply," Agamemnon announced.

"That is not a failing," Thanatos replied.

"Perhaps not."

"It is not of Menelaus that I wish to speak. I bring grave tidings. I would ask that you trust my feelings for I have no proof to lay before you."

"I trust you, Thanatos. You can be assured of that."

"The Hittite empire is a ravenous beast that looks to consume ever more land. Treaties have kept them from moving toward these lands in the past, but that is all about to change."

"In what way?" Agamemnon moved to the edge of his seat.

"King Priam of Troy is dying. The only heir of any worth is Hector who has refused the crown. Priam is desperate to ensure his city and his household continues. He must find a powerful ally that will protect his legacy. He hopes that the ally will oversee his lands but leave his family to rule, if only in name.

"Priam is right not to look to me. I have no love for the man."

"And he knows that. He also knows that these city states are almost in constant war. Not one of them can offer Troy stability."

"And what of the Hittites?" Agamemnon asked.

"They will use Troy to control trade, and I believe, as a base to launch attacks against every state in the west. They have vast wealth and armies. It will be like trying to hold back a great wave."

"What can be done?"

"Troy must not fall into the hands of the Hittites. With the wealth from that city alone they could fund an entire campaign against these lands. Priam is no fool, he already suspects that forces may move against him. He will welcome the Hittites but resist any other. Only you, Agamemnon, can move against him. Only you can bring other states beneath your wing."

Agamemnon considered the words spoken by Thanatos. "Menelaus will not go to war with Troy."

"Then we must make it his ambition. We must give him a reason to take a blade to Troy."

The End of the Beginning

COMING SOON

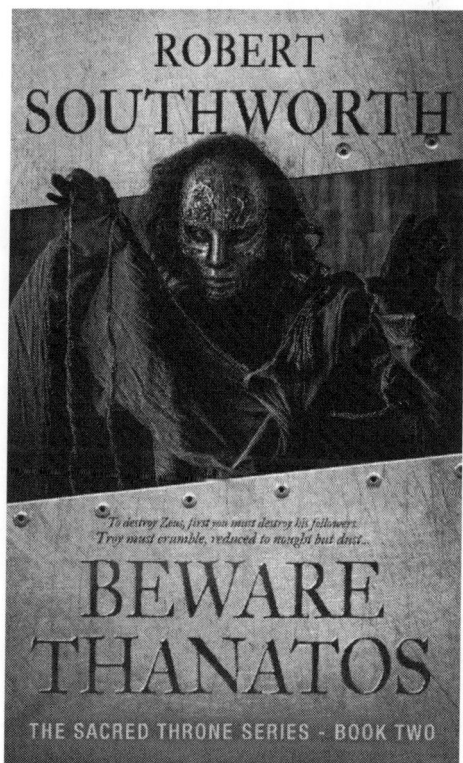

ROBERT SOUTHWORTH

To destroy Zeus, first you must destroy his followers.
Troy must crumble, reduced to nought but dust...

BEWARE THANATOS

THE SACRED THRONE SERIES - BOOK TWO

Afterword

I do hope that you have enjoyed the first book in the Sacred Throne Series. I have tried to bring fantasy to the ancient world. Whether I am successful or not, will be down to you, the reader. The second in the series will be released Autumn 2022. This has been a new experience for me, leaving the world of historical fiction has been both exciting and soul destroying in equal measure.

Contact

If you would like to discuss this book or my other works.
robius1@sky.com

Books By This Author

The Reaper's Breath

The Reaper's Touch

The Reaper's Breath

Wrath Of The Furies

Spartacus : Talons Of An Empire

Spartacus : The Gods Demand Sacrifice

Spartacus : The Pharoah's Blade

Printed in Great Britain
by Amazon

65974430R00298